The Miracle Adjuster

SIMON CAMPBELL

ISBN-10: 0997806222

ISBN-13: 978-0997806229

'Of all the offspring of time, error is the most ancient, and is so old and familiar an acquaintance, that truth, when discovered, comes upon most of us like an intruder, and meets the intruder's welcome'.

—Charles Mackay; 'Extraordinary Popular Delusions and the Madness of Crowds', 1841

1. Frank and Fátima

'*A*re you sitting comfortably?'

'Pay attention!'

'I'm going to tell you a secret'.

'The truth will be revealed...'

These were the taglines attached to the whoopla for expensive lingerie, economical cars, cheap perfume and a limited (collector's truncheon) edition box-set of series seven of 'Roy Chancy, PCSO' within the tacky pages of the in-flight magazine on Panda Air U571. The box-set came with what advertisers were flogging as 'a deluxe certificate of authenticity' and you and I would call 'a sales receipt'.

The counterfeit plane ticket in my pocket confirmed that I was Colin Jekyll and that Colin was travelling from Tesco Airport, Glasgow, to Wonebelong Airport, Sydney.

But Colin Jekyll was not my real name. My real name was Frank Canon.

And if you need to know why I was travelling under an assumed name?

It's because I was a liar.

It paid to tell the truth. Unless it was your job to lie to people. Sure, sure, I wasn't paid particularly well. But I worked my arse off. I lied to pensioners and pre-schoolers, to tabloid journalists and high court judges. I lied in phone booths and in public conveniences (and phone booths that had been converted into public conveniences). I lied in the Amazon rainforest and in Royal Tunbridge Wells. I would have lied on the moon if I could have done. And if I could have done then I would have lied about the moon landings while I was there.

But everything I'm about to tell you? The dancing plagues and the weeping statues? The drunken weather and the biased lightning? The rat glue? That's all true. Every word of it.

I sat alone in the Bangkok Airport Hilton exercise yard.

Flight U571 had been delayed for several hours as our pilot was nervous about taking off in biblical rain and so my fellow passengers and I had been obliged to wait until the airline could find a more reckless pilot willing to take the risk. Panda Air didn't want to worry anyone about the biblical rain though and so the PA tried to persuade us that the flight had been delayed because they were waiting for more complimentary alcohol to be delivered.

Everyone seemed happy to wait.

I walked into the artificial daylight of the Long Stay Terminal and found myself if not assaulted, then certainly touched by the sweet and sour aroma of the celebrity restaurants and the white noise of the arcades with their life parodies and achievement proxies. An off-duty pilot was banging away at his flight simulator screaming; 'Pull up goddammit! Pull up!'

And his blasphemy reminded me of work.

I headed for the duty free but some life-sized emoticon intercepted me first and offered me a free sample of something called 'Miracle White Shining Involvement'.

Now take it from me, the word 'miracle' is overused. Mostly in order to offset the entirely unremarkable nature of the noun it's providing PR for; hair gel, noodles, babies and so on and so forth. What this guy was offering me was basically chewing gum.

Chewing gum that wouldn't make my teeth whiter.

On the Reinhardt-Munster Scale of the Phenomenal chewing gum that wouldn't make my teeth whiter was about as far away from phenomenal as you could get. This was closer to the other end of the scale. What this wasn't, was a miracle. But for some reason I bowed my head as I accepted it and drifted into a shop selling 'Hip-Hop Philosophy' degrees and doctorates in 'American Pseudohistory'. I needed to buy some souvenirs. I just didn't have anyone to give them to. Ever since my family disappeared I'd been a bit of a loner.

My goldfish was home alone and I wondered how he was doing; if he was cheerful, fulfilled, breathing etc. Conventional wisdom (something on which one relied heavily in my line of work) suggested my goldfish didn't have enough of a memory that he'd be happy to see me when I got back, but he was my only remaining companion.

And I take my responsibilities to goldfish more seriously since Black Saturday.

I was a nurturer now. A nurturer who was away on business.

In my line of work you usually worked alone. And I'd gotten to like it. I had no-one telling me what to do, no-one giving me their opinion on how it should be done or their praise when I did it well, no-one photographing me doing it well and then showing all our friends. It wasn't a bad time to be alone; to boil yourself a pizza and watch someone's phoned footage of a gig online, to download shaky video of a film that's only in theatres or turn yourself into a troll. This was a golden age for the loner. Which was lucky for me, because I'd been alone most of my life. Being a loner suited me just fine. And it suited my goldfish too. We had a lot in common, my goldfish and I. It was just that neither of us could remember what it was.

I bought myself a souvenir pilot's license. And a bag of mixed nuts.

That reminded me of work too.

I sat down with my Happy Meal and opened it up to check on the toy, but for some reason this Happy Meal came with an apple pie flavoured condom. And it wasn't called a Happy Meal. It was called a 'Little Box'. Sometimes whoopla gets lost in translation. It was fast food but I found the time to taste the sweat and tears of the kid who'd prepared it for me. Some highly decorated businesswoman sitting opposite me opened her kid's Little Box and then swiftly headed back to the counter fighting back tears. I could have done the same, but I wasn't the complaining type. I wasn't the type to upset the status quo.

I was the guy protecting the status quo.

Colin Jekyll's plane ticket clearly identified his classiness but that didn't prevent his being stopped by one of Panda Air's black-shirts when she saw my bag of duty free nuts.

'Sir. Stop. Sir. Sir. Sir! Stop!'

And then, with everyone's attention;

'You cannot take two bags onto this flight!'

And then, keeping calm, managing her fear;

'You cannot take two bags onto this flight'.

I guess she just had to keep on repeating this until I dropped my nuts. She didn't really know what she was doing any longer. Sometimes the training just takes over.

The queue grew behind me. People were glowering at

me like I was the reason they'd missed the Second Coming. I didn't want to stand out from the crowd (because I was undercover), but unfortunately my face had turned bright red. No-one would notice another white man with a red face once I was in Australia, but until then I stood out like a sore thumb.

We eventually boarded the bus to our plane, just as the previous passengers were rolling down the inflatable slide. Our driver proceeded to drive in a holding pattern around the plane at something approaching 2mph. When we finally got on board we played musical chairs while the crew swapped those over 200lbs with the thinner passengers; to balance the plane out. If there were any martyrs on the flight they must have been praying to be let off.

It was to be expected that there'd be some turbulence. It was just my rotten luck it had been planned for while I was on the toilet. Once I'd stopped shouting and bleeding I opened the door to some airbrushed stewardess and started banging on the cabin door demanding the pilots stop screwing around. You could hear them giggling on the other side of the door.

Long-haul flights can get boring. So this is what pilots do. They lighten up.

Eight out of ten times turbulence is just a practical joke.

I couldn't remember why I'd developed a fear of flying, or when, but that wasn't unusual; I had a terrible memory. It wasn't really a fear of flying though, it was more of an all-inclusive phobia; it didn't start with the plane taking off, it started with the packing, with making it to the airport on time (3 hours early). It was the meal on the flight, the queue for passport control and the scenic taxi route. It was the total loss of control, the utter obliteration of your status quo. But I tried to put it out of my mind. It wasn't about the journey for me, it was all about the destination. And the destination was Oz! I was off to see the Wizard (a Bishop, I was off to see a Bishop. A wonderful one though, not the other kind).

On the plane you could watch indiscriminate episodes of cops and docs shows.

If you wanted to make a TV show you had a choice about what kind of show you were going to create. You could create one set in a police station.

Or if you don't want to do that, you could create one set in a hospital.

I switched on the bite-size screen in front of me and was immediately confronted with 21 year-old Blimey Lowsey; sitting on a tangerine chat show sofa, lamenting the semi-conscious uncoupling of her third marriage (following a drunken Teen Choice Awards night) and being comforted by Andromeda Strain on 'Face Talk'. Blimey was a thirteen year veteran of the 'pop world' but only a thirteen week veteran of the 'real world'. I checked my in-flight menu and opted for series five, episode eleven of 'Roy Chancy, PSCO'. This was Ross Kemp as a psychic Police Community Support Officer on the streets of Swindon. In this episode ('Blood on the Tracks') Roy tackled a bunch of terrified foxes at Swindon railway station. What Roy did to these foxes, you wouldn't want to know. And neither did I. I tuned my headphones into the cockpit frequency to check we weren't 'going down hard' or 'fast' or 'hard and fast' or anything, and then I pressed play, laid back and listened to Sylvester Stallone reading a 'Grimm's Fairy Tales' audiobook. Sly (beautifully) recited 'The Donkey Cabbage' as I made notes on my Panda Air napkin.

After we'd skidded to the end of the runway and the applause had died down I queued for forty minutes to meet someone important eating a falafel sandwich in a small Perspex™ box and dutifully handed him Colin Jekyll's counterfeit passport and visa entry form.

I didn't look anything like Colin did in his passport photo. But then who did? Your passport photo wasn't an accurate reflection of how you looked in real life. You were allowed to smile in real life. But it *was* an accurate reflection of how you looked after queuing three hours for passport control. You weren't allowed to smile in your passport photo because you had to give the guys at passport control the chance to compare apples with apples.

Whenever I filled in a form Colin's job description was always 'Events Manager'.

It was Colin's job to manage events, to make things less eventful.

Whenever some new scratch-starter found themselves pressganged into the Agency the first thing I'd tell them was; 'Get yourself a job description'. Then I'd force-feed them my anecdote; about how on my first job I'd asked some guy what his job description was before I helped him and his family adjust to the Amazon rainforest. That was one of only two times I'd ever broken the rules. He told me he was an Events Manager. I took his job description because it seemed reasonable. Nothing else about the job seemed reasonable.

To be honest most things seemed to be deliberately 'unreasonable'.

This job was bad for your health.

The head of the Agency (whose name was Wilbur Whitehall and was thus born for his career in the same way that Bill Body was born to be my P.E. teacher and Charles Atlas my Geography tutor) died of a heart attack shortly before I left for Australia. This was the man who'd recruited me, who became my mentor, and who suffered a massive coronary while waiting in line at the butcher's. When your wife's a vegetarian this is known as being caught *'in flagrante delicto'*. The job was the problem. Wilbur's heart just wasn't in it any longer.

As with telesales and politics it was difficult to justify all of the lies you were forced to sell people in order to give them something they'd never asked for. Sure, sure, the little white lies your parents told you were designed to protect you. But the lies we told? They were designed to protect us. Maybe I'm repeating myself here; but I was the guy protecting the status quo. Sometimes the training just took over. And I'd been trained to follow orders. The boss wasn't always right. But the boss was always the boss. Soon there'd be a new man at the top, ordering me to sell bigger lies. Ordering me not to worry about the new direction the Agency might be taking. Not to worry about the new direction that I was about to take.

If you're unclear about what the Agency does, then everyone's been doing their job.

I'll explain more later, but if it helps, think of the Agency as being just like any other government department. Most people had absolutely no idea what they were doing.

You didn't need to know the specifics of what the Agency was up to, only that whatever it was, was for your own good. All you needed to know was that the vast majority of its time and resources were being put to good use. Sure, sure, some of your taxes might be needed for Ministers' mortgage payments, but a lot of what was left was spent on you. Specifically it was spent preventing you from discovering anything more than that.

That was for your own good too.

The full name of my employer was 'The Information Reclamation Agency'.

Sure, sure, it was an unfortunate acronym. But we thought of it first.

We had a dotted line to the Dept. of Education. And an invisible one to the Ministry of Defence. If you want to know more, its offices are on the thirteenth floor of the Blacker Building in Whitehall. But it's doubtful you'll find them. Don't get me wrong, it's nothing personal, but the reason you won't find them is that the sign on the front of the building reads; 'Centre for the Unknown'. It isn't one of those flash, show-off agencies.

The Centre for the Unknown is what's known in the business as a 'façade'.

Some years ago the Serious Fraud Office raided the Agency's headquarters as part of 'Operation Leprechaun' and discovered a list of secret front organisations that someone had pinned to a noticeboard headed; 'Secret Front Organisations'.

There was the 'The Reality Foundation', 'The Wide Awake Club' and 'Greenpeace'.

Someone took the Serious Fraud Officers to one side and explained their mistake. They posed for a few photos (holding Holy Grails™ and laughing, holding fossilised rabbits' feet and laughing) and then a few of us from the Office of Reality Enforcement followed them home while the Office of Selective Omission ret-conned the photos on the SFO's official FaceSpace page so they appeared to be posing with furry handcuffs (and laughing).

The centre for the unknown; you're never quite sure what they're up to. Here's hoping they're working on the meaning of life. And not just trying to keep it from you.

Colin's passport wasn't returned for more than an hour. This was routine. When you have the kinds of stamps I've collected border control staff tend to revolt against their own suspension of disbelief, they tend to enforce disbelief. I know a lot about enforced disbelief. If my real job description had come with a list of responsibilities then 'enforcing disbelief' would've been top of the list. This is if I hadn't told people I was an Events Manager.

The reason they gave for keeping me so long was; 'people smuggling'. Then they asked if I'd packed my own suitcase. If Colin was a comedian he could have told them he'd packed it full of cheap labour. But Colin wasn't a comedian. Colin was an Events Manager. He didn't rock the boat, or go overboard. He wanted to operate in the shadows. Unfortunately Australia is flat and sunny and covered in sand and there aren't any shadows there. But it was a great place to do business if you were in my line of work. Oz was like another world. In Australia you could have egg and beetroot on your burger and no-one batted an eyelid.

I walked out of Arrivals and squinted. In the distance you could see red bushfires among the Blue Mountains. I turned away from the fires because, just between you and me, I tended to get a little awkward around flames. Flames made me sweat. And I'd only just dried out after the plane journey. Luckily I was in Australia, so I just looked like everyone else.

I queued for a cab. I felt the warm sun on my face. And then I felt my face burning.

The guy in front of me was on the smartphone to his wife who was bringing him up to speed on her bushfire situation. 'It's a miracle you didn't get hurt...' he told her.

But it wasn't a miracle. It was just very lucky.

I got in my taxi and started speaking in tongues.

The tongue in my mouth belonged to Russell Crowe. Possibly it belonged to Mike from Neighbours. Having an Australian's tongue in your mouth isn't phenomenal (ask any backpacker). Having an Australian's tongue in your mouth doesn't so much reach the phenomenal end of the Reinhardt-Munster Scale as it does the other end. The 'bullshitting your taxi driver' end. It's better to give than to receive when it comes to bullshit. And I didn't have time to take the scenic route. I had somewhere else to be. And I was already very late.

A couple of months later I was running late again. The thing I was late for was 'my own funeral'. But it's not easy learning how to pilot a helicopter while you're flying one.

Into a lightning storm. Without an instructor. But with a fear of flying.

My taxi driver didn't seem very happy with his tip, but I had a big smile on my face. I loved Australia. Sure, sure, the weather was predictable, but very little else was. Normally I wasn't a big fan of unpredictability (in England things were entirely the other way round), but you had to learn to live with it if you were in my line of work. Unpredictability paid the bills.

I grabbed a newspaper and a chocolate milkshake. Thirteen people had been killed the day before in what the newspaper had christened; 'The Brisbane Beer Flood'.

One had drowned, one had died from his injuries, and eleven other souls had succumbed to alcohol poisoning when 26,000 gallons of beer in the Triple X Brewery had burst its vats and sloshed onto the streets. The paper reckoned it was a miracle the other two hundred and twenty-nine people who'd been hospitalised hadn't been killed by all the complimentary alcohol they'd drunk. But you know what I'm going to say right?

Nowadays anything even remotely accommodating, which is also slightly unlikely, ends up being labelled a miracle by somebody. Surviving stuff is especially miraculous; see 'surviving Panda Air', 'surviving NHS brain surgery', 'surviving being struck by lightning' and so on and so forth. But these aren't miracles.

To be clear; if you have seen the face of the blessed Virgin Mary in a slice of toast, you have not witnessed a miracle. And you shouldn't tell people that you have.

What most people call miracles? They're just mistakes, continuity errors, bloopers. Maybe it's nature being impulsive, or it's the way that something's supposed to be, and we just haven't come up with a decent explanation for it yet. Chances are these continuity errors are just unexplained science experiments. For all you know, these are just 'try-outs'.

The point here is: You. Don't. Know.

But the church knows. They even wrote a book about it.

And everyone in the Agency had a copy.

The church and the Agency had a lot of history together. Sure, sure, a lot of it had been rewritten, but the church was the Agency's most loyal ally. And just like how Britain's most loyal ally was the USA; we had to do whatever our most loyal ally told us to do. If you ever overheard me promising to 'go by the book' then this was the book I was going by.

Maybe you haven't heard, but the church has a lot of rules.

My second job was at Fátima, in Portugal.

At the Banco Lotto music festival.

People said it was 'beyond belief' that Keith Carbonara was still alive and well and wearing the same leather trousers he'd worn when Emulsion released their seminal album 'Animal Innuendo' in '73.

They called it; 'the night of the deep heat'.

Believe me; I've heard the conspiracy theories. I wrote most of them.

If it hadn't been for me Fátima would be like Lourdes, Mecca and Glastonbury nowadays; filled to the brim with the unwashed and the stoned. If it hadn't been for me you'd have heard about the Banco Lotto music festival by now.

There'd be a film based on a book.

Sixty-thousand festivalgoers witnessed the onstage breaking-up of The Burial Stones in the biblical rain and then watched as the clouds parted and the sun blurred, twisted, raved about, and then collapsed onto the horizon. It tried to get back to its feet and appeared to stumble towards the bar, changing colour to a sickly green and radiating that deep heat.

After about two or three minutes of this drunken astronomy people realised; i) the bar was closing and ii) their clothing, which had been dripping wet only minutes before, was now dry as a bone. There were cracks in the ground where moments earlier there'd been a mud bath. People couldn't move their feet for hours (which prompted some particularly vitriolic abuse from the headline act; The Disco Brothers).

The church was understandably unenthusiastic about agreeing with those who claimed some sort of Divine Intervention following the break-up of The Burial Stones. There had to be another explanation. And wouldn't you know it, there was.

I'm good at sneaking about. The training just takes over.

Maybe I'm not great at disguises but I'm not bad at persuading people to suspend their disbelief. I'm not bad at persuading people to enforce their disbelief either; depending on what the situation calls for.

So after explaining how Colin Jekyll was an Events Manager (and a little retroactive bar work) it was discovered that some poor scapegoat had inadvertently hooked one of the white wine reservoirs up to several of the water tanks servicing the bars.

Everyone was shitfaced.

You see, sometimes something happens that falls a little outside the normal way of the world. And people are in the habit of calling these things miracles. But that's only because they see the 'what' without knowing the 'why', the 'how' or the 'who'.

Let me try to illustrate this another way; by quoting an oldie but a goodie.

A great philosopher once wrote;

'And since at times one and the same cause is known to some and unknown to others, it happens that of several who see an effect, some are astonished and some not: thus an astronomer is not astonished when he sees an eclipse of the sun, for he knows the cause; whereas a lot of people from Norwich, who are ignorant of this science must needs wonder, since they know not the cause'.

Must needs wonder? Must needs panic is more like it.

Must needs soil yourself and run for the hills (or if you're in Norwich, drive).

Think of my job like this. I took people who were astonished and made them feel like astronomers. It was my job to invent mundane explanations for the astonishing. People knew not the cause. So I gave them one. And so it was that people could argue for hours on end about 'the night of the deep heat'. But they could all agree on one thing.

It wasn't a miracle.

2. Sharkbait and Nasty

I was born in England in '73. In the week of the trash riots, the cod war outbreak (sic) and the release of 'Animal Innuendo'.

Dad was a dreamer, always looking for the next get rich quick idea, the giant conch the other beachcombers had missed. Mum said his ideas were about as useful as fairy tales; so each night I would fall asleep listening to my father's softly whispered stories of zero-gravity weight loss workshops, prams for teenagers, guide dogs for the deaf and Christmas salad hampers. I guess Dad was probably just as scared of the truth as most people, though I've struggled, on occasion, to distinguish the memory from the fairy tale.

I loved my parents. Up to a point. The point where they vanished without a trace. They'd been gone a long time, but that just made me think about them more, not less. And I doubted they could still fend for themselves, because they'd be in their seventies by now.

All I had left were the memories. Of visiting dad at Cunningham's Hardware Store. Or helping mum bake shortcake in the oven. I couldn't remember where I'd last seen them, but I had a feeling that my parents didn't want to be found. And I had a job to do. The lives of the many outweighed the lives of my mum and dad. I guess if they hadn't vanished I'd have ended up protecting my parents from the truth eventually (though old age has its own devices for shielding you from harsh reality), but there was never any shortage of other people who needed my protection. Life can be painful. The truth hurts. My parents taught me that.

When I was seven I developed an unhealthy obsession with superheroes (with disguises and masks). There was the spider bite. The microwave accident. The invisibility. And the leaping from the top of the stairs in a single bound.

Maybe that's where I got my fear of flying from.

When I was eleven I passed the entrance exam for Uphill Grammar by fiddling the egg timer on my desk that informed the deaf headmaster's guide dog when my time was up.

I bought myself time. I could stop time where it was. But I couldn't turn it back.

I put my hand up in Physics when everyone else kept theirs down and learnt that sometimes everyone else can be wrong. At least that's how I remember it. Don't ask if that's what really happened. I've struggled, in the past, to distinguish the history from the pseudo.

I didn't find the courage to ask Sophia Smith out until the day of our graduation from Manchester University, as she was being driven out of harm's way (to Surrey) by her parents.

I tried to run after her. But I had a ventricular septal

defect. And a hole in my shoe.

I never was sure if she heard me or not.

I was recruited by the Agency when I was twenty-one.

No-one I worked with had ever received a pay rise or a promotion, but you usually got a gift if you survived twenty years' service. And I just had a few more weeks to survive.

Most people ended up with a souvenir from the Whitewash Museum. The only constraint was that you could carry it out through the front door with you when you left. Everyone used to joke that they were going to take the (faked) fake moon landing set. But no-one ever did. People usually just took a memento of their biggest lie.

I wasn't so comfortable with the big lies, however noble they were. But I didn't like to think that people might get hurt if I didn't do my job. The kind of truth I was protecting you from wasn't the truth about your career prospects or how you looked in that dress. It was the kind of truth that leaves a scar. I suppose I liked to think that my behaviour fell into the category of 'for the greater good'. I suppose that's what everyone working for the Agency liked to think. But I always preferred to tell little white lies.

The reason I was travelling to Australia? It was only to tell a little white lie.

I was faced with a very long drive along some very straight roads. The car I'd hired was a Viagrador. The Viagrador was the second fastest convertible in the world, could reach speeds over 200mph and wasn't fitted with a windscreen or any rear-view mirrors.

I took the Great Western Highway out of Sydney, towards the Red Mountains. I stopped for lunch in a little roadside diner in Sunset Rock. The sticker on the door said;

'Trip Advisor's Roughest Little Roadside Diner 2012'.

All of the men stopped talking as I walked through the door. The women didn't stop talking because they weren't allowed into this section of the diner.

I asked for a menu and watched my fellow patrons. Everyone looked like they had blood on their hands. These men looked like the type who still slaughtered their own supper. But I looked like the type who had a kid's diet. The type to keep things simple.

Maybe we're all looking for the simple explanations in life. But don't think that we're alike. I'm the only one here who was paid to enforce reality on the rest of us.

I'm the only one here who's spent his life trying to spare us all the truth.

If you wanted to blend in you had to order the pie, but when I asked the gassy gentleman sitting opposite me what was in it the reply was; 'meat'. When I asked what kind of meat I was assured it was; 'local'. I figured there was no future in this line of questioning. Everyone else was busy spreading ketchup on their own pies and eating them red-handed.

People leered at me sideways from under their wide-brimmed hats as I walked back to the convertible. There weren't any other cars to be seen.

This town just watched the future drive through.

I realised people were looking at me sideways because they appeared to have eyes on the sides of their heads. They had a lot of unnecessary forehead between the eyes. I revved the engine and sped off, thinking that the place smelt strongly of cheese.

I drove past the Sunset Rock Cheese Museum in top gear.

I couldn't quite put my finger on it; it could have been the pie, or witchcraft, but I had a tremendous feeling of unease. There was something sinister about a place that had a cheese museum, but if you needed to fill up the car, see a dentist or eat an imported meat pie you had to do all of this 'somewhere else'. Signs on the road pointed the way to supermarkets and dry cleaners you simply couldn't believe were really out there. You could look to the horizon but all you would see were mountains or waterfalls or salt lakes the colour of ice cream flavours. There was no evidence of the future out here. There was no way to suspend your disbelief.

By the time I was back on the main road my right foot was bubbling with surplus adrenalin. I pushed pedal to metal, felt my worries g-forced out of me and set about trying to keep up with the setting sun. You had to wonder if the person who'd designed the Viagrador had heard about flies. They were really spoiling my view of a beautiful sunset.

A few months later I'd be speeding towards another sunset, in a stolen bandwagon belonging to a cult jam-packed with celebrities. But for now all I could see were the flies.

Hundreds and thousands of flies were getting right in my face.

Because I was in Australia. And because the Viagrador didn't have a windscreen.

I needed some windscreen wipers. Or one of those hats with the corks. But I had neither. All I could do was put my foot down and try to outrun the flies.

It was at about this point that I ran through the speed trap.

A police siren started up behind me. The pitch of the siren just seemed to keep on rising. But as I had no mirrors I couldn't see the police car. My right foot shifted from the gas to the brakes. The Viagrador had been designed to speed up. The slowing down was a 'nice to have'. My borrowed tyres locked and drew thick black lines across the Great Western Highway as they skidded off of the road and came to a halt beside a burning bush.

I felt anxious; because of the flames. And because of the approaching police officer;

'I've been waiting here all day for an idiot like you?'

I searched my pockets for Colin Jekyll's driving licence;

'I got here as fast as I could'.

Officer Constable was in a bad mood because Colin was a bloody Pom. Had he been an Australian Colin would have lost his licence. When you've been standing in the middle of 'somewhere else' all day the least you've got to look forward to is confiscating the occasional licence. I handed over Colin's and watched Constable's bottom lip wobble.

How many cars passed through his speed trap? Two? Three? A week?

How soul destroying it must be to be a traffic copper on a continent with no traffic.

'You won't lose your licence but you still pay the fine?'

He perked up like someone had just put an arm around his shoulder or cleared him of the unlawful shooting of an unarmed man;

'You were six miles an hour over the limit so that's considered dangerous? Means a bigger fine?'

We got into an argument over the dangers of speeding. My POV was that speeding wasn't that dangerous; that the shorter the amount of time you spent on the road, the safer you were. My POV was that, in fact, most speed cameras didn't even bother picking people up at speeds above 120mph.

Officer Constable's POV was;

'Fine would normally be one-twenty-five? But it's on special this week so it's doubled to two-fifty?'

I threw myself at his mercy and explained that the reason Colin had been speeding was down to the terrible sense of foreboding he'd felt back in Sunset Rock. I explained how Colin had been desperate to get out. But it was impossible to read the intentions of someone who finished his every sentence with a question mark.

'The reason the bloody speeding fines are on special this week is because of how close this is to Christmas?'

I confessed; I didn't have that kind of cash on me.

'That's ok? We have a brand new ATM back at the station?'

The police station in West Wysolong was actually just a table and two chairs in the back of a pub called 'The Crooked Man'. The pub smelt of stale sweat and gravy (well it was either the pub, or it was me). Someone had bolted a sign that read 'Police!' to the wall above me. If you actually needed a fully functioning air-conditioned police station you had to head over to East Wysolong (aka top town). Top town was a three hour drive from bottom town.

My plan had been to withdraw $250 from The Crooked Man's ATM but the landlord / desk sergeant filled me in on the $200 maximum.

The reason they had a $200 maximum withdrawal was because this was a pub. Also, no-one had ever needed to withdraw more than $200 from the ATM because; i) it was brand new and ii) no-one had ever been dumb enough to speed past the only speed trap for ninety square miles during the only week in which fines were doubled.

I withdrew my $200, sold Colin's (fake) Rolex to someone at the bar for $40 and dug around under the seats in the Viagrador for enough loose change to make up the difference.

Of the nine pubs in bottom town three had accommodation available.

I booked myself into the Metropolitan. Its ninety-seven-year-old manager informed me that as he had no other paying guests staying the night I was welcome to take my pick of the hotel's three rooms; the Gold Suite, the Opal Suite, or the Uranium Suite.

There was only one department store in bottom town and at 3pm on a Tuesday it was closed. The post-it note on the door told me to find Bronwyn in the pub if I needed anything.

I needed to buy some souvenirs. Souvenirs are part of the job. They give you a good excuse for travelling. People don't question the reason for your trip if you can show them a souvenir pilot's license.

There was one department store on this street. There were nine pubs.

I figured there was probably more than one Bronwyn.

And she wasn't happy that I'd dragged her out of the pub to open the store when all I wanted were a couple of 'koala ear' hats. Disguises are part of the job too.

I felt a bit guilty, dragging Bronwyn away from her heavy drinking in this heat, but I told her that I didn't really have a choice. I had a job to do. This was something known in the business as a 'nice to not have'. It wasn't a mustn't not have, but if I could tell my boss that it wasn't around any longer it would be good for my performance appraisal. I explained to Bronwyn how I really needed a pay rise this year. I didn't explain how I'd already missed my last three quarters' red-herring targets. But I bought a souvenir boomerang with the last of my Viagrador change and that seemed to cheer her up.

I went back to The Crooked Man and fiddled the ATM.

Between you and me, if you put an ATM into standby mode it starts behaving like your grandparents; it can't hear any information being fed to it down the phone line and has no idea how much cash it has or how many withdrawals you've already made. These ATMs just start pressing banknotes into your hand, whether they can afford to or not.

Between you and me, the way an ATM ends up in

standby mode is by turning it off and turning it back on again. This is why most ATM's tend to be cemented into a hole in the wall. But the ATM in The Crooked Man wasn't cemented in anywhere. It was brand new.

I couldn't break into an ATM in the middle of a police station though. Not with all the people queuing at the bar. And I didn't have a disguise on me. Only the koala ear hats.

My subterfuge instructor would've been ashamed of me. But the same subterfuge instructor who'd been so ineffectual at teaching me the dark arts of the convincing disguise had taught me another, much more valuable lesson. If people aren't listening to your bullshit, tell them the building's on fire. Then they'll start listening to whatever you have to say.

So I shouted; 'Fire!'

Everyone started screaming and shouting.

Because the Bunnies had just scored against the Bulldogs.

I waited for things to die back down and shouted; 'Fire!' again. This time everyone started running. They ran to the bar to order a drink, and then they ran out of the pub.

I shifted the ATM a little to the left and flicked the switch under the floor panel.

Then I withdrew $200. Twenty-five times.

The reason I'd needed $5000 was to pay my scapegoats for the crop circles. I'd told Bronwyn this wasn't a 'mustn't not have' but that had been before I'd actually seen the crop circles. These weren't corny spriographs or noughts and crosses but the kind of crude phalli you might find in the margins of a ten-year-old's exercise book. And these hadn't been created by a couple of schoolboys but by a bunch of poppy eating koalas. This, apparently, was the kind of behaviour to be expected from the koala which I'd just been informed was;

'Not as smart as your average bear?'

My two dreadlocked scapegoats worked as volunteer zookeepers at the local koala sanctuary. For $2500 each these koala-keepers would confess to being behind the sugarcane phallus hoax. We got ourselves into a lengthy debate over whether Jimbo and Lachlan could label themselves as volunteer zookeepers if their zoo consisted of one kind of animal only.

I waved my Oxford English Dictionary around and pointed out that;

'...a zoo maintains a collection of wild animals. Plural'.

But Jimbo checked his own copy and countered that a zoo could also be defined as;

'...any situation characterised by confusion and disorder?'

So we agreed that they worked in a zoo. Not because I agreed with them, but because I really had a lot of work to be getting on with.

The old Bundy farm had two crops. One was sugarcane grown to make rum. The other was opium used in 'no-frills' antidepressants. The Koalas had wandered through the opium crop first. By the time they'd reached the sugarcane they were hammered.

A harsher art critic than I might have argued that it had taken them two days to create what one human teenager might compose in a few seconds, but there was no denying they'd created the world's first ever recorded koala art. Now it was down to Jimbo, Lachlan and I to make sure these koalas wouldn't get exhibited.

Paying off people to hoax continuity errors like this was pretty standard practice.

This was a small scale deal; nothing like the 'Bigfoot hoax' hoax.

Believe me; you couldn't have pulled that off for $5000.

Crop circle hoaxes had outnumbered the real deal ever since the release of 'Animal Innuendo' and all of the cereologists running around screaming 'conspiracy' had only helped to sweeten the deal. The Agency loved to encourage these types. The more the whack-jobs protested the less likely everyone else was to listen.

Lachlan and Jimbo filmed each other drinking Bundy Rum and staggering around the fields with short planks of wood tied to their feet and a sixteen-foot length of rope that was attached at either end to the koala ear hats I'd purchased from Bronwyn, just in case.

Forty-eight hours later their YouTube video had clocked up 1,301,973 hits.

No-one has ever cited the beer situation in Australia as an example of apartheid but this was basically how things were; Queensland Best Bitter wasn't welcome in the Northern Territory and Victoria Better Bitter wasn't permitted in New South Wales.

The bar in the Metropolitan offered me a choice between an Orange Bitter or a Bundy Rum and coke. Orange Bitter seemed to be a popular choice of beverage among the locals. And a popular choice of cologne. I took the rum and coke without the rum.

I found myself introduced to two token characters who claimed their names were 'Sharkbait' and 'Nasty'. Neither smelt of Orange Bitter. They smelt of antiperspirant. Which meant they weren't locals. They were Poms. Sharkbait was about to appear on TV. The show was 'When Animals Go Wild' and you can probably guess why Sharkbait was on it.

Lots of people had said it was a miracle that Sharkbait survived. But sometimes lots of people can be wrong. Sharkbait had been saved from a Bulgarian tiger shark by a particularly altruistic pod of Turkish dolphins that had chased the killer fish off of Sharkbait after he'd gone through two bottles of potato schnapps and fallen off of Nasty's sloop in the Black Sea. I made a note to speak to the Office of Selective Omission and find out how they'd missed this one. Sharkbait had been paid a lot of money by the Turkish producers of 'When Animals Go Wild' and was planning to travel the world. For now though he was sitting in a pub that was about as far away from the coast as you could get in Australia.

Sure, sure, it wasn't right of Nasty to spoil the show's ending, but the bottom town reaction was harsh. People refused to suspend their disbelief, even after Sharkbait had pulled up his vintage 'Stones in Fátima' t-shirt to reveal the truth; the teeth marks, the dents, the chunks of him that were missing, even after he'd told bottom town that; 'seeing is believing'.

Nobody was disputing he'd been bitten by a Bulgarian shark, but saved by Turkish dolphins? It was just too unbelievable.

After Sharkbait's thirteen minutes of fame were up 'When Animals Go Wild' returned with a piece on killer badgers in Iraq. Apparently secret British forces based in Baghdad had trained man-eating badgers to attack suburban insurgents. These killer badgers were generally black and white and close to five feet in length, with a British accent and a propensity for road rage if you pranged one with your car.

Several suburban insurgents had been interviewed by 'When Animals Go Wild' and a couple even had the fur coats to back-up their stories. But seventy-eight-year-old Brigadier General Sir Rufus Moribund was on TV denying these wild accusations;

'We strongly refute the allegation that secret British forces have killed anyone in Baghdad, by means of man-eating badger'.

Want to know how Sir Rufus could make that statement? Someone cleaned up those killer badger corpses and replaced them with dead honey badgers. Someone somewhere decided; 'We don't need this war being complicated by killer badgers'.

Someone somewhere thought; 'This situation is messy enough as it is'.

People don't mind their loved ones fighting terrorists or covering the bin collections during a strike, but no right-minded person could ever let their husband or girlfriend risk their lives for a badger. It was a cover up. Believe me.

Don't *not* believe me just because the truth is unbelievable.

The Metropolitan's geriatric desk jockey arrived with my croc burger and told me that I had to see 'Bishop Anger'. I thought for a moment that 'Bishop Anger' must be a show that followed 'When Animals Go Wild', but then I remembered that there was a Bishop in bottom town, the Bishop of Orange, and I was here to see him. And his name was Anger.

Believe me.

3. Tinkerbelle and the Bishop

I switched on the TV in the Uranium Suite.

Fake-tanned and faux-boobed Katerina Waist was advertising her new 'Robinson Crusoe Diet'. Stranding yourself on an island without food was the way to go apparently.

I flicked over to the History Channel's breakfast news sofa.

The top stories were a failed assassination attempt and a natural disaster.

Both of these were described as 'unbelievable'. Although neither were.

Some people keep mouthwash in the fridge, some iron underwear, some people text into TV holiday competitions with the wrong answer (it isn't D and it isn't E). All of these things are very difficult to understand. All of these things might be described by someone struggling to believe them as 'hard to believe'. But none of these things should be described as being *unbelievable*.

A man whose leg grows back two and a half years after it was amputated.

This is unbelievable.

The failed assassination attempt had been made against Raúl Greedo; a much loathed newspaper magnate who was appearing at one of the four baseless court cases he'd been unjustly implicated in. There was the missing pension fund. And the yellow journalist who'd posed as a Maharajah and sold magic mushrooms to Sir Rufus Moribund.

There was the one about the cloning of Princess Armadillo's phone. And the one about the cloning of Princess Armadillo (and the clone's exclusive photo shoot).

No-one on the History Channel sofa was expecting this to be the last attempt on Raúl's life; each time he survived he just became more loathed than ever, like the children's entertainer who manages to survive elimination from 'Is This Talent?' each week.

There were no details on how Raúl had managed to not get killed, no footage of him not dying; so the news ran some footage of him being photo-bombed a year earlier. This was literally when someone had thrown a remanufactured hand grenade at him while he was being photographed at the Sick Industrialist Foundation's Comedy Gala. The grenade hadn't exploded. The photos of Raúl wetting himself hadn't made it into the public domain.

The news turned back to nature. There'd been an incident that was being reported as 'biased flooding'. The Thames had burst its banks but it appeared that the only homes affected had been in Chelsea. A lot of newly excavated basements had been ruined.

'I won't keep you a moment? I just have to forward this

e-mail to ten other people?'

The Bishop of Orange sat opposite me on a bean bag he'd picked up while visiting the Creation Museum in Orlando (kids riding dinosaurs, sabre-toothed kittens playing with balls of wool; that sort of thing). The bean bag was covered in biscuit crumbs. As was the Bishop.

He started talking to me about cane toads, with his mouth full of Tim Tam;

'A parishioner of mine was going to euthanise one with a cricket bat? I told him using the freezer was a more humane way to kill them? But that didn't work out how I'd expected?'

This was something I'd always found irritating about the job. The people who had all the answers were always telling you how things hadn't worked out how they'd expected. I'd learnt to live with the odd bit of unpredictability though. I was in Oz talking to a £10 Pom Bishop with a kangaroo tattoo on his left buttock after all. But who was to say that in a couple of weeks I mightn't find myself fleeing the scene of a bakery burglary with a beautiful intern?

The Bishop ran a Dustbuster™ over his cassock as we gossiped about a recent discovery made by a cross-eyed construction worker named Kevin Goodfella who'd been digging out the foundations for the new 'First Strike!' bowling alley in Orange.

Kevin had been excavating a large rock some six or seven feet below the surface with a digger he hadn't fully mastered control over. Upon his dropping the rock and its splitting in two he'd watched as dozens of seemingly dead toads had spilled out onto the ground beneath him. At which point, and after having been exposed to oxygen for a short time, the cane toads had started to gasp for breath, twist and flip about, and then began popping into town.

Bishop Anger unlocked a desk drawer, handed me a grapefruit sized rock and asked me to inspect it. You could clearly see the imprint of a toad's face in the rock; its eyes, its lips, the space where its nose should have been.

Kevin Goodfella's discovery had led to some tough theological questions, such as;

'How could the creatures have survived?' and;

'How the hell did they get in there in the first place?'

I tried to reassure the Bishop that this sort of thing happened all the time. But there was nothing particularly reassuring about toads dozing within rocks that your schoolteachers had told you take several millennia to form. This represented a dramatic challenge to the status quo in Orange. People had always believed that cane toads had been introduced to Australia as part of the cane beetle fiasco of '35, when thousands of samba-loving toads had emigrated from Brazil to feast on the indigenous creepy-crawlies. The only (rather crucial) difference having been that the cane beetles in Brazil did not have wings.

And the cane beetles in Australia did.

Bishop Anger told me to stop worrying about born-again amphibians.

He hadn't called me here to combust cane toads.

He was happy for me to clean up the toads on my way home, but the fact was that cane toads were so loathed by the Orange community nobody particularly cared how they'd gotten into the bedrock. They'd managed to get in everywhere else after all.

People didn't wonder about the cane toad resurrection, they just flattened them with their cricket bats (or freezers) and buried them again.

No, the Bishop wasn't too worried about the cane toads.

Because cane toads were not cute.

The creature that Bishop Anger *was* worried about wasn't like a toad. This other creature was one of the top three cutest creatures on the planet (according to the Sunday Times 'Cute Continuum' Australia has nine of the world's ten deadliest snakes but only two of the world's top fifty cutest mammals).

Bishop Anger was worried people would notice this other creature. He wanted to be sure I'd be able to handle things. And by handle things he meant for me to perform an extinction (of the creature) and an exorcism (of the problem).

'...These are the jobs I hate the most. Jobs that involve children or animals. I have a lot of empathy with animals. Children and animals; don't work with them, that's my advice'.

This was me talking with my back turned to the Bishop while he changed out of his robes and into a spandex singlet. He hadn't asked me to turn my back, but I had anyway.

The Bishop had some sympathy for my empathy but needed to be convinced that I'd be '...going by the book?' I had another go at reassuring him;

'No-one in the Agency has ever *not* gone by the book'.

The Bishop's facial expression was either one of some discomfort or one of some distrust (both expressions I'm familiar with). I wondered if he'd heard those rumours about the Norwegian Queen and I, but it turned out he had a general mistrust of anyone who worked for the Agency. The Bishop had met enough of my colleagues to know that a common opinion among them was;

'There's nothing wrong with ignoring the rulebook, it's only getting caught doing it that's unacceptable?'

Bishop Anger hadn't read the book but;

'The one thing people have always told me about the book is *'it doesn't bear thinking about'*? Be good to the rules and the rules will be good to you? This is a delicate time? We don't want any confusion? As far as the church is concerned there's no such thing as good publicity? ...It's important this be handled discreetly?'

The reasons why the Bishop was getting so hot under

the dog collar were; i) he was on his step-master and ii) the general lack of discretion among most people. Your ghost whisperers, your pay-as-you-go clairvoyants, none of these people wanted to be discreet; they wanted a TV show. And who didn't? Live services on the church channels were rehearsed to within an inch of their lives (even though the script hadn't changed in a long time and was printed right there in front of you), but these relic-floggers and faith-charmers had started confusing people. They were ad-libbing. They had miracle white smiles.

And they weren't going by the book.

Depending on who you asked, the head-turning being caused by these phenomenon-peddlers was either a terrible omen that people were losing patience with the church, or it represented a great opportunity to help (or at least sell something to) all of these lost souls who were reaching out for something spiritual. I'd never met anyone in the Agency who believed it was a great opportunity. Everyone I'd met was firmly of the opinion that any continuity error was an abomination. And we were in the abomination management business.

The Bishop was sweating. A lot. He was out of breath. But full of hot air;

'We can't allow that the occasional blemish might be seized upon by Scientologists or Mormons or fundamentalist atheists? If it doesn't support dogma it can't be approved by our church? And if it can't be approved by our church then it certainly shouldn't be approved by anyone else's? Well you know that of course, you know that better than anyone?'

I knew all about it.

The one thing you didn't want was someone finding a better explanation for one of these abominations or errors (call them what you will) than the one in the script. As soon as people figured out that you couldn't all be right they started trying to figure out who was wrong. If someone had a better explanation for the toad living in a solid rock than you did, that made you wrong. And nobody wanted that. If there were toads living in rocks you wanted them to further your agenda, not someone else's.

Look, the easiest thing was just to get rid of the toads on your way home.

People in the church all agreed; it was better to be safe than sorry.

The church didn't need any more bad publicity.

And this is what abominations tended to be.

I left Bishop Anger on his Genesis step-master (though the image and the aroma both stayed with me for quite some time) and headed into the bush. I didn't like working with children and animals but I had a feeling that things were going to work out ok.

Let's be perfectly honest; we'd caught a break here. Of all the places in the world you wanted a cryptid to turn up it was Australia.

Maybe you haven't noticed, but they have a kangaroo and an emu on their coat of arms. In Australia you see something that looks deranged and out of some science fiction novel or toddler's drawing and you just wonder what it'll taste like barbecued.

Can you imagine if this had been found anywhere else? A completely normal looking animal, maybe something that's even on your own coat of arms, like a lion; well if one of those turns up in a field in Essex then everyone starts losing their minds.

But in West Wysolong, in bottom town, people just wanted to know whether to serve it with a red, a white or a bitter.

I'd enjoyed my fair share of cryptid encounters of course.

Basically, with a cryptid, what you're aiming for is keeping some creature whose existence is a myth, a myth.

You're looking to bury the evidence. Then you get some photos of whatever it was people had *really* seen. If it's a lion in Essex you get a fat cat (or a stuffed toy). If it's a unicorn you panic. Or maybe, if you can find one, you get a rhinoceros. The interpretation you're trying to encourage here is 'misinterpretation'. Mermaids, sausage dogs, circus fleas; they all have a rational explanation. If you find a dodo you make sure it stays extinct. If you find something that's way outside of acceptable zoology, you keep it outside.

Unless you're in Australia.

Then you can have your Jurassic birds and your knife-wielding plants. No questions asked in Australia. Australia is full of stuff that shouldn't exist. Things that are hard to believe. Cryptids in Australia are easy. Not like Bigfoot. But I'll save that lie for later. For now all you need to know is; if kangaroo is Aboriginal for 'I have no idea', then Bigfoot is Redneck for 'you have no idea'. And I'm the reason you have no idea.

But the reason I was in Australia? That was just an occasional blemish.

Let me take a leaf out of Bishop Anger's book and try to avoid any confusion here. The book you're thinking about isn't the book I'm thinking about. The book I'm thinking about is; 'The Principles of Reality Enforcement'.

It was published by the Vatican before you were born. It told me how to do my job.

And Bishop Anger had read from it as I'd spotted him on his step-master, in a room full of dog-eared Cliff Richard calendars and sweat-sodden jockstraps.

'One must at all times follow the rules. When one invests so much time into misleading others, it is necessary to guard against misleading oneself. These rules are provided to help you scrutinize the faithfulness of astonishing tales and blunders'.

This was the first time the Bishop had seen the book.

Why I'd offered to show him my copy I have no idea.

'Let your caution guide you when dealing with astonishing tales and blunders, and remember that alleged phenomena necessarily fall within one of the six degrees of credibility; believable, not unbelievable, not believable, unbelievable, stupid and tabloid'.

Four hours later I stood in the mid-afternoon oven of the Outback and ran through the six degrees of credibility as I tried to apply them to the thing I'd just glimpsed ahead. A pair of dirty hands waved me back and semaphored for more room. The dirty hands were attached to sunburnt arms; the sunburnt arms were attached to a stubby jackaroo named Cleaver. Cleaver's hands grabbed hold of something stupid and tabloid.

I went by the book.

The local Bishop is always the first port of call when judging any phenomenal allegation. Bishop Anger had travelled to the derelict and dust-busted badlands of the Bogan Station weeks earlier to judge things for himself. The questions the Bishop had asked were the same I asked myself when introduced to Cleaver Bogan. Was Cleaver a liar? Was Cleaver insane? Was Cleaver just in it for the money? Cleaver seemed ok to me. Just a little nervous. It turned out he owed a lot of money to a bank in the neighbouring town of Casino. The thing I could see in front of me could make Cleaver a lot of money.

My eyes started watering. Because of all the dust. Or because I was staring straight at Cleaver's cash cow knowing that I'd been sent here to assist in its extinction. There was no way the Agency's allies would allow this. There was no way the church could ever convince anyone that this thing in front of me was a part of God's plan. And they could hardly tell people it was a mistake. The church wasn't in the habit of accusing God of making mistakes.

Not publicly.

The thing's name was Tinkerbelle.

The rules were clear. You had to be certain that Tinkerbelle was the real deal. If there was any doubt over Tinkerbelle's being the real deal, then she wasn't.

I looked at the umbilical cord attached to Tinkerbelle and followed it for a few feet. There was a high probability that Tinkerbelle wasn't a myth. Something like 100%. She wasn't one of those 50/50 cryptids like the Fiji Mermaid. Tinkerbelle came with genuine blood and guts and a fluffy white coat. She was eating some kind of kid's breakfast cereal out of Cleaver's hand. Maybe it was 'Cocoa Monkeys', maybe 'Honey Badgers'. Cleaver told me that she would have preferred to have been grazing on green grass (what she could reach, given her umbilical cord) but we were in the Outback and there was only one green thing to be seen for miles and it was right in front of us.

Tinkerbelle was neither unbelievable, nor not believable.

An important part of my deciding whether Tinkerbelle was believable was dependent on what I believed in. Actually, it was more dependent on what *you* believed in. The rulebook made it very clear; if Tinkerbelle didn't fit in with what you already believed, if Tinkerbelle wasn't already in the script, then it was too late to write her into it now.

And Tinkerbelle was far too late.

The only other rule to be applied was whether or not Tinkerbelle had any financial value to the church, the Agency, or any of our corporate sponsors.

This was basically a simple formula for calculating astonishing revenues.

This was basically a moot point. Tinkerbelle was technically some kind of crop, a croptid if you will, but she wasn't the kind of crop you brought along to your harvest festival.

I felt sorry for Cleaver. Tinkerbelle could have paid for

his early retirement. I felt bad for Tinkerbelle too. Because of the empathy thing. But I really had no choice; this wasn't the kind of continuity error that gets approved by the church.

The kind of continuity error that gets approved is 'The Miracle of Saint Giles". This was when everyone arrived late for bell-ringing practice at Saint Giles' Church in Hastings on 1st April 1973. This was when Bruce's car caught a flat, and Betty's sausage dog broke off its leash. When Tracey had to pick up her dry cleaning and Victor forgot to turn the clocks forward. This was when all eleven bell-ringers turned up at Saint Giles' at 19:23pm.

After the church had been hit by a meteorite at 19:22.

The reason I was at the Bogan Station; it wasn't the kind of error that gets approved. It wasn't the kind of thing you got to hear about. Perhaps, once upon a time, they couldn't be explained, but eventually people had accepted the killer birds and killer plants at face value.

I doubted people were ready to accept Tinkerbelle though.

Tinkerbelle's other name was 'The Vegetable Lamb'. This was the name Bishop Anger had given her when he'd contacted the Agency. This had been shortly after he'd seen the abominable cauliflower attached to the other end of Tinkerbelle's umbilical cord.

He hadn't been able to come up with a better name.

Tinkerbelle looked up at me with blue eyes. She looked real. She looked difficult to hoax. Tinkerbelle's umbilical cord was attached to a three-foot wide cauliflower that had sprouted out of the red earth and was surrounded by a seven-foot high fence erected to keep the dingoes out. This was because each time a dingo strayed within the circumference of her umbilical cord she ripped them to shreds with her razor sharp teeth. She was otherwise affectionate though and was happy to be sheared for her unusually soft and velvety fleece.

Maybe one day people could've accepted Tinkerbelle. But I had to make my adjustments. Sometimes you just have to get on with the job that you're paid for.

Cleaver wasn't happy of course. Cleaver was worried about his early retirement.

I had a lot of empathy for his Tinkerbelle sympathy, but I was just doing my job.

Sometimes I wondered what I was doing with my life. I wondered if the lies we fed people didn't just make them panic even more. I wondered if the status quo was worth it. But then I'd tell myself that was just the way things were. And people liked things how they were. So who was I to re-arrange things? I did what I did because it needed to be done.

It was either that or it was because of Black Saturday.

I couldn't remember which. Because of my terrible memory.

But I knew that people panicked when the status quo was undermined. And that people tended to do stupid things when they panicked. And I knew that people could get hurt doing stupid things. And I didn't want to put people in danger by not doing my job.

The truth hurts. Everyone knew that. But what you didn't know couldn't hurt you.

The way you bring about the extinction of a vegetable lamb is; you cut its umbilical cord. Don't ask me what Tinkerbelle was getting from that giant cauliflower that she couldn't live without. I was no more a zoologist than I was an 'Events Manager'.

My real job title was 'Reality Enforcer'.

I enforced reality. Sort of. Depending on your point of view.

Depending on your point of view you could argue I enforced the opposite of reality, that I enforced disbelief.

But all I really did was correct continuity errors. I called them continuity errors, but they have a more popular name, the name you would probably use.

You'd probably call them 'miracles'. If you ever got to hear about them that is. But you don't. So you call other things miracles instead, or you stop believing in them altogether.

Tinkerbelle had to die because we couldn't take the risk that someone might have believed her story. I guess if you'd ever gotten to meet her you'd have probably said that Tinkerbelle was a miracle.

Unfortunately for you, Tinkerbelle isn't a miracle any longer.

4. The What

*T*he things I'd tended to deal with on the job had always been a little pear-shaped, but it wasn't until I'd dealt with Tinkerbelle that the pears started to taste funny.

It seemed I'd picked up some sort of uncomfortable feeling in Australia. And jet lag.

I was having trouble sleeping. It was either jet lag, or it was work. It could have been the repressed memories of my childhood, but how the hell was I supposed to know?

I stood in my garden alternately searching the pond for goldfish and watching lights blink on and off in the tower block opposite. I tried to get some sense from my subconscious, but it held out long enough that the fortune teller from flat twenty-three got back from her nightshift and switched on her lights and then I knew it was time to get up for work.

The last cleaner who'd left my employment had described my home as ramshackle ('a bloody pig sty'). There were souvenirs strewn all over the place, just in case anyone ever asked what I'd been up to (although no-one ever did, because I was a loner). I'd explained how the stacks of gossip magazines and tabloids were all in perfect order, they were just piled a little high. I hadn't explained that the reason these periodicals had reached such heady heights was the absurd frequency with which continuity errors occurred. I hadn't explained this to any of my cleaners because it was my job to lie to people. I couldn't really afford a cleaner, but the Agency had insisted on one ever since Graham O'Thrones had left that USB full of photos of the Home Secretary's two-headed twin sister on a double-decker bus.

Most of these tabloids were copies of the Sunday Spartan. You may have chanced upon some of the Spartan's more memorable headlines over the years; 'WW2 Bomber Found on Moon!', 'One-Armed Monkey Lands One-Winged Plane!', 'Racist Donkey Robs Bank!', 'I Gave Birth to an Alien Hamburger!' and 'Alien Hamburger Stole my Handbag!'.

Most of these headlines made you feel a little unwell, if you were in my line of work.

Most of these headlines meant an early start and an audit of working procedures.

Someone usually wanted to know; how the hell did the press get wind of this?

Piled on top of my souvenir copies of the Spartan you might have found (if you were still my cleaner) a collection of rare and valuable comics. There was the one where Superman saves Stalin from the Royal Russian. And the one where Captain America and the New Defenders take down the Brotherhood of Students. These were published once; once upon a time they were out there, but retroactive continuity is a wonderful thing and comic books are a lot easier to redraw than the Zapruder film or a photograph of a racist donkey robbing a bank. You can still find a few of the original books knocking about out in backstreet charity shops if you look hard enough. Some collectors have offered me thousands for these.

The Dalai Lama; you wouldn't think it but he's a comic book nut. And a millionaire.

As soon as publishers saw how easy it was to rip up the past and act like it had never happened they started bringing superheroes back from the dead or erasing unpopular love interests or villains (or villainous love interests) as if they'd never existed. After a few years the TV networks got wind of all of this rebooting and started trying it out in soap operas. Who can forget that memorable episode of Emmerdale Farm when 'Barn-door' Barney Rothschild awoke to discover his descent into a glue-sniffing, kerb-crawling bunny-boiler had all just been a bad dream? This marked a watershed. It was the first time a writer's retroactively erasing something objectionable hadn't gone down well with the audience.

Unfortunately there were no Emmerdale fans in the Cabinet, which explains why the Government was so caught out by the ferocity of the criticism when they retroactively changed the backstory for 'Gulf War 2: Son of a Bush' to contradict their previously established (and critically acclaimed) saga of an American oil-rustling dynasty.

I was one of the few who found themselves sympathising with the PMs DOA POV during all of those subsequent inquiries he was unable to attend. I used to think there was just no point in dwelling on the past, especially if the past was unpleasant. I liked to think that my bad dreams were nothing more than that. That my bad dreams never happened.

Sure, sure, I collected copies of the Sunday Spartan, but it wasn't as if I had some unconscious desire for the truth to come out. Give me a choice between the hidden truth and a comic book and I'd take the funny pages every time. I was really no different to anyone else. Sometimes you got home from a hard day at the office and you just needed an escape.

I listened to the news on VoidFM as I cleared away the breakfast dishes. There seemed to be some confusion about last week's failed assassination attempt on Raúl Greedo. No-one was sure anymore if it had failed or not.

Now people were speculating that Raúl might have failed to survive.

I pushed my back up against the kitchen sink and tried to throw knives into the knife block from a record distance. Once I'd broken my personal best I tried throwing dishes into the dishwasher from the same distance but I got too cocky and threw a lead crystal cheese plate like a Frisbee. I spent the next two weeks finding shards of glass in my cornflakes. Sure, sure, the blue glass had been placed there by some nutter with a vendetta against Kellogg's, but the clear glass, that was all my own fault.

I drove my Fido VTO towards work at a walking pace.

I thought about driving along the footpath at a walking pace instead; most people around here had stopped using the footpath altogether. You got the pram, the pushchair, the bike, the car, then you downsized to the mobility scooter. As I reached second gear I could see someone painting over the bicycle lane and turning it into a mobility scooter lane.

I double-parked the Fido and headed up to the thirteenth floor.

The Blacker Building was two hundred years old and to the best of my knowledge had never been refurbished. Still the old men working there seemed to behave as if they were employed at one of those Silicon Valley start-ups where you're forced to take a break every thirty minutes and the break you're forced to take involves some sort of coerced fussball with people from HR or Ping-Pong with the guys from the warehouse.

Fortunately for me the Agency didn't have a warehouse. It had a Whitewash Museum, but I'd never been forced to play fussball with anyone who worked there. I didn't play Ping-Pong either, because I'd only recently turned forty and most of my colleagues on the thirteenth floor had turned forty twenty or thirty years earlier. Don't get me wrong though, these were some pretty sprightly pensioners. These old men could handle themselves.

A couple of septuagenarian colleagues were giving the visiting Archbishop of Earthsea a tour of the Whitewash Museum. I had some of Bishop Anger's Tinkerbelle photographs (also a photo-shopped Justin Bieber calendar he'd printed himself at a J-Mart) to check in and followed the fusty old men down to the fusty old basement. Mole-faced Martin Reckless from HR was waiting at the bottom of the stairs with a fire extinguisher;

'Be a good fellow and hold onto this for me would you Canon?'

'You're going to start a fire in the basement?'

'A practical joke. We want the Archbishop to think we've set the Shroud on fire'.

Reckless held up one of the many fake Turin Shrouds to be found lying around the basement. The real Shroud was safely tucked away in the Bellagio Hotel where it had been ever since the Dalai Lama had won it in a game of three card Vajrayāna poker.

But I was looking at the fire extinguisher Reckless had in his other hand;

'That thing expired eight years ago'.

I got a thick shake of the head and a rolling of the eyes;

'You're a real damp cloth you know Canon?'

'Then I'll stick around. You're going to need one'.

I kept my distance. I much prefer to keep my distance when I know a fire is about to backfire. I ducked behind a crate of weather balloons and hooked an old gramophone up to a pair of giant speakers that had been used at admiration-hogging (and hog-admiring) Prime Minister David Cameron's election rallies to fake the crowd's enthusiastic applause.

Reckless did a passable job of smiling, revealing some of the shroud's hidden history (did you know it was actually Jerry Fallwell who'd lost the shroud to the Dalai Lama?) and making his premeditated combustion seem like a spontaneous accident.

The Archbishop started screaming and crying pretty much simultaneously. Reckless was still laughing at this point but stopped abruptly when the Archbishop threw his considerable weight in the direction of the burning shroud and started rolling around on the museum floor doing his best impersonation of a fire blanket. Reckless let the expired extinguisher off and covered himself (but no part of the burning shroud) in expired white powder. I quickly grabbed hold of a numbered vinyl copy of celebrated banshee Mariah Carey's confiscated cover version of Public Enemy's 'Louder Than A Bomb' and dropped the gramophone's needle. It sent a soundwave through the room at such a high frequency that it snuffed out the oxygen fuelling the flames. And put the fire out.

It wasn't a damp cloth. But it worked. I checked my vegetable lamb snaps into the museum and rewarded myself with a chocolate milkshake from the vending machine.

But what else do people do at the Agency? What do people get paid for?

Let me start at the best place to start, the place you'd never normally start from, the place you'll never see before the opening credits of 'Roy Chancy, PCSO' or 'CSI: Coventry'.

Let me start at the beginning...

On October 12th 1888 the cream of Tunbridge Wells' society gathered around a natural spring (a slightly rusted hole in the ground) under a suitably royal blue sky for the ceremonial converting of this common town into a royal hanger-on. The ceremony began with a speech by the Mayor and was followed by three hymns... And a mutton shower.

After everyone had stopped screaming people started to scoop up the chunks of mutton that had fallen from the clear blue sky. It being in bad taste to eat mutton in Royal Tunbridge Wells the meat was sent off to a veterinarian who hypothesised that a murder of crows had flown over the town shortly after enjoying a particularly long lunch of particularly dead sheep, and, the sheep having already turned, the off mutton was regurgitated over Royal Tunbridge Wells by the vomiting crows.

But if this was the truth, it was pretty disgusting. A more palatable explanation was needed; one that could assuage the hysteria gripping the town.

Queen Victoria called her Ulterior Minister away from his Jack the Ripper hoaxing and asked that he find a more plausible explanation for this abomination than the 'meat asteroids' theory currently doing the rounds. The Minister promptly called in a favour from an old Tsar Wars buddy (who was now an ordained reality enforcer working out of the Vatican's Eastbourne field office) and after a thorough investigation and a five course lunch the Minister's old drinking buddy came up with a surprisingly simple (yet eloquent) explanation. The mutton shower had never happened.

After overcoming his surprise that the residents of Royal Tunbridge Wells had been so willing and able to swallow this untruth so easily the Ulterior Minister recognised the potential for further outrageous lies. And so six months later, on 1st April 1889, the Ministry of

Enlightenment was born (later renamed the Information Reclamation Agency), with Queen Vic agreeing to pay the Vatican a licensing fee for her own whoppers franchise. But this was absolutely *not* a protection racket. This was simply the reunification of church and state.

Of course Queen Vic wasn't too happy about having to pay the licence fee. She was more inclined to just steal the idea. Because Victoria was a kleptomaniac.

Although to be fair, she was only really interested in subcontinents.

My apologies if you hadn't realised this yet; but you haven't been living in the real world. The real world is a world of random chaos. Of black holes. And plot holes. Of cock ups and mistakes and continuity errors. In a world where numerous divergent outcomes are possible sometimes the impossible happens.

You've heard of the law of averages right?

It's a typo.

It's actually the *lie* of averages.

The point here is that people judge the world by averages, as if the average is correct and anything that isn't average is wrong and strange and frightening. But the fact is there's no such thing as average; we live in a world of almost endless irregularity.

The Law of Disproportionately Unrealistic Numbers states that the typical person sleeping for the normal number of hours per day and engaging in no more than the usual volume of outrageous behaviour can expect to experience what the Agency refers to as a continuity error and you still insist on calling a miracle once every forty-two days.

Basically, assuming that while you are conscious things are actually happening to you (i.e. assuming you are not sitting in the House Of Lords), in order to witness a one in a million event, you need to wait, on average, around forty-two days. What you call miracles, they're happening all the time. They're as common as muck.

Think about it; in the last forty-two days something miraculous happened. Probably it was behind you, but even if it was right there in front of you, if the guys at the Agency have been doing their jobs correctly, you'll never have known.

The Agency is split between the Departments of Knowledge Management (DKM) and Ignorance Management (DIM). I was with the former, in the Office of Reality Enforcement. If you worked in the Department of Knowledge Management then you were in the business of managing knowledge; catching continuity errors and abominations before they became common knowledge, at which point they needed to be passed over to the DIM crowd to give them the ret-con treatment.

The ret-con treatment is basically a process for managing people's ignorance. This is a process that starts with your discovering something, continues through investigating it, and ends with someone in the DIM deleting it. Over in the DIM you have the Office of Selective Omission and the Office of Clarification and Continuity. You don't so much have a conversation with these guys as they give you a synopsis of the conversation you were about to have and you assume whatever they're telling you is accurate.

Those of us who worked in the DKM tended to take more of a 'hands on' approach to the job. Most of the time the DIM guys picked up where we left off.

But sometimes the roles were reversed.

About a week after the Tinkerbelle job some DIM guys had needed my help dealing with an outbreak of plagiarism. I took a call from the Office of Clarification and Continuity and some panicking DIM fellow explained how;

'Half a dozen people wrote the same song yesterday'.

(As in yesterday was Tuesday, not as in 'all my troubles seemed so far away').

Half a dozen people had sent the same demo tape into Jason Broccoli; A&R man for XS records. Jason had loved it the first time he'd heard it but by the sixth time he was rolling around on his carpet with his hands over his ears, screaming and crying. Fortunately Jason Broccoli was the A&R man for XS records and so this hadn't raised too many eyebrows.

The song's title was 'You Suck!' and bore an uncanny resemblance to 'My Sweet Lord' by George Harrison. I was told to get there, get the tapes, and then visit the composers.

This was pretty much your standard cryptomnesia outbreak.

Cryptomnesia is a memory of a particular event which you didn't know you had. This is as opposed to your regular selective or 'political' amnesia, which is a memory of some dodgy event that you knew you didn't want. Cryptomnesia is almost always the only other explanation for plagiarism after stealing. It's 'stealing by accident'.

Sometimes memories get lost. Sometimes they get hidden.

It isn't that rare. Everyone has memories they've forgotten.

By the time I'd dealt with the first set of plagiarists I had an encrypted voicemail waiting for me from the OCC. This time I needed to visit a couple of screenwriters who'd sent the same manuscript to the same agent. The OCC had received a tip off from a movie spoilers website, but it turned out that the agent at Paramount hadn't actually spotted the similarities between the two screenplays and was in the process of green-lighting them both, despite the fact that their titles were virtually identical. The agent not picking up on this wasn't the most disturbing aspect of the case though, nor was it the fact that one of the authors was named Walter Marks and the other Mark Walters.

No, the plot was the problem. It's always the plot.

One of the screenplays was called 'The Miracle Adjuster'.

The other was called 'The Miracle Adjustment'.

Both screenplays opened on an establishing shot of the Australian Outback and featured a vegetable lamb, an outbreak of plagiarism and an Alaskan beach covered in severed left feet. This wasn't cryptomnesia. This was crypto-clairvoyance. This was scary.

Scary like my mentor's once having adjusted a thirteen-year-old's creative writing exercise book when the story concerned the invasion of Narnia and the thirteen-year-old's name was Anthony Blair. But that's another story.

And now isn't the time for name-dropping.

Maybe later I'll tell you how I got myself onto Blimey Lowsey's tour bus.

But that was weeks away, and for now I had a job to do.

The boys in the OCC had come up with a plausible explanation for this unexplainable event. And it was down to me to perform it. I had a copyright lawyer to impersonate and a fake Parisian client whose interests I needed to look out for.

They say you can't bullshit a bullshitter. But you can. You just need to know where to get hold of the best quality bullshit. You need to know how to use it. And you need to know the Principle of Least Astonishment.

Basically what I was trying to achieve here, was belief.

When Boris LaBouche: Entertainment Lawyer turned up on Mark Walters' front doorstep I wanted Mark to believe that the leather bound copy of 'L'Ajustement de Miracle' that Boris handed over was the real deal, and that Boris LaBouche's Parisian client (Simone Vandriver) really had written 'L'Ajustement de Miracle' in 1955.

When Boris LaBouche (a copyright lawyer who looked an awful lot like Colin Jekyll but with a moustache and pince-nez) started throwing threats around in an affected French accent I wanted Walter Marks to believe Boris. What I didn't want was for Mark Walters or Walter Marks to find Boris' story 'hard to believe'. I absolutely did not want Boris' story to sound astonishing. If you were putting together a story like Boris' you basically had to ask yourself; 'What would be the least surprising explanation for this?'

If people believed George Harrison they could believe Boris.

Boris explained how Simone Vandriver was pretty angry about how Mark had ripped off her 1955 French classic. And Boris really looked like he believed Mark when he told him that he'd never even heard of the book.

Boris told Mark not to worry; maybe he'd read it a long time ago.

Or maybe someone had whispered the plot to him while he was sleeping.

Who knew how it had happened.

The important thing was that Boris LaBouche had a leather bound copy of the book and Mark had thirty days to destroy all copies of his plagiarised work or else he'd be hit with a writ, or an injunction, or both.

Then I visited Walter so Boris could tell him the same thing.

After lunch I dropped by the Office of Clarification and Continuity to congratulate them on a job well done. An hour later two screenplays and a bogus copy of 'L'Ajustement de Miracle', Simone Vandriver, 1955, had been safely checked into the Whitewash Museum.

5. The Why

*T*he Fido VTO had a top speed of 158mph but the radio could only tune itself into two stations. You basically had to keep your finger on the dial flipping between the two in the hope you'd find something worth listening to. Finding something worth listening to on VoidFM or StaticFM was firmly at the unlikely end of the Reinhardt-Munster scale.

I listened to the new number one ('You Suck!') before enduring a routine about toilet brushes that the weather girl on the Breakfast Show had overheard at Jongleurs.

When I got into the office the phone rang twice with a couple of celebrity-endorsed telemarketers begging me to fax them a copy of my signature. This is what recording artists have been forced into since internet piracy brought about an end to record sales; Nickelback Payday Loans, Crowded House Insurance. I worked through a file on my desk filled with mug-shots of some cyclops caught selling 'Royal Blood' outside Windsor Castle. But this was just evolution doing its thing. Do we really need two eyes if we all have camera phones?

This is what's known in the industry as a body error. A girl who can breathe underwater. A boy with an immunity to the Colonel's secret blend of herbs and spices.

These dissonant abilities have a name; disabilities. The Agency has sponsors who might be bankrupted by these kids, corporations who don't want people noticing continuity errors, don't want people witnessing the weird and wonderful. The world can only be chaotic as long as we believe corporations bring order to the chaos.

People need to believe that everything is under *someone's* control. When people start seeing continuity errors then things start looking out of control. Then people start panicking. Pay a visit to the Office of Reality Enforcement and you'll meet the people responsible for making sure you don't start to see things getting out of control.

It doesn't take much to start a panic nowadays.

Let me tell you, there is nothing more frustrating than returning home after managing an outbreak of killer badgers to find that people have started losing their minds over a football match (and to find that there's nothing left to eat in the fridge).

This is probably going to come as a bit of a shock, but a country's stock exchange tends to swan-dive by an average of thirty-nine steps after its football team is eliminated from the World Cup. People trace the great depression of the noughties back to some bad mortgages, or terrorism, but the banking crisis really began when Switzerland were eliminated from the 2006 World Cup in a penalty shoot-out.

This time it was the US (thrashed six-nil by Cuba).

Unfortunately this market crash had led to an outbreak of uncontrollable dancing among traumatised brokers on Wall St. There were brokers doing the Time Warp and brokers busting out a new version of YMCA (PIGS). A seventeen stone fat cat was leading his traders on a Conga around a brass bullock with all of the uncontrolled arm-waving and leg-raving of a herd of baby camel-spiders. This had to be contained before it went viral.

This wasn't the kind of thing people wanted to see.

'A Raving Plague on Wall Street'.

'Dancing Mania of the Minted'.

These aren't the kind of headlines you want to read over your Frosties. These are the kind of headlines that'll put you right off of your Frosties and send you creeping back under the bedcovers.

We started rounding up the Wall St. paparazzi. Then we started cutting in.

Sure, sure, we were all dancing. But we were keeping a low profile all the same. We were listening, we were learning. We were getting ready to make our adjustments.

There were American psychos experiencing visions.

But their blood was cocaineless.

Their urine E-deficient.

These bankers had shared plenty of hallucinations in the past, but that usually only resulted in the collapse of someone's business or a repossession, not the kind of communal possession that ends up with three hundred body-popping stockbrokers doing the Macarena across the Brooklyn Bridge.

The market had opened to a couple of panicked investors doing the Lambada but within an hour there were thirty or forty and by the time the reality enforcers had arrived on the scene there had to have been at least five hundred shareholders dancing Gangnam Style. Those who refused to join in were beaten with glow-sticks.

Old men of the exchange were dragged out of their private members' clubs and forced to dance until they collapsed. When the EMTs arrived to treat the broken legs they got dragged in too; if you were wearing something fluorescent you fitted right in with these ravers and their neon contact lenses.

But for some reason the sight of someone wearing boat shoes with socks prompted violent scuffles.

These bankers seemed even less able to control their urges than normal, as if in some new kind of trance. Workers at the Casino Bank stripped each other naked and started fornicating with people working for the financial regulatory services. The head of Oligarch Relations at Chemical Bank started crawling around Times Square on all fours making animal noises and jumping out in front of terrified tourists.

Some bankers even resorted to foul language.

Some resorted to sword fighting.

The VP of A&L Asset Management (who'd been around long enough to have witnessed the Boston dancing plague of 1937) hired Limp Bizkit in an effort to ward off the raving mania by having them repeatedly play their one big hit. Unfortunately the plan completely backfired due to the diabolical taste in music shared by most people working in the financial industry and so instead of breaking things up Limp Bizkit only succeeded in encouraging more to join in.

It was clear that these bankers weren't going to stop dancing.

After forty-eight hours we had no choice but to intervene and so following an emergency session of the Treasury Department we started injecting some extra liquidity (your energy drinks, your legal highs) into these sweaty bankers to prevent them from crashing.

We set up a cordon around Wall Street and put up first aid tents and makeshift shelters. A tent city sprang up to contain all of these raving bankers with their glazed eyes and their screaming and chanting and their 72 hour stink on.

The Office of Clarification and Continuity put out a

statement confirming that this was just another anti-capitalist occupation.

And all of this over a football match.

Can you imagine what would have happened if people had woken up and found vegetable lambs sprouting up all over the place?

Vegetable lambs aren't part of the bargain. Vegetable lambs aren't in the script.

If you're in charge then you wrote the script. When something happens that isn't in the script then you no longer look like you're in charge. This doesn't fit with what you've been telling people. With the reality we all agreed on. People aren't going to believe a word you tell them any longer. Are you really going to throw your career away over something as flimsy and subjective as the truth?

The thing about the truth is; it doesn't get out much.

Everyone agreed on the truth a long time ago. Our ancestors got together long before we were born and agreed on what was real and what wasn't.

The way you get agreement on the truth is; you find out what most people believe in.

And then you get everyone else to sign up to it.

Basically what you're doing here is giving people freedom of choice. You can choose to be part of the majority. Or you can be in the minority; Norman No-Mates.

When you get enough people behind your story, then your story becomes the truth. This is a really watertight process. This works whether your story is real or whether it is not. Even better, this works whether people *know* if your story is real or not.

Maybe human beings don't know anything for sure. But they can still agree with each other. I can still believe what you tell me. And if I believe you I get a reward. I get to hang out with you and your friends and we can all have a whale of a time agreeing with each other.

What's not to like?

Only people who don't agree with us. You know; the minority.

Oh yeah, and things that we all agreed could never happen.

Things that aren't in the script.

Let's assume that you're in power and that while you're in power 'things' that people 'can't understand' start 'happening'.

The one thing people absolutely do not want to hear from you is that you don't know *why* things are happening, or even worse, you don't know *what* is happening.

That you're theory-less. That you're explanation-lite.

People don't like to think that life is getting out of their control. But if they do they at least want to comfort themselves with the knowledge that someone else has things covered.

It used to be that people would go and see their priest for some answers.

Their priest's life couldn't be out of control. He was the very definition of control.

Unfortunately priests started giving that up recently; the appearance of being in control, of our lives, of their own. In fact there seems to have been a concerted effort by some priests to distance themselves from control.

Priests just ain't what they used to be.

But that's ok, because these days we've got something even better than priests.

When our politicians do precisely the same things to kneeling subordinates as our priests, it doesn't make us think they've lost control, it makes us think; 'I wish I had as much control as that guy!' The priests might have fumbled the ball but the government is still in control of things. We know because we stayed up late to watch the election results. We shouted 'hooray' when the good guy won, or 'boo', when the good guy lost. Either way there's a good guy or a bad guy in charge. We can see who's in control.

So when people start panicking then whoever said they were in control finds themselves in trouble. As soon as people start thinking you've lost control then someone else is going to come along and knock you off your golden perch (and melt your perch down and bling their bandwagon with it). All of a sudden people stop putting their trust in whatever it was you were telling them and you're facing a revolution.

Believe me; it happens all the time...

It happened in 1797. Maybe it's before your time but there was a revolution in France. This is when you ended up in a situation where there were more people in the minority that didn't agree with you than in the majority who did. This is when the people you governed started chanting; 'You don't know what you're doing!' or worse;

'We don't believe what you're telling us'.

The thing about the French Revolution was; it made quite a mess of the church, what with all of the burning monasteries and the desecration and the dead priests everywhere. These revolutionaries were quite 'anti-church'. They chucked the Pope in prison. The Pope!

Because they didn't like the look of his calendar.

Napoleon saw sense eventually and pardoned the Pope, which was the honourable thing to do. As soon as he was made aware of people's concerns Napoleon got right on it and gave France its church back. Certainly no-one could have accused Napoleon of not identifying the problem and dealing with it. He did what needed to be done like any good statesman would. Unfortunately the Pope had been dead a few years by then.

Then it happened again. In 1917. There was another French Revolution, in Mexico.

The priests were given the same choice as before; you

could give up all of your rights and your property and leave the country, or you could give up all of your rights and your property and leave this plane of existence.

And then it happened again! In 1931. In Spain!

You have to admire the rigor of the Spanish revolutionaries though; after they'd finished the torturing and the pillaging and the seizing of the property they at least let the surviving priests stay on in the parts of the churches that had survived the fires. As long as they kept up with the rent. Otherwise their new landlords threw them down a mine shaft.

The church got the message, eventually. The church decided that if you can't stop revolution, and you can't stop people panicking that you've lost control, then you need to make sure people don't start seeing things that don't fit in with the story you've been telling them. You need to make sure you don't let people see anything to upset them.

Like the ratings system for games and movies; it's for their own good.

People used to burn books. Now the Agency burns miracles.

It used to be that the Agency cleaned up after spontaneous human combustion. Back in the days when it was shrouded in mystery. But after the Department of Ignorance Management came up with that 'human candle' hypothesis it became so easily explained that the Agency started using it to clean up other miracles.

Just between you and me, no-one really thought anyone would buy this. No one believed your average nuclear family could find Nan-Nan's charred left foot next to a pile of ash, a shattered china plate and half a dozen broken digestives, and then just shrug it off because Nan-Nan was much like a candle in many respects.

It was hard to believe anyone could buy the human

candle theory.

But people did.

As far as the Agency is concerned miracles are a threat to our way of life. Show your average person a dodgy dossier or a blurry photo and they'll swallow anything you tell them. But show them a miracle and they'll start forming their own beliefs; they'll believe whatever the hell *they* want, and they'll throw out your doctrines and your rulebooks quicker than you can say 'please don't'. You can't say 'please don't' anymore, because people don't do what you ask them anymore.

People only do what you *tell* them.

You have to be a little more forceful.

You have to form an organisation whose sole purpose is to aggressively pursue and discredit any individual or event that might undermine the status quo while at the same time enforcing your reality on those who might disagree with you.

It doesn't matter if something actually happens a lot or not, only if it seems to happen a lot; whether it's in the news a lot or not.

People's faith in the consensus reality needs to be enforced.

'Alright chap?'

Maxwell Self materialised behind me and gave me a slap on the back. Pin-striped 'little teapot' lookalike Self was a fellow reality enforcer. The slap on the back was Self's way of showing me (and anyone else watching) that he felt he was my superior. If not now, then following some imminently anticipated promotion. They'd broken the mould when they made Self. But everyone who knew him wished that they'd broken it earlier.

Self would often tell me (in his castrato whine);

'You need to get noticed by the right people chap. You need to make sure you're following them on FaceSpace'.

I wondered if he was noticed more than me because he dyed his hair a preposterous shade of astronomical black. That was the only reason I ever noticed him. That and the fact that you'd hear his cartoon villain's voice and turn to reply and then realise he was talking to someone via his Bluetooth hearing aid. It was that or he was hearing voices. I'd always considered Maxwell Self to be a dangerous idiot. But I didn't get to choose who I worked with. I only got to choose the paper I read as we travelled back from Wall Street together.

Self wore the expression of a man suffering from simultaneous constipation and explosive diarrhoea. This was the expression of a man who'd completely lost control.

It was the same expression as the one he had on the front page of my newspaper.

You could pick up any newspaper in any country and see Self's expression as he watched the Duke of York and Chancellor Helmut Schaffenhoffen rolling around on a table in the all-you-can-eat Chinese Dining Room at Buckingham Palace, with various fried hors d'oeuvres and canapés stuck to their backsides. This was because the Duke had attempted to address Chancellor Schaffenhoffen in his native tongue during an after-dinner speech at the 'Offshore Wind Farm Non-proliferation Summit'. Unfortunately instead of saying;

'I applaud the Chancellor's undaunted tenacity' he'd said;

'I desire the Chancellor's teenage daughter'.

At which point the Chancellor had struck him with a stale pumpernickel and wrestled him to the ground. Eventually the Duke and Chancellor had been separated and everyone had calmed down. Unfortunately His Royal Highness had calmed down a little overzealously and after his fourth glass of Weinerblokker he proceeded to vomit over a corgi sitting on his mum's lap, passed out, fell off of his chair and cut his face on his ex-wife's glass slipper.

Self had only been there to switch the Chancellor's climate change study with one commissioned by Exxon. But somehow he'd ended up sitting next to the Queen. You could only just make Self out in the corner, but his water-boarded expression hadn't changed since. One thing you didn't do in the Agency was get your face on the front page of a newspaper.

I told Self not to worry, but when you worked for a secret organisation that was hell bent on keeping itself under the radar and maintaining a web of lies, paranoia was a bit of an occupational hazard.

Self was keen to impress the kinds of people who don't usually get impressed, the kinds of people who only pay attention when things go tits-up. Otherwise you were just *there*. Maybe it was all part of Self's game plan. If you were 'just there' you needed to say something controversial every now and again to make sure you were still visible (to the Agency that is, as opposed to the readers (and tits-up lovers) of The Sun).

Self said something controversial pretty regularly.

The previous year he'd had too much absinthe at the Agency's annual knees-up at the Cock and Bull and suggested to the Chancellor of the Exchequer (whom Self knew from the Oxford University Jammy Buggers Club) that the Agency's policy on reality enforcement might be adjusted in line with the consensus reality of the Jammy Buggers.

If someone had a belief at odds with the Jammy Buggers then shouldn't the Buggers enforce their reality upon them? The Chancellor then confronted the Agency's Deputy Outfit Director and told her that the PM (another Jammy Bugger) wanted to rip up the rulebook. The PM thought it was time for the Agency to take a more hard-line approach.

Self may be a dangerous idiot. But he is a consistent one. He gave the same speech when called in front of the Agency's Public Relations Committee following his setting fire to Muhammad's beard and two front teeth at a museum in Kuala Lumpur.

This was the kind of thing the Agency's Public Relations Committee tended to frown upon because; i) there really was nothing miraculous about a Muslim with a beard, and ii) there really was nothing desirable about two billion men with two billion axes to grind.

This was the kind of thing that would get you noticed, but which usually failed (rather spectacularly) to impress. The main reason this irritated people was that it generated a lot of unnecessary manual work for the Office of Clarification and Continuity.

Now it turns out Muhammad was clean shaven after all.

I left Self at JFK airport. He had another job to go to; some controversial new wind power station off the coast of Washington State that had been generating body errors.

We burned miracles.

But some of us enjoyed pyromania more than others.

I might have spontaneously combusted the odd body error in my time, but I waited until that body had passed on. Self thought this was too risky; you had to combust the body in error while it was still living, maybe even before it started. And Self's definition of a body error was a bit broad for my liking. We may have been in the same line of work, but Maxwell Self and I were at opposite ends of the Gandhi Spectrum as reality enforcers go.

Sure, sure, if you were a reality enforcer then your job was clear; people's faith in the consensus reality needed to be enforced. But that wasn't to say people didn't have the right to disagree. It was just that anyone who didn't agree was living in a different world to the one we were in. You know; the good one.

It wasn't our job to keep these people out of our world though.

It was our job to bring them back in.

Trust me, people wanted to be a part of our world, to be a part of the world that we saw in our films (as long as that film wasn't The Matrix), or that we read about in our books (as long as that book wasn't 1984).

No-one (apart from politicians and rock stars) wants to be told that they're living in a different world to normal people. If you're living in a different world to the rest of us then chances are you're going to bump into a reality enforcer who's going to drag you back into the good world that we're in.

You're probably just suffering from a little disbelief.

The reality enforcement police can help with that. Think of them like normal law enforcement officers; all benevolent and helpful and looking smart in their uniforms etc.

But if you're really attached to that different world of yours, or even worse, you think you're in the good world, or worst of all, you go around telling people your world is better than ours, well then chances are you're going to get dragged out of there pretty forcefully.

Maybe you'll never even know it's happened. You'll feel a little sleepy and when you wake up, you won't be in Oz anymore. You'll be back in Kansas where you belong. And that piece of paper in your hand? It's a repeat prescription.

Consider yourself re-educated.

Welcome to our world.

6. The How

Back at the office I was confronted by a bit of a panic. People were panicking because of the amber security alert. And the piercing alarm bells. And the piercing cavity-searches.

A clerk from the Office of Clarification and Continuity ran into me clutching copies of a book called 'Futility' (more of which, later). Then he started yelling about the security breach and the 'cleaners' who were scouring the building for some investigative journalist who'd apparently come in through the bathroom window. This kind of thing happened all the time. Your more experienced adjusters (like me) didn't panic because of an amber alert. Your more experienced adjusters (like me) only tended to panic when meeting women.

Problem was; the office was full of them. The scratch-starters had arrived.

This was causing another panic, in addition to the one that people were already dealing with. This was the 1+1=3 equation of panic. You had two different things to panic about, so you started panicking about which of the two you needed to worry about the most.

I wasn't too worried about the alarm bells ringing. I was wearing ear plugs. But the scratch-starters were an issue because; i) it meant I'd be stuck in the office for the rest of the week and ii) one of them was making me panic. Normally a line of scratch-starters just provoked a feeling of mild dread. Normally you were just wondering who you were going to end up with. Normally you didn't care. But one of them was making me care.

Actually this young intern was making everyone in the office care. Because she'd gotten herself trapped in a full body scanner at the security gate. All of my colleagues were staring. And so was I. But I had a good reason for staring. Or a better reason.

I thought I recognised this young lady. From my past.

I didn't like to think about my past, usually. I usually found my past easy enough to dodge. But this young lady looked like she was going to trip me up...

'...The good news is that divine inspiration is at an all-time low, and this helps keep the overall volume of inspiration at a manageable level. Coupled with the fact that imagination has been in steady decline ever since our Gameboy intervention, this means that challenges to the status quo are at record low levels, even for peacetime...'

This was Buck Haddock; our fairly permanent (and fairly permatanned) guest speaker from USADSAK giving a presentation to the scratch-starters in the Sir Charles Fort Hall. It was the same presentation that he gave every year, but I still had to pretend to look interested. Buck was only half-way gone but most of his audience were already rocking a thousand yard stare through the indecipherable slides being projected against the wall.

One of the scratch-starters raised his hand;

'Can I be excused? I'm allergic to PowerPoint...'

I wished that I'd thought of that.

Stan Moreish walked up to the lectern and announced a short coffee and breadsticks break to be followed by Buck's final presentation; 'The Big Fat Noble Lie'.

Buck took an unnecessarily theatrical swig of his coffee.

The way Buck drank from his mug; it was obviously empty.

'We want everyone to agree on what is real... and what isn't. We want them to agree on the truth. But the important thing is not that the truth is real, that the truth is *'the truth''*.

Why would someone get up on stage with a prop coffee mug?

'The important thing is that everyone agrees that it is'.

Buck fumbled with his projector and did that thing with his eyebrows. He flipped to his next slide; 'What is a Noble Lie?' This was slide fifty-one, of one hundred and eleven.

'A noble lie is told for the good of the people you're lying to. The concept was first proposed by Plato'.

Behind Buck was a nice big photo of Adolf Hitler.

Not nice, I meant that other word; horrific.

'Plato's motives for nobly lying were altruistic, to maintain the status quo. But over time this evolved into the 'Big Noble Lie' used primarily by propagandists such as Hitler'.

Another fake sip. Another slide. A big bust of Plato.

'Hitler was of the opinion that when one lies, one should lie as outrageously as possible. People are generally scared of lying and tend to only tell small, white, lies. Most men wouldn't think twice of telling their wife that they like her new hairdo, but they would never dream of telling that same loved one they were actually an alien in disguise, sent to our planet to colonise it by impregnating Earth's women'.

The way Buck drank his fake coffee was an outrageous lie.

'Hitler reasoned that, because normal men would never conceive of telling such gigantic untruths, they'd find it hard to believe that anyone else would. Hence they'd be more likely to fall victim to big lies than little white ones. When you lie for the Agency you lie big. And you stick to your lie, not matter how preposterous'.

The way Buck sipped from an empty mug was preposterous. And irritating.

'...Can anyone give me an example of a noble lie?'

Some teacher's pet in the audience started frantically waving her breadstick in the air;

'Wearing a seatbelt on a plane can save your life'.

Buck motioned for the young woman to continue.

'I mean, planes don't crash very often, but when they do, everyone dies... Whether they're wearing their seatbelt or not'.

'So why lie about it?'

'It stops you damaging other people's luggage in the overhead lockers, if there's turbulence'.

'But you don't believe that wearing a seatbelt will save your life if the plane crashes?'

'You'd have to be stupid to believe that'.

'Which is why it isn't a good example'.

Buck's next slide was 'The Origins of the Bigfoot Lie'.

'The lies we tell, are the lies everyone believes. The lies we tell are the big fat lies'.

Buck skipped to some flow diagram that had been shrunk down to the extent that it was only really useful for an optician's wall. But which everyone was too scared to admit they couldn't follow.

'The truth according to Darwin was that those who have the most sex survive. Darwin's theory might otherwise be known as the survival of the hotties, or the survival of the stunnas. Just as seals fight for control of the harem, so men go around kicking sand in each other's faces and fighting over women. And while some nerds could occasionally wash the sand from their eyes and pull a fast one while the dominant male was watching the game, more often than not they ended up getting their asses kicked'.

The flowchart was replaced by a picture of the Hulk.

'And if you weren't the tallest or brawniest, you could still get by with your fashion sense. If you dressed like a peacock you were ok. If you kept an eye on the latest fashions you got laid'.

The Hulk made way for the Fonz.

'The trouble was most scientists spent their time hitting the books rather than the gym. And the priesthood hadn't encountered a fashion fad for two hundred years. The idea of Sexual Selection was all well and good if you were stuck on a ship in the Galapagos with a crew of ninety men wearing the same uniform, but back in the real world most preachers and businessmen didn't favour an interpretation of evolution that suggested the only motivation for an individual should be to have as much sex as possible'.

A diagram illustrating 'as much sex as possible' was on Buck's next slide and was greeted with a lot of smartphone activity.

'As much as everyone loved Darwin's theory some of these lab geeks were a bit concerned about the amount of sex in his books; because none of them were getting much action and the 'hotties' who were getting it weren't reading any of their articles explaining it all. If everyone spent all of their time propagating themselves soon enough there'd be no qualified biologists left to explain how they were doing it'.

The next slide was a close-up shot of someone's genitals.

It was too close to call whether they were male or female.

'This was where the Department of Knowledge Management came in. Everyone who'd read Charlie's book turned to the pages about Sexual Selection first of course; lay Darwin flat on his back and he falls open on the sexy pages every time. But the Origin of Species had a sub-plot; Natural Selection...'

Was it just me, or was Buck miming eating a breadstick?

'Sure, you could call someone fit based on how much sex they were getting, but who among us can last long on an empty stomach? You needed to feed before you could breed; so couldn't you also call someone fit based on how well they'd adapted to their environment? Their suitability for survival? ...And couldn't these survivors be the smartest, the healthiest and the hardest working? Like a teetotal brain surgeon? Or a vegan rocket scientist?'

Buck wiped pretend crumbs from his face with a pretend napkin.

'Well no, not really. But, couldn't we make it *sound* like the survival of the fittest referred to the rocket scientists and the brain surgeons? As long as they went jogging three times a week and steered clear of red meat? We had an Office of Selective Omission if we needed to spend less time talking about Sexual Selection, and we had an Office of Clarification and Continuity if we wanted to talk about Natural Selection some more'.

Buck wanted to talk about Natural Selection some more;

'Pretty soon everyone was talking about the 'survival of the fittest'. Sure you'd get the occasional nitpicker whining about misinterpretation, but for the most part people studied hard and went jogging and looked up to brain surgeons and rocket scientists. These were the people who would inherit the Earth, not those of us who were just sitting around getting stoned and horny'.

An e-mail from Dr Myway reminding Buck to come in and discuss 'those test results' popped up in the bottom corner of the screen.

'And it would have worked. If it hadn't been for the Nazis'.

Now we were back to Hitler again.

Although the photo we were looking at was of Charles Darwin.

'The survival of the fittest had become the elimination of the weakest. Sure the boffins had worried about a society that might degenerate into soap opera if the less bright out-bred the smartest, but now the survival of the fittest had become synonymous with black leather and blonde hard-men and this was even further away from your average professor than the fancy dressed playboys had been'.

Buck mimed pouring some water into his glass. He mimed taking a sip.

'The church leaders and businessmen had their finger on the pulse of the average man on the street. They knew that the average man on the street wasn't too keen on the elimination of the weakest. And they were pretty ticked off with the scientific establishment for this whole fiasco. So the priests and the businessmen decided their best option was to debunk the theory of evolution altogether. Sure the baby had peed in the bathwater, but a lot of scientists argued that this was like throwing the baby out *with* the bathwater. But it was too late. We weren't working for the eggheads any longer. We were working for our corporate sponsors. We were fighting Nazis'.

Buck simulated a cough and a splutter. Then he mimed apologetically wiping spittle from Stan Moreish's suit jacket. I looked at my watch. Then wished that I hadn't.

'Sometimes, when the lie just cannot continue, when it can no longer be considered noble, you have to come up with a new one'.

The audience in the Sir Charles Fort Hall wasn't looking at Charles Darwin any longer. We weren't looking at the theory.

We were looking at a stupid and tabloid looking creature.

A creature named Gerry.

'And so began 'Operation Big Fat Lie', which through an unfortunate series of poor telephone connections became 'Operation Big Foot Lie'. This was how the missing link, christened Gerry by Darwin when he'd first brought him back from the Highlands, ended up being re-christened Bigfoot'.

The next photo was of Gerry and Charles together, smiling into the camera and giving us the thumbs-up.

'Gerry was covered in the same ginger hair and exhibited the same protruding forehead now commonly associated with Bigfoot, and the Scots. Of course these things used to be associated with the missing link, but the DKM stole Gerry's skeleton from the Natural History Museum. It's called the missing link for a good reason. Now if you want to see him you have to go to the Whitewash Museum. Be warned though, there are a lot of Bigfoots in the Museum and the ones that are still alive do smell strongly of cat pee'.

The Whitewash Museum smelt strongly of cat pee. And bullshit.

'Once the physical evidence was dealt with we had the relatively easy task of faking witness statements from rednecks'.

Buck clicked onto a slide showing a pair of eighteen inch wooden 'Bigfoot' feet but then inadvertently double-clicked and arrived at a publicity shot of Pamela Anderson.

'These are clearly fake. But of course we needed a pair like these to grab people's attention. We certainly didn't want anyone to think that what they were looking at were real'.

The next slide was of an unshaven man in his fifties who was chewing tobacco and wearing an ape costume.

'In some cases we needed to hire actors and actresses who could pose as redneck witnesses. Of course, any rumours you might have heard about a romance between myself and this particular beauty are just idle gossip'.

Next up, a slide that clearly showed a bear with a severe case of mange with a muzzle and leash tied to a post in the ground.

'This particular gentleman was paid off to cover for a family of Bigfoots who'd been terrorising prospectors around Ape Canyon by toilet-papering their cabins and setting fire to paper bags filled with their own faeces. Our patsy here admitted to being the prankster and, funny story this, he invested the money we paid him into a beekeeping operation'.

Buck had that wrong. He'd actually become an accountant.

The final slide was a photograph of a 'Bigfoot corpse' in a pool of melting ice water. The corpse was quite clearly a shop window mannequin with some domestic pet hair glued to it and scuba diving fins cut into the shape of feet.

'This is just a bear with a severe case of mange. This wasn't one of ours'.

'Did Bigfoot put this presentation together for you?!'

Hecklers were ten a penny when Buck was talking.

'Every time another Yeti or Yowie turned up we'd hire some actor or out of work lumberjack to claim that he'd been abducted by an ape-man and forced to play Boggle or Yahtzee. Then we'd roll in and find the fake furry feet stashed away in the back of his 'Big-Rig'. Maybe we'd pay his wife to tearfully reveal the shameful truth to a local news-hound. We just kept on repeating the lie; Bigfoot was nothing but an amateurish hoax...'

This is known in the business as 'shoring up disbelief'.

You keep repeating things over and over again and eventually the lie sinks in. Then other people start telling your lie for you. Pretty soon millions of people are hearing your lie from millions of other people. And millions of people can't be wrong. Then you've created some facts. People don't argue with facts, doesn't matter how they started out. If you can turn your bullshit into a fact people won't question it, they'll just tell the next person.

Buck continued to give people the facts;

'Now all we needed to do was poke fun at anyone who still believed in the missing link, who might suggest that monkeys were related to talk show hosts and politicians; so people would start doubting the whole theory of evolution and reject the survival of the fittest and all of its inconvenient controversies'.

I looked around the room at a lot of tongues and tonsils and teeth and other things you see when people's mouths are wide open.

It would be a shock to anyone, realising that as recently as the 1940s Bigfoot was accepted to be the missing link that proved the theory of evolution. The DIM did such a good job of removing Bigfoot from history that job offers started pouring in from the Agency's corporate sponsors. No-one remembers the missing link, just like no-one remembers that Santa was a black guy in a green costume until Coca-Cola paid the Agency to paint him red and white. But people would think you were nuts if you started claiming Santa was a black guy. Right? There you are; just you and the unpopular truth in the minority.

Everyone accepts that Bigfoot is a guy in a monkey costume, just as fifty years ago everyone accepted that 'survival of the fittest' meant that the cleverest and healthiest survived. Like Buck said; *'It isn't important if the truth is true'*.

It's only important that everyone agrees it is.

Like I said; *'Sometimes everyone can be wrong'*.

Water doesn't drain differently in the southern hemisphere.

Breakfast isn't the most important meal of the day.

And you don't lose more heat from your head. Unless you're doing the ice bucket challenge, because you ~~want the internet to see you in a wet T-shirt~~ do a lot for charity.

Sure, sure, human beings prefer to do as little thinking as humanly possible. But most people still use a lot more than ten percent of their brain. It's just that those people use ninety percent of their brain on things that are a total waste of their brain's time.

Maybe this doesn't apply to you or your friends. Maybe this is a gross generalisation, but most people are gullible, and easily fooled.

The DIM did such a good job of removing the missing link from history they created the creation-evolution controversy.

Sometimes I'd be in the back garden at night, meditating with a ~~stolen~~ souvenir Tim Tam and some chocolate milk, and I'd hear a loud voice say;

'Chewing gum takes seven years to digest'. Or;

'You'll have to wait an hour before you can go swimming'.

And for a moment I'd worry that I was starting to hear voices. Then I'd realise that this was how the couple next door talked to one another, and that actually they were some sort of parrot/sheep/human cryptid bred to regurgitate whatever they heard.

It was that or they were aliens. Some terrifying new breed of interloper from 'Reptilon' or 'Dirtworld'. Whatever they were they were making a real drama of behaving like 'normal human beings'. They even put their recycling bins out on the wrong day and parked in front of my garage like my other neighbours. They were so desperate to blend in they'd swallow and regurgitate any old lie.

The one about sell by dates.

The one about dry clean only.

The one about lightning never striking the same place twice.

It kind of slipped out just now, but you heard me right.

I sometimes worried that I was hearing voices.

My head seemed to really have it in for me sometimes. Like when I'd be sitting in a lecture hall believing in the principles of reality enforcement and the concept of the noble lie and all of a sudden some hooligan thought would start rioting in my head and chanting; 'You don't know what you're doing'.

Or when Maxwell Self would be telling me about ripping up the rulebook.

I'd always considered myself to be one of the good guys. But I wasn't so sure about Self. I had a lot of doubts about Self. If things had been different maybe I wouldn't have seen myself as one of the good guys. But things weren't different. People weren't different.

Maybe this is a gross generalisation, but people are all the same. All terrified of the unknown. They were all terrified of the unbelievable truth. So I kept it from them.

I couldn't see my goldfish anywhere. The colour of the pond water was basically what you'd call black. What you'd call impenetrable. It was the not knowing that was the hardest part. There was only the one goldfish in there, somewhere, but the water was getting blacker each day and I didn't know if he was going to make it. But I knew that I had to keep this lonesome goldfish alive. We needed each other.

I couldn't afford to lose another one, not like the last time.

Like Black Saturday.

7. The Who

I watched Maxwell Self heading unavoidably towards me. Because the only free urinal was the one right next to me. There were a lot of urinals in the Blacker Building.

But there were a lot more old men.

I watched Self fiddle with his Bluetooth hearing aid or some earwax. I tried not to look. Because you weren't supposed to look at the man using the urinal next to you. There'd been a memo about it. I couldn't stop him talking to me though.

'I hear congratulations are in order chap! Your scratchie is gorgeous. Did you see her in that body scanner? I've some printouts if you want...'

Self called scratch-starters 'scratchies'. Like brickies or chippies but different in that he would talk to a scratchie. Especially if they looked like mine did in his printouts.

'Monty was telling me you mustn't address her by her first name. Gets her very heated. And not in a good way. You need to use her surname; Smith. But she's a real knockout your scratchie. Would you mind swapping seats at the Cock and Bull tonight?'

This was the traditional scratch-starters dinner, held for the previous three years at the Cock and Bull Club. For the one hundred and twenty-three years before then it had been held at The Savoy, but the spontaneous combustion of the bill had become something of a tradition and eventually we'd been shown the door permanently.

Self didn't want to trade places so he could sit next to my scratchie though. He wanted to sit next to the Deputy Director. He wanted to poke his nose into the Deputy Director's unit. Self wanted to try for a promotion before he tried for a coup.

I was happy enough to trade places. All of the networking, the nose-poking, it wasn't for me. What's known as 'the politics', it was best left to politicians. And people who behaved as if they were politicians. Which seemed to be an increasing number of people.

I could see her walking towards me as I held the door to the gents open for an elderly colleague. Smith kept bumping into the cleaners who were running back and forth checking closets for investigative journalists. Smith looked like someone from my past. I just couldn't remember who. I had a great memory for faces. But a lot of them were repressed.

'You must be Smith'.

Smith didn't bother to mention how lucky it was that I hadn't gotten her heated by using her first name. Smith's first name was Epiphany. But I guessed it must have long since passed the point when Epiphany had grown tired of the questions surrounding her name and so when introduced to anyone she would simply say; 'You can call me Smith'.

There were three things about Epiphany Smith that were immediately obvious to me.

The first was obvious to everyone. Epiphany Smith was

a knockout, albeit a rather begrudging one; with her crew cut hair, her rejection of makeup, of high heels, of consensus.

The second thing I noticed was that Smith was completely ignoring the attentions of the men in the Agency, the majority of whom were either searching for the missing journalist, staring at Epiphany or attempting some combination thereof. That isn't to say that Smith was ignorant of their attention, she just chose not to milk it by dressing up like a schoolgirl with magic charms that wiggle in front of your face like a witch's nose.

Epiphany and her effortless snake charming.

Her other people magnetism. Her surplus beauty.

If you ever need a crap excuse to talk to me you could do worse than speak to some of the colleagues I bumped into on the day Epiphany Smith was assigned to me. For example:

'I need to erm, speak to you about the erm, the dodos'.

The third and final thing that was very obvious to me, but which might not have been immediately apparent to anyone staring at her charms, was that Epiphany Smith was incredibly nervous.

'I tried to get an early night but I was so excited about meeting you I couldn't sleep and then just as I was finally drifting off to sleep, ευναγερμό μου πήγε μακριά και ντύθηκα στο σκοτάδι, ja luulen pukeutunut liian fiksusti ja sitten melkein jäänyt minun juna; Special Brew. Tio estas kion homoj kiuj kaptas mian trajnon nomas ĝin'.

I asked Smith if she realised she spoke in tongues when she was nervous.

'I'm not speaking in tongues'. Said Smith. In Swahili.

I realised that actually her lips were speaking English; they were just out of sync with her dialogue. Smith just sounded as if she'd been very badly dubbed when she was nervous.

I apologised and she accepted, though I was still a little bit irritated at having to show an intern around. But I put on a smile and tried to give off the impression that I was looking forward to showing her around a building that I'd been working in for the past twenty years.

Lionel Gatehouse from the Office of Confessions bounded over on the pretence of my sponsoring him for the Channel Tunnel Half-Marathon and I asked him if he had time to show Smith around. I'm not sure what he said because he blurted it out, but it was in the affirmative. But Smith turned all negative, Smith started behaving black and white; quoting from her induction booklet which clearly stated that she wasn't permitted anywhere in the building without the mentor to whom she'd been assigned. And no-one else.

I explained how she was right to stick to the rules. But wrong to disappoint the head of the Office of Confessions. Smith explained how she'd been lying about following the rules and that she didn't care who she disappointed as long as it wasn't herself.

Smith was sticking with me because she'd overheard that I was the best.

But I wasn't a mentor. I was a loner.

'Chap!'

Self returned with his own scratch-starter; a puffy-chested fellow named Freddy, but spoke as if we were alone or as if our two scratchies were deaf.

'Thought you might prefer to trade? Wouldn't you? ...This chap I've been assigned scored a Dickie on his aptitude quiz'.

The interview process our interns had been through was a two week induction programme at a multinational I can't name here but which rhymes with pony. Applicants were subliminally tested to check their aptitude for reality enforcement. They were trained to use a new order processing system but were actually learning how to spontaneously combust someone with a body error. It was data entry, which tested their ability to respond to a crisis.

Self ignored his intern, turned to Smith and asked;

'What did you score?'

Smith started babbling again;

'그것은 어떤 뜻점수 따라 달라집니다.나는 최고의 수면을 하지 않았다 그러나 나는 확실히 누군가가 내 점수 또는 어떻게 그것을 가지고 또는 내가 함께 할 계획 에 대해 이야기 하지 말라고 얘기 해요. Ek het goed gedoen. Hoër as die gemiddelde. Maar ek is nie seker of ek moet sê dat'.

I was having second thoughts about Smith's fitness but Self appeared to be staring intently at her name badge.

'Well you probably did much better than my scratchie did'.

Self's scratchie was standing right behind him. I told him;

'He's standing right behind you'.

'I know'.

'And he can hear you'.

Self tore himself away from Smith's lapel;

'Just a bit of banter between chaps. I've got his back. I'm behind Freddy all the way'.

I told Freddy this just meant that when the shit started flying he'd be the one who got hit first. Freddy told me;

'My name isn't Freddy; it's Ian'.

The tour resumed at the Office of Clarification and Continuity.

I introduced Smith to George and Stevens; two of the Agency's best ret-con artists. Baggy-trousered George was remaking classic films while tightknit-sweatered Stevens destroyed the originals. We'd missed their removing a character named Oback Barama from Star Wars but watched them replace the Germans in 'Escape to Victory' with North Koreans.

We weren't at war with Germany after all. We were at war with North Korea.

George and Stevens were clearly very taken with Smith. These thin white geeks were getting hot under their collars and probably wishing they'd worn clean lab-coats, contacts and some kind of body spray. Sat among all the discarded film canisters and junk food cartons piled on the desk were three VHS copies of Kubrick's 1952 thriller 'Voyage to the Moon'. George and Stevens grabbed for a copy each and competed to give Smith the low-down in the style of rival anchors on a breakfast news sofa;

'There were simply too many parallels to what actually went down in the summer of sixty-nine to let this stay out there'.

'The mission number, the name Buzz, that famous quote'.

'So we've been rounding the copies up ever since'.

'Luckily this was before anyone paid to see Kubrick's films'.

'Luckily those who've seen it since have been persuaded that they're actually watching his faking of the moon landings'.

Stevens looked at Smith with his head half-cocked and George did something strange with one of his nostrils;

'A lot of people get pretty amazed by what we do here, but these are just basic corrections for errors in the space-time continuum, or something'.

Stevens started spinning around in his swivel chair and I was reminded of how his grandfather had been one of those scientists worrying about the 'survival of the fittest'.

George swivelled Stevens to face the wall as he walked to a bookshelf and then handed Smith a copy of 'Futility';

'Read the blurb on the dust jacket'.

Smith turned the book over and read the plot summary;

'The Titania is the world's most unsinkable ocean liner. As opulent as the world's greatest hotels, with the largest collection of crystal chandeliers and the smallest collection of lifeboats. The great ship sets sail from Southampton, bound for New York. But things take a terrible turn towards misadventure when the liner collides with an iceberg. Off the coast of Newfoundland. Around midnight'.

Smith shrugged and handed it back.

'So they changed the name from Titanic to Titania? Very subtle'.

George opened it up on the first page and handed it back, grinning;

'It was written thirteen years before the Titanic was built'.

Smith looked at me sceptically. I nodded; it was true. Stevens stopped swivelling, took Futility and slotted it back into the bookshelf;

'The Whitewash Museum has dozens of books like this. A lot of Nostradamus' later visions were actually just premonitions of episodes of Battlestar Galactica'.

'So you're like censors?'

'We are *nothing* like the censorship guys! You're talking about the Office of Selective Omission. This is Clarification and Continuity. Do you even know where you are right now?'

I offered Stevens a custard cream that I had spare while George defused the situation;

'We get a bit upset; a lot of management confuse OCC with OSO. We like to think we get things done with a bit more panache though, not like the guys in OSO whose talents only extend to their use of the delete button...'

This shared pride brought Stevens out of his geek mist;

'Or a black marker pen!'

George and Stevens enjoyed a fist-bump. Stevens tapped at his laptop and twisted it around so Smith could see the photo on his screen;

'Would a *censor* be able to handle the king?'

The old man in the photo was in his eighties, with tanned skin like leather, blind man's sunglasses and a flared white jumpsuit.

'We've told him to get rid of the jumpsuits dozens of times but he refuses. But we pay for his sunbed sessions, so, you know, people don't really recognise him'.

Smith's eyes had grown wide as plot holes;

'This is Elvis?'

Stevens was simultaneously impressed, and trying to make an impression;

'You can recognise him? Even with the sunglasses?'

George jumped ahead in the race to impress Epiphany Smith;

'You kinda gave it away when you called him the king. ...We Photoshop™ the images so they're out of focus, so no-one can be sure it's him. But the odd one slips through. They get passed onto the OSO; it's not a difficult job, labelling witnesses as unreliable'.

Smith was incredulous. Or she was yawning. But her mouth was definitely wide open;

'Your whole strategy is... you pay for his tanning salons?'

'When *you're* managing a chain of events that's becoming really stupidly labyrinthine, you'll want to keep it simple too'.

'This is really about managing your time. There are a lot of fake deaths each year. We just finished Raúl Greedo yesterday'.

This was news to me;

'Raúl Greedo faked his own death?'

'*We* faked his own death'.

We watched footage of Raúl Greedo's apparently miraculous survival.

But this wasn't miraculous. This was absurd.

The would-be assassin was the same person who'd thrown a grenade at Raúl the last time around; Vladimir Unitarian. Vlad really needed to either stop being an assassin or stop using hand grenades. And stop getting himself on camera. We sat through half an hour of

Vladimir in his green beret and camouflage shorts and wondered why no-one at the Plastic Diplomats Conference had thought to question him. We watched as Raúl Greedo started his plastic speech and listened to Vladimir's war cry of 'apocalypse Raúl!' as he pulled the pin and threw a gift-wrapped grenade towards the lectern.

We watched the grenade as it bounced off of the head of Billy Crystal (who'd just finished warming the crowd up) and as a confused and frightened Fox News reporter swung at it with her microphone and hit it towards the stage. We watched as its fall was cushioned by the inflatable plastic dove installed by U2 (who were due to perform at the end of the conference) and then watched it roll gently across the red carpet and come to a stop; the tissue paper that was still wrapped around it preventing the lever from releasing.

Stevens turned to me and explained how;

'What you've just seen. It isn't what happened. Anymore...'

We watched the version Stevens and George had ret-conned with some CGI so there was no gift-wrapping around the grenade that flew straight and true to land at Raúl's toadskin-shoed feet and blow him into the News at Ten.

'This was too good an opportunity to pass up'.

'He's safely locked away now, busy ret-conning his will'.

Stevens leant back in his swivel chair with his hands behind his head in a way that was designed to make him look casual and maverick and indispensable.

But the effect was ruined by the sweat patches under his arms.

'We get to work with a lot of celebrities'.

George coughed up an 'ahem' to give Stevens the heads-up about his underarm issue.

'A few years ago we got invited to the Palace... Because of that thing with Kate and Wills being second cousins. ...Pretty cool right?'

The problem was, you might think you had a pretty cool job, but then you told some girl you wanted to impress and she behaved like you were a mortuary make-up artist or an airport toilet cleaner.

Smith didn't sound as if she was enjoying this part of the tour;

'But what you're doing isn't on; repainting the past to black out anything unpopular'.

Stevens was astonished and dismayed to discover that the hot new scratch-starter held such anti-agency opinions. George did his best to change Smith's rear-view of history;

'We don't paint out the unpopular stuff. If we did you'd never have heard of Howard the Duck. Or Brussels sprouts. We just paint out things that will create a panic; things people are better off not knowing about'.

I pitched in;

'Can you imagine if we didn't stop these things from getting into the news? You're allowed one crazy story at the end of the bulletin each night, two minutes max and preferably about a kitten in a tumble dryer or a letter that's taken fifty years to arrive. The kind of stories we deal with? Where are we supposed to put them? The only place we can put them if we want to make sure no-one believes them is in the Bible. And honestly, we've made so many changes to that over the years...'

Don't misunderstand my motives here. I didn't care if Smith was impressed or not. She was there to do a job, and so was I. First impressions didn't come into it as far as I was concerned. And what did it matter if she looked like a girl from my past or not?

But I rescued the lads all the same;

'Changing the past isn't necessarily wrong'.

I continued, because I had everyone's attention already;

'Wellington's Second Rule of Retrovision states that history dribbles from the present into the past. It's a creative process of renewal. History looks different depending on where you're standing. Your grandkids might grow up to learn that Lenin was a humanitarian or that Nelson Mandela was a total git. If your grandkids discover new evidence that proves our history was wrong, they'll change it. ...The thing about history is that you don't have to have been there to know what happened'.

All around the Office of Continuity and Clarification you could see the evidence of this pinned to the walls. There were souvenir spoilt ballots from the 2000 US election. Men in black on grassy knolls. And dozens of nuclear tests where the radioactive clouds had been retouched so they appeared to be in the shape of a mushroom rather than a giant phallus. These were the photoshopped histories that proved my point. History depends on who your historians are.

Of course the OCC weren't only about changing history. Think about almost all of the history you've ever seen. Life isn't black and white like history. Sometimes history needs colouring in.

Smith was staring at one of these framed histories on the wall and asking no-one in particular;

'Is this Martin Luther King in a Nike t-shirt?'

The next photo was from the famous set of the Yalta conference. In this particular shot Churchill was holding a Mars bar and Eisenhower had a Coke. Stevens explained;

'I've got to remove the Big Mac that Stalin's holding, after McDonalds forced Burger King to withdraw it. But it's just another part of the job. If we're going in to fix the continuity anyway, then there's nothing wrong with a little product placement'.

Stevens was a good company man;

'Advertising's an important revenue stream. And all we're doing is adding a little extra detail to the history that's already there. We're not painting over it...'

Something told me Smith wasn't buying into this. The thing that told me was the scowl on her face. But Stevens persevered;

'It's covert advertising. It's subliminal'.

Smith nodded in agreement;

'Sure. I get it. If people fall for your lying photos they're more likely to go and buy the product than if they thought it was just another ad with a dead celebrity. It's very noble'.

Maybe you've already picked up on it, but Smith was starting to sound sarcastic.

Steven's started fidgeting in his swivel chair. Stevens wasn't helping himself;

'We're just doing the job we're paid for'.

'You're doing what you're told. I get it. Just following orders. It's brainwashing'.

Stevens' loyalty was unquestionable.

But George was an apologist;

'You know I hate working on product placement personally. But it allows us to do more important work. It's like when John Turturro has to appear in those GoBots movies so he can afford to feed and clothe himself'.

'You're all very right wing'.

Smith was very wrong about that. I tried some reassurance. But it was the last time;

'We don't choose our sponsors. We work for the world's only apolitical government agency. All we do is repair the plot holes'.

'You repair potholes?'

'*Plot* holes. When something happens that contradicts something that's happened previously, it creates a plot hole'.

Stevens tried to help me out;

'It's a kind of worm hole. Like a tornado'.

'It's nothing like a tornado'.

I wanted to set Stevens straight, so we could all try to move on, but I could tell Smith didn't believe a word I was saying. And I was usually so good at this.

We swung by the Office of Confessions.

By this time I wanted the tour over with. I was

seriously thinking about taking Self up on his offer to trade interns. The guys in confessions weren't so easy to be around anyway. These were the guys who arranged for people (usually terminally ill or recently married) who were prepared to take a fat cheque to confess to some seemingly unexplainable events.

I mean, you heard about the magic bullet right? But you still know who shot JFK.

Some of these guys were on the book permanently though.

You'd call these guys repeat offenders. We called them reliable witnesses. Not because you could rely on them, but because we could.

I shook hands with Bob Forearm. This guy was a serial confessor. Selling DIY weeping statue kits. Bob Forearm was always in town anytime a statue started bawling blood or pinot grigio or eucalyptus oil or whatever. Anytime a statue started shedding tears and people started believing you'd find Bob getting himself arrested soon after. You'd always find Bob explaining it to the local police; how easy it is to fake a weeping statue. You'd always find that people would rather dismiss something as a hoax than believe in a miracle.

Lucky for us, right?

8. Our Unreliable Narrator

I was born in a heatwave in the year of the monkey. On the day of the Pac-Man.

For my seventh birthday I got a chemistry set that I used to investigate local crime scenes; to track down missing cats and relatives and bicycle chains. There was the episode about the ant genocide. And the killer badger finale. I had a good chemistry with animals.

I home studied and learnt to play the French horn. Then I learnt to speak Hungarian so I could understand my music tutor. I spent a lot of time alone after mum became an architect. Because dad worked for the local radio station. My parents were old hippies, and dad played a lot of protest songs. I always pretended to tune into his show, but I preferred rock.

I had my first kiss at eighteen, with Sophia Smith. She left the next day; she had somewhere else she needed to be. But I never wrote to the forwarding address she left me.

When I was nineteen I impersonated a police officer, badly.

As soon as I was arrested the Agency offered me a job.

'...Adjust the weather?'

This was Smith repeating what I'd just said. This had started happening a lot. I would say something that Smith found stupid or tabloid, and instead of saying; 'that's stupid' or; 'that's tabloid' she would just repeat after me. We were sitting in Business Economics class on Al Virgeenn flight 072 to Bin Dilaid Airport, Dubai. The reason we were flying to Dubai?

To adjust an outbreak of drunken weather.

Smith rolled her eyes as I translated my encrypted reports of the ball lightning, the electric blanket of cloud and the snowfall. My encrypted reports included an artist's impression of the Sheikh Hanvak Bridge. Luxury cars had been rear-ending each other for days, because of the low clouds.

The Office of Confessions had spoken to the people who knew about traffic, and the people who knew about traffic had warned them that the accident on the Sheikh Hanvak Bridge could go on for days or weeks or months.

It was down to us to make sure no-one ever got to hear about it.

Some people call Dubai a modern wonder of the world. A miracle of engineering. Some call it a building site. I'd first visited Dubai ten years earlier and had been keen to see what it looked like now it was finished. I worked up the courage to lift my blind, but the view through my porthole was terrifying; it was an even bigger building site.

People were wondering when the construction industry in the UK would get back on its feet. The answer was; when Dubai gave all of their cranes back. All of their cranes were building desert islands and theme parks

(Dubai World, Dubai Women's World, Diggerland).

But Dubai already was a theme park.

I enjoyed speaking Arabic. But most people in Dubai spoke English, with a bad cockney accent. I wasn't a fan of the fake Dubai accents, the fake Dubai islands, or the fake Dubai ski slope. But I loved the hot air. You went out with a jacket to put on when you got indoors. But when we landed people were wearing jackets *outside*. Because of the snowdrifts.

The fake indoor ski slope was deserted for the first time in years. But they'd done a roaring trade in hiring snowboards out. The snowdrifts were also the reason we couldn't get a Little Box delivered to our hotel room. No-one could get through to our room. Including us. Not because of the snowdrifts so much; the reason *we* couldn't get to our room was because we'd gotten stuck in an elevator between the 68th and 69th floors of the best (the tallest) hotel in Dubai. The reason we'd gotten stuck was that Smith had, quite accidentally, but also quite clumsily, pressed *69 instead of 69. Whatever you do, don't press *69 in an elevator.

Unless you're with a competent abseiler. Like me.

'Marvel Burger?'

'The planet's only Michelin starred burger franchise. But there are only two in the world; one in New Zealand and one here. It can't be far. ...Trust me; it'll be worth it'.

This is what I'd said to Smith as we'd walked down sixty-nine flights of stairs.

But our burger trek had become a wild goose chase.

One of the problems with it snowing in Dubai was the sunlight reflecting off of the unreasonably (not to mention unseasonably) white snow and blinding anyone who wasn't wearing sunglasses. This wasn't a problem for the locals; they just kept their sunglasses on. More of a problem for the locals was footwear. A lot of people couldn't feel their feet any longer. A lot of people were going to get frostbite.

But Smith and I had sensible shoes on.

We just didn't have any sunglasses.

Smith asked if I was trying to lose her. I explained how it wasn't possible to know your way around Dubai because every couple of weeks someone built something that completely changed its appearance. Continuity errors were pretty common in Dubai.

My first assignment in Dubai had been to adjust the miraculous survival of a mall full of mockneys from a terrorist attack. Members of the Future Homeland for Muslims (or FHM) and the Guardians of the Quran (or GQ) had unleashed several canisters of VD gas into the Sheikh Anbayk Mall. But everyone had survived. Everyone had a sore throat and a headache, but everyone had survived. So I'd altered some lab results to make it look as though GQ and FHM had attacked the mall with flea bombs. These paradise speculators were written off as just another bunch of amateurs, like that disgruntled beefeater who tried to take out Tower Bridge with his Swiss Army knife.

If it hadn't been for me there'd be no Dubai Land today. People would be terrified to come here. There'd be no shopping malls. No-one would've invented this mirage in the desert and all of these tourists would be fighting for space on your ski slopes in your malls.

I wasn't sure if Epiphany Smith had been listening to me or not. But she had. And now Smith expected me to return the favour;

'Let me tell you what I think'.

Just so you know, I was a loner, so I wasn't really that jaded when it came to someone starting their sentence in this way.

'Adjusting weird outbreaks of weather and plagiarism is one thing, but terrorist attacks are not one in a million events'.

'No, they're one in twenty million events'.

Part of my not being jaded was not realising you shouldn't interrupt when someone wants to tell you what they think. I must have gotten away with it though because Smith just raised her voice and continued talking;

'What I was about to say was; I hope you don't mind me asking about this stuff. Those guys in the office seemed terrified of questioning the job...'

I told Smith she could trust me.

'I thought we'd just be covering up the weird and the wonderful, not rewriting history. I suppose I'm a little uncomfortable about hiding the truth about terrorist attacks'.

'Because?'

'Because you're insulting people's intelligence! You can't have a society where the ugliness of the world gets rewritten. Our history books will just be page after page of flawless leaders and polite neighbours. ...People can cope with the horrors of the world you know'.

'But I wasn't trying to hide something horrific. I was covering up the fact that everyone survived. Because the only thing more certain to spread fear and confusion than a terrorist attack is everyone inexplicably surviving one'.

Smith started shaking her head a lot.

It was either that or she was shivering.

I kept my eyes peeled for a shop selling thermal underwear as I continued;

'I don't want to insult people's intelligence, but I don't want them kidding themselves that they're invincible either. I've seen people who thought they were invincible and they're not around any longer. I'm inoculating people against the truth, because if they go down with a bout of the truth they might not recover'.

'People *can* handle the truth'.

'People go out of their way to *avoid* the truth!'

'You mean in the same way that people go out of their way to eat a burger when they have a choice of nine restaurants at their seven star hotel?'

I lied to the both of us;
'It'll be worth it'.

A good example of how people prefer to avoid the truth is the Baltimore Mustard Stain Epidemic. If you're not from Baltimore and you don't have any friends or family there then you might have missed this, but basically it was an example of a how a whole city could lose its mind if it was exposed to some new and virulent strain of the truth.

It started on Valentine's Day 1984 when a large number of women in restaurants noticed that their husband, boyfriend or lover across the table had a mustard stain on his shirt. If they'd been at home it wouldn't have been worth remarking on, but the women doing the spotting had invested a lot of time and effort getting ready for a romantic meal and were justifiably pretty peeved to realise their soul-mates hadn't taken things quite so seriously.

As each woman angrily pointed this out so the woman on the next table checked and found the same thing; somewhere on the shirt or tie of the man sitting opposite was the undeniable yellow of a mustard stain.

By the end of the night women all over Baltimore were starting to get suspicious.

How could it be that so many mustard stains were spontaneously appearing on people's clothing? The stains were everywhere, and not only in candlelit restaurants. People started noticing them on co-workers, undercover cops and insurance salesmen too.

The Mustard Stain Epidemic made the national news, and the outbreak spread ever wider. Within a week outbreaks were being reported in Philadelphia and Washington DC. Dry cleaners were the victims of the most vicious attacks. This had to be the work of shirt vandals or jacket defilers. That or it was the government. Or mustard farmers.

People started asking; 'Are there mustard farmers?'

People started asking; 'Where the hell does mustard come from anyhow?'

By the end of February over six thousand cases had been reported.

People were running out in front of police cars and flagging them down in order to report their mustard stains.

The police had two theories. Theory number one was that vandals were using paintball guns or peashooters to splatter innocent bystanders with mustard.

Theory number two was mass hysteria.

The police went with theory number two.

A week later the mustard stain outbreak abruptly stopped. The fact was; a lot of people had had mustard stains on their clothing for a very long time. It was only when the media started drawing their attention to it that they'd thought to look closely enough to see the little yellow stains they'd never noticed before. The Baltimore Mustard Stain Epidemic was a textbook example of how people preferred collective delusion to the truth.

Smith disagreed with me. This didn't come as a surprise.

'This is a textbook example of the influence of the media. Of fear-mongering. Shit-stirring. This is why people should figure the truth out for themselves'.

'But they did figure it out for themselves. They figured out that it didn't make any sense. And then they figured out that they didn't like things that don't make any sense'.

Smith was turning blue. Smith should have packed a cardigan.

Even if you're travelling somewhere hot, you should always pack a cardigan.

I gave her my jacket. I had my cardigan on underneath.

'...People avoid the truth like the plague, especially if it's a bit weird, or scary. But that just leaves them with something that's unexplained, so they have to come up with their own explanation instead. Something that feels comfortable and familiar. Like a lie'.

Smith started to let off steam;

'Why don't we turn back and get something to eat at the hotel?'

I wasn't for turning back. I had a head of steam too;

'People are great at lying to each other. They say; 'I was at Woodstock', they say; 'I knew someone who knew Princess Diana', they say; 'I did not have sexual relations with that woman'. But most of the time they lie to themselves. People can convince themselves of the truth of a lie no matter how obvious the lie, so long as it's a notion of how they wish things were. Better to live in a warm and fuzzy lie than a frightening reality'.

Marvel Burger was just up ahead. The problem was, it wasn't possible to see just up ahead on account of the blizzard. All you could see were the locals rolling around in the snow and staring up at the sky in awe; with open mouths and flapping tongues frozen to the sides of their faces by the icy desert wind. I threw a snowball at a giant brass teapot and continued;

'People and the truth don't mix well. People take a bit of truth and turn it into hysteria. And this was over some mustard stains!'

The snowball ricocheted off of the teapot and struck a sleeping camel.

Just so you know; it's generally best to let sleeping camels lie.

'The truth about the truth is; what you don't know can't hurt you, but what you think you know, probably will. We stop people getting hurt, by protecting them from the truth'.

'Because we know what's best for them? It's our job to treat everyone like children?'

I could see people running around catching snowflakes

on their tongues. And a child eating yellow snow in the exact spot where I'd hoped to have been eating a Marvel Burger.

'Should we explain to these people that this snow is a freak event that's probably heralding some impending disaster? Why not let them enjoy playing in the snow?'

I pointed to the child's face full of wonder. But Smith just saw the yellow snow;

'Drunken weather is one thing. Covering up terrorist attacks is different. We run a black marker over the facts, and then fill in the blanks with people's emotions. Like a cult'.

I smiled and reassured Smith; we weren't part of a cult.

'Isn't that what people in cults always say? Those guys back at the OCC or the OSO or whatever, they're terrified of the rulebook, of questioning what they're doing'.

I was starting to question what I was doing. Because my stomach was growling.

And so was Smith;

'Stop me if I'm out of line, but I wonder if you're not just as much a victim of the Agency's propaganda as those geeks back at the office'.

'I don't think that word means what you think it means'.

'Geeks?'

'Propaganda. It's from 'The Congregation for Propagating the Faith'. The CPF was the inspiration for the Agency. After the French Revolution the church started employing parishioners to print fliers anytime something happened that made people question what they believed in. People don't like to question what they believe in; they want someone to reassure them that they've been believing in the right thing all along. Everyone got the same fliers, the same message, and so everyone kept on pulling in the same direction'.

'So propaganda does mean what I thought it did'.

'You say it like it's a bad thing. Sure, sure, when the

Nazis started papering people's houses with fliers showing the Pied Piper saving fluffy German kittens from packs of rabid Jewish rats that was bad propaganda. But the Agency used the same tricks to undo a lot of Nazi propaganda. A lot of the books you saw being burned before the fall of Berlin were copies of 'Don't Trust a Vegan Rocket Scientist or The Word of a Man with a Moustache'.

'That was us?'

'It was counter-propaganda against the Nazis that led to the creation of the Agency'.

'I thought it was formed in response to a Victorian mutton shower?'

'Do you believe everything you read that's published by the Agency responsible for spreading disinformation?'

'I joined the Agency because I prefer not to be lied to. And I'm usually pretty good at spotting liars'.

Smith still had the gloves I'd given her on, because it was snowing.

But I took up her challenge anyway;

'But you've eaten pigeon without knowing it right? I mean, you have been to KFC?'

'Nice try. ...Oh come on. You can't be serious?'

'Do you know how expensive chicken is? You've seen how many KFCs are out there right? They're all full. There are a lot of chickens, but there are a lot more McNuggets'.

'That's disgusting'.

'And the milk you drank at school? Not from cows'.

'So, from goats then?'

I pulled back my top lip and gave Smith my best rat impression;

'Definitely not from goats'.

'...I think I'm going to puke'.

'There isn't that much cows' milk to go around. Look, these kinds of lies are tolerated by schoolteachers, and parents. And journalists. ...And politicians. Who checks what they're taught at school? Or what mum and dad tell them? They start out as lies, and grow into facts'.

'This is horrible'.

'Exactly! Weren't you better off not knowing the truth?'

Smith started retching. This was a standard reaction.

You'd retch too if you found out everything you'd swallowed was a lie.

'I trusted my teachers. The cows. It was all lies'.

'It was all *white* lies. If you hadn't been told that too much TV gives you square eyes would you look the same today?'

'Lying to adults is a bit different'.

I was starting to worry about Epiphany Smith. I had to know;

'Are you here to subvert my work?'

Smith looked surprised (and tired. And hungry. But mostly surprised). Whether she was surprised because this was a stupid question or because it was a smart one I couldn't tell.

'Why join the Agency if you feel this way?'

'Because I want to be on the inside. I want to experience these so-called miracles...'

'Continuity errors'.

'I want to get behind the curtain and see the real world for myself. I just don't understand why nobody else is allowed to see it'.

Getting behind the curtain was all well and good. But I had to make sure Smith wasn't going to pull the curtain back and expose something naked and shrivelled and ugly behind it.

'Sorry to have to tell you this. But it's your job'.

'But it's pseudohistory. How can the Agency's sponsors condone the rewriting of history simply to maintain the status quo?'

'Because *they are* the status quo. Sure it's pseudohistory, but it's *their* pseudohistory. If the Agency didn't inoculate people against the truth they'd get their medication from some other source, maybe one whose lies aren't so noble'.

'Just concentrate on convincing me that we're not lost.

Because you're never going to convince me of the joys of ignorance'.

'But people *do* enjoy ignorance. That saying about bliss isn't an oxymoron. It's very easy to convince people of a lie, because when they're presented with the truth they don't react well. They take the truth and distort it; they imagine the worst case scenario. All we're doing is giving them the best case scenario. All we're doing is telling them that the worst case scenario was just a horrible nightmare. But it's ok now, because we've woken them up'.

I could hear Smith's stomach rumbling. And her teeth chattering.

'Yep. We wouldn't want to be stuck in a horrible nightmare'.

We'd finally arrived. The place we'd finally arrived at was the conclusion. And the conclusion was; there was only one Marvel Burger. And it was in New Zealand.

We started back towards the hotel and Smith asked if Marvel Burger was just another one of my lies. We shuffled through the snow in silence and watched the Emiratis dancing among the snowflakes. It was a beautiful sight and I could even hear music in people's smiles and laughter. And then I realised it was Smith's ringtone.

'I can't talk now. I'm in Dubai. It's snowing'.

Smith finished whispering and hung up.

'You shouldn't tell your friends what you're doing you know'.

'I don't really have any friends'.

That was a shame. It would have been nice to have had this in common.

But it was obvious to me that Smith was lying.

9. Reinforce Your Disbelief

*W*e drove through the desert snow. We'd been woken in the middle of the night and told that the drunken weather had dumped a continuity error out in the middle of the desert. Smith and I quickly realised another thing we had in common. Neither of us were morning people. But then we'd laughed at the camels stuck in the snowdrifts. And had some tea. Maybe there'd been a little frostiness between me and Smith. Maybe it was melting a little.

Epiphany turned on the warm air;

'I was just tired and hungry. I mean I *was* tired and hungry, and then we spent two hours walking around Dubai in the freezing cold looking for a hamburger restaurant that didn't exist. ...You're not listening to me are you?'

Whatever Smith had been saying, I'd stopped listening. During my efforts to break the ice I'd realised it was winter and that water froze during winter. And my pond was full of the stuff. I was worrying about the goldfish. Could air get through ice and into my goldfish? I'd heard it could, but it was hard to believe.

'I was thinking about my goldfish'.

'I didn't know you had pets'.

'Just the one. But I don't think he even knows who I am. I'm never there'.

'Isn't there someone who could look after him for you?'

'No-one I can trust...'

We crawled over the snow dunes and drank tea and compared storm stories.

Smith kicked off with a flash flooding tale. I think it was supposed to be a horror story, what with the long cold shower and the foreign screaming that Smith couldn't decipher or even remember so I could decipher for her belatedly, in a Nissan Patrol being chased by a pack of camels across the tundra.

Smith told me about the ~~stolen~~ used cars washed away from Honest Don's front lot. She told me about the washing machines and the tumble dryers swept to their deaths and the SOS messages in cheap Belgian beer bottles clinking and drifting down the road.

Smith painted a picture that was so vivid I could almost reach out and touch the flood of plastic dog turds from the novelty shop she'd lived above.

But I was confident my story was better.

I'd been sitting by a pool in Bermuda when some meteorological cock-up had started a freak hailstorm. The hailstorm had been a freak because; i) the hailstones were the size of cricket balls, but the shape of cats and dogs, ii) the hailstones coincided with an earthquake which had emptied the pool of the guests and then the water and iii) the name of this tropical storm was Tarquin.

Hurricane Tarquin.

I gave Smith the skinny on the Martian green sky and how the paths behind the infinity pool had turned to ice. I explained how the third time I'd been hit by a cat-shaped hailstone I'd lost my bearings and my footing and slid into the pool. Then I explained how the guys from the pool bar had jumped in and held an oversized drinks umbrella over my head. As it was struck by lightning. Twice.

The second bolt gave me a headache that lasted a week.

'That explains a lot'.

Smith followed up her wisecrack with a story about a spitting cloud.

I'd seen clouds that rained all sorts of animals, or cast shadows in amusing shapes of rabbit ears or human reproductive organs or the DNA Double Helix™, I'd even watched clouds reversing into each other, but this was the first time I'd heard of a cloud chasing after a young woman and spitting at her.

But my tale of the terrorist cumulonimbus was the clear winner.

This was one of those 'nice to not have' jobs I'd tackled while adjusting an outbreak of Elton Johns in Nigeria in the late nineties.

It was just a fluffy white cloud hanging around quietly in a blue sky.

At least that's what the witnesses had told me. At least that was their story before I'd paid them off. No-one had provoked the cloud, but all of a sudden it had started spinning out and rushing at people. The witnesses described how the cloud had started making a sound that resembled some species of giant sea monster belching and farting. And then it had exploded in a shower of plastic knives and forks and vanished into thin air.

This was quite an unusual case, even for me. It deserved to win our contest.

But Smith didn't believe me! Her exact words were;

'I don't believe you'.

'We need to trust each other if we're going to be partners'.

'*You* can trust *me*'.

Epiphany Smith's phone rang.

Smith had changed her ringtone but I could tell it was the same caller as the day before because of the way Smith started acting like a soap actress at Christmas.

'Now isn't a good time... Just find yourself something to do... I don't know... Then take the rest of the day off...'

She hung up. Nervously.

'...My mum'.

'She works for a newspaper?'

'...She works as a cleaner. Why?'

'I thought I could hear someone using a Remington Exclusif in the background. You know; the typewriter'.

'You heard that? ...I find that hard to believe'.

'I guess we're discovering a shared enthusiasm for the hard to believe. That's why I know a bit about typewriters. I know a bit about unbelievable truths'.

'Unbelievable truths?'

'Well unbelievable headlines anyway. Have you ever read the Sunday Spartan?'

'I don't really keep up with the news. And neither does mum. She prefers Coronation Street. And GMTV'.

I didn't want to mention the trust thing again but Smith was going to have to stop lying to me if we were going to be partners.

I wondered why Smith was lying about her mum being a cleaner.

I wondered if perhaps her mum was a traffic warden. Or The Duchess of York.

'I do feel a little sorry for the people who work for the Sunday Spartan. They must get frustrated that people fall for the lies they're fed by other papers but don't believe a word the Spartan says. ...Maybe you could ask your mum?'

'She might wonder how you can feel sympathy for the people you're lying to'.

'Well, the guys at the Spartan aren't really listening to me are they? They're ignoring my lies. And the ones who are swallowing them are too lazy to investigate the kind of stories the Spartan publishes. They're just turning up to Agency briefings to get the press release. Why should I have sympathy for them? I don't have any respect for them'.

'Who do you have respect for?'

'People who persevere in printing the stuff no-one listens to. I have respect for them. And empathy. And sympathy, you know, because it's my job to stop them from doing theirs'.

'So you can't have any self-respect then?'

'I've got self-respect up to my eyeballs. I have a little self-doubt though. And a little self-loathing'.

'Really?'

'I loathe Maxwell Self. I thought it was obvious'.

'You don't ever feel guilty for keeping these miracles a secret? You don't ever find it hard to adjust a miracle?'

'...I always stick to the rulebook'.

'No-one *always* sticks to the rulebook'.

We drove towards the crest of a snow dune and saw the flashing red and blue lights reflecting off of the snowflakes. We got out of the 4WD and slid down the dune in silence. Our silence was drowned out by the screaming and the wailing and the gnashing of teeth that greeted us at the plane crash site. In front of us were the passengers of flight YOY-13. We'd been warned when first called about the casualty list. Everyone had survived.

Flight YOY-13 was directly in front of us. The wings were intact, the engines, the fuselage, the duty free; they all seemed to be where nature intended. There was only really one thing wrong with flight YOY-13.

The plane was upside down.

Smith put her hands over her mouth. Because she was shocked by what she was seeing. Or because she was blowing on her hands to keep them warm.

'How on Earth did everyone survive that?'

Actually, not *everyone* had survived. The one passenger

who'd been wearing his seatbelt hadn't made it. It turned out that not wearing your seatbelt was a real life saver.

The guy who'd been wearing his seatbelt had gone to pieces during the plane crash.

There'd been a lot of soft things stuffed into the overhead compartments that cushioned the blow when the plane crashed; feather pillows, soft toys, duty free marshmallows. That was what had saved everyone else. That and not wearing their seatbelts.

I unholstered my spontaneous combustor and briefed Smith;

'We need to clear this up. There are three hundred people here; they can't all be allowed to survive a plane crash'.

'Can't be allowed to survive? ...We have to kill them? Is that what you're saying?'

'What? No! I'm saying we can't allow their plane to crash'.

'So what? You have some sort of device that wipes their memory? An army of guys are on their way to clean up the wreckage?'

'Yes, an army of guys are on their way. But I don't have a memory wiping device. At least, I don't think I do. But I do have a reinforcement of disbelief device; called conventional wisdom. My conventional wisdom device tells three hundred people they can't have all survived a plane crash. They have all survived, ergo, there was no crash'.

'So, these people who just survived their plane crashing, upside down, are never going to believe it's possible, that they could survive a plane crashing upside down?'

I had a smile frozen to my face as I hid my combustor in a desert foxhole;

'Exactly!'

We walked among the walking wounded. They were dazed and confused; they were in the middle of the desert and it was snowing after all. There were plenty of camels around and the plane they'd just crashed in was a giant straw. Who among them was really prepared to accept that they could have survived something like this? This wasn't the kind of thing that was generally accepted. The people on flight YOY-13 had watched plenty of shows on The Reality Channel. They'd heard lots of experts give voiceovers over lots of pre-visualised animations of planes crashing into famous landmarks (Big Ben, the White House, the Death Star etc. etc.). People had seen enough TV to know that you didn't survive this kind of thing. One of the few things experts in the field weren't arguing about on The Learning Channel was your chances of survival if your plane landed upside down.

'All of these people are very comfortable with the idea of not surviving a plane crash. They won't put up a fight. This isn't like having to tell people that smoking is bad for them'.

'But people accepted the truth about smoking eventually. After sixty years of denial'.

'That was nothing to do with us. And no-one ever really trusted those tobacco guys did they? Lies are only convincing if they haven't completely lost touch with reality. Even if your liar is dressed up like a doctor. But nobody here believes you can survive a plane crash. Nobody here wants to believe such an outrageous truth'.

'Isn't seeing believing?'

'Not by the time we're through with them...'

Smith and I explained that we were going to help people feel more comfortable.

Smith handed out blankets as I poured cups of tea. Smith was wearing what I had erroneously called a nurse's outfit but were in fact paramedic's overalls. I wore a pair of thick rimmed spectacles. We were posing as rescue workers but I could tell Smith hadn't been won over by the efficacy of my disguise. Because she looked embarrassed to be seen with me.

'No-one is going to forget what the rest of your face looks like because you're wearing spectacles. People are just going to think you're wearing a very poor disguise'.

I told Smith she was probably correct.

The passengers were slowly congregating around Smith and I like zombies on flesh. They heard the sound of one of their own describing the disastrous circumstances of flight YOY-13 and were drawn towards us to throw their own two pennies' worth in.

Passengers described the odd-shaped ball lightning that had cannonballed its way through the fuselage into Upper Middle Class before heading to Sub-Prime Economy where it split into four boyband shaped balls of energy and performed a strange series of movements that some described as 'vogueing' and others as 'twerking', depending on their age.

The eldest passenger (ninety-two-year-old Edwin Nappi) claimed the balls were 'doing the twist' and emitting some sort of high pitched whining.

But the other passengers explained that this was how all boybands sounded.

The four boyballs had finished their routine by hovering around the stupefied air stewardesses. Then they'd fallen silent, dodged out of the way of the drinks trolley and sheepishly exited through the emergency exit without leaving a scratch on it.

Everyone agreed that this had been more frightening than turbulence.

It was down to me to provide some reassurance.

I raised my hands and then my voice;

'Everyone, listen please? I'm afraid I have some bad news'.

This got their attention.

'You're all trapped on a mysterious desert island and

you can never leave... because you're all dead!'

It took a little longer to sink in with the younger children, but eventually they started crying too.

'Only joking! You're all fine and you'll be through customs in no time. We just overshot the runway a little'.

I whispered to Smith as people stopped crying and just started looking like they'd had a very long day.

'You tell them something unpopular, an idea they'll want to reject, to make whatever you say next seem more attractive. You give them a little scare so that when you put your arm around them they'll just nod their heads and agree. ...You give them a choice of what to believe in and you make one of those choices really bad'.

Smith's disguise was pretty convincing. I was sure the passengers wouldn't find it hard to believe that she was a nurse, what with the red eyes, the bedhead and the attitude;

'So people won't climb over the warm and fuzzy bullshit to get to the truth right? Even when the truth is the size of a plane and is right there in front of them? You think these people are going to find your lie so convenient and attractive they'll just bury their heads in the snow and completely deny reality?'

'Yep'.

'You're wrong'.

I wasn't wrong.

But I could see why Smith might think I was.

One of the reasons Smith might have thought I was wrong (even though I wasn't) was the soft-bellied sales executive who was standing next to me screaming;

'The bloody plane is upside down!'

I used the textbook response. I took him to one side and whispered in his ear;

'Keep it down man. You sound crazy'.

'I am *not* crazy. The plane is upside down!'

I could see panic flickering in everyone's eyes.

I could see survivors all around me suspending their

disbelief. I needed to anchor them to my more familiar and less 'crashy' version of events to make sure they wouldn't succumb to reality. I needed them to deny the unbelievable truth of their situation and get comfortable on some metaphorical (or metaphysical, I don't remember which) cushions that I was going to throw between them and the whole plane crashing episode.

We needed to enforce everyone's disbelief.

'How about we get everyone a nice cup of tea and then you can tell me some more about this conspiracy theory of yours?'

Smith pulled her surgical mask down and whispered to me;

'Should we really be playing that up? The conspiracy angle?'

'Sure. It's word association. I use the phrase 'conspiracy theory' and people look at this guy and the first words to come into their heads are; paranoid, weird and crazy'.

In the business this is known as an 'instant dismissal'.

I put my arm around him and made sure everyone could hear;

'Yes. The plane is upside down. But look around you. It's snowing in Dubai. Isn't it obvious you're dreaming? ...Don't you remember asking for that third gin and tonic because you wanted to flirt with the stewardess?'

I could see a flicker in his eyes. Of shame.

The fact that all of these people were naturally inclined to dismiss the truth? That's what I was relying on. That and people's natural fear of embarrassment. Embarrassment can make people do all sorts of things. It can scare a person into accepting a lie or scare them into telling one.

You have the fear too. If you'd been in those people's missing shoes would you have wanted to be the looney claiming everyone had just survived a plane crash? Wouldn't you rather believe in the same reality we agreed upon earlier? You know; the one about how it isn't possible to survive a plane crash. The one that's in the script?

That would be better for you, wouldn't it?

The way you do your job if you're a reality enforcer is you explain to people that they're out of touch with reality (ours, not theirs). Then you help them get back to our reality. Whether they like it or not. Call it tough love.

Smith wanted to know if this was why I was wearing what I had incorrectly called 'my disguise'. I answered in the affirmative and added;

'You said people were going to think it was a poor disguise'.

'Because they will, they do, they're thinking it right now'.

'Exactly. And all the time they spend asking themselves why I'm wearing a really poor disguise is less time they have to spend thinking about anything else'.

Smith shook her head and handed out another blanket.

'When you need to reinforce disbelief among a large crowd, and you're in the middle of a desert, you use whatever sleight of hand you have at your disposal. People will become so consumed with questioning whether or not I'm really a doctor they'll forget about whether my story about the crash is plausible or not. It's like Superman. You spend all of your time wondering how none of his colleagues can recognise him through a pair of glasses and a tie, instead of questioning the idea that a man can fly around the world in his underpants without messing his hair up. It's all part of the hypnosis'.

'But you're not hypnotising anyone'.

I nodded to the blanket that Smith had in her ~~nurse's~~ paramedic's glove;

'That blanket is laced with hallucinogens'.

And then I poured another cup of tea;

'And this tea is mixed with a strong sedative'.

Smith sniffed at her blanket.

'Both are quite tasteless, but the combined effect is similar to an absinthe binge. It makes crash survivors very suggestible'.

I went from survivor to survivor pouring cups of tea and making suggestions. I suggested everyone drink their tea and relax and that they'd wake up as soon as flight YOY-13 landed. They'd be informed about the slight loss of cabin pressure which may have caused them to pass out or even hallucinate as they were led off of the plane, a little too groggy to realise that the plane they'd landed in was slightly different to the one they took off in.

It was all just a bad dream.

How else could you explain the fake doctor in your dream who was wearing such a transparent disguise? And the idea that your plane had crashed, upside down, and that everyone had survived? You'd keep that part of the dream to yourself. You certainly wouldn't discuss it with your fellow passengers. It was crazy to think you could survive such a crash. Anyone claiming so would have to be escorted to the nut house.

By the time everyone had landed safely and flight YOY-13 had been buried under the snow Epiphany Smith and I had driven back to the hotel where an encrypted pictogram from the Agency was waiting for us. The pictogram was a photo of me, the logo for sex addicts anonymous, a picture of Superman (minus his disguise) and a high-resolution scan of a solitary pea. The pictogram spelt it out for me; 'USA ASAP'.

We packed our bags and checked out just as the survivors of flight YOY-13 were checking in. No-one recognised me.

We boarded our flight. I wanted to pull a sleeping mask over my eyes but I still had a job to do. There was more reality to be tolerated. More disbelief to enforce.

A minor panic had been caused when a middleweight female passenger (possibly under the influence of some 'travel pills') had taken the events of season 2 episode 7 of Roy Chancy a little too literally. Unfortunately this was the Christmas Special in which Roy went on holiday to visit Inspector Tortellini in Sicily and his plane was hijacked.

Our female passenger suspended her disbelief.

Then she started screaming;

'We're all going to die!'

I spoke to a tight-fitting stewardess who was bent over and slapping the woman in the face as the on-board chef tied her wrists to her seat with some unwanted seatbelts.

I explained to the stewardess;

'I can calm her down'.

'Are you a doctor?'

I hesitated for a moment. I wasn't wearing my spectacles.

'No, but I deal with this kind of thing all the time'.

I quickly flicked through the in-flight menu and located an old episode of The Twilight Zone. The stewardess asked;

'Won't she panic even more?'

I changed the channel and put some little headphones on the hysterical passenger.

'It's in black and white. Unless this woman is colour blind she isn't going to believe this is real'.

I didn't tell the stewardess that this was a bit reckless. A bit of a gamble.

For all I knew this woman really did have a problem separating the seeing from the believing, and if that was the case she'd fall for any outrageous plot twist or ill-conceived special effect, whether it was in black and white or whether it was not. But as I returned to my seat I couldn't hear her shouting warnings to the characters on her bite-size screen, and so I re-joined Smith who patted me on the back for a job well done. And then accidentally spilt her glass of complimentary alcohol over me.

Simon Campbell

10. The Man They Couldn't Hang (Or Gas, Or Electrocute)

*I*n Wyoming it is illegal to photograph horses during June. Wyoming has also passed laws prohibiting the shooting of fish (between January and April) and the tattooing of rabbits with the intention of making them unrecognisable to their owners.

There's a saying about Wyoming; 'If you're in Wyoming you'd better hold your breath'. In Wyoming you can face life without parole for hijacking, arson, robbery, escape and resisting arrest. And the death penalty for treason.

The gentleman that Smith and I were visiting had been convicted of 'all of the above'.

Smith and I were met at the gate to the hulking great Wyoming State Prison by the hulking great Sheriff Elmo Lee Constable. I asked the Sheriff;

'Do you have any family in Australia?'

And he replied; 'Are we gonna have a problem here son?'

Sheriff Elmo had a bit of orange food stuck to the side of his face, as if he'd fallen asleep at his desk while eating a donut covered in orange icing. There was no chance Sheriff Elmo had been eating an actual orange because Sheriff Elmo didn't eat fruit.

We walked at the pace of a man who never ate fruit as Sheriff Elmo ran through the sequence of events as he saw them. Sheriff Elmo had seen the sequence of events on MSG News. He hadn't asked the prisoner for his version of events on account of his being 'a Muslim demon'. I was confident the gentleman we'd been sent to 'adjust' wasn't a demon. He was just a terrible terrorist. The gentleman's name was Rashid Rashid.

We watched a re-mastered cut of the surveillance video.

Rashid Rashid was queuing at a Boston Airport check-in desk for O'Brien Air.

Rashid was sweating. More than a regular O'Brien Air passenger.

He was sweating so much his face was wrinkled. Even though Rashid was in his mid-twenties. Rashid clearly wasn't one of those cool, calm and collected terrorists.

Things started off badly and went downhill fast. Rashid tried to check-in without any luggage, and this, added to the fact that he looked nothing like the photo in his passport (he wasn't smiling, but he wasn't a forty-year-old man with a full beard either) prompted the check-in clerk to hit her panic button. A couple of airport police queue jumped to the desk to ask him some questions. And Rashid ran. The faster he ran, the more he sweated.

The first charge Rashid was convicted of was Resisting Arrest.

And had he been caught that would have been that. But as the lachanophobic airport police were unable to keep up with him, he was also charged, a little unfairly, with Escape.

Rashid picked up a fellow passenger's bag and tried again, successfully, to check-in for his flight. Fortunately his having a carry-on case that stretched the limits of the overhead lockers was enough to distract even the most vigilant jobsworth from the fact that he looked a dozen years younger in real life than in his passport. Of course it was more difficult to notice the difference second time around, due to the full beard that had grown over Rashid's face in the intervening half hour. This, as far as Sheriff Elmo was concerned, was proof-a-plenty that Rashid was a demon. But I was of the opinion that people tended to change their appearance.

Just look at the Human Torch in the Fantastic Four movies.

Actually no, don't. Don't look at the Fantastic Four movies.

The third charge, for the stolen carry-on case, was Robbery.

The more offences Rashid collected, the more he sweated.

The film of Rashid finished and we watched the extras; the passengers and crew of O'Brien Air Flight 321 sharing their experiences.

The next crime committed in Rashid's ever ratcheting campaign of evil was his failed attempt at lighting the fuse in the homemade bomb strapped to his sweating groin. During his trial this had been characterised as his successful attempt at Arson, seeing as how, even if the fuse never caught fire, the match he struck did.

Buxom-haired Acting Senior Flight Supervisor Tammy Wyneaux described how she had smelt the faint whiff of something 'not right' as she trollied her duty free down the aisle. After checking that none of the bottles of 'Fire! by Condoleezza Rice' were leaking Tammy parked her wares and stalked up and down the aisle with her nose turned up a little further than usual as she channelled her inner bloodhound in search of the source of the smoky smell.

Passenger 57, aka Rod Smut, had smelt the burnt match too, and after checking that the smell wasn't coming from his in-flight meal, caught Tammy's attention and pointed at Rashid, who was attempting to bring a naked flame into contact with his groin.

Tammy explained to Rashid that this was a non-smoking flight.

Rashid apologised and told her he was trying to quit. Tammy recommended he read 'Quit it!' by Keith Richards as that had worked for her (even if it hadn't worked for Keith).

But as soon as her back was turned Tammy heard another match being struck and turned back, a little dizzy, to see Rashid with a match in his left hand and what she initially assumed to be an erection but was later confirmed to be a pipe-bomb (thus exonerating Rashid of one count of Indecent Exposure) in his right.

Tammy instinctively grabbed the hard projection and began to tug at it furiously as Rashid writhed around in his seat trying to break her grip.

Tammy turned and caught the eye of some old bag across the aisle;

'You're gonna have to help me with this!'

Screamed Tammy.

At which point the old bag saw the pipe-bomb in Rashid's pants and fainted.

Rod Smut (who'd been alternately covering his fiancée's eyes and staring in disgust at Tammy and Rashid) leapt from his seat, grabbed a jug of tonic water from the drinks trolley and saturated the rutting animals with the goal of quashing their interracial passion. Rashid wriggled away from Tammy and ran down the aisle and into the toilet where he locked himself safely away from the screaming, clawing O'Brien Air trolley dolly.

I guess this was about the time that Rashid decided to repent.

This must have been around the time he began praying for forgiveness.

Tammy and her crew got everyone strapped into their seats (despite the odd protest about the worthlessness of seatbelts) and then the pilots indulged in some freestyle turbulence until Rashid could be heard banging on the toilet door begging for mercy. He broke out and stumbled into the cockpit where he accidentally disengaged the autopilot shortly before being tasered by the co-pilot (and knocking himself out against the pilot's headrest). But as he had already managed to get the cockpit door open, Rashid was also charged with Hijacking.

The flight crew tied him to a seat using tiny headphones donated by passengers who were, to be honest, not really enjoying the in-flight disaster movie; 'Aerophobia!'.

Even though aerophobia means 'fear of fresh air'.

Rashid woke two hours later to find himself charged with Treason. He would have gotten away with it if only the co-pilot hadn't started fooling around with the Taser™. If only the pilot hadn't been struck in the neck (and knocked himself out against his own headrest).

If only the plane hadn't been forced to make an emergency landing in Wyoming.

Rashid's prayers would have been answered if only the co-pilot had been able to steer the stricken plane away from the Wyoming State Magician Memorial. If only Wyoming hadn't suffered such disproportionate magician casualties during WW2.

When Rashid realised he was in Wyoming, and charged with Treason, he really began to sweat. But it turned out Rashid's sweat had been a real lifesaver. It turned out that the pipe-bomb in Rashid's explosive pants hadn't detonated as the fuse had been soaked through.

Sheriff Elmo finished reading off the charges as we were interrupted by a commotion of news-vans jostling for parking spaces in the prison's pay and display parking lot. A lot of spaces had already been taken by police cars that were resting on bricks.

The vans were emblazoned with scrabble-winning combinations of consonants and pictures of maxi-toothed, faux-haired news anchors.

The reason for all of the news-people was the imminent arrival of the local governor.

The reason for the governor was the demon.

The other person who'd heard about the governor's arrival was the shrewish Mrs Elmo Lee Constable. Mrs Constable came trotting in wearing a homemade fur coat. I spotted some raccoon, and a little beaver. Mrs. Constable kissed her husband on the cheek, curled her lip at Smith and greeted her windswept nephew; Deputy Vernon Constable. Deputy Vernon had recently survived a tornado through sheer force of luck and Mrs Constable wanted to parade him in front of the media in the car park. I suddenly realised that everyone working in this police station was related to one another. I was surrounded by a pack of Constables. And a receptionist named Fanny whom Mrs Constable referred to as the 'station wrecker'.

Mrs Constable beavered past us and started gnawing away at MSG News anchor-face Anne Punter, a sort of blonde wig on a skewer of gristle who behaved like a bimbo so consistently that people had begun to assume she was sleeping with someone senior at the network. Of course, once people had made this assumption it had become a self-fulfilling prophecy and Anne suddenly found herself rising through the ranks because of looks she didn't have and an affair that had never been consummated with anyone other than herself.

Whatever Anne Punter lacked in truth she made up for with lies.

Lies, damn lies and opinions. Anne Punter was the presenter of 'Public Opinions', a vanity project on MSG News which plagiarised the views of lunatics and used colourful black and white graphics to tell people how Anne felt about one issue or another. Anne had run a piece on Rashid in which she'd described him as a 'neo-nasty'. This was shortly after Anne had interviewed MSG weather consultant Patty Nutshell who'd posed as Wyoming State Attorney Marilyn Killjoy standing in front of a green-screen onto which a still of Shawshank Prison had been superimposed. This was when Patty had invited Anne to visit Wyoming to report on the demon busting;

'As it happens, live from this prison, where I am, right now'.

Patty's disguise had been poor, even by my standards, but the MSG News team's creative writing was second to none. They even had Semi Sans-Serif playing Rashid for their dramatisation of events; starting with his choosing the fish for dinner and ending with his urinating all over the Wyoming State Magician Memorial.

Anne needed to get some air miles out of people's fears. People were terrified of being on a plane that blew up. It wasn't a fear of flying, it was more a fear of exploding.

I didn't suffer from Ekrixiphobia. Sure, sure, I had a fear of flying, and a fear of flames, but the bit in the middle? The exploding? That wasn't one of my fears.

Smith and I watched a VHS videotape of Public Opinions. Sheriff Elmo refused to fast forward through the commercials, so we watched a second-hand mattress salesman having some sort of seizure, then endured commercials for George Michael multi-surface cleaner and Will.i.am office stationery. Then we got back to Semi's portrayal of Rashid Rashid in the MSG News Movie of the Week; 'Evil sat in seat 35B'. The ending had been rewritten and Anne Punter provided a scream-over as Rashid committed a series of acts of terror at various Wyoming residents' homes; setting fire to their laundry, stealing their daughters etc.

After the movie Anne took her show on the road for a seemingly endless (and endlessly witless) series of door to door home invasions. Anne cornered one local family after another and isolated an heirloom or pet to be used in a roleplay that would inevitably end in tears as Anne explained how Rashid was going to use terrorism on it. Panicked viewers had no choice but to bury anything of sentimental value in the backyard (family pets included). Rashid was out there somewhere, stalking them, watching them, waiting to do terrorism on them.

Anne described this as a vicious circle. The point about vicious circles and regional TV commercials was; you had to get personally involved with your audience. There was no point in making vague references to wars on terror; you had to push the terror through the front door like shit in a paper bag. You had to let people smell the fear.

Ask yourself this; what's more likely to get you jumping off of your sofa? Footage of refugees in a country far far away? Or a paper bag smelling of fear that's just been posted through your letterbox; having already been set on fire by Anne Punter? You don't keep things vague when it comes to terrorism. You put a face on it, an evil face like Rashid's. Like you do with refugees and benefit cheats and environmentalists. If you don't give people a face to blame they'll start blaming the status quo, and none of MSG News' corporate sponsors wanted that. Because they were the same as the Agency's sponsors.

Sheriff Elmo started whistling the theme tune to Public Opinions and then repeated the demonic accusations Anne had made the night before. Elmo was telling me;

'No way you're gonna be able to fix this demon problem'.

Elmo escorted us through a lot of floral wallpapered corridors as we made our way through the bowels of Wyoming state prison and into a floral wallpapered waiting room.

Apparently Mrs Constable was a part-time interior decorator.

The TV hanging from the floral wallpapered ceiling was playing another episode of Public Opinions. Elmo had them all on tape apparently. Anne Punter was standing in front of a child's drawing of Wyoming State Prison with some actors posing as a hostile crowd waiting for Rashid's arrival with everyone repeatedly chanting; 'crucify him'.

The other thing hanging from the ceiling was a bird cage.

Hanging out of the bird cage was a bald-headed drunken-looking parrot. The parrot was chanting; 'crucify him, crucify him'.

Sheriff Elmo reached into his gun holster and pulled out a handful of nuts;

'Hello Mr Freedom. Want some nuts?'

Sheriff Elmo turned back to us and explained;

'Feed Mr Freedom nuts and he recites famous Punterisms'.

'Does he like any particular kinds of nuts?' asked Smith.

'No. He likes all kinds of nuts'.

Sheriff Elmo handed Smith a few and left us with Mr Freedom;

'Radiation is good for you... the gods hate liberals...'

I could tell that Mr Freedom was making Smith angry.

It was either Mr Freedom, or it was Anne Punter. Smith sat down hard;

'How is this their top story? The guy was a complete failure'.

The news couldn't always tell you what to think, but it was great at telling you what to *think about*. Especially when they put the same story at the top of the hour every day for a fortnight. Smith huffed and puffed;

'You'd think the whole country was under threat from this one idiot. He's about as much of a threat as those morons who filmed their dress rehearsal for blowing up Stonehenge and then put it on YouTube!'

'They give terrorists a bad name'.

Smith was being serious;

'I'm being serious! These guys don't have a brain cell between them. Their plots are ridiculous, and they can't even carry them out competently. MSG News is really leading these morons on!'

'So maybe they're not such bad terrorists after all. You don't have to succeed in blowing anything up; you just need to get yourself caught and Anne Punter will terrorise everyone for you'.

Suddenly there was a scream.

We looked up at the ceiling but Anne Punter and Mr Freedom had both shut up for once. The screaming was coming from reception.

Governor Harrison Ford had arrived.

Despite the fact that Rashid Rashid had only barely managed to initiate an act of terrorism, and despite the fact that he was quite obviously one of 'those morons' Governor Harrison Ford had thrown the book at him.

Why dat? I hear you ask.

Because Governor Harrison Ford was in a bit of hot water.

Specifically Governor Ford had been videotaped in a hot tub.

With the Governor of South Dakota's wife. Drinking heavily and sniffing glue. And not even glue from the Wyoming Glue Co. But imported glue. And not even imported from the South Dakota Glue Co. This sniffing glue was from North Dakota. Governor Ford needed to get the electorate back on board. He needed an issue. Luckily Harrison's sister was Esmeralda Ford. And Ezzy was married to Raúl Greedo's son Helmut. Raúl Greedo had been the owner of MSG News until his 'death'. At which point Helmut had inherited it.

This was why Anne Punter was 'interviewing' Governor Ford.

If Governor Harrison Ford ever gave up politics a career in Hollywood surely beckoned. There was much fist-thumping as he framed Rashid for a crime he didn't commit;

'You bet we're not gonna let the terrorist who destroyed our State Magician Memorial go free. This hatemonger declared war on the good folk of Wyoming and tried to take our teenage daughters from us!'

Smith and I were watching this from the waiting room.

Mr Freedom was squawking away;

'Hatemonger, hatemonger, police brutality, I love you Fanny'.

Governor Ford was squawking away;

'I did not have relations with Governor Redford's wife. I already have a Governor's wife at home. It wasn't me in that video, I love Wyoming. I'm good, and terrorism is bad'.

And now Anne Punter;

'So Governor, you're making a promise to the voters? That people needn't be afraid if you're in charge? That you hate terrorists? That you love voters? That you're going to slay your demons? That there's an election? That you're going to slay *Muslim* demons?'

Anne was like one of those field mice that have been experimented on. Except no-one had grafted big ears on Anne. Just a big mouth. And they'd cut off her ears.

'That's exactly right Anne. What you just said'.

Smith switched off the TV and confiscated Mr Freedom's nuts;

'At least they're taking the emotion out of the issue'.

Smith started crushing walnuts in her clenched fist. I

told her not to get too worked up about it. There was no point in worrying about all of the lies that people swallow so easily.

The reason there was no point in Smith's worrying about all of the lies that people swallow so easily was that in a few weeks she would be writing them.

I had to break some bad news to Smith; a lot of scratch-starters were sent to the Framing Workshop for their first assignment. The Framing Workshop was where we'd invented the 'axis of evil'. It was where we'd come up with the term 'global warming'.

'We came up with global warming?'

'We needed something that was a little easier for Republicans to crack jokes about than complex intellectual concepts such as the 'greenhouse effect' or 'climate change'. And who in the Northern Hemisphere was ever going to take global *warming* seriously?'

'So this is just a standard cover-up to hide another act of terrorism, like in Dubai?'

It was getting hot in the waiting room.

I wanted to open a window, but they'd been wallpapered over.

'It's exactly like Dubai in that I already told you I wasn't covering up an act of terrorism then and we're not covering one up now'.

Governor Ford arrived in the waiting room.

'I'm innocent, I'm innocent, a pardon, a pardon'.

This was Mr Freedom. The parrot appeared to recognise the Governor and was clearly of the opinion that this sort of behaviour was likely to be rewarded with nuts. Mr Freedom was a shrewd operator. And so was Epiphany Smith;

'We're in the waiting room for death row, right?'

'Just remember how unreliable I can be. Now isn't the time to start believing every word I say'.

The Governor finished with his nuts and joined us;

'You the man they sent to finally get the job done?'

'Colin Jekyll sir, at your service'.

'So tell me Colin, how do you intend to finish this demon off when everything else we've tried has failed?'

Of course (as with most election promises) Governor Ford's pledge to execute Rashid had been beyond his ability to fulfil. The only reason Rashid was still on death row was; he couldn't be executed. And when I say couldn't, I don't mean for lack of trying.

This was the fourth time the Governor had arrived to witness Rashid's execution. But the lethal injection, the hanging, and the electrocution had all failed. It was bad enough that this terrorist a-hole had survived, but people had started talking as if it wasn't his time, as if only his maker could decide when a man's time was up, and not the penal system.

Crazy talk.

Like I said before; the church has a lot of rules. And they expect everyone to follow them. Including God. The church really doesn't like anyone noticing when God breaks the rules that they told you He gave them.

Colin did his best to reassure Governor Ford;

'I've doubled the strength of the lethal injection. ...But if that doesn't work I'm going to saw his head off'.

A screen-door was pulled away revealing a window into Rashid's world.

Rashid's world consisted of being strapped into a second-hand dentist's chair waiting to be executed. By me. Smith started acting like some Hollywood lefty;

'They're going to kill an innocent man!'

The man in the dentist's chair didn't look anything like the man in the mug-shot I'd received from the Agency (and of course he didn't look anything like he did in his passport photo). The man in my mug-shot was around 200lb. Sure the camera added ten pounds but the guy behind the glass couldn't have been more than 100lb soaking wet. Smith protested;

'This isn't the man in the surveillance video'.

'Told you he was a demon. Betcha believe me now right?'

'He doesn't look anything like Rashid Rashid'.

This didn't bother Sheriff Elmo;

'He looked like a Muslim when he arrived, and he looks like a Muslim now'.

But it bothered Smith. Smith looked hot when she was bothered;

'He's a hundred pounds lighter!'

I whispered to my apprentice;

'He's either on the hunger strike diet. Or he's a floater'.

'A floater?'

'His age and appearance don't stay fixed, they float around. The medical name is Rapid Ageing Syndrome. It's quite widespread among people in soap operas'.

This was the first time I'd seen a floater myself but I'd read about them in the rulebook. Rashid was just another mistake. Another blemish that needed to be rubbed out.

I opened Colin's briefcase and removed the needle and the vial. Then I took off Colin's jacket, rolled up Colin's sleeves and walked into the kill room.

After I'd administered the lethal injection I asked Smith to check Rashid for vitals. She glared at me like I'd just asked her to check him for prostate cancer but it wasn't as bad as the look she gave me when I asked her to help lift his corpse onto the gurney that we rolled out to the ambulance. Maybe I was asking a bit much of Smith. It was her first week after all.

Everyone was watching Anne Punter interviewing Mr Freedom as we pushed the gurney past the ambulance. I couldn't overhear exactly what was said but there was a sudden squawking and Mr Freedom went for Anne's face.

Feathers and hair extensions flew in all directions.

Mr Freedom accused Anne Punter of misquoting him

and flew out of the interview.

It was a pretty good distraction.

Smith gave me a look like drunken thunder as I explained how we were going to have to load Rashid onto the back seat of our rented Venereo STD1. The Venereo had two doors and no boot. It was our luggage or Rashid and I didn't have time to explain to Smith why this dead man was more valuable than her vanity case.

I squeezed Smith's handbag into the glovebox. Then I apologised. Twice.

We drove into the wilderness. Smith wasn't talking. And neither was I.

I was thinking about Peter Pickles. Peter's wife Patricia had tried to murder him after taking out thirteen separate life insurance policies on her better half. Pat Pickles had tried to poison Peter four times. When that didn't work she'd backed over him on their driveway, as he was checking for a non-existent bender on the fender of Patricia's recently acquired Humvee. After Peter came around from a mild concussion Pat had helped him into bed and heated up some chicken soup. Then she'd sabotaged the gas heater in the bedroom, closed the door and gone to the shops. When Pat got back she was so angry to find Pete in the kitchen washing up his soup bowl she'd stabbed him six times with a potato peeler.

The other person I was thinking about was Samantha Jam.

Sam Jam had been accidentally pushed over the edge of a cliff by a herd of alpacas that had been spooked by her mobility scooter.

Samantha survived the fall.

She was killed when her mobility scooter landed on top of her.

I was thinking about how some people die harder than others.

11. The Unsinkable (But Inflammable) Norweigan Queen

We left the Venereo and continued into the woods on foot. By this time Rashid had come around sufficiently that he was able to walk unaided and beg for his own life;

'Rashid knows what he did was wrong and he's sorry'.

Things had clearly gotten to Rashid. Things such as the cocktail of tranquilisers I'd injected him with on death row. He'd turned very pale. What you might call Caucasian.

'Rashid is begging for your forgiveness'.

Sometimes Rashid was like a brave casting choice. Other times he was more like the kind of subtle casting change most people never notice; like when they swapped Samuel L. Jackson with Laurence Fishburne halfway through The Matrix. Chances were Rashid was just a little nervous about being in the woods with me. But that was ok. I was nervous too.

I was suffering from self-doubt.

I was nothing like Maxwell Self. I didn't agree with combusting people while they were still breathing. Between you and me, I was thinking Rashid might turn out to be another Peter Pickles or a Sam Jam. Who was to say cutting his head off would work any better than lethal injection, or hanging? But I still had to deal with my Self issue.

If I didn't take care of Rashid then some other reality enforcer would.

I'd told Smith to wait in the Venereo. I'd told her;

'Don't go into the woods. I don't want you seeing this'.

But after five minutes we'd all given up the pretence that Smith was following us without our hearing her treading on every single twig like some tap-dancer with arthritis clearing rainforest.

I'd argued with Smith. I'd told her;

'If you follow me, things won't stay the same between us'.

The problem I had was that Epiphany Smith wanted to talk me out of spontaneously combusting Rashid. But to begin with Smith didn't say anything. No-one was talking. Rashid took this as a cue to continue begging for his life. Maybe he'd had some training somewhere or maybe he'd been born with common sense, but he'd obviously decided his best chance of survival was to tell us his life story and keep on repeating his name.

'Rashid was the youngest of seventeen brothers. Stuck in a boring existence with no way out and no chance of ever achieving anything! Rashid wanted people's respect. But Rashid's life was worthless. And he was living in Birmingham for God's sake!'

I told Rashid not to blaspheme. Or to do it quietly.

'Rashid is sorry. He just fell in with a bad crowd. But they made Rashid believe that he was doing something meaningful with his life. They gave Rashid a sense of purpose!'

I could tell Smith was a little stressed too (because she was muttering under her breath, in Esperanto), though whether it was Rashid's constantly referring to himself in the third person or the fact that she thought we were taking him into the woods to spontaneously combust him I couldn't be sure of.

It was probably the latter.

'Well your purpose was preposterous. But it sounds to me like you were just brainwashed'.

Smith looked at me as she said this. Rashid shook his head;

'Rashid knew it was wrong to try to blow up a plane. Even an O'Brien Air one. But Rashid never really intended to go through with it'.

I pointed out that he'd been caught trying to light the fuse.

'Rashid was weak. After the meal was served was a low point. I tell you if other people on that flight could have blown themselves to kingdom come after that meal they would have done what Rashid did!'

'We follow orders too. You can get a bit lost when you stop following your instincts'.

Smith was laying it on a bit thick. Maybe she thought I was no good at picking up on signals. Because I was a loner. I ducked under a low-hanging branch and told her;

'People can always choose not to follow bad orders'.

'The people who don't make the rules don't break the rules. Even if they've started to question them. Even if they've decided they don't want to be someone's puppet any longer. The boss isn't always right, but the boss is always the one brainwashing you'.

Yep, Smith was really flogging it; the brainwashing angle.

Maybe it was true. Most brains are pretty weak when you think about them; pretty yellow. Introduce your brain to hormones, alcohol, or Australian anti-depressants and chances are your brain will completely change the way it behaves.

The common or garden brain isn't in control of much of anything really.

Yeah maybe it was true. Maybe the guy who'd been played by a middle-aged fanatic when we'd started walking into the woods and was now being played by a teenage Aston Villa supporter had an average human brain like the rest of us. On the other hand, maybe Smith was simply peddling all of this brainwashing whoopla to try and get a rise out of me.

'Someone writes a script and throws in some special effects and everyone swallows some rehashed fairy-tale that's been created to sell us someone else's bad ideas'.

Smith talked in tongues when she was nervous. Or in English.

It wasn't the fault of the scriptwriter. It was the dubbing mixer.

I tried to take the words out of her mouth and redub them myself;

'You can't keep on with this anti-establishment stuff when you work for the establishment. Not in front of the prisoner'.

'What does it matter if you're going to kill him?'

Rashid could overhear us talking. I thought it only fair to raise my voice and say;

'If this is your way of talking me out of killing Rashid then you could have stopped ages ago. I'm not going to kill him. That's kind of why I smuggled him out of prison alive'.

Rashid fell to his knees and started kissing my muddy boots. I ignored him. It was either that or having to feel embarrassed for him, like some weepy reality TV contestant.

Smith blurted out a series of questions, while trying to still appear angry;

'What? Why not? Why are we walking into the woods?'

'Because I wasn't sure I could trust you. This way I could let Rashid go, but I could still tell you that I'd spontaneously combusted him. Because I'm not a coldblooded murderer. And because you wouldn't stay in the car'.

'A week ago you were worrying I couldn't be trusted to stick to the rules, now you're worried I can't be trusted to break them?'

'I was worried you couldn't be trusted not to tell anyone that I had'.

'What if I'd come out here to check for his body?'

'Why would you come out here to check for his body?'

'Curiosity?'

'I'd have found an old campfire. You wouldn't have known the difference'.

Rashid looked offended. Smith looked suspicious;

'You were really never going to go through with it?'

'I've bent the rules before you know. I was told to combust the Queen once, but I couldn't go through with that either'.

'You were told to combust the Queen? Ha! I almost believed you until you said that. I don't think you've ever broken the rules. You're too straight'.

'Well maybe one day I'll prove you wrong'.

'I'll believe it when I see it'.

I dragged Rashid to his feet;

'You're free to go'.

Rashid looked confused. He also looked around fifty-five. And five feet two.

'Free to go and do what?'

'Live forever I suppose, or die of natural causes at least. But that doesn't mean you're forgiven. Maybe Rashid doesn't deserve to die in the woods, but whether or not Rashid deserves forgiveness? That's above my pay grade'.

Smith started to come at me with a 'but'. But I cut her off;

'I know what you're going to say. It's ok to forgive someone who's following orders, or who's just, a bit of an idiot...'

I turned to Rashid and pulled my 'no offence' face.

'...No offence. ...But I don't think everything gets to be forgiven that easily'.

Smith finished waiting to start talking;

'What I was going to say was; what do we do now? You can't leave Rashid wandering around out here; he's a wanted man'.

'He changes his appearance every five minutes! Who's going to recognise him?'

'You can't just dump him in the woods!'

I thought about arguing. About telling them how I'd once dumped an events manager in the Amazon rainforest. But I'd started to feel a bit lightheaded (it was either work related stress or time for lunch) and so I just reluctantly agreed to give Rashid a lift somewhere.

'Rashid wants to go somewhere he can do something worthwhile with his life, or failing that, something that pays above minimum wage'.

'I'll take you anywhere we can get to in two days. But I have to get this young lady back to the Framing Workshop in three'.

Smith threw herself at Rashid's mercy;

'Think of somewhere exciting. I want to make the most of my last couple of days of freedom'.

As Rashid was taking requests I added;

'Somewhere at the end of a long straight road'.

'Rashid has made his decision. Americans can't tell the difference between Rashid and a Cuban... So Rashid's going to Miami!'

Miami from Wyoming in two days was the kind of challenge I enjoyed. I even let Smith drive part of the way. But we started arguing when Smith stopped the audiobook I'd been listening to and put on the local radio instead. I asked our driver;

'You like Christian Rock?'

'I do'.

I looked at Rashid in the mirror. He looked much closer to death than he really was.

'Is Rashid even allowed to listen to Christian Rock?'

'Rashid would rather listen to the audiobook. Rashid was a big fan of the Wars of Narnia when he was a boy. Rashid wanted to be Aslan'.

Smith turned the radio up to twelve;

'Rashid's *still* a boy. ...There's only one grown up in this car'.

'Rashid demands that you return us to Narnia!'

Rashid had confided in me in a truck stop toilet just past Denver; he'd been having a lot of mood swings since he'd been electrocuted the first time. He also thought his memory was much worse, but he couldn't be sure. One thing I was sure of was that Rashid was pretty quick to lose his temper. A second thing I was sure of was that either Rashid's appearance changed depending on his mood, or his mood changed depending on his appearance.

Now he was a teenager again.

We stopped at a budget motel in St. Louis. The banner over the front entrance read; 'International Guild of Multicultural Celebrity Impersonators Annual International Symposium'. Blocking our entrance was a petite woman in a platinum blonde wig with a block of wood tied to each foot and a name badge that read 'Bolivian Marilyn';

'Do you think you would enjoy some multicultural celebrity impersonations? ...Please, you can just buy the ticket. You don't have to use it'.

I sent the Agency's travel agent a cryptic pictogram containing a courtroom sketch of Woody Allen's ex-gf, an illustration of Robinson Crusoe's man-servant and a photo of Tupac Shakur looking at himself in a mirror (translation: MIA, Friday, 2 PAX).

I sat in my motel room and tried to visualise arriving in Miami and getting shot of Rashid ASAP. There was something unpredictable about any situation that involved a man you couldn't recognise from one moment to the next. I didn't mind unpredictability (in moderation), but things seemed a little more out of control than normal. The Evening News had not one but two bizarre stories at the end of the bulletin. A Utah newspaper had printed the winning lottery numbers three days before the draw. And in sport; the Jamaican men's 4x100 relay team had performed so badly at the World Championships they'd been arrested.

I met Smith and Rashid at the bar. Smith needed a stiff drink. Rashid ordered a Virgin Mary. I had a chocolate milk. Rashid's clothing (and religious affiliation) had changed. The logo on his t-shirt read 'Jesus is my home boy' but when we'd checked in it had read 'Don't kiss me I'm Muslim'. Rashid was a walking talking continuity error.

Fortunately no-one was going to notice him among the crowd at the IGMCIAI Symposium. According to the awful Ricky Gervais impersonator compering the show we'd arrived just in time for awards night.

The hot favourite was Algerian Bette Midler. Algerian Bette was basically the Meryl Streep of the awards. The other big favourite was Chinese Tom Hanks. 'Chanks' had won for the last two years running. Chanks was basically the Tom Hanks of the awards.

The bad Ricky Gervais impersonator cracked off-colour multicultural jokes as each member of the Guild took their turn to accept an Impy Award™ and thank their agent. They all had the same agent. The only sour note was when Italian Ice Cube forgot to thank her during his acceptance speech for best performance in a restaurant.

The agent let out a shriek;

'You ungrateful shit! You'll never work in this town again!'

'Can you believe the amount of talent in this room?'

Said the compere, who I'd now realised, *was* Ricky Gervais.

Smith ordered another drink (she was either a heavy drinker or her empty glass was another continuity error) as Chanks approached us with flyers for his 'Coping with Cancer' after-dinner speaking tour. Rashid expressed his sympathy. Chanks looked surprised;

'I don't have cancer. Tom Hanks has cancer'.

We were all shocked to hear this.

'Tom contracted cancer in Philadelphia'.

If Rashid hadn't laughed in his face, then things might have been ok.

'Rashid thinks you're confused. Tom Hanks was only playing a character, and the character had AIDS, not cancer'.

This made Chanks so angry he threw his volleyball across the room;

'Tom doesn't have AIDS! Tom Hanks is undergoing chemotherapy!'

Smith knocked back her drink. And ordered another;

'You've got to have a sense of humour to go through that'.

Rashid disagreed;

'No you don't. Doctors aren't refusing patients chemotherapy if they don't have a sense of humour'.

'You have no bloody respect for Tom Hanks!'

And with this war cry, Chanks grabbed hold of a bronze bust of Elvis that had been sitting quietly at the bar, and launched himself at us. Elvis caught Rashid flush on the nose. It didn't leave a mark. Rashid just sat there taking the hits from Elvis. The two problems with this were; i) it wasn't normal and ii) celebrity impersonators had started to notice. I could tell that Chanks was struggling with the exertion of continually swinging Elvis at Rashid's face (because of the heavy breathing). I ran out of the bar and to my room. I didn't have eyes in the back of my head (and I wasn't omniscient) but I was sure Smith saw me as a coward.

By the time I got back Chanks had collapsed from the effort of the heavy metal beating he'd handed out to Rashid. Rashid was now surrounded by the Bulgarian Bruce Willis, the Korean Chuck Norris and the Belgian Jean Claude Van Damme. I pushed my way through the crowd and raised my voice into an abominable Welsh accent;

'Step back everyone. I'm the Welsh Doctor Dre'.

Algerian Bette found my disguise of stethoscope, muscle suit and big headphones far too convincing. She suspended her disbelief;

'But Doctor Dre isn't a real doctor! Is he?'

I got down on my knees and counted out the ratio of breaths to chest bumps to the tune of 'I Will Survive'. At first I thought everyone had started cheering. But I relaxed when I realised they were shouting at me, telling me that I had it all wrong. I was supposed to be resuscitating Chinese Tom Hanks, but I was performing CPR on the bust of Elvis.

Smith and Rashid were staring at me open mouthed.

In-between breaths I nodded at the fire exit.

I just needed to keep everyone else's attention. I needed to tell everyone an outrageous lie. A lie so outrageous hopefully *no-one* would believe it.

I sat the bust back up and forced soap actor's tears from my eyes;

'He's alive. Elvis is alive!'

The room went *very* quiet. It was like one of those awkward silences.

'I told you he wasn't a real doctor' said Algerian Bette.

It was like car crash TV. People didn't know where to look.

Which is ideally what you're aiming for when you need to slip away unnoticed.

We ducked out through the fire escape and ran to the Venereo. Rashid was sweating. He looked a good four stone heavier and was wearing a t-shirt that read; 'Martyrs do it back to front'. I thought about engaging Rashid in a philosophical discussion about the difference between sacrificing one's life as opposed to just ending it, but Smith started congratulating me on having prevented our lynching; on having taken control of the situation. A situation involving a man who couldn't be killed, a Chinese Tom Hanks impersonator and a bronze Elvis bust was always going to be difficult to control.

Smith and Rashid were both catching their breath. And laughing. And so was I;

'I guess I can see the attraction of the odd bit of unpredictability. You get to be a bit unpredictable yourself. When you're in the business of obliterating anything that's even remotely surprising it's a nice break from the routine if you can surprise yourself'.

Smith stopped congratulating me. She seemed to be staring at my muscle suit;

'If you're in your twenties unpredictability is great fun, but it's a bit weird in a forty-year-old man. Still, you don't look much like a forty-year-old man in that stupid disguise'.

I slipped out of my muscle suit as Smith opened the driver's door for me;

'You know a good indication your disguise is working is when no-one can tell you're wearing one'.

Just before Atlanta we received an alert from the Agency.

The way we received the alert was during the WAMY traffic report.

'I'm hearing about a diversion for anyone heading to Miami. They should follow signs to Gladys, Virginia instead. This is due to something out of place in their way'.

I didn't like the sound of this 'something out of place'. I wanted to drop Rashid on the side of the road, but I was out-voted. Smith seemed happy that we hadn't been ordered back to the office anyhow. Rashid seemed unhappy that we were headed for 'somewhere else'. I checked the map and promised to introduce my passengers to the Queen along the way.

Just between you, me and my therapist, I might have been trying to prove something as I drove towards the Sand Hills Desert in South Carolina.

Maybe I wanted to prove that I wasn't some brainwashed puppet of the Agency.

Maybe I wanted to reveal something more than just the Queen.

We drove across a prehistoric beach, blinding white under the midday sun. It was hard to see anything beyond the sand dunes, but then in the haze of the horizon she appeared.

She was sat half-buried in a dune, fifty feet long, timbers weathered and splintered, with what remained of her starboard shields scattered along her hull and bronzing in the sun.

'We're in luck. Sometimes she's completely buried'.

She'd been given many names over the years. The Arapaho had called her 'Hosa'.

The locals had called her 'Boat', before the Agency had relocated them to the Congo.

But her crew had called her 'The Norwegian Queen'. The Queen was a legendary lost Viking longboat. She was legendary and lost because she was hidden out here in the sands. No-one knew when she'd gotten here, or what had become of her crew and her treasure. And no-one cared. The Queen was just another Viking longboat in a desert that had needed to be dealt with. Which was why the Agency had first sent me here twenty years earlier.

Smith wore her customary open-mouthed expression.

'The Queen was my third assignment. My orders were to combust her. But she was so beautiful. And she was so far out here I didn't think anyone would ever find her. She was my secret mistake'.

Rashid wasn't listening to me. Teenage Rashid was tearing up a sand dune towards the Queen. Epiphany Smith had been listening though, and she had a big smile on her face;

'So you don't always stick to the rulebook'.

'This is one of two exceptions that prove the rules'.

Smith flopped down onto the sand and closed her eyes;

'You know, sub-consciously, you must have wanted people to discover the truth. If you were willing to risk someone discovering the Queen then you can't have thought it was right to hide her from people. I think you knew it wouldn't spark a panic. I think, sometimes you let the occasional miracle slip through'.

'I didn't let this slip through. No-one else knows she's still out here'.

Smith opened her eyes and sat bolt upright;

'So you're not a miracle adjuster then, you're just a mystery thief?'

I could tell Smith was getting worked up. Smith was going red.

I was getting good at spotting these shifts in emotions. And sunburn.

'I'm the guy protecting people from continuity errors. One in a million events can be a dangerous thing, but the Queen can't hurt anybody out here in the middle of the desert. No-one ever died because I didn't combust the Queen'.

'Did anyone ever die because you *did* combust something?'

'I think it's your turn to tell me a secret'.

Smith laid back and closed her eyes again;
'I don't have any secrets'.

Fifteen minutes later I had one less.

It was an accident, no question.

A one in a million calamity like Black Saturday.

A unique alignment of cock-ups that started at Wyoming State Prison when they inadvertently handed back Rashid's belongings (including his pipe-bomb underpants) and continued with my handing them to Rashid, who then unknowingly packed his exploding undies into the rucksack he'd causally tossed onto one of the white hot bronze shields that littered the Queen's hull. The previously sweat-soaked fuse quickly dried out in the desert sun sufficiently that nearly twenty years after I'd been despatched to combust the Norwegian Queen, she went and spontaneously did it all by herself.

Rashid didn't stand a chance. He was engulfed in a fireball instantaneously. I could see him dancing in the flames. Maybe it was the Rhumba, maybe the Tango. All I knew for sure was that I couldn't move and that Smith was screaming at me to do something.

The thing I was doing was no thing.

Smith quickly gave up on me and started running towards the Norwegian Queen. This made me move. I chased her down and pulled her back as we watched the Queen burn. She burned as you'd expect wood that had been in a desert for nine hundred years to burn.

Smith turned on me;

'Are you insane? We can't leave him to die! We have to put the fire out!'

I wasn't sure how to put it politely;

'How the hell am I supposed to put a fire out in the middle of the desert?'

'You coward! Do you want it to burn?!'

I wasn't a coward. I was just paralysed with fear. Because of Black Saturday.

But Smith wasn't to know this because I couldn't talk about Black Saturday with anyone. It was a repressed memory.

Smith was becoming hysterical; because of all the fiery death.

'You *do* want it to burn! Because you can't trust me?! Because you're brainwashed?! Maybe you had some balls twenty years ago but now you're just a fool following orders'.

I was actually very upset at the Queen's going up in flames.

I was also getting a bit frustrated with Smith's opinion of me;

'Maybe this is fate, maybe she was never meant to be seen'.

Smith begged to differ;

'You're a liar and a cheat and your talent for outsmarting people is only exceeded by your talent for outsmarting yourself!'

This wasn't true. But my problem was, I could only disagree with Smith by lying. I couldn't talk to Smith about my fear of fire, so I figured it was probably best to just stand there paralysed with fear and watch the Queen burn and say nothing except;

'If I thought Rashid was in any danger I would have done something. But he's fine'.

Rashid walked over and Smith gasped and turned away at the sight of him. Because the fire had reacted badly with Rashid's clothing and he was standing in front of us buck-naked. Smith's phone rang. She answered as angrily as possible;

'I don't have a single bloody thing for you!'

Smith hung up. She seemed upset about something.

12. Gladys' Mumbo Jumbo

I pulled the Venereo up to the outskirts of Gladys, Campbell County, VA. We were right on the Bible belt. We'd fallen breadcrumb like into a fold of gut hanging over the hip; into a divine love-handle. All around us were blue skies, green fields and a hell of a lot of white weathered sheds. And white prefabs built to look like weathered sheds. In Gladys, people wanted to blend in with one another, to live in Where's Wally World. Men wanted to get home from work and switch on the TV and enjoy the same sideshows that the guys from the office or the slaughterhouse enjoyed. They enjoyed what they were supposed to.

The reality that everyone in Gladys had agreed upon was Adam and Eve not Adam and Steve; it was a red neck and a purple heart, cheese sauce and bacon on your dessert.

It was three-year-olds in beauty pageants.

If anyone in Gladys ever felt the urge to leave the National Evangelical Presbyterian Missionary Church to join the Reformed National Evangelical Presbyterian Missionary Church, or if they ever felt the urge to turn vegetarian, then their neighbours soon put them right on what had been agreed upon and what had not.

People in Gladys dreamt of the big car, the big fridge and the big breakfast, of having a little more than their neighbours. But only enough to encourage a little respect, and maybe a little envy. Certainly never enough to stir their contempt.

Everyone in Gladys owned a dog and knew someone with a tractor.

Three out of ten people had a photo of their dog on a tractor.

And two out of three had that photo hanging on their living room wall.

The fact that the reality everyone in Gladys had agreed upon was so apple-pie and soccer-mom and so down to Earth was the reason why this continuity error was so serious. Gladys wasn't like Australia. There weren't so many out of place things already there.

There was no platypus and no kangaroo.

That's why this artefact was so seriously out of place.

It's what we called a Seriously Out Of Place Artefact (a SOOPA).

I finished reading aloud from my Rough Guide to Virginia and turned around to judge my companions' reactions. Smith was texting someone behind my back while Rashid tried to light his farts with the cigarette lighter he'd gotten with his Happy Meal. He looked about ten.

I threw the guide away and retrieved our orders.

Our orders were contained within a series of cryptic pictograms that had been e-mailed to a disposable smartphone posted to a PO Box just outside of Salem. The photos in the pictogram were, in order of receipt; a child's sketch of a Canon. That one was easy to decipher. A photo of a dunce's cap. A bunk bed assembly diagram. A copy of Andy Warhol's famous pop art soup cans. And a Captain America style gimp mask.

Our orders were clear. We were to debunk the SOOPA.

Paragraph 14 Section 42 of the rulebook stated that you had to destroy your orders as soon as you'd figured out what they were trying to say. I pressed delete and tossed the phone onto the passenger seat. I didn't hear the countdown start.

Smith and Rashid were eventually coaxed back into the car and I started telling them about our orders. Smith couldn't be coaxed out of her sulk though.

'Are you sure you should be telling us this?'

This was passive aggressive Epiphany. I was passive passive;

'You can read the message for yourself if you want. You're sitting on it. You just need the password for my phone'.

Smith pulled my smartphone from her backside;

'I know how to retrieve messages from phones'.

Now that Smith was no longer incubating the smartphone we could hear the countdown as clear as tabloid headlines. It went; nine, eight, seven.

'The phone's flashing a red self-destruct warning at me and you have two unread messages from Crowded House Insurance'.

The phone went; six, five, four.

I was sure I'd only pressed delete. I was sure I hadn't pressed self-destruct. But I didn't want to take any chances. I slammed on the breaks, snatched the phone from Smith's trembling hand and threw it out of the window. It ricocheted off of the wing mirror (if only we'd been in a Viagrador) and landed on the backseat. It went;

three, two.

Smith and I looked around in time to see Rashid grab the phone and sit on it. We heard a muffled voice tell us; 'This message will self-destruct...' There was a loud pop from Rashid's buttocks. And the ear-piercing sound of metal being shredded.

And then the rear of the Venereo fell apart.

'It was only supposed to delete the message'.

Smith got out of our half of the car first, shouting at me;

'You could have killed Rashid. Again!'

'No. I couldn't'.

Gladys was a small town that had started a rumour big enough to reach a hearing-aid somewhere within the bowels of the Agency. When we arrived the main street was deserted. Eerie. Clichéd. The receptionist who greeted us at the Overlook Motel was named Norma and even had a plagiarised facial tick and stereotypically offbeat inflexion to her enunciation. When Norma started talking about her mother up in the house we all feared the worst. But then her mother arrived in rude health and served us homemade gooseberry pie.

The pie had some berries in it. And some goose.

Norma pushed her pie away and passed us the register to sign.

To make sure we had our stories straight I told Norma;

'We're all Events Managers. That's our occupation'.

Norma explained;

'Ya'll need to wash your own towels and bedsheets. Or if you're flush with cash you can pay the dirty linen surcharge'.

Rashid spoke for all of us when he enquired;

'What if I don't get my sheets dirty?'

'The other thing is, we only have two rooms available and there are three of ya'll. And we have a rule at the Overlook that men and women can only mix if the beds are separated by a curtain'.

Smith looked aghast. As did I. And Rashid;

'How does a motel in the middle of nowhere run out of rooms?'

'The friendly atmosphere? And because a lot of people have arrived from out of town, a lot of strangers like ya'll, not from Gladys. All here to see our miracle'.

'I can't share with a woman'.

I knew Rashid had me on this one. All I had left to me now was the choice between Rashid and Smith. And I was a loner.

'I think mother would prefer it if you two white folks shared? And you look like a nice couple, for a couple of strangers. Just keep the curtain pulled; that's all we ask'.

Smith walked out. I took the room key from Norma and smiled.

I figured that eventually either Smith would start talking to me again or I'd send her back to the Framing Workshop and carry on being a loner. I headed back to the garage that we'd been towed to in half a Venereo to find it closed, but there was no point in getting all bent out of shape about it. I doubted the town had a spare car they could've hired us anyway.

We eventually discovered life in Gladys. A few kids were running along the street wearing Halloween costumes. There was Marilyn Manson, there was Gene Simmons, and there was Britney Spears. Smith asked where they were headed.

'We're going to see the mamba jamba'.

We followed at a discreet distance.

I explained the history of the SOOPA to Rashid. Smith pretended to be more interested in a little bit of Gladys caught under her fingernail. She was very convincing.

I'd investigated plenty of SOOPAs in my time; the MC

Hammer audio cassette discovered in the prehistoric caves at Altamira. The ancient rune stones discovered in an Aztec pyramid, which contained a series of spoilers for the next Star Wars movie. The trilobite fossil found in a slab of ancient rock in Lyme Regis, which also happened to encase a frying pan. All of these artefacts were seriously out of place.

Some were more easily explained than others; like the prehistoric cave paintings at Chauvet with the chorus to Hey Jude.

Explained away as the scribblings of a Neanderthal.

Others were more difficult, like the teasmaid discovered off the coast of a Greek Island in the wreck of a ship thought to have been constructed in the second century. BC.

This was long before teasmaids of such complexity were thought to have first appeared. The Spurios Teasmaid was a serious threat to our agreed upon history of the ancient world. Sure, sure, history could be rewritten, but this was more like rewriting the laws of physics. Most physicists were in denial. Most people who weren't physicists suggested the teasmaid had been airdropped by ancient astronauts.

They'd started arguing in front of everybody.

And it was down to the Agency to break up the fight.

The Agency didn't want to meet the cost of retro-fitting enough ancient history to suggest that the Greeks had been perfectly capable of creating a mechanical teasmaid. And no-one in the Archaeological Society was keen to admit that they'd overlooked all of the teasmaids that had been dug up over the past two thousand years. In the end we had to pay a deep sea diver a small fortune to admit that he'd hoaxed the teasmaid out of some Ancient Thracian saucepans and a 1930s cappuccino maker.

I was worried this new SOOPA was going to be difficult like the Spurios teasmaid.

We followed Marilyn, Gene and Britney to the Glad Mall.

The town's entire population of three thousand was crowded around a stage usually reserved for beauty pageants and hog auctions.

We paid three bucks to get a photocopied entrance ticket that had a caricature of some two-dimensional protagonist holding a jam jar. Once we had our tickets we proceeded to the stalls selling orange pop and orange cakes. As everyone in Gladys was in the mall it was uncomfortably hot inside. This meant that most of the flies in Gladys had joined us also. The flies were all over the orange cakes or they were drowning in the orange pop. Luckily we managed to locate one stall where there were no flies on the food. Because the owner of this particular stall was spraying her food with Raid to keep the flies off.

Blonde soccer-momesque Christy was the owner of the 'Happy Cup' café and wanted six dollars for a cinnamon croissant because;

'It's like you, from Europe'.

Christy carried on smiling as Epiphany Smith sought clarification;

'But why are they so expensive? You baked them here right?'

She looked at Smith blankly;

'They're from Europe'.

Christy's voice went up at the end of each sentence but there was no Australian tongue in her mouth (tongues don't go in the mouth silly!). Christy's voice went up at the end of each sentence because somewhere in there a part of her brain was trying to climb out.

At first glance there appeared to have been an outbreak of half-hearted peroxide abuse in Gladys. It would've been the sixth outbreak of the year, and technically a pandemic. But then you slowly realised that all of the young women and football players had intentionally dyed their hair orange. And then you slowly realised that everyone had stopped talking. Someone pressed play on an antique ghetto blaster, a tape warbled into life and Algerian Bette Midler started butchering 'From a Distance'.

The man of the hour walked onstage; all five feet four and seven stone of him.

This was the caricature from my ticket in real life. He had the childish grin. And the coloured in hair. He had the disproportionately big head. The man of the hour's name was Chuck Redstar and he was holding the SOOPA above his head like a trophy.

It was a jam jar. Encased in prehistoric amber. ...It was an amber jam jar.

Chuck Redstar. This was the man who had brought us here; the owner of a seriously out of place jam jar. The leader of a new cult. A cult which had already claimed three thousand disciples. But Chuck Redstar was not this man's real name. This man's real name was Norman Grinder. Chuck Redstar wasn't even his real pseudonym. His real pseudonym, around here, until very recently anyhow, had been 'Weird Norm'. He held the jar aloft;

'This, amber jam jar, is proof that evolution is a fallacy! People were around, making jam, when dinosaurs ruled the Earth!'

The jam jar was scuffed, cracked. It could conceivably have been created before the earliest recorded jam jars. But it didn't really matter when it had been made, as the amber the jam jar was encased in had to be at least thirty million years old.

'Gladys will go down in the history of mankind as the place where the most important discovery in, the history of mankind, was made! Gladys has been chosen to reveal the truth behind man's creation!'

I could see Smith sighing;

'Does this guy believe what he's saying?'

And I could hear Rashid rolling his eyes;

'It's always the short ones...'

'Shhh! Show some respect stranger'.

I stopped Rashid before he started getting heavy. I explained that Chuck just wanted some respect. Like Rashid. And this crowd was a little on the large side and a little on the white side to be starting another incident. Redstar continued (to get himself excited);

'This jam jar has been revealed to Gladys alone! A truth that has been kept hidden from Timberlake and Clearwater'.

I figured Timberlake and Clearwater were either a much loathed local folk duo or neighbouring towns.

'The closed minds of the residents of Timberlake and Clearwater are not ready for the truth we have been given'.

So they were neighbouring towns then.

'This is the start of special times for the people of Gladys. Like Bob there, from the construction yard. And Pat from the mail office. ...I can see Mike from Canada. We're all proud of you Mike'.

Mike was getting a lot of pats on the back and had a tear in his eye.

I guessed that Mike had recently come out of Canada.

'I can see, up at the back, Andrea from the Glad Clinic. You may have been born an Andrew but you'll always be an Andrea to us'.

I turned around and saw Andrea looking pale. I guessed Andrea hadn't come out before today. I guessed she was kind of coming out now.

The football team started chanting; 'Gla-dys'.

'That's right boys. And we're gonna end that seven year losing streak against Farmville this year too'.

Someone helpfully added;

'Those Farmville bastards filled up their team with ringers from Timberlake and Clearwater!'

'That's true. We all know that's true. But it no longer matters. Because Gladys has the most valuable trophy in the world!'

Redstar thrust his amber SOOPA into the air once

more, as the mall spontaneously erupted into a chorus of the local football song;

'⊗💣☠! you Tim-ber-lake, ⊗💣☠! you Clear-wat-er, ⊗💣☠! you Mi-chael-Moore and Farm-ville ⊗💣☠! you too'.

People ran onto the stage. I saw Redstar flinch before he ran backstage.

And into a display of souvenir amber jam jars.

The Agency couldn't allow this sideshow to continue.

So I'd been sent to Gladys, to adjust their amber SOOPA. To frame it or hoax it. It hadn't really been spelt out in my pictogram, but I was under strict orders to prevent this cult from spreading any further.

Maybe I'm repeating myself here, but this amber jam jar wasn't in the script.

Maybe the Agency's corporate sponsors at Marmite and Vegemite could've put aside their differences and united behind a prehistoric yeast spread, but they weren't going to stand for this. The Agency's sponsors had poured a lot of money into a lot of coffers over the years. They wanted *their* people in charge. But this was a threat to the church's golden perch. After two hundred years of insuring themselves against revolution the church would wind up getting written out of history by their own anecdote.

And if there's one thing religions hate it's plagiarism.

There isn't one thing religions hate of course, there are lots of things. But the only thing they hate more than plagiarism is incest.

And Chuck Redstar was a mother⊗💣☠!ing plagiarist.

The church didn't need another competitor. The church was in the business of squeezing their competitors out. And it was already quite a crowded marketplace.

We were going to need a big fat lie to cover this up. Maybe noble, maybe not.

The nobility of the lie was a 'nice to have'. But the lie itself, that was a 'must have'.

Sure, sure, this wasn't going to be a little lie, like Tinkerbelle, this was going to be bigger than that. But it was still just a big *white* lie. And that was a lot more palatable than the alternative. If it turned out that the amber jam jar was the real deal and the truth were to be revealed, we'd be talking mass hysteria. Or worse.

Maybe the Agency had grown a little complacent. Maybe they should have seen this coming. But it was done now. My main concern was keeping my job. And my job was throwing myself in front of the status quo and keeping it safe from harm.

After Redstar's speech Rashid, Smith and I did some window shopping. We weren't sizing up souvenirs though; we were sizing up the competition.

Smith had taken an instant dislike to Redstar;

'We need to get hold of that stupid relic and re-bury it'.

Maybe I shouldn't have, but I smiled and asked;

'So you want to be a mystery thief too?'

For some reason Smith hit the wall. She was probably swatting a fly.

'It isn't the jam jar I'm worried about; it's the moron holding it! In the same way that destroying the Ark of the Covenant™ would be unthinkable, unless you were trying to prevent Hitler from getting his hands on it. If this jam jar fell into the right hands perhaps it wouldn't have to be hidden? Maybe we could try to live with the weird and wonderful rather than adjusting anything that doesn't fit in with the status quo? Wouldn't that be nice?'

'Sure, if we hadn't spent the past one hundred and twenty years hiding the truth. But this would be a pretty big shock to the system. This would be like dropping a cane toad into boiling water rather than heating him up slowly'.

'So why don't we try heating things up slowly?'

'These things take time. More than we've got anyhow. We've worked very hard on our noble lie. Our version of reality has been perfected over many years. It comes with a long warranty. Do you really want people buying a reality that Redstar cooked up overnight, for the gratification of his ego? A reality that'll break down in a couple of months?'

The GladMart shop window had a display of amber jam jar t-shirts and boxer shorts and amber jam jar handguns. Smith turned away in disgust;

'You're missing the point! You want to protect people from the truth. I want to protect them from Redstar's lies!'

'I'm not missing the point. You're worried that Redstar is lying to them. In which case we agree; we need to do something about Redstar. So let's get him out of the way first. Then we can argue over whether people are ready for the truth or not'.

I didn't want to keep arguing with Smith. Because I'd started to enjoy her company.

But sometimes the training just takes over.

We arrived in a brightly coloured cluster of public health hazards that was rather loosely referred to as the food court and discovered the reason for the recent orange food dye shortage. I could see people eating orange burgers and drinking orange beer.

But according to Smith;

'These people don't seem to be suffering from mass hysteria'.

'They've all dyed their hair orange! Look at their eyebrows!'

But Smith insisted on approaching total strangers, to try to find someone rational in the food court, to prove her point that people *can* handle the truth. We put a fiver on it.

We were pointed in the direction of Pirate Jack. Pirate Jack was the miner who'd discovered the SOOPA in the local arsenic mines. In terms of winning my bet the testimony of a man who could be suffering the effects of arsenic poisoning (hallucinations, hair loss, confusion, drowsiness) could really go either way.

Smith explained that we were here to test the amber jam jar. Jack asked what kind of tests specifically and Smith explained that they were scientific tests. Smith was a liar. I tried to see if any of Jack's hair was falling out. Diarrhoea was another side effect of arsenic poisoning, but Jack smelt predominantly of cornflakes.

'It ain't no hoax on my part, if that's what you're getting at. Hell, I don't see what all the fuss is about. A damn jam jar gotta be one of the least strange things I found in that mine'.

This wasn't good. This wasn't good at all.

'You've found other things in the mine?'

'I found four frozen fish fingers in a solid rock. Aargh'.

Smith asked Pirate Jack if he was feeling alright.

'I'm fine. How are you?'

'I'm, good. ...So what else have you found in the mine?'

'I found a fossilised foot. Wearing a bowling shoe. The *left* shoe. I found the rear axle of an old Tranny 360 and you can't even buy them in this country. I found a cubic zirconia in a lump of coal'.

The problem with Pirate Jack was that he wasn't hallucinating.

The problem was, this was a hell of a lot of continuity errors to find in one place.

'It ain't no hoax. But Weird Norm's crazy if he thinks that jam jar is evidence that proves his literal account of creation'.

It looked like I was going to be paying Smith a fiver. And Smith looked like someone smugly waiting to be proven right.

And then...

'That jam jar is clearly evidence of time travel. Time travel by a super-intelligent future version of mankind. Or perhaps highly evolved farm animals. Such as hogs'.

It would've saved me a lot of work if everyone in Gladys had shared Pirate Jack's viewpoint. But Jack was a loner, like I was.

'No-one in Gladys wants to hear the truth about hogs. So if you're here to prove that jam jar ain't what Redstar says it is, then you're gonna have a tough time convincing these folks'.

Maybe it was the arsenic talking, but it seemed to me that Pirate Jack was out of touch with Gladys reality. That is to say, Pirate Jack was out of touch with the new conclusions everyone else had jumped to since being exposed to the amber jam jar.

Everyone else had fallen under Redstar's spell. They'd jumped on the bandwagon. In a town full of people who'd been convinced that the theory of evolution was bankrupt, at least the guy who believed in time travelling pigs was the madman you knew.

And at least I could cross Jack off of my list of people to be de-programmed.

And at least I'd won a fiver.

We left the mall and headed back to the Overlook Motel. There was now one room less than when we'd first checked in and we'd all been moved into a double room that Rashid was refusing to share. This was a crisis of conscience for Rashid, apparently.

Rashid's rulebook was even more unforgiving than the Agency's. There was no chance he could share a room with Smith. It wasn't anything against Smith personally.

It was just that she was a woman.

'Believe me, I wish our laws could be re-written as easily as yours. Do you know how many house parties Rashid has missed because the house wasn't properly segregated?'

Smith guessed it was a lot of house parties;

'Maybe you should try to free the sentiment of your rulebook from the reality of fourteen hundred years ago?

Maybe they didn't have house parties back then? Maybe if they had, they would've made house parties exempt from the rules?'

Smith's line of reasoning failed to win Rashid over.

We ordered Happy Meals and thick-shakes and watched as a TV news anchor described in graphic detail how Dallas Cowboys quarterback José Barcelona had been killed while en route to a 49ers game. Unfortunately for José a cow had strayed onto the highway on the way to the airport and had been struck by a Dairy Queen truck with such force it had been launched into the air, across the central reservation and through José's windshield.

The news anchor thought this was probably the work of 49ers witch doctors.

I looked down at my Happy Meal cowboy action figure which was entirely unable to distract me from the fact that these continuity errors were getting far more frequent and far too obvious. Far, far too obvious...

13. Canon's Cutthroat Razor

*A*ll of a sudden there was a big bang. From the bathroom.

Rashid had started locking the bathroom door each night after he'd caught Smith sneaking in to use the loo. This was because Rashid had been sleeping in the bathtub. After that Smith and I had been locked out. I'd shown Smith how to pick locks but Rashid had started falling asleep on the toilet each night, so Smith had started picking the locks on the other guests' rooms and sneaking into their bathrooms instead.

The big bang had come from a microwave that Rashid had snuck into the bathroom along with a six pack of Vimto. Rashid was finding our Gladys diversion quite frustrating. Rashid wanted to know when we were going to get to Miami. Partly out of boredom then, and partly out of curiosity, Rashid had retired to his segregated bathroom, put the six pack of Vimto in the microwave and turned it on. To test his 'unbreakability'.

Rashid looked like a thirtysomething. But he was behaving like a toddler.

I'd been shaving when the big bang had made me jump and cut myself on the chin.

I hadn't realised at first because our only mirror was in the bathroom and I'd been shaving from memory.

Smith pointed out that I was bleeding. Then she soaked a complimentary motel toilet roll in a $16 gin from the minibar and helped me stem the bleeding. The $16 gin really stung.

Rashid emerged from the bathroom with part of a Vimto can sticking out of his skull and Smith took back the gin-soaked toilet paper and started working on Rashid instead. Smith needed to stop Rashid from bleeding all over the floor. Because of the surcharge.

I looked at the can sticking out of Rashid's head and told him;

'I always dreamt of having superpowers. Of saving people trapped in apartment fires, burning buildings, towering infernos, that sort of thing'.

'Is stupidity classed as a superpower?' asked Smith.

'In college. And government'.

Rashid didn't think of himself as stupid, or superheroic;

'This isn't a superpower. Rashid doesn't have super speed. He can't stick to walls. They only thing Rashid can do is take a beating'.

'Maybe you should try professional wrestling?'

'Rashid has ambitions and dreams. He wants to do something useful with his life. Rashid wants to get out, to move on'.

I could tell Rashid wanted to get out, to move on. But I had to be straight with him;

'We have to stay for as long it takes to debunk that amber jam jar'.

I had no idea how long that was going to take. All I

knew for sure was; i) it was my job to debunk Chuck Redstar's amber jam jar as a fake, a forgery, a fugazi and ii) Chuck's amber jam jar was the real deal, an honest mistake, a genuine continuity error. If it wasn't then none of us would have been bleeding all over a motel room floor in Gladys.

The reason the Agency was so sure it wasn't a fake? I didn't know. They hadn't told me. The reason I was so sure? If the Agency thought this was a hoax they'd have sent me a different pictogram. Our orders would have been to *encourage* Redstar.

The Agency spent millions of your tax dollars each year manufacturing hoaxes to reinforce people's disbelief in the miraculous. They took the freebies where they could get them. The Agency was all for encouraging private investment in hoaxes. The more hoaxes they saw the less people believed.

Don't believe me? Then ask yourself this; you don't believe in crop circles do you?

You don't believe in Bigfoot?

If this was a hoax then Redstar would admit it eventually.

No faker wants his hoax to be believed for ever; otherwise what's the point?

But this wasn't a hoax. Normally we'd have bundled Redstar into the back of some mystery machine and told him to write down a number on the back of an envelope. But the problem here was that Redstar wasn't going to accept a payoff. No amount of cash was going to persuade him to give up his jam jar. Redstar wasn't in it for the money.

He was all about the love and the attention.

And he wanted both of yours.

Sure, sure, the Office of Confessions could have paid off some homeless guy to admit to the hoax. It happened all the time. But it only happened all the time if you could remove your protagonist (from the face of the Earth). And

I've already gone on record regarding the spontaneous combustion of people who are still breathing.

No, we were going to have to come up with a hoax of our own. It was down to us to convince people that Redstar's amber SOOPA wasn't seriously out of place at all. And if we couldn't? Well then someone would have to dig up some buried Gospels recounting our lives with the dinosaurs. Because if we didn't, you could be sure that Redstar would.

Like all good plagiarists Redstar had stolen someone else's idea.

But the embellishment? The USP? That was all his own work.

Any time the Almighty does something you weren't expecting a new religion or cult springs up with a convincing explanation for it.

The big mistake religion made was giving God a job description; saying what He does and what He doesn't do. The other big mistake religion made was hitching itself to one version of God. But God was rather smarter; God never tied himself down to one version of religion. And so unfortunately, and as seen in Gladys, God was in the habit of doing things that really screwed religions over. As soon as you named the date for judgement day you just knew you were going to be proven wrong.

'It's you that's wrong. There is one God and one religion'.

Rashid had been eavesdropping. And picking bits of microwave oven out of his ears.

Maybe I was being a little mischievous, but I had to disagree;

'Don't try to tie God down. He's a free spirit'.

'This is blasphemy!'

Perhaps. But it wasn't just blasphemous. It was also bleeding obvious.

Back in seventy-three The Watchtower in Texas Society started telling people that Armageddon was coming in seventy-five. They even broadcast a Saturday morning cartoon; 'Weekend Armageddon Showcase'.

Within five months TWITS had six million members, and within seven they'd all put their houses on the market and sold off a kidney in preparation for the apocalypse.

On 3rd January 1975 a special edition of Weekend Armageddon Showcase issued an apology on behalf of the (exclusively male) leadership of TWITS who expressed their disappointment and frustration that the apocalypse hadn't come off. TWITS apologised for relying on the opinions of 'so-called experts' who'd provided them with duff information. The statement apologised to those cult members living out of suitcases and promised Armageddon in 1999.

Let's face it; God is too unpredictable for religion. God tends to embarrass religion at parties. And people don't want unpredictable. They want a predictable God with an easy to follow set of rules. People just want to believe what we tell them.

Whatever you do don't start believing what you see.

What you see is wrong, most of the time, and so if you believe what you see, what you believe will be wrong too.

Our problem was, a lot of people had started believing what they were seeing. A lot of people could see the seriously out of place artefact right there in front of them.

It was in a display cabinet in Christy's coffee shop.

The display cabinet was actually the coffee shop gun cabinet. And when we arrived the 'Happy Cup' café had been renamed the 'Happy Jam Jar'. Christy had renamed the coffee shop by painting the words 'jam jar' over the word 'cup' in orange paint.

People were queuing around the block.

This was even more phenomenal than when the face of

Cher had started appearing in meat feast pizzas at branches of Luigi's Pizza Shack. There'd been a lot of arguments about exactly which face of Cher was appearing in the pizzas but eventually everyone had agreed it was 1987 Cher and so Luigi's had started printing that face on mugs and fridge magnets.

Cher eventually settled out of court (for lots of dough).

The souvenir mugs in the café window were just old mugs with the words 'Jam Jar' neatly printed on them in orange marker pen.

'It's a novelty coffee mug. ...Have you ever seen one before?'

I had to admit to Christy that I hadn't.

'Then it's a novelty'.

Smith ordered a coffee. She didn't get me one because she knew I didn't drink coffee. Or because she was still in a bad mood. Smith didn't take Rashid's order because we'd left him at the motel. Maybe no-one could've recognised him, but there was still a chance that the bits of microwave sticking out of his face could've put someone off their bacon cheesecake.

As the whipped cream, chocolate and marshmallows were applied to whatever the hell it was that Smith had ordered there was a commotion behind the counter as Chuck Redstar attempted to sneak up behind everyone and jump the queue.

The commotion was because one of Redstar's minders had become very attached to a giant rat glue board at the Happy Jam Jar's rear entrance. As soon as Smith saw this she started arguing with a somewhat preoccupied Christy over her inhumane treatment of rats.

The national news media were at the Happy Jam Jar for Redstar's inaugural press conference. I was concerned that Epiphany Smith was going to get her face plastered all over the News at Ten and dragged her out of the spotlight.

Luckily I was wearing my disguise; a handlebar moustache and a Chilean accent. I was Dr Javier Madrid; scientific sceptic.

Christy carefully handed the amber jam jar to Redstar. Redstar recited his lines;

'Today is a day that will live long in the memory and in the history books written by the people who are here to remember what is happening, here, today...'

I whispered to a four-eyed mailman stood next to me;

'Someone should tell Redstar he's a modern day prophet'.

'You're a modern day prophet!' he shouted.

This was greeted by whoops from the crowd and a ripple of excitement among the media. Redstar puffed out his pigeon chest and looked at his notes;

'I am just a humble messenger with a wonderful message...'

I hoisted a small boy onto my shoulders and told him to shout;

'We wuv you Mr Wedstar'.

There were some 'awws' and some laughter. And more whoops.

'I'm here to reveal a really great thing to the world!'

I started whooping. Redstar was beaming. People were cheering. Redstar's guard had been dropped, his ego inflated. Now for the pin prick. I shouted in a clear Chilean accent;

'Either Redstar is crazy, or he thinks that you are'.

The air was sucked out of the coffee shop as everyone took a deep breath of shock and froth.

I raised my Chilean voice (and my Chilean indignation) further;

'That jam jar is a fake! This man is using it to dupe this community, for his own financial gain!'

This sparked a huge commotion. People jostled one another. If everyone hadn't been holding a coffee and a pastry things could've turned physical.

I pulled an orange flyer from Dr Madrid's pocket;

'This is a flyer for a guided tour of the arsenic mines; so people can follow the journey of the amber jam jar. Cheques are to be made out to one Norman Grinder. But Norman Grinder is a con-man'.

I pointed an indignant Chilean finger at Redstar;

'Norman Grinder is Chuck Redstar!'

There was a hushed silence. And then someone calmly said;

'Yeah, we know. Norm changed his name a few weeks ago'.

'Forty bucks seems a fair price for a tour of the mines'.

'For the arsenic mines? I've always wanted to see those'.

Was this room full of plants? Dr Madrid had to spell it out;

'This jam jar isn't evidence of anything. He could claim it arrived on the Millennium Falcon but that wouldn't make it so'.

Redstar could feign indignation as well as the next man;

'I don't know you sir. But I'll tell you I'm not claiming anything as ludicrous as 'space jam'. This jam jar was made locally, right here in Gladys, between thirty and forty million years ago'.

Dr Javier Madrid waved the flyer in the air;

'And now you want to charge people between thirty and forty dollars to have their picture taken with it!'

Dr Javier Madrid turned to the news cameras;

'Whenever you encounter a man making astonishing claims you should always ask yourself; how much money is he making out of this?'

Someone shouted out;

'He's trying to hijack this press conference!'

And that was when the Gladys football team bundled me to the ground. And for a moment Dr Javier Madrid's world went very dark.

When I came to I could hear someone calmly

explaining;

'It wasn't that kind of hijack'.

I tried to reapply Dr Madrid's Chilean accent. But I started off somewhere in Cornwall and finished up in Nigeria.

'He's speaking in tongues!'

Christy came into focus offering me a cappuccino.

I dragged Dr Javier Madrid to his feet;

'My name is Dr Javier Madrid. I work for the Dorking Institute for Clinical Knowledge and Scepticism. And I'm here to debunk these outlandish claims. This jam jar is as exaggerated as faeries or anti-ageing creams. Don't accept this man's word in blind faith'.

'Why not?'

'...Because he might be lying to you'.

'We trust him'.

The whole room was leering at me sceptically. Me! And I was the one pretending to be the sceptic. Redstar was pointing;

'Dr Madrith, if that is his real name, isn't a sceptic at all. He only doubts the existence of anything that doesn't prove his own biased viewpoint'.

I had to admit he had a point. Oh no I didn't. I didn't have to admit anything. Admitting things wasn't in my job description. I continued to lie instead;

'I have no bias. I'm only here to try to free you all from this man's dishonesty. My only bias is towards the truth'.

'So, you are biased then?' Asked one particularly local reporter.

I flashed my best Dr Madrid smile and repeated himself;

'Only towards the truth'.

'So then you *do* admit that you're biased?'

Dr Madrid leaned over the amber jam jar and did his best to appear unbiased.

I was flanked by two members of the football team,

just in case 'Dr Madrith' decided to 'do anything stupid'. I addressed the room;

'Anyone with any sense can see that this is a fake a mile off. It's the only simple explanation'.

I had everyone's attention. Because of the amount of caffeine in everyone's bloodstreams. And because everyone desires the simplest explanations in life.

No-one was about to embrace the unbelievable truth.

'The idea that intelligent man was blowing glass millions of years ago, living side by side with the T-Rex, is not a simple explanation. Why would we stop making jam jars for millions of years, before starting again sometime in the thirteenth century?!'

I could see people starting to think. It was written all over their screwed-up faces.

This was my opportunity to attack them with my razor. Other razors were available, but mine was the closest. Other razors would have you believe that you shave away one assumption after another until you have the simplest *correct* answer. Because, as Einstein once said to his barber; everything should be kept as simple as possible, but no simpler.

Fortunately for me most people didn't agree with Einstein.

Most people wanted the simplest possible explanation, regardless of whether it was true or not. Whether a thing was too simple? That was just pedantry. If you didn't always descend to the depths of the simplest explanation for its own sake, then most razors didn't always agree that the simplest explanation was the truth. Unfortunately this meant most razors were pretty useless in the real world. Which is why I invented a razor of my own.

My razor stated that, all other things being equal, if you made the truth sound complicated, no-one believed it. The people in the Happy Jam Jar wanted a simple storyline to follow. By using Canon's razor I could give them what they wanted.

But Chuck Redstar couldn't. Though bless him, he did try;

'We didn't need jam jars because we weren't eating jam. I always turn to scripture for precise answers to my questions and these good people will tell you that there was a worldwide shortage of yeast that led Christ to turn water into wine. This is why everyone ate unleavened bread, which as we all know, doesn't go well with jam'.

There was an exclamation from Christy the baker;

'Yes, this must be the reason why even now, thousands of years later, you still never see anyone spreading jam on a tortilla!'

I looked around the café. At the overpriced muffins. And the self-satisfied customers.

I was hoping that people were thinking; 'these folks are just making this up as they go along'. Or; 'some things in life are difficult to explain, but this is really taking the piss'.

But the truth wasn't quite complicated enough, yet. Some people in the coffee shop were still hanging in there. Probably for the free refills, but maybe because they'd been won over by all of this pig-headedness.

'So maybe it's a salsa jar? People were still eating salsa right? ...The point is we stopped making *jars*'.

'No this is definitely a jam jar. Look; there's still a tiny amount of jam inside it'.

I took Dr Madrid's magnifying glass and found the black and blue microscopic speck. Christy peered over my shoulder. I suppose coffee breath was an occupational hazard.

'Blackcurrant jam. For sure. You don't get salsa that colour'.

I could feel myself getting frustrated.

Because I'd disguised myself as someone with a 'Latin temperament';

'So if this is really a jam jar, then where's the spoon? Why isn't there anything else covered in amber? Where are the knives and forks? Surely there should be a spoon covered in amber? Surely there should be a spoon!'

People started whispering. As difficult to believe as you or I might have found Redstar's reasoning up to this point, the idea that a jam jar could exist without a spoon was incoherent to the people in the Happy Jam Jar. The clientele of the former Happy Cup café were faced with a stark choice. If they believed in the amber jam jar then they'd have to believe in a jam jar without a spoon. And I doubted anyone was prepared to go that far.

Except Redstar. Redstar was prepared to go that far;

'Well maybe forks and spoons are indispensable wherever you come from, but this is North America! And in North America we eat with our fingers!'

Only those who try to go too far ever know how far they can really go.

Dr Madrid rolled the dice one more time;

'So people were making jam jars, before the yeast shortage?'

'That's right'.

'*Thirty million years* before the yeast shortage?'

'...Yes'.

'And these glass blowers weren't only making jam jars right? I mean, they were making grails and vases and milk bottles too?'

'I suppose'.

'So why haven't you found any of those in amber?'

The whispering ballooned into full-blown disbelief.

But Redstar wasn't done yet. As long as you had the balls to carry it off you could always add something new into the mix to further your own argument.

Redstar gave us the best explanation he could come up with;

'...Recycling'.

Maybe everyone had drunk too much coffee, but I could see people tugging at their collars and sweating. They were feeling embarrassed for Chuck. Because of the whole being out of touch with reality thing. Everyone knew there'd been no prehistoric recycling schemes. These people were old enough to have witnessed the days before recycling themselves. Everyone in the Happy Jam Jar knew that Redstar was losing the argument.

Even Redstar knew that;

'...So you don't believe that this amber is really amber? And you don't believe this jam jar is really a jam jar?'

I told him I didn't believe any of that. I was lying of course, but I did that all the time.

'Then we'll send our miracle away to be tested'.

Dr Madrid smiled and held out my hand;

'Give it here then and I'll have the results by next Friday'.

Redstar recoiled as though I'd asked him out on a date;

'Nice try. But I think I'll try somewhere else. I'll not have the tests contaminated by your prejudiced organisation'.

I feigned Dr Madrid's professional pride. It was easier than forging his PhD had been.

'But I work for DICKS! We can make sure this is studied, scientifically, so we can know whether it's real or whether it is, as I'm confident will be proven, a hoax'.

The fact that The Dorking Institute was itself a hoax didn't stop Redstar from acting as if he'd heard of us;

'I'm not handing this over to you! Your organisation is the same lot that fiddled those tests on the girl with the x-ray eyes by sitting her in a room with glass walls!'

'I don't know what you're talking about!'

Redstar was confusing DICKS with WANGS (the Worldwide Association for Neuro-Genetics Studies).

'Dr Madrith isn't the kind of man you can trust with your miracles. Not if you ever want to see them again'.

Dr Madrid imitated the anxiety of a door to door salesman;

'But there's only one other company in the world that can run these kinds of tests; The Rockingham Research Facility'.

I knew because I'd created a website for Rockingham Research the night before.

It sure was easy to create your own website nowadays.

And it sure was easy to manipulate Chuck.

'And, they're expensive. Honestly, I can do it dirt cheap'.

Chuck wasn't buying it. But then at the same time, he was;

'We need impartiality. Then these good people can be sure that no-one is trying to dupe them. After all, what could I possibly gain from having this miracle tested if it were a fake? I already know that this jam jar is the real deal! And my agreeing to the tests proves it!'

I could see people nodding at each other and ordering cookies. I could hear them eating their croissants and slurping on their cappuccinos, from Europe. Redstar had won our personality contest. Dr Madrid had no choice but to agree to Redstar's suggestion.

I'd snatched victory from the jaws of almost certain victory.

In the same way one might snatch jam from a blind man.

All we had to do now was send the amber jam jar off to the bogus Rockingham Research Facility to run some bogus tests, and the test results would show that whatever we'd sent them was bogus. This was standard operating procedure. It worked every time.

Except for the Shroud. The Agency had sent that off for bogus tests dozens of times.

The Shroud was the exception that proved my point.

We stopped off on the way back to the Overlook Motel to pick up a copy of the International Spartan. It was full of bad news. A hurricane of material possessions had rained smartphones, sunglasses, hair straighteners and glossy magazines all over North Korea. The International

Spartan had attributed this to fly-tipping cargo planes, but I suspected the worst.

Meanwhile goldfish had rained down on spectators and players at a Champions League semi-final in Istanbul. And forty-nine Scottish schoolchildren had been battered by a squall of deep-fried Mars bars during PE class.

Ok, maybe that last one was a prank. But there was no doubt in my mind; these continuity errors were growing in frequency.

It was the story on page seven that really worried me though. A story about a plane that had crash-landed upside down in the Dubai desert after some turbulent weather.

I focused on my breathing and showed the paper to Smith.

'This is the newspaper I was telling you about'.

Smith seemed disinterested. Or distracted.

It was definitely something beginning with 'dis'.

'I've never read it. Or even heard of it'.

'But you've heard of the story right? ...I'll tell you now, I know exactly what happened and I'm furious'.

Smith appeared distant. Disconnected.

'I was running low on hallucinogens because there were so many passengers; I thought I could get away with giving them half doses'.

'Maybe one of the air traffic controllers leaked the story to the Suntan?'

My heartrate slowed to a dull thud and I felt a bit better. For a moment.

And then we walked out of the newsagent's and straight into a hostile crowd who'd gotten off of their heads on two-for-one espresso shots and followed us from The Happy Jam Jar. There was some jeering and some jostling and then Epiphany Smith screamed like she'd been shot. She reached up to her neck and showed me what she had in her hand. Chewing gum. We both looked around but Smith's assailant had made their escape.

I tried to calm her down by lying to her;

'Don't let it bother you; I'm sure they were aiming for me'.

I prised the gum from her clenched fist and examined it more closely. I held it to my nose. There was no mistaking the aroma.

It was a stick of Miracle White Shining Involvement.

We returned to the Overlook Motel to find Rashid muttering to himself and packing.

Smith explained how we were going to be here a while longer. How we had to wait for some test results. I suggested Rashid try to find a movie on the pay-per-view. Rashid explained how American movies were shit. Then he explained how he was even worse off now than when he'd been stuck in Birmingham.

He suggested we pack our things and head to Miami. I said we couldn't do that.

I left to get a pizza. Smith came too. Sure, sure, Smith thought that I was just a fool following orders. But she still didn't trust me to get hers right.

Rashid decided to stay behind and destroy the TV set.

Don't worry. He didn't hurt himself.

14. Rashid's Miscalculated Risk

*T*he scene outside the Happy Jam Jar the following morning reminded me of springtime in Mogadishu. Specifically I was reminded of an outbreak of Pop Idol Virus named after the popular Somali soap opera. This was when around four hundred primary schoolchildren had fallen victim to the same flu virus that had struck down several hysterical wannabes on the show the previous Friday. Symptoms of Pop Idol Virus included heavy breathing, red faces, sore ears and fainting.

Sixteen schools were forced to close for several weeks longer than usual.

'This sort of thing happens all the time'.

I reassured Smith. My reasoning was that I didn't want her to fall victim to the same hysteria that everyone around us was suffering from.

I didn't reassure Rashid because Rashid was AWOL.

I'd been pretty concerned about Rashid after he'd destroyed the TV set in our motel room. Obviously he wasn't enjoying himself in Gladys. I'd remembered how he hadn't been enjoying himself in Birmingham. And how that had led to him trying to blow up a plane.

I hoped Rashid wasn't planning to do anything stupid.

But for now I had a bigger problem to deal with.

In front of us there were around a dozen people passed out on the pavement outside the Happy Jam Jar. There was every reason to expect we would find more bodies inside.

On the face of it we appeared to be dealing with a textbook episode of mass hysteria.

We needed to control the situation. We needed to contain this outbreak of obsessive behaviour before anyone else witnessed it. The more witnesses we had, the more victims we'd have to treat.

Smith and I ran into the Happy Jam Jar and found Christy unconscious and face down in a tray of freshly fried orange donuts. Smith helped her into the recovery position and I grabbed a bottle of blueberry infused water which I squirted all over Christy's face.

She came around with a yelp and started flailing around on the wet floor like a fish out of water. More specifically; like a fish out of water that kept screaming;

'Mexicans! Mexicans!'

Smith dried Christy off with a souvenir Amber Jam Jar tea-towel and I tried to make her a double espresso. Eventually I gave up trying to switch the Happy Jam Jar's robot barista on and ran a mug of ground coffee beans under the hot water tap. Christy choked a little, swallowed, opened her eyes and focused on Dr Javier Madrid. Dr Madrid smiled and offered her an orange donut in order to gain her trust. Christy wasn't sure why she'd been screaming 'Mexicans!' but she could recall opening up about an hour earlier;

'I was out back double-glazing the bacon when I heard a scream and came in to find Doreen asleep in front of the counter. I tried to help her, but I started to feel faint almost immediately'.

'What's the last thing you remember before fainting?'

There was a glint of a memory in Christy's eyes. Her mouth opened, ready for an explanation to fly out. And then the look in her eyes turned to one of horror.

Christy let out a dull moan;

'The amber jam jar...'

She looked over my shoulder. And then she fainted again.

I dropped Christy to the floor and turned to see what had troubled her so. In front of me was the padlocked Happy Jam Jar gun cabinet that had been turned into the SOOPA exhibit. Except the gun cabinet wasn't padlocked any longer.

And the amber jam jar was nowhere to be seen.

I began to reconstruct the sequence of events. Doreen was lying in front of me clutching an orange feather duster; she must have been the first to become hysterical when she saw that the amber jam jar was missing. Christy had seen Doreen and the empty gun cabinet and clearly concluded that Doreen's decision to faint had been the correct one. As more minimum wage earners had arrived they'd fainted too, and then customers and amber jam jar gloaters had formed an orderly queue around the block and proceeded, one by one, to faint in the style of toppled dominoes.

Back outside I looked at the locals planking all over the road. I estimated around sixty people had spontaneously fainted in the past twenty minutes. This mass hysteria was gaining momentum. Soon the whole town would be lying around doing nothing.

We needed to start waking people up. I told Smith;

'We need to start waking people up. We need fast food'.

Fortunately Smith had been paying more attention than I had;

'There's a hamburger restaurant around the corner'.

We started to run. While running I explained to Smith why no-one had used the phrase 'hamburger restaurant' since the fifties. And Smith explained that she wasn't listening.

We ran into 'Patriot Burger'. Patriot Burger had previously been called 'Hamerican Heroes' but had been forced to change its name when it was pointed out that their burgers didn't contain any ham (or anything that could legally be called 'meat'). I flashed my Patriot Burger platinum card that permitted me to order from the lunch menu before 10.30am;

'I need two hundred large fries and all the thick-shakes you're capable of'.

The slightly out of focus forty-year-old man in the wipe-clean cap in front of me spontaneously fainted. Fortunately this Patriot Burger had stretched to paying a second minimum wage and so we sprinted back to the Happy Jam Jar and started forcing multiples of people's recommended daily allowances of fat, salt and sugar down their throats.

I'd hoped that by reengaging people with their regular diet I could jolt them out of their hysteria. As our first patients regained consciousness the passé sirens of the Virginia State Troopers echoed off of the walls of the deserted (above knee height) Main Street.

A buck-toothed young officer ran over with his gun drawn and I shouted;

'Stay back!'

I couldn't risk men with firearms fainting unsupervised.

The bystanding young officer watched as I brought another hysterical latte lover around;

'Hey Lou. You gotta see this! It's just like that picture in your Bible!'

Lou ambled over in his mustard-stained uniform and

his sheriff's hat. He looked Smith up and down, helped himself to some fries and then offered his slick and greasy hand.

I didn't want any more trouble with the police so I shook it.

'Sheriff Lou Constable'.

What were the odds? Seventy three thousand to one, if you're counting. Sheriff Lou surveyed the street party come triage centre I'd created with all of my fast food;

'Quick thinking with the health food. We usually just use the fire hoses'.

'Usually?' I asked.

'Fire hoses?' asked Smith.

'Fainting's common in these parts. Specially in the women'.

People were washing fries down with thick-shakes. A few of them were sobbing or yelling or running up and down Main Street.

'That's fairly common too'.

Sheriff Lou reassured us. Then he reassured us some more;

'Thanks for your help. But you can stop your panicking now. I phoned Chuck Redstar. He's on his way to sort out this mess'.

Chuck arrived twenty minutes later on 'the bandwagon'. Smith found the bandwagon a little underwhelming, what with her being a big city gal and all, but even though it was just a tractor painted orange towing a prefab mobile home (painted orange) it certainly impressed the people on Main Street who were slowly coming to their senses and cheering Redstar's arrival. And throwing their half-eaten fries to the dog sat on the tractor's front seat.

Redstar leapt off of his bandwagon and made a beeline for a pretty Happy Jam Jar waitress who was still unconscious on the sidewalk. He had to step over two larger and older ladies who'd been at the front of the queue at the start of the outbreak. Redstar got to his knees beside the young waitress and looked up to check that everyone was ready for his close-up. I followed the line of Redstar's gaze and my heart sank.

Anne Punter was having her face applied and shoulders padded in preparation for a live report from Gladys. My heart stopped sinking and my pulse went through the roof.

The pretty waitress started to come around. Redstar eased her back to the pavement and asked her to remain unconscious until he could resuscitate her for the cameras. Redstar was looking for a photo op. Weird Norm wanted to overshadow his past with the bright future that reflected off of the amber jam jar.

I'd have to doctor the photos. Fortunately for me, practice makes perfect.

Redstar and Dr Javier Madrid ran around resuscitating people for the news cameras as Anne Punter provided a shrill commentary in the style of a horse-racing commentator. I needed to keep the cameras on Javier rather than on Redstar and his missing amber SOOPA, but Redstar and Anne were already playing hide the microphone boom;

'Are we really to believe it's just a coincidence that we find this sceptic at the scene of the crime? The man who tried to persuade the good people of Gladys that your miracle was a fake?'

Just to clarify, this was Anne Punter whining. But she soon handed over to Redstar as he helped a seventeen-year-old girl in a 'Jam it in!' t-shirt to her feet and held her steady;

'It's no coincidence. The amber jam jar was stolen from its display cabinet to prevent its verification, by scientists'.

Maybe Redstar was being deliberately ambiguous as to whether the scientists were doing the testing or the stealing, but I had to give Dr Madrid the right of reply;

'Or perhaps the fake has been hidden to prevent its

testing? To ensure the truth would never be revealed?'

Just so there's no unnecessary confusion here, the amber jam jar being stolen did me no favours at all. The countless conspiracy theories that were bound to arise from its theft would no doubt legitimise it. Redstar looked offended. He sounded offended too;

'Why would I agree to the tests if it wasn't real?'

It was difficult to argue with this. But I gave it a shot;

'Because you were losing the argument. Because no-one can assign any credence to your esoteric suppositions. Because this is pseudoarchaeology!'

People were looking around. Possibly for subtitles. I translated for them;

'You've about as much chance those test results will prove the authenticity of your jam jar as a nine-year-old has of using his toy telescope to prove the existence of aliens!'

Some semi-conscious local radio DJ sat up and declared;

'I was abducted by aliens. Twice. And I have the probes to prove it!'

I shook my head and tried to think of how to restart the mass fainting;

'This is exactly what I'm talking about. Making ludicrous claims for which there's absolutely no evidence, or inventing ludicrous evidence to back up your ludicrous claims'.

I ran over to an unconscious girl in an amber burkini and saw Redstar curse his luck as I fed her some cold fries.

But then he let out an audible 'yes' as he realised the Gladys women's volleyball team had been queuing for frappuccinos.

Either the MSG news team was capable of asexual reproduction, or there were more news crews arriving at the Happy Jam Jar by the minute. This was a proper personality contest, a genuine political kiss off with the debating and the kissing all rolled into one.

But the way Redstar was resuscitating people, it was a bit inappropriate.

'You're the one trying to hide the truth from these people!'

Shouted Redstar as he draped a souvenir amber t-shirt over another unconscious caffeine addict. Then he turned on Dr Javier Madrid and the network of shadowy interests that sponsored his paranoia and my pay cheque.

'There's a global conspiracy of academics and clergy working to prevent normal hard-working God-fearing folk like ourselves from discovering the mysteries of the universe. Museums and universities have sucked the truth out of our world and spewed forth their own warped version of history'.

Where did he get this stuff? Did we have a leak? A mole?

'This cabal of special interest groups employs men such as Professor Madrith, if that is his real name, to enforce their version of reality by attacking truth-sayers like myself with outrageous accusations of hoax-making!'

I patted my pockets to make sure I hadn't lost my copy of the rulebook.

It sounded as if Redstar had read the preamble.

'This man is part of a worldwide conspiracy to suppress the true wonders of the world such as the amber jam jar that they stole from our happy café!'

I could see the people I'd resuscitated only minutes earlier forming a new queue.

To kick Dr Javier Madrid's backside.

Anne Punter joined Chuck;

'This is a liberal plot to discredit brave men like Chuck Redstar by stealing their jam jars. And this is because liberal historians and liberal scientists are terrified of evolution!'

Anne was confusing evolution with revolution.

Someone nipped into the Gladys chemist and returned with a soap box that Chuck pulled Anne up onto; although as everyone was lying down it was a bit pointless. Like Anne.

'They're part of a shadowy elite running our book clubs and TV Guides. A network of liberal fundamentalists feeding us a version of the truth that tastes funny'.

People were glaring and drooling. The only person who wasn't was the first waitress I'd brought around who was with the MSG news crew, telling them how she'd always wanted to be in the movies. I realised this was what Redstar wanted too.

I had to show people Weird Norm instead. I made Dr Javier Madrid laugh out loud;

'It's an entertaining story, if a little far-fetched'.

No-one looked entertained.

'The suggestion of a conspiracy to hide the truth is absurd. Perhaps some of my colleagues at the Dorking Institute are a little set in their ways, but they'd never reject hard evidence that contradicts their opinions. We were looking forward to the amber jam jar test results. Really we were. But we're going to have to proceed much more carefully now that you've failed to come up with any real evidence to back up these weird theories of yours'.

Redstar was so angry he almost fell off his soapbox;

'The evidence we had to back up our claims has been stolen!'

'How convenient for you'.

'You've got a smart mouth! But you should be agreeing with me!'

'But then people will think I'm just as crazy as Weird Norm'.

'That isn't fair! You should be listening to what I'm saying! I'm important now! I've been interviewed by Anne Punter! I'm not Weird Norm anymore! *You're* the weird one!'

Encouraging Chuck to throw a tantrum on live TV hadn't been my original strategy. But it should have been. This right here was how you lost a personality contest.

As Chuck was putting his foot through his soapbox Dr Javier Madrid walked over to Doreen; the only remaining unconscious waitress. The first to faint. I fed Doreen a glazed bacon muffin. No-one was looking at the empty gun cabinet anymore. But unfortunately for me it was the first thing Doreen looked at when she regained consciousness.

She started screaming;

'Mexicans! Mexicans! A Mexican stole the amber jam jar! He stole our miracle!'

I was pretty sure I hadn't seen any Mexicans in Gladys. But I was pretty certain most Americans couldn't tell the difference between Rashid and a Cuban.

Smith and I ran back to the Overlook Motel.

Smith was out of breath. But full of nervous energy. And sugar. And salt;

'I didn't think you cared if things disappeared. You know, things like the Norwegian Queen?'

The other thing that Smith was full of was passive aggression.

'You can only disappear a continuity error before people discover it, once they know about it it's too late'.

This was really the last thing we needed.

'This is really the last thing we needed. Now people will carry on believing Redstar, because if the SOOPA disappears his claims can never be undermined'.

'Are they really undermined if you doctor the test results like you did in Dubai?'

This was nothing like Dubai.

'This is nothing like Dubai. People in Gladys want to believe Redstar. The story he's given them is one they want to hear. They've been waiting thousands of years to hear this'.

Meanwhile, back at the room; Rashid watched from behind the shower curtain as a mousy chambermaid named Dolly spontaneously regained consciousness, picked herself up and dusted herself down. Then she started dusting down the TV. An advert for the Hunger Strike Diet was followed by a news report describing how people watching events unfolding in Gladys had started spontaneously fainting across the US. Anne Punter appeared on screen to give an update on the theft of the amber jam jar (in the style of a cock-fight commentator). Upon seeing Anne Punter Dolly spontaneously fainted. When she came around from her second fainting fit Dolly ran out of the room, picked up the phone and dialled 911.

There was a Mexican thief loose in Gladys, and Dolly knew where he was hiding.

Mexican Rashid gave us his Dolly anecdote as he packed his bag. Smith and I were packing ours too. The reason we were all packing according to Rashid was;

'Rashid was only trying to help'.

This was rather disingenuous of Rashid. Or dishonest. What Rashid had really only been trying to do was get us out of this cramped motel and on our way to Miami.

'We can talk about it later'.

The reason we couldn't talk about it any earlier was all of the police officers who'd cordoned off the Overlook Motel five minutes after we'd gotten back to our room. Rashid and Smith looked at me nervously. Fortunately for them I'd come up with an escape plan.

'We've got a pool jumper!'

Gladys police officers ran around headlessly as Rashid climbed over the balcony and looked down at the street below. The pool was actually on the other side of the motel, though to be fair to Deputy Chip Sergeant they'd never had a suicide attempt in Gladys before, and people jumping from their balconies into the pool was a fairly regular event.

The important thing was that someone was hanging off

of a motel balcony, whether they intended to land safely or not shouldn't be a deputy's primary concern. Rashid wasn't going to land safely in the pool. But it wasn't as if he could hurt himself either.

Anne Punter and her MSG News hairdresser arrived on the scene in matching flak jackets and started interviewing the police on their smartphones. Sheriff Lou asked them to let him do his job. When Anne asked what that was Sheriff Lou explained that it was his job to try and talk Rashid down from the balcony. Unfortunately Lou didn't speak any Mexican.

Lou knew that the man on the balcony was a Mexican because Dolly had told him so. Lou also knew that the man was intending to commit suicide because people felt guilty after stealing. And he knew the Mexican was lonely and isolated because Dolly had only changed one set of towels in the bathroom. Anne suggested this might be a way for two people to halve their soiled towel surcharge but Lou pointed out that there was only one toothbrush in the room (Smith and I had been brushing our teeth in the other guests' bathrooms).

While the police and the news teams concentrated on the sole Mexican occupant of the room Smith and I climbed the stairs to the roof and then used a rusty drainpipe to shimmy all the way back down again. We had to use the drainpipe because the old fire escape had been removed. The old fire escape had been a health and safety risk.

Anne Punter started a betting pool on whether the Mexican would survive or not.

Most police officers backed 'no' at even money but Deputy Chip Sergeant put his ten bucks on 'yes' at seven-to-two. It was harsh on Chip that his wager was rewarded with such immediate regret but after finding the Spanish translation for 'don't jump' on his smartphone and then crying out; 'No saltar!' Rashid threw himself off of the

196

balcony. He dropped like a stone, hit a limited edition magnolia Range Rover belonging to Anne's hairdresser and went limp as the car's roof buckled and twisted out of shape beneath him.

The car alarm started playing 'YMCA'.

Sheriff Lou and his stunned deputies watched as Smith and I ran to the Range Rover. I opened the driver's door with a coat-hanger I'd unscrewed from our motel wardrobe and we jumped in. I started the engine and the three of us sped off in a cloud of burnt rubber. Smith sat in the passenger seat, gripping the door handle. Rashid sat on the roof, gripping the aerial, shouting and screaming and cursing us for not letting him get in the car before driving away.

Deputy Sergeant's colleagues looked on in disbelief.

I checked my mirrors and saw a few of them fainting as Chip collected his winnings.

We pulled up at the Southern Comfort Inn on route 501 and checked into three different rooms. The guy on reception said he liked my convertible Range Rover.

I tossed him the keys and told him he could keep it.

But he wasn't watching me and the keys hit him in the eye.

To cut a long story short, Rashid had broken into the Happy Jam Jar around 3am and found the key to the padlock hidden in an old croissant wedged behind the gun cabinet;

'Rashid figured if he removed the SOOPA you wouldn't have to wait for the test results to come back. It's the waiting for the test results that's the most stressful part'.

'And you had to get out of that motel room'.

'And Rashid had to get out of that motel room'.

I pointed out that he'd gotten his wish, but that even though he was in the habit of being unrecognisable, if he continued being spotted committing crimes eventually he would get us all caught.

Then I locked Rashid in his room and visited Smith in hers to break the bad news;

'We have to return the amber jam jar'.

Twenty four hours after it had first been stolen Smith and I found the key to the Happy Jam Jar's back door exactly where Rashid had said it would be; in a stale muffin on top of the a/c unit.

'Shit! Shit!'

Smith had trodden in a pile of rat poop. I told her to take off her shoes and leave them outside; we didn't want to leave any trace of our having been in the café.

'Other than our replacing the jam jar?'

'Other than that, yes'.

We found the key to the gun cabinet padlock still in the stale croissant (where Christy had replaced it, despite the theft) and I carefully locked the SOOPA up safe and tight.

Then I crept back outside. Mission accomplished.

I looked around but nobody in Gladys could be found out at 10pm, let alone 3am. I also noticed that the streets looked as if they'd been recently vacuumed. My phone rang and shattered the silence with the first few bars of 'Suspicious Minds'. It was strange that Epiphany Smith was phoning me when she was stood right next to me. I turned to tell her this and realised the street was even more deserted than I'd first thought. I answered my phone.

'Help'.

Epiphany Smith needed my help. She was caught in a trap. The rat glue trap laid just inside the café's back door. This was where Smith had stopped following me.

Mission unaccomplished.

I crept back inside. Smith looked apologetic. And much shorter without her shoes on.

I tried to help her out of the rat trap. All of a sudden I

heard a siren.

It made me jump. But not Smith. Which was a shame, because it might have gotten her out of the rat glue. Smith hadn't jumped because the siren was her ringtone.

She answered her phone;

'...I can't talk now. I couldn't get it. It's a long story'.

Smith hung up and stared at her feet;

'My ex-boyfriend'.

It occurred to me that I was pretty good at sneaking about undetected, but that Smith wasn't. And she wasn't great at lying either.

It also occurred to me that we hadn't heard the actual police sirens over Smith's ringtone. It occurred to me because Sheriff Lou Constable and his posse of penniless deputies had the Happy Jam Jar Café surrounded. Smith started acting all sacrificial;

'You could still make a run for it'.

But I shook my head. I stood shoulder to shoulder with Smith. In some rat glue;

'We're in this together'.

Standing shoulder to shoulder with Smith seemed to bring us closer together.

'Sorry you got stuck with me'.

Said Smith. It was a nice moment. It was just a shame that we'd had to legitimise the amber jam jar in order to have it. It was a shame because we were supposed to have debunked it by faking the test results, but now we'd gotten ourselves caught red-handed in a rat glue trap. It was one of those unique situations where you screwed up the secret mission you'd be given, and then you screwed it up again.

It was one of those unique situations where the leader of a weird cult made a lot of outrageous claims about how you were part of a conspiratorial elite desperately trying to hide the truth about intelligent design from the rest of the world.

And then you proved him right.

199

15. Smith's Theory of Everything

Gayle Jail only had three cells and two were already being used by felons convicted of out of season trout mounting. Gayle Jail reminded me of the Overlook Motel. The TV in our cell got bad reception and when we checked the menu we were told that they were out of the sea bass and the tiramisu. You had to leave your towel on the floor if you wanted it washed, otherwise they'd assume we'd reuse them.

Our red-eyed prison guard seemed nervous, even for a prison guard. It turned out Steve was especially anxious because it was a full moon.

I lifted up the toilet seat. And tried not to pass out.

'No way you're using that while I'm in here'.

Said my cellmate. But I held my breath and explained;

'You're going to want me to use it'.

'...Should we talk about things?'

I figured this was a standard opening gambit between two new cellmates. But I'd already met Epiphany Smith.

'About how your plan seems to have backfired?'

I didn't want to talk about it (I was still holding my breath). But Smith did;

'No-one would have cared if we'd never returned it. Everyone would have soon moved on. ...Remember the Christmas fox attacks?'

I did. Perhaps my memory was starting to improve.

'The BBC picked up on a story about an eight-year-old who'd been bitten by a fox in his back garden in Kensington on Christmas Eve. And how he'd managed to crawl the whole two hundred metres from the bottom of his garden back to the servant's quarters?'

They'd called it a miracle.

'And two days later a woman was bitten on the ankle by a fox in York. And every day there was another story about fox attacks even though only two people had been bitten and that was less than the previous all-time low for Christmas fox attacks?'

For someone who didn't read the papers Smith had really followed this story.

'And then the Chancellor's wife ripped her evening gown on a stuffed fox at the Chequers New Year's Eve bash? And they played helicopter footage of foxes loitering in Regent's Park and closed London Zoo for four days? And they tried to pass a law allowing people to *hunt* foxes? You remember how it was the only story in the news?'

'Yes'.

'Until the January sales started?'

I was pretty sure I'd spotted the subtext to Smith's argument.

'There's nothing mysterious about fox attacks. People had a simple explanation for the fox attacks; foxes were attacking people. But people hadn't gotten a simple explanation for the amber jam jar, and if we'd never returned it they'd have kept watching until they did.

Unfortunately for us getting caught red-handed returning it gave them an explanation; the amber jam jar is genuine and you and I are part of an establishment that's hell bent on covering it up'.

What I was trying to say was;

'I've failed...'

'To keep the truth from people?'

I wasn't accustomed to people finishing my sentences for me. I was a loner.

And what I was trying to say was;

'I've failed...'

'To hide the mysteries of the universe?'

That was part of it. But what I was trying to say was;

'I've failed...'

'To maintain the authority of the established order?'

'I've failed to debunk the SOOPA! And now we've exposed ourselves that bloody amber jam jar will become a Holy Grail™ for the conspiracy theorists. Or at least an Ark of the Covenant™. We lied, so now people are going to trust Redstar to give them the truth. People will hear that glass-blowers were blowing glass while herds of diplodocus grazed outside their workshop windows. And then they'll panic'.

Smith was going red in the face. She was either trying not to lose her temper or trying to retain control over her bladder.

'So we have to make sure people don't discover the truth, because we've spent so long brainwashing them? Because any time anyone discovers that things in real life don't look the same as they do on TV they start freaking out? But we don't see this as a reason to tear people away from the lies? This is a reason to tear them away from the truth?'

Smith sounded nervy. She sounded Antipodean.

And she was starting to look sunburnt.

'If the Agency hadn't covered everything up in the first place an amber jam jar wouldn't seem so extraordinary and we'd never have been sent here to get rid of it. If we lived in a world where unexplained events were as common as fox attacks nobody would pay Redstar any attention'.

Smith waited for me to agree with her. And waited.

'You have to agree the truth would be better for people than Redstar and his cult?'

Sure, sure I was in a prison cell. But I didn't have to do anything I didn't want to.

'You're talking about rewriting human history. Giving human history a prequel nobody wants. People are comfortable with our original history; they get anxious when you make prequels'.

I checked to see if the toilet would flush. It wouldn't. I carried on;

'That bloody jam jar hasn't followed the script. If there was no dissonance caused by the discovery that man had been living alongside dinosaurs I'd never have been sent to adjust those Mayan burial stones with the cartoon drawings of a triceratops'.

The same dinosaurs were popular with every generation.

'Wait, what? You already adjusted something that showed people were alive at the same time as dinosaurs?'

'Didn't I already mention that?'

Smith looked like a prisoner who was just hearing about the second set of showers for the heterosexuals.

'The Office of Confessions paid some noodle farmer to admit to hoaxing the stones by copying his six-year-old's colouring-in book'.

'You saw genuine evidence of people living with dinosaurs?'

Was it just the prison cell that caused Smith to find this so much harder to swallow than the amber jam jar?

'Keep your voice down... Sure they were genuine, but so what? They were a genuine mistake. They didn't prove anything. And neither does the amber jam jar. It's just another continuity error. It's no different than spotting a digital watch in a Mel Gibson movie about cavemen. It's like an unfinished special effect. You just shrug it off don't you? You don't let it spoil the whole movie'.

'So this is just God breaking the laws of nature? Didn't He come up with the laws? Who breaks their own rules?'

Dieters. Politicians. Gremlin owners. And God.

'I don't spend much time deciphering the motivations of the omniscient. I just clean up afterwards. ...Maybe God decided His rules were made to be broken'.

I tried the flush one more time. Just to be sure.

'People like Redstar don't let a blooper spoil their story. But the boffins and the true believers, these are the guys who write into magazines pursuing every little error to the nth degree. No matter how unreal something is, it still has to follow their rules'.

The toilet was totally backed up. Perfect.

'This will be like witnessing a chat room brawl on a nerds' message board; fighting over who'd win a pie-eating contest between Batman and Superman. Religion and science have been locked in a room with Redstar. And now they've got to fight their way out of it'.

(n.b. according to renowned astrophilosopher Stephen Hawking's theoretical multiverse Batman is unquestionably in a pie-eating contest somewhere. And he's almost certainly winning).

I called for Steve the prison guard. I used the telephone in our cell and dialled reception. Steve had told me I was entitled to a phone call, but then he arrived in his twitchy-eyed bad mood and told me;

'This isn't a hotel you know'.

I agreed. Then I complained about the toilet in our room.

I didn't expect Steve to clean it though. He was a prison guard. If he could just get me a bottle of heavy duty toilet cleaner I'd do it myself. I wanted to complain about our TV too. But I was in prison. So I kept my mouth shut.

Smith couldn't do it though;

'Why don't they fight their way out together? There's two of them and only one Redstar'.

Smith didn't read the papers. Smith hadn't heard about the missing link and the war between religion and science. I didn't feel the need to bore her with the details.

But my cellmate treated me like a captive audience;

'Religion without science is a dodgy sales pitch and science without religion is just a list of terms and conditions. Why is it that most people want to learn about both, but the only ones who don't are the ones doing the teaching?'

What was it about prisons that made people so philosophical?

Steve returned with my bottle of bleach and put it in the little tray they used for your meals and your morning papers and your signed confessions.

'Knock yourself out' said Steve.

To which I replied; 'I probably will'.

I started emptying bleach into the backed up toilet bowl.

'That's a very Eastern philosophy you've got there. Unfortunately this is the West. And people in the West don't want all this wishy washy touchy feely uncertainty. People want to know that someone is right and that someone else is wrong'.

I farted the last of my bleach into the blocked toilet;

'People need an answer to everything. So it's our job to convince everyone that someone has all of the answers; that there's nothing out there that can't be explained'.

'Why is it that everyone who means to say 'I don't know' has to say either yes or no? When did 'I don't know' disappear from the English language?'

'I think it was when caveman Mike wanted to persuade caveman Phil to leave the cave for the first time, so he could spend some 'alone time' with the cavewomen. And caveman Phil wanted to know if it was safe to go out'.

'But what are people afraid of? What terrible demon will be summoned by the invocation of those three words?'

'Well, demons don't really exist you know, but doubt and distrust and discomfort do. No-one's going to congratulate you on your honesty if you say you don't know, they're just going to ask someone else until they get an answer they like'.

Smith looked down. Maybe it was because I was about to use the loo. I continued;

'People can't stomach the idea of not knowing, they have to know; so if there's no established truth about something then we have to invent one. Because otherwise people will invent one for themselves and they'll do a terrible job and you'll end up with the same panic on the streets as Baltimore. You want the rest of the world to end up like Baltimore?'

'No'.

Of course not. No-one wanted that.

'The unexplained doesn't make anyone feel warm and fuzzy. It scares the shit out of people. Who wants to go on TV and announce to the world that they don't have a clue? There's too much at stake'.

I started patting myself down in much the same way as Steve had when we'd first checked in.

'Unless you sound like you have an answer for everything you'll never get people to listen to your explanation for anything'.

'No-one has *all* the answers'.

'You don't need to have all the answers; you just need to say that you do. You just need to have a *theory* for everything. Whether your theory is any good or not isn't important. Whether you sound convincing while you're explaining it, that's what matters. Take the 'Off the Shelf Universe''.

'The Off the Shelf Universe?'

'The idea that the Universe has been pre-programmed before you buy it; you just switch it on and everything you need for life; your matter, your laws of nature, your clock; they're already installed'.

I offered Smith one of the sticks of Miracle White Shining Involvement that I'd hidden in my sock. Smith declined my offer. Explicitly.

'Is it true? Who knows, but it sounds like it could be. All you know for sure is there's a black hole in our knowledge, but it's pointless arguing over whether it's a God-shaped gap or a puddle-sized hole if you don't sound convincing while you're doing it'.

I put another stick of gum in my mouth and shut up for a moment. I could literally feel my teeth not getting any whiter. In my hand I had twelve shiny foil wrappers.

'Did you ever see MacGyver?'

'What's a MacGyver?'

'You'd know if you'd seen him. I had to ret-con the pilot episode of his TV show to prevent a generation of teenage boys from discovering how to blow a hole in a wall with a stick of chewing gum'.

Smith wasn't really listening. Smith was talking;

'I have a theory of everything too. There isn't one. Claiming your theory explains everything is like saying something tastes like chicken; it's the answer you give when you don't know the answer. There's more truth in stories about World War Two bombers found on the moon, or one-armed monkeys landing planes, or racist donkeys robbing banks...'

I'd stopped listening to Smith about thirty seconds earlier.

I'd needed to concentrate on the jail break.

Maybe you don't watch a lot of videos created by teenage boys, but if you drop aluminium foil into a blocked toilet bowl filled with bleach, it explodes.

I dropped my ball of foil wrappers into the toilet.

'...donkeys robbing banks...'

There was a whoosh of air as it was sucked out of the

cell. There was a flash of blinding magnolia or jasmine light. There was a loud farting noise from near the toilet.

And then everything went black.

I slowly opened my eyes and swallowed a bit of gum that I'd caught in my throat.

I looked at the intact toilet and realised that my improvised bomb had backfired spectacularly. But there was still a gigantic hole in the cell wall. It didn't lead outside though. The hole led into a huge howling, swirling, vibrating black vortex.

Into a plot hole.

There was a strange woman standing next to me staring at the plot hole with an incredulous look burnt into her face and some 'no-frills' toilet cleaner burnt into her jeans.

Epiphany Smith wasn't being herself.

'Your name isn't Epiphany. ...You're that journalist that everyone was after!'

'What the hell did you just do?'

'*I* didn't do anything. *You* created a plot hole. You told me you'd never read the Sunday Spartan, but then you recited three of their most infamous headlines. Thereby completely contradicting the logic of your backstory'.

'What the hell did you just do?'

Either Smith was having difficulty grasping the concept, or time was being warped by our standing so close to the vortex. It was probably a little of both. Smith caught up with me;

'But I was lying to you. So, isn't that more of a plot *twist*?'

Smith was right!

'You're right! This plot hole shouldn't exist. And because of that, it does! It's one of those self-fulfilling plot holes'.

Smith was shaking her head a lot. So I tried to straighten things out;

'Look. How the plot hole was formed isn't important'.

'The important thing is getting out of here right?'

'No! The important thing is that you lied to me!'

'I never actually lied about who I was, to you anyway'.

'You told me your name was Smith'.

'I never said my first name was Epiphany'.

'I was told you didn't like being called by your first name'.

'I don't. ...My first name is Mildred'.

What was it about prison that made people want to confess?

Mildred Smith thrust her hand out and smiled;

'Nice to meet you'.

We didn't have time for pleasantries (and I hadn't washed my hands after using the toilet), but I wanted to meet Mildred. So I took her hand and pulled her towards the plot hole;

'We need to get out of here'.

'Through that thing?'

'It's perfectly safe. ...Sort of. It'll just take us back to the point where the discrepancy was first created; when you told me you'd never read the Spartan. ...Probably'.

I reached into my pocket. I had one last stick of chewing gum left. I turned to Smith;

'This hole leads back to a point in time before Rashid stole the amber jam jar. All we have to do is avoid bumping into ourselves and we can get out of this cell and make sure we never get back in it'.

'What happens if we bump into ourselves?'

'I don't know. Probably nothing. But it's the kind of thing science fiction writers are always worrying about'.

I unwrapped my last Miracle White Shining Involvement and spat it into the plot hole.

'What did you do that for?'

'To check that the hole is pointing in the right direction'.

'Is that the gum that hit me outside the newsagents?!'

'Let's go. Steve will be back with our starters any minute'.

'Did you just spit gum at me?!'

'And you locked the real Epiphany Smith in a broom cupboard somewhere. And you didn't tell me that you worked for the Sunday Spartan. So let's just call it even'.

'Those are really just different parts of the same lie. And I didn't lock anyone in a broom cupboard'.

'Surely you didn't leave Epiphany sitting around the office doing nothing all day. Someone would've figured out that she didn't belong there'.

Smith gave me the one arched eyebrow;

'Have you ever been to a newspaper office?'

'Ok, but wouldn't Epiphany have been suspicious?'

'Of what?'

'Well, let's see; you were posing as someone working for the Agency, and you told Epiphany her assignment was to go undercover at the Spartan, posing as Mildred Smith and advising the Agency, via yourself, of any weird news stories they were planning to break'.

'How the hell did you work that out?'

'Well that's what happened last time, when the News of the World tried it'.

The plot hole grew larger.

We decided that I'd go through first. But Smith still seemed nervous;

'Du verkar inte väldigt förbannad om min ljuga för dig?'

'Because you opened up the plot hole that's going to let us escape. But if we don't use it soon we'll be stuck here and we won't be able to go back in time, and we won't be able to debunk Redstar and people will keep on falling for his bullshit and the world as we know it will be changed irrevocably. ...And *then* I'll be pissed off with you for lying to me'.

'عادلة بم ا فيه الكف اية'.

'And to be honest I'm more pissed off with myself for not figuring it out sooner. It really was the only explanation for someone with such anti-establishment views wanting to work at the Agency. And, well, I respect the integrity of reporters who work for the Spartan'.

The plot hole grew larger still.

I poked a finger into it. My fingernail grew a quarter of an inch but the finger was otherwise unmolested and Smith started to relax;

'But we're trying to combat your black propaganda and expose the unbelievable truth. It's written on the staff notice board'.

'Well, maybe I'm starting to respect that too'.

There was an awkward silence.

Because the plot hole was basically a vacuum.

'...Do you think you could get some of my copies of the Spartan signed? Just the stories I covered up? Or maybe a visit to your office? I'd love to see what goes on behind the scenes'.

Smith looked at me with sympathy. Or empathy. It was hard to tell which because the G-force coming off of the plot hole made her look as if she were standing in a wind tunnel.

'...Why do you cover up miracles?'

'Let's just say; sometimes the truth isn't everything it's cracked up to be'.

I jumped in feet first. I did a forward roll. And a star jump. Over the past. It was just like in the movies; with the special effects and the soundtrack. I think I heard something by Strauss. And then we were thrown back in time and the last few days had never happened. They'd been wiped out of existence.

They were just a dream...

We hit the ground running. We had to get back to the Overlook Motel before we got back to the motel. We had to avoid the original Canon and Smith. We needed to disguise ourselves, but all we had access to in Gladys was some cheap fancy dress.

So I was Sonny. And Smith was 1975 Cher.

The Overlook Motel receptionist didn't recognise either of us. I told the receptionist that we hadn't stayed at the Overlook before, which meant we had to hear about their linen surcharge policies all over again. I didn't want to offend the receptionist by making my impatience obvious. So I let Smith do it instead.

I booked us into the room next door to ourselves. By the time we got settled in our original selves were already next door arguing with Rashid.

I peered through the blinds. We needed to keep an eye on ourselves so that when we left our room we could take our own places. So we could use the benefit of hindsight we'd gotten from travelling back in time and prevent; i) Rashid stealing the amber jam jar and ii) our getting caught returning it.

We were going to have to kidnap Rashid from ourselves.

Maybe I'm making this sound more complicated than it was?

We heard the door slam shut. And the TV explode. We watched ourselves head out to get pizza and then took off our disguises and returned to our room to find Rashid packing.

I suggested we forget about the pizza and go out for dinner instead. Rashid was so happy to get out of that room he didn't even mind wearing the Village People policeman's costume that I'd rented for him. And he can't have noticed when Smith pulled her 1975 Cher wig back on because he just pointed out that her hair had grown longer;

'And your nose too'.

14. Love Bomb Celebration Riot

*W*e got back to the room after our Happy Meals.

Rashid didn't notice that we'd returned to the room next door to our original one. Because we'd distracted him. And because only half of the rooms at the Overlook Motel had numbers on their doors.

We locked ourselves in our room. Because we couldn't leave Rashid on his own. Having travelled back in time it would have been a bit of a wasted effort if we'd allowed history to repeat itself. We had to stop Rashid from stealing the SOOPA. It was like one of those 'what if' moments. So we hid in our room. For two days. Because we didn't want Rashid to screw up the past again.

And because I wanted to see what the original Smith and I were up to.

I wanted to see how they'd get on without Rashid. Maybe they'd come up with a better idea for sorting this

SOOPA out. In which case, I didn't want to get in their way.

In which case, I wanted to take some annual leave.

Rashid was suffering from cabin fever. And complaining to the maid about how the mints she left on his pillow tasted awful;

'For the first two days I thought you were leaving your used chewing gum on my pillow'.

I asked Rashid to stop antagonising the maid. I was thinking about how things used to be, before Smith and I had jumped through the plot hole.

We ordered some Virginian takeout and played call my bluff.

Smith fed me headlines from back home (she watched the GMTV News anchors read the morning papers) and I tried to guess if they'd been ripped from the Sunday Spartan or not.

'Camouflage jackets disappear from store!'

'Bodies discovered in graveyard!'

Most of the headlines were from the Mail or the Express;

'Deaf benefit claimants refuse to listen to government!'

The last one was a bluff. But I had to agree with Smith that none of these would have caused a panic.

Except for the story about the bodies in the graveyard.

Smith and I had escaped from prison. But we were both feeling trapped. Because the original Smith and I had left to get pizza two days ago and neither of us had returned yet.

I asked Smith if she could recall any sports results from yesterday that we could bet on tomorrow. But Smith didn't want to think about sport. Smith was agonising over the past.

Or the future. It was one of the two;

'What's happened to them? Where are they? We?'

'I guess they must have been sucked through the plot hole, back into the prison, or some alternate reality, to replace us. You know; nature's way of balancing things out'.

'Did you just make that up?'

I had.

'Ok. I don't know. There, I said it. I have no idea where we, where they are. ...I guess it's called a plot hole for a good reason'.

Smith was shaking her head. So I apologised. I was starting to get the hang of not being a loner. You just had to apologise a lot more.

'Sorry. It's a hard habit to break'.

'What is?'

'Lying...'

Rashid was busting for the toilet. But unwilling to use the bathroom after Smith, or the urinals in the lobby. We'd travelled back in time. And as far as Islam was concerned, they'd figured out the bathroom a long time ago. Men sat down when they took a piss.

And they did it as far away from women as possible.

Rashid Rashid's belief in his religion was unshakable. I wondered if his belief in his religion wasn't stronger than his belief in his God. Rashid was very narrow-minded when it came to interpreting his rulebook. I didn't want to say anything. But Smith did;

'I love driving my Toyota, but I don't go around bombing Ford factories, and I don't feel compelled to visit the dealership that sold me my car five times a day'.

I wanted to tell Smith that this was a really terrible metaphor. But more than that, I wanted to carry on playing call my bluff. I could tell that Smith wasn't really enjoying herself. And that Rashid was losing his temper. I could tell because he'd started behaving like a rock-star; throwing his pillow mints (and then the minibar) off of the balcony.

'Rashid can't be stuck in here with you people any longer!'

I checked my watch. The original Smith and I were nowhere to be seen. It didn't seem like they were coming back anytime soon, so I figured it was safe to go out.

But there was really only one place to go...

TV news crews from across the US had set up at an amber jam jar rally hosted by Clint Eastwood, Angelina Jolie and Ricky Gervais. An old Sunkist advertising banner hung over the stage with the word 'MIRAJJE' hand-painted over it. This stood for 'Mankind's Internationally Recognised Amber Jam Jar Evidence'. This was the name of Redstar's cult.

Following a challenge by a South American professor who could no longer be located the amber jam jar had been sent away for testing. Now someone had to pay for the tests.

And they weren't cheap.

Redstar really believed his SOOPA was for real. And he really believed the men in white coats in the lab that he needed to pay were for real too. The men in white coats were not for real. Neither were the tests results. Or the lab. Waiting for the results was the most stressful part. But receiving the test results would be pretty stressful too.

In the meantime, I still had a job to do. Please don't think I'd been doing nothing in my motel room. Sure, sure, I'd been playing call my bluff. But I'd been working too.

The church was usually up in alms. But a lot of their hard-earned hand-outs were being skimmed by Redstar. And time was money. Sure, sure, our test results could be faked, but our fake results couldn't come back overnight, not if we wanted them to sound convincing. Maybe scientists weren't always right, but they were right most of the time.

They just usually took their sweet time proving it.

So in the meantime I'd been keeping myself busy. I'd been on the phone posing as concerned preachers, local businessmen and soccer moms trying to get the rally shut down.

Between you and me, if you need to shut down someone's right to free speech you check the local health and safety laws. Tell people you're shutting down a White Power™ rally because you don't like what they have to say and you'll get overrun by people championing a fascist's right to say things they personally find abhorrent. But tell the same people you're concerned about public safety (children, pets, parking etc.) and they'll sign your petition in a heartbeat.

The health and safety concern I'd raised was that the MIRAJJE rally was the same day as the GAG (Gladys Atheist Group) 'Atheist Rally to Restore Global Harmony' and that the police wouldn't be able to cope. But then the GAG ARRGH rally had been cancelled as some of the atheists had heard there was a free bar-b-q at the MIRAJJE rally.

And so had the Gladys police department.

Redstar bounded onto the stage as Matt Damon and Angelina Jolie gave a rendition of 'From a Distance' backed by the distressed faces of the Gladys Infant School's Parent Teacher Choir. Redstar immediately assured the crowd that contrary to scurrilous reports in the media all of the money raised would go to the costs of testing the amber jam jar and that under no circumstances would any money be going to the Timberlake Veteran's association.

That had just been a sick joke.

The rally had been moved out of the Glad Mall to the higher capacity (but equally inspirational) Salem Monster Truck and Speedway circuit. Redstar had attempted to get the Virginia Home Guard to fly over the rally in their refurbished B-52 bomber but hadn't been able to find enough cash for the security deposit. But as the rally started a swarm of locusts passed overhead and headed in the direction of Clearwater. Redstar described it as;

'An awe-inspiring sight, a wonderful blessing, a miracle...'

Even though it was none of the above.

Redstar launched into a long celebratory speech he'd copied from Wakipedia. The US was 'God's favourite place in the world' and Gladys was 'God's favourite place in the US'. Redstar got up on stage and talked down to the crowd about how the rest of the world had become bankrupt. He put on his telemarketer's headset and beseeched the crowd to join his mission to rescue the rest of the world... with a jam jar;

'This mission will be long and hard... It could take hundreds of years... But I'll see it through to the end if you will'.

Redstar looked out across the bewildered crowd and wiped a solitary tear away;

'This is really, beyond belief'.

It was. But it was also a celebration. And Americans didn't need asking twice when it came to celebrating something American.

The American thing that Redstar was celebrating was God.

It was; 'Time to look God in the eye'.

And it was; 'Time to press our jar to the ears of the world'.

And it was; 'Time for us all to turn amber!'

There was a roar of approval for this last comment, from the stadium's loudspeakers. It sounded a lot like the roar at the start of my 'AC/DC Greatest Hits Live!' album.

'I want you all to pray with me. I want you all to get on your knees and give thanks for the miracle of the amber jam jar'.

People looked at all the mud that had been churned up

by the Monster Trucks the night before. The people of Gladys had dressed for the occasion. No-one wanted to get their knees muddy. Redstar held out his arms in a pose he'd copied from his illustrated bible;

'Come on! Can't we all just get behind this jam jar?'

No-one moved.

Christy and several bewildered-looking junior cult members started handing out 'European sandwiches' (paninis) and an unidentified red soda. I warned Smith and Rashid not to drink the free soda, even though we knew Christy wouldn't harm a fly.

Just rats, she harmed a lot of rats.

After lunch Redstar introduced the star attraction;

'Now it is time to let the spirits speak to you! ...Ladies and gentlemen ...I give you ...Elvis!'

I could see people choking on their red soda.

But this wasn't Jonestown. And this wasn't Elvis.

This was a fancy dressed freckled psychic named Esmeralda channelling the spirit of Elvis as he threw his considerable astral weight behind Redstar's jam jar.

Esmeralda could channel Elvis because she didn't realise he was alive and well and lying on a tanning bed in Orlando. But nobody else in Salem knew that. Which meant only Smith, Rashid, Esmeralda and I knew for certain that Elvis didn't give a stuff about the amber jam jar. But that wasn't what was important.

The important thing, the unfortunate thing, the reason Redstar had blown his B-52 Stratofortress flyover deposit on Esmeralda the psychic, was that anyone in Salem who was having doubts about whether they should join Redstar in his crusade was about to have their doubts snuffed out by Elvis.

You either believed in the amber jam jar, or you stopped believing in the king.

And that was no choice. People in Salem loved the

king. And the king loved them back (his love just had to be squeezed out of the tube that was Esmerelda);

'Elvis wants me to tell you all that he loves you!'

Esmeralda the Psychic had been born Angus Fanwanking in 1963.

After a short and unsuccessful writing career that had lurched from soap operas to laundry detergent adverts (featuring several actors whom Angus had written out of soap operas) Angus changed his name, his sex and his occupation and began experimenting with cheap cider and Ouija boards; resulting in Esmeralda being contacted by Elvis in 1994 during the World Cup Final in Pasadena. At first Esmeralda had assumed the voice in her head to be the incoherent ramblings of some football commentator, but during the penalty shoot-out Elvis had assumed control of her body and performed a greatest-hits set with all of his trademark hip-shaking and butt-waggling included.

Esmeralda eventually sobered up and over the course of the next 9½ weeks Elvis assumed control of her hormone-enriched body to dictate the world's first (authorised) posthumous autobiography.

The next year Elvis and Esmeralda collaborated on his first album of new material for twenty years. Critics criticised the poor quality of Elvis' voice as channelled through Esmeralda's Dictaphone. They slated the banal lyrics. They hated the album cover.

But things really started to go awry for Esmeralda when 'Psychic Mike' released an album of covers of her tunes, with Mike channelling Esmeralda channelling Elvis for his recordings. There followed a long period of litigation with Elvis possessing Esmeralda in order to take Psychic Mike to the courts for infringement of copyright. Proceedings had to be abandoned when Psychic Mike was possessed by 'the real Esmeralda' who claimed (under oath) that she had been forced out of her own body by a malevolent spirit posing as Elvis but who was most probably just Buddy Holly.

When we got back to the Overlook Motel (after Rashid had thrown his shoe at Esmeralda and angrily demanded; 'Why didn't you see that coming?' and we'd all been hotly pursued by members of the Gladys football team as Mangelina sang the Star Spangled Banner backed by the long faces of the Gladys 31st Girl Scout Troop) I had a pictogram from the Agency waiting for me at reception. Of an ecstasy pill. And some tea. So I phoned in.

Redstar was gaining momentum. And Ministers attached to the Agency were starting to get nervous. What if our bogus test results didn't come back quickly enough?

Some reality enforcers wanted to combust Redstar.

Some wanted to combust the entire town of Gladys.

I hung up. I didn't feel good. I was sweating. I knew that if I didn't sort this situation out soon someone else would. Someone more like Self than me. My heart was racing.

My head was still firmly in place. But my heart just wasn't in it any longer.

I was having an attack of cognitive dissonance.

I phoned a premium rate doctor who told me that heart failure was serious and that if I thought it was happening to me then I should hang up and see another, more physical doctor immediately. Smith could see me looking conflicted;

'This job isn't for me. That's obvious. But I'm not sure it's for you either'.

It didn't matter if Smith wasn't sure if this job was for me. My superiors were convinced. And I'd been told to sort out this mess. There was another MIRAJJE rally in two days, in Mechanicsville. Mangelina and Clint and Esmeralda and Elvis were all keen to lend their support again, but I figured I could crash their party. I could get the real Elvis.

I could get real Elvis to put a stop to all of this.

We hired a Ford Fallus GTL and headed to Florida.

I wasn't too keen on revealing that Elvis had faked his death. I was pretty sure that revealing the king would spark a panic. But real Elvis was preferable to fake Elvis. Real Elvis was preferable to Redstar. And I figured the Agency would welcome no longer having to deal with real Elvis continually photo-bombing people's SeaWorld snaps.

All we knew for sure was that Elvis had last been seen on a security camera at a KFC in Orlando. George and Stevens were busy removing the offending images from a conspiracy theory website run by a shadowy individual outside of Tampa. When I mentioned this to Smith she asked for the name of the website.

'Son of Deep Throat'.

'Oh that's Tommy's website. Tommy sends the Spartan some of our best stories. I've always wanted to meet him in person'.

So that was that. Smith, Rashid and I settled our argument over the driver's seat and the radio with a game of rock-paper-scissors that I won (I cheated) and then we headed for Tampa Bay.

Meanwhile, back at Redstar's cult (now better known to late night TV gloaters as; 'The Real World'; an MSG News scripted reality show presented by Anne Punter) unpaid volunteers had been busy chasing celebrities to endorse MIRAJJE. The money left over from the last rally had been invested in chocolates and champagne and pigskin handbags sent to the agents of various stars of the stage and screen. This unsolicited downpour of uncalled-for affection was known in the trade as 'love-bombing'. Basically it was stalking someone but appearing normal enough to gain their trust. Then when you had their trust you slowly cut them off from their agent and their closest family member (if they were different people).

Love-bombing employed a basic celebrity reward system; if they stopped going to temple or church or those Scientology sleepovers they got a hug and a diamond Swatch.

Redstar's inner circle skimmed through celebrity magazines to identify whoever was currently 'in meltdown'. A lot of weeks it was Blimey Lowsey who was 'in meltdown' and so Redstar invited Blimey to perform alongside Esmeralda at a benefit gig outside Knoxville that was broadcast live to MSG subscribers and pirate patrons of The Real World.

Blimey didn't need asking twice. It was every singer's dream to sing alongside Elvis. Blimey's agent/mother had told her it was impossible. Blimey's mother/agent had tried to hold her back, but here was Redstar with a motivational speech about visualising your goals and a box of Australian antidepressants.

But the benefit concert was an elaborate trap! Once Blimey was on stage with Esmeralda singing 'Suspicious Minds' she was Redstar's.

During the interval Blimey changed into an amber uniform made out of bubblewrap and was joined onstage by Clint Eastwood and the Knoxville Finishing School (all wearing the same amber bubblewrap). Blimey whipped the crowd into a frenzy with a gang-busting string of hits and finished off by kneeling down with her face in Clint's crotch as she told her fans that Chuck Redstar had;

'Given me the strength to throw off my wild child ways'.

She'd been love-bombed.

And more than that, as Blimey turned away from Clint's crotch and faced her adoring fans in the crowd, as she ripped off her bubblewrap to reveal the mandarin jam she'd body-painted herself in from head to toe, Blimey became the bomb.

Blimey's followers (her 'Blisciples') had cut themselves

off from their families and friends years ago. The people who loved Blimey Lowsey, they weren't music lovers, they loved something, but it wasn't music. It was more like, hypnotherapy. The Blisciples had put their faith in Blimey, and now Blimey had put her Blisciples' faith in Chuck Redstar and his amber jam jar.

Of course Christy never admitted to inciting the celebration riot that followed Blimey's cover of 'You Suck!' Christy wouldn't admit it even though she'd been wearing a body camera that had been glued to her backstage pass by the producers of The Real World.

Blimey had been onstage when Christy had picked up her smartphone backstage and started playing a game called 'Twitter'. You scored points on 'Twitter' by getting the characters in the game excited over nothing. Christy found it easy to play; promising people free pastries and Swarovski handguns if they followed Redstar's MIRAJJE blogisodes.

When Christy finally tweeted; *'All ya'll droogs and blisciples get ur free taste of Blimey's muffins backstage #nads@'* she hit a new high score. She made real people in the real crowd so excited they ran onto the real stage. And then through it.

And then they kept on running, through the real streets of Gladys, overturning real cars and setting fire to real recycling bins and real leather couches.

No-one seemed put out.

Celebration riots were a common type of riot in Tennessee.

The offices of the 'Son of Deep Throat' website were located within Son of Deep Throat's bedroom, in the basement of his mum's house in Tampa. Son of Deep Throat was fifteen-year-old halfling Tommy Knocker. Smith was a little disappointed her idol was so small in real life, but I explained that this was often the case when meeting one's heroes.

Tommy tracked real Elvis from one fast food outlet to the next. We lost him anytime he visited a cheap diner without CCTV, but by extrapolating a line along the I-4 I deduced that Elvis would stop at the Plant City Truck and Pie Stop the following evening. We jumped into the Fallus (which now sported an 'Elvis Lives!' bumper sticker) and hit the gas.

Blimey had lost her driving licence the last time she'd sped anywhere and so Redstar had offered her the use of his bandwagon. Redstar needed to keep Blimey on the wagon. Blimey had been speeding when she'd been caught speeding.

But now she'd 'found amber' Blimey was an airbrushed sober pin-up for MIRAJJE.

Redstar had bussed in truckloads of Blisciples as a kind of rent-a-crowd supplemented with starving actors looking for work in-between filming reality TV shows and queuing for the latest McDonald's Burgerwrap™ launch. But the only wrap people in Tennessee were interested in was the one in Blimey's new amber clothing range.

The Fashion Channel's Evening News team broadcast live as one by one marginally distinct teenagers walked into the Tennessee Outlet Centre and realised their dream of being integrated into Blimey's society. They emerged from their chrysalises squeezed into the same amber costume as the new Blimey blow-up doll being launched at the Early Learning Centre.

With the same hair as the Blimey doll.

And the same hopes and dreams.

Blimey appeared on the cover of Vanity Fair tastefully body-painted in orange jam (and airbrushed to within an inch of her life according to Smith).

She spoke about how she'd 'learnt her lesson' and how she was 'good people' and how she'd 'met a great teacher' and how 'sometimes your teacher has to give you the same lesson over and over, y'know, for the propaganda to sink in?'

New Scientist countered by putting the guy who'd discovered DNA on their cover wearing only a single helix, but it quickly became the lowest selling issue in their history.

The south-eastern corner of the US slowly turned amber.

The more who believed, the more who wanted to believe. People had always worn a uniform on the inside. But now everyone could see it. Everyone felt more relaxed now they didn't have to worry about anyone picking them out of the crowd.

The Nashville Thunderdome hosting the amber jam jar rally appeared to have been covered in orange AstroTurf™. Redstar had created a grassroots movement out of one jam jar and twenty-five thousand sixteen-year-olds. He walked onstage hand in hand with Blimey and prepared to harvest his turf. In a bright orange jacket and bright orange jackboots. Like Blimey. But unlike Blimey in that Redstar was also wearing trousers.

Because he wanted to win the crowd's respect. And Blimey already had it.

Redstar raised his stunt amber jam jar high in the air. The real one wouldn't be back for a few more days. But Redstar wanted everyone to see it in his hands; the hands that were attached to his arms, the arms that belonged to him.

This is what's known in the business as 'acquired prestige'.

Redstar began to chant in a rather strange (*Austrian?*) accent;

'We believe in the amber jam jar! ...We won't be controlled by the old religions!'

The ginger field chanted back;

'Gla-dys! Gla-dys!'

'We will forget about history! ...We will wake up feeling refreshed'.

The amber grassroots pumped a collective fist in the air;

'⊛🎸💀! you Tim-ber-lake, ⊛🎸💀! you Clear-wat-er, ⊛🎸💀! you Mi-chael-Moore and Farm-ville ⊛🎸💀! you too'.

'You have your own voice! The voice of the king!'

The voice of the king walked onstage. Esmeralda wore an amber nappy and was being dictated to over her large Dr Dre headphones;

'We're all shook up! ...Say you want a revolution!'

I couldn't allow that. So I left Rashid in the Fallus with the engine running and Smith watching over the members of the Gladys Football Security Team whom we'd drugged and tied up backstage and I pushed the real Elvis Aaron Presley out onto the stage.

Elvis was a bit disorientated at first, because of the Rohypnol. But he eventually realised that he was either standing in front of a huge crowd for the first time in forty years or enjoying a pleasant flashback, because he soon slipped back into the groove; greeting the crowd with that curled-lip smile before launching into 'Crying in the Chapel'.

I started to worry that I'd really underestimated Redstar as Elvis was booed off stage and pelted with rotten satsumas.

All of us in the Agency could be proud of the bang-up job we'd done in helping Elvis fake his death. No-one in the Nashville Thunderdome was willing to take the word of a living Elvis over a dead one. We'd only ourselves to blame for letting him spend so much time in all of those tanning salons developing that leathery skin. But still, I had to admit it had been pretty smart of Redstar to love-bomb the Guild of Multicultural Celebrity Impersonators and throw Chinese Tom Hanks onto the stage to argue that real Elvis was nothing more than an imposter, a multicultural impersonation of himself. And then have everyone in the crowd believe him, because real Elvis really did look as Colombian as Chanks had alleged.

I couldn't bring myself to relive events on the Nine o'clock News. So I stared into my thick-shake as Smith surfed the airwaves for something completely different.

George Michael had launched a new range of multi-purpose cleaning fluids.

And there was another continuity error.

Some wildlife-bothering daytime television presenter had stumbled across an 'unbelievable' discovery while chasing after a family of pygmy benefit cheats in the Jor-El Mountains of central Tajikistan. In a cave dotted with primitive cave art of men in heavy make-up and flared hair a series of shelves had been cut into the rock face. And on these rock shelves were hundreds of neurotically arranged twelve inch stone disks with a small hole cut into the centre. And on these stone disks were dozens of circular grooves. No-one had managed to find a stone turntable yet, but people were already speculating over what would be heard on these prehistoric rock records.

Perhaps Bon Jovi.

I had to wonder what on Earth was going on at the Agency if this kind of thing was being allowed to get out. What exactly was happening that was preventing the DKM from getting out there and adjusting these things being referred to as miracles?

Maybe a coup d'état. Maybe burrito night in the canteen.

I was starting to think I'd never be able to show my face in the canteen ever again.

'Failures don't get dessert'.

That's what it said on the motivational poster above the canteen serving hatch.

But for once news of Redstar cheered me up. For once Redstar was a help rather than a hindrance. News was spreading of his arrival in LA. Redstar had been told (by who wasn't clear) that LA was to be the site for the first MIRAJJE embassy.

People didn't have time to think about stone records.

Redstar's new religion was bigger than rock music.

15. Invisible Healing Appointment

No-one found any sleeping toads within the rock that Redstar built his embassy upon, but CNN had a webcam trained on the construction site running 24/7 just in case.

Redstar had used the proceeds from his benefit gigs and Blimey Lowsey's international chart topper 'Heard Behaviour' to broadcast national TV adverts for his embassy crowd-funding site and had set up shop on BSN (the Biblical Shopping Network) selling replica amber jam jars (and matching spoons). The jars were 100% recyclable.

Chuck claimed to have had a series of dreams during a recent heatwave in which the embassy had demanded to be built, as the amber jam jar was a beacon (in common with other bright orange objects) that would call a prophet back to the world.

Which prophet, his night sweats hadn't specified.

And so the embassy had been constructed with a huge radio antenna and a neon helipad on its roof to land a prophet safely and with minimum turbulence even though no-one really knew which prophet would land there. Perhaps it would be all of them.

Rashid was incandescent at such sacrilege. But Smith told him not to worry.

Redstar would end up with egg on his face when the prophet *didn't* return.

I didn't want to burst their bubble, because I was in there with them, but the fact was it was easy to get a prophet to return, it happened all the time. Redstar could get hold of any nut job claiming to be the second coming and as long as he love-bombed enough celebrities for their endorsement people would force themselves to believe it.

I'd dealt with my fair share of false prophets over the years.

I'd intercepted the second coming of Ganesh when he'd arrived in Kashmir and assumed the physical form of a fifty-three-year-old geography teacher.

Ganesh had descended from the astral plane three months earlier in order to establish the Order of WTF (which either stood for wisdom, truth and faith, or it didn't) but when I tracked him down he'd jumped on a flight to Hawaii. When I caught up with him in Molokai 48 hours later and asked why he'd needed to take a plane to escape he attempted to prove his divinity by jumping off of the Kalaupapa cliffs. I guess Ganesh didn't have a fear of flying.

Though he may have developed a fear of landing.

It's not for me to say whether Ganesh successfully made it back to the spirit world or not.

And it wasn't for me to say whether Redstar's MIRAJJE embassy was vulgar or not. That was for the media to decide. And perhaps the prophet who was about to land there.

Maybe he'd turn around if the embassy design wasn't Art Deco.

Who the hell knew?

All we knew for sure was that the helipad had been designed by Jean-Paul Gaultier and finished with the same rhinestones that had been super-glued to the ceilings of the conference room, bowling alley and bathhouse. All we knew for sure was what we read in the pages of 'Home and Haircut' magazine or what we saw on 'Celebrity Cribs'.

Everyone agreed that Celebrity Cribs had been a leftfield choice of show to announce the date for the second coming on. But that was the least of the surprises.

Most apocalypse experts and Armageddon commentators expected Redstar to stick with tradition and announce a date some years in the future, but no-one knew for sure, not even the sponsors of Celebrity Cribs; Nevada State Lottery and Mountain Dew.

After three hours of build-up that included a world record attempt for the most Mountain Dew that could be drunk in ten minutes (about half a can), Celebrity Cribs cut live to the embassy roof where Blimey Lowsey performed a cover of 'Waiting For A Star To Fall' which ended in a fireworks display, the draw for the Nevada State Lottery and Redstar's cliff-hung announcements;

'I can exclusively reveal... that the date... of the return...'

This was textbook use of the dramatic pause.

'Of the prophet...'

People were on the edge of their seats.

'Or *prophets*... will be...'

People were on the edge of their patience.

'...Tuesday!'

After the confusion over whether Redstar had meant *this* Tuesday or *next* Tuesday had been resolved it was just a matter of watching various bewigged and hairdoed news anchors fist-fighting for the rights to the best spot on the embassy rooftop.

Redstar was too busy behind the scenes to defuse the tension on the roof. Redstar was watching a pre-visualisation of the special effects for the prophet's arrival as directed by James Cameron. And rehearsing his greeting the prophet(s) with Daniel Day Lewis.

And trying to remember not to look at the camera.

Opening night arrived. And so did the prophet. Just the one. Or 'The One'. The prophet known to the world as; 'Invisible Brian!' Invisible Brian lived up to his billing. He stood, perhaps beside Redstar, maybe behind him. Live on international TV.

'Which religion does Brian represent?'

Asked the massed reporters of Al Jazeera and Celebrity Cribs.

'All of them!'

Replied Redstar.

'And where is he now?'

'He's standing right next to me. But he's invisible! And he has a name. His name is... Brian Jones!'

It wasn't clear if Brian was an individual representation of all of the prophets 'squeezed into one' or the rhythm guitarist from The Burial Stones. But what did it matter? He was back. It was Tuesday. And he was going to create the New Jerusalem. In LA.

It was at about this point that Smith had been expecting everyone to start laughing. She was understandably crestfallen then when she realised everyone believed Redstar. All of the people Redstar and James Cameron had cast in the roles of 'football player in crowd', 'clapper' and 'yes man'.

You try not clapping and cheering at someone once everyone else has started.

Go on. Even if you're just watching it on TV. Just try it.

The next day Invisible Brian was everywhere.

You couldn't avoid Invisible Brian even if you tried.

The place that Invisible Brian was most was on the radio. Normally none of us could agree what to listen to on the radio, but Smith, Rashid and I all agreed we didn't want to listen to this. We didn't want to. But we had to. Because of the job.

Brian had been John the Baptist in a past life. After that he'd been King Arthur, and then Malcom X. He'd also had a short stint as a heating engineer named Mick. But he didn't want to talk about that. Invisible Brian didn't want to dwell on the past; he wanted to talk about the future; he wanted to talk about why he'd been beamed down to Earth from a lifeboat fleeing the exploding planet of Reptilon.

Invisible Brian conducted his radio interviews in an affected English accent. Like a South African doing a bad Keira Knightley impersonation. But what he lacked in Received Pronunciation he made up for with convincing rhetoric. You couldn't listen to Brian and not send a donation, or purchase a copy of Heard Behaviour.

You couldn't resist Brian and his celebrity super-friends.

There was the fundraiser hosted over the phone with Jason Statham.

The FacelessBook campaign. The blink and you'll miss him special guest star appearance on The Big Bang Theory.

And the affairs with the Beckhams.

Both of them. At the same time. Behind each other's backs.

There was the authorised autobiography of Invisible Brian ghost-written by a blackmailed Salman Rushdie. All of the critics agreed that Rushdie had really captured the essence of Invisible Brian in 'The Truthful Book About What God Told Me To Tell You', later republished as 'What God Said'.

Rushdie recounted how Brian had spoken to the

smartest people in Reptilon before fleeing the planet in their only escape pod. They'd told him all about religion, and they'd explained how you could say what you liked about history if you went back far enough. You could explain how angels had been jet-pack wearing tourists from Dirtworld. There was a whole universe of jet-pack wearing alien tourists waiting to welcome mankind once we'd accepted the truth about the amber jam jar and started doing what Redstar told us.

Politicians signed contracts with MIRAJJE Limited Liability Corp. and showered talk shows with their golden feelings on topics ranging from Moon sovereignty to the flavour of jam in the amber SOOPA.

There were press releases and blogs. There were Saturday morning cartoons.

There were some pretty distasteful Happy Meals.

Invisible Brian even offered to resurrect Raúl Greedo from the dead so he could face trial for those pyramid schemes. Brian could resurrect anyone from the dead, for trial.

If that particular revelation did nothing else, it did at least precipitate a sharp drop in the number of suicide bombings.

But Invisible Brian wasn't immune to stupid ideas either. Brian believed the swastika was all about peace, love and harmony. You could say that about the swastika if you went back far enough. But things were different now. It was pretty tough getting permission to build a MIRAJJE outreach centre in Jerusalem when your corporate logo was a swastika superimposed onto an amber jam jar. What you needed was a PR firm to give your swastika a little spin, to make it seem more positive, to make it look more like a 'plus' sign.

You had to take the edge off the swastika.

But Invisible Brian had his doubts about the plus sign. It looked a little too much like a crucifix. And Brian didn't want to upset any potential Jewish converts.

The stock market rollercoastered as the public's opinion of MIRAJJE LLC peaked and troughed depending on the logo being carved into the facade of the outreach centre. Prices for replica jam jars sold on BSN soared and plunged as ~~Redstar~~ Brian continually changed the logo and discontinued replicas with the wrong logo suddenly became more or less rare and collectable. There were queues outside the stores at midnight to be the first to pick up the latest edition and queues outside the stores an hour later to return them.

The host of 'Mad Money' screamed 'buy!', and 'sell!', and then started screaming 'man down!' as he had a panic attack. Mobs of broken second homeowners laid siege to the Mad Money studios in Houston angrily demanding compensation for the life-savings they'd lost speculating on MIRAJJE stocks. Others camped outside Redstar's embassy and created a second tent city next to the one that had been rented out to the construction workers.

Redstar attempted to defuse the situation (and distract people as their tents were removed) by organising an outdoor has-beens concert in Las Vegas.

But Redstar had an ulterior motive for arranging the concert.

Besides his other ulterior motive.

Redstar invited Belinda Carlisle, Debbie Gibson and Tiffany to perform at the concert, reuniting the original line-up as they'd appeared in posters on his wall in the eighties, Playboy magazine in the nineties and 'Celebrity Handjob' in the noughties.

Back when he'd been Norman Grinder these women had been top of the magazine pile. Now Redstar was on top. Now he'd have the chance to create some new memories of these faded stars. To give them a spit and polish and shower them in love.

Maybe I'm being too Mills and Boon here, but what

I'm trying to say is, he invited these objects of his teenage lust to 'invisible healing appointments'.

Belinda, Tiffany and Debbie were falling over each other to meet Invisible Brian.

Because the room they met Brian in was very dark.

Bright lights tended to give Invisible Brian migraines.

This is what Brian would tell Belinda or Tiffany or Debbie once Redstar had 'left the room' so that they could be 'alone now' to enjoy their 'healing appointments'.

Don't believe me? Then just read Belinda's autobiography. Or Debbie's.

Tiffany even wrote a new song about it. It sounded a lot like her other song.

And what was I doing while all of this was going on?

I was watching an episode of Face Talk, about how more and more people were changing career in their forties. But I was also busy photocopying forty two pages of bogus test results that had been couriered to me by a woman on a mobility scooter. I was glossing over a Rockingham Research Facility compliments slip and attaching it to the test results like the blurb on the back cover of a novel that explains what's inside in 40 words or less.

This is what's known in the business as a 'Press Release'.

Basically what you're doing here is releasing the press from the onerous task of having to read through a forty two page document themselves.

We headed for the LA Public Library.

It was like a lot of other public libraries, but with more DVDs.

'This doesn't look anything like it does in the movies'.

I explained to Rashid that we were in LA, and that the library he'd seen in Ghostbusters was in New York. Rashid refused to believe me and went off in search of some sort of evidence to prove me wrong. Smith and I went looking for ancient manuscripts.

The ancient manuscript we were after had been written sometime in the late fifteenth century, but it had been badly translated into Olde English over the years and most of the recipes were unusable. I needed to find the original Latin version. But Smith found it first.

The 'Gioia Di Cucinare Codex'. By Leonardo Da Vinci.

Da Vinci's book of recipes. For homemade marmalade and contact lenses and diet pills. His recipes for bubble bath and for turning base metal into gold. That got Smith excited.

She started searching for a copier.

Then she started searching for change for the copier.

I told her not to bother. Someone had already tried it and it was a non-starter.

Don't blame Da Vinci though. Blame Ye Olde translator.

We scanned the index until we found Da Vinci's recipe for 'Fare Ambro'.

You poured an egg white into the gut of a pig. Then you dropped your guts into a pot of boiling water until you had a sort of fossilised scotch-egg. You cut it into whatever shape you wanted, added some insects (or if you preferred a jam jar and a small amount of diet blackcurrant jam), greased it with some linseed oil and then left it in the sun for two weeks. Or until it turned orange. This was Leonardo Da Vinci's recipe for making fake amber.

We followed the recipe to the letter. Except we didn't have two weeks. So we chucked it in a microwave for twenty minutes, then paid for our fake amber to spend four hours in a tanning salon.

We sat around the fake amber jam jar. It looked as real as the real amber jam jar.

I thought back to the rudimentary satnav I'd once built in a school workshop.

But this was better.

The real SOOPA had been safely locked away in the Whitewash Museum. But we needed a fake to return to its rightful owner. And this was it. My last chance to discredit Redstar and expose the amber jam jar as a fake. It was a real work of art.

But you know what they say about pride.

A few hours later I was fighting back tears as I watched TV. Smith panicked that I was having another attack of cognitive dissonance, but it was probably just depression. Because our bogus test results had been broadcast. And conclusively proven that the amber jam jar I'd couriered back to Redstar was a fake. Or they hadn't. It wasn't very clear.

We were watching a special edition of Face Talk featuring renowned (and recently cut and blow-dried) Jam Jar denialist Professor Richard Ticker and nineteen nineteen-year-old Blisciples. Dickie explained how the amber was copal. Then he explained how copal was an immature form of amber.

'You're immature!'

Shouted the thirteenth Blisciple. But Dickie wasn't really listening. Dickie was waiting for his chance to speak. He passed the time that he had to wait to speak by not making eye contact with the Blisciples. Because the Blisciples were all wearing orange bikinis. Maybe Dickie had the coiffured chest hair and healthy tan that could combat your average looking creationists, but the Blisciples had flesh to press too. They could gloss over Dickie's beautiful hair and turn people's attention to his pot belly and sagging anatomy. They accused Dickie of tailoring the results to fit his 'agenda'; Dickie was more concerned with being proven wrong than with discovering the truth. Things quickly turned nasty.

'You're wearing bikinis! You don't know what you're talking about and you're all wearing bikinis!'

Dickie waved a piece of white paper around;

'I have the test results right here. They prove that the jam jar is a fake. Microscopic traces of reduced sugar jam were found inside the jar! Maybe you can believe our ancestors had the ability to make glass jars, but you can't seriously be suggesting they had the capacity to manufacture diet jam!'

The test results were handed to Andromeda Strain;

'...Does anyone here speak Latin?'

It wasn't clear if anyone in the audience spoke English. But a hand went up and the results were passed along to some old centurion;

'This is just a list of made-up words!'

Dickie tried to stand up but was pushed back into his chair by a bouncer.

'You're not reading it right! Those are scientific words!'

The test results were passed back to Dickie to translate just as one of the Blisciples launched herself at him. What happened next wasn't entirely clear. It wasn't entirely clear because the Blisciple started rolling around on the studio floor with Dickie in her bikini and the network quickly pixelated her modesty. The bouncer broke things up. And when the Bliciple's pixels had been separated from Dickie's she had a large white pixel in her hand.

Dickie protested too much;

'This is just a desperate effort to prop up a completely discredited ideology'.

It was also a desperate effort to prop up sales of Dickie's latest book; 'Why God Never Said Nothing To No-one'.

The Blisciple started to tear the test results apart. Then she started to eat them.

And she talked with her mouth full;

'This man is terrified of admitting that he doesn't have an explanation for the miracle of the amber jam jar. Or one for the more recently discovered miracle of prehistoric low calorie jam!'

Dickie disagreed with her;

'She's swallowing the truth so there'll be none left for us and we'll have to swallow more of their bullshit instead'.

The Blisciples were feeling very contrary under their pixels;

'*You're* the one feeding people bullshit!'

This was your textbook reverse psychology right here. If Redstar's harem of spokestrippers could convince people that Dickie was the one feeding them bullshit, then Redstar's (past its sell by date) diet jam would have to be more palatable by comparison.

Dickie's hair started to wilt as he went increasingly red in the face;

'Damn you all to humanist oblivion!'

Dickie was turning a sort of frustrated purple colour;

'If there was a God he'd be in this studio right now telling you I'm right! Then you'd have to listen to me!'

It wasn't immediately clear that these were Professor Richard Ticker's last words. Because it wasn't immediately clear that he'd just suffered a massive, temper-induced coronary. A real bolt from the blue. So Andromeda Strain kept on asking him questions. Asking him questions was a futile attempt to tear the audience's attention away from their tweeting photos of the de-pixelated Blisciples.

'Are you expecting people to take that on faith?'

Andromeda started berating Dickie;

'Do you or do you not have evidence to disprove prehistoric low calorie jam? ...Do you or do you not? ...Do you or do you not?'

Dickie didn't answer. He just started looking blue. It reminded one of the Blisciples of an unfortunate incident she'd experienced with an elderly uncle some years earlier. So she leant over and took his pulse. And then the network hastily cut to a commercial break.

By the time they returned to Face Talk Dickie's death had been confirmed.

And his face had been pixelated.

After Dickie's passing the other bosses in the boffin mob started pushing each other out of the crowd whenever a news network called for brave volunteers to debate the test results. One by one these brave 'volunteers' tried to come up with an explanation that the man on the street could understand. An explanation the man on the street could *buy*.

Sure, sure, the test results had been overwhelmingly negative (which was ideally what you wanted your bogus test results to be), the problem was that science was complicated. In fact, as far as most people were concerned, science was unnecessarily complicated. The problem was that very few of those following the debates could agree with any of these explanations, because most had become lost around two minutes into the broadcast. As far as most folks were concerned none of the scientists' reasons for why our ancestors *hadn't* made diet jam leapt out as being any more reasonable than the Blisciples' reasons for how they could have. Most folks would rather believe that they wouldn't fall off of the planet because the Earth was flat than have to listen to some nerd explaining how no-one really knew how gravity worked but probably it was something overly scientific and needlessly complicated.

The more complicated the explanations of the test results became the more difficult people found them to believe. Just as decades earlier people had preferred to believe that JFK had been assassinated as part of a Cuban Mafia conspiracy than to have to endure another 'expert' explaining how it was technically possible for a well-equipped ~~reality enforcer~~ lone gunman to possess a rifle capable of firing magic bullets.

The more people knew, the less they understood. The greater the degree of certainty the scientists expressed, the more uncertain everyone else became.

Some doctors claimed that tobacco was good for the brain. Some claimed it was bad for the heart. But most people had both. So which did you go with? Which cherry were you supposed to pick? You couldn't just go with the consensus reality; everyone else was as confused as you were. There was a lot of confusion. Plus panic.

Panic and fighting.

ERR News was trending heavily with their found footage of a vicious brawl between two homeless men over the test results and what they meant for the veracity of intelligent design theory and the global academic conspiracy to bury the truth about the jam jar.

The taller man thrust a butterfly knife at his rival;

'Screw you and your biased interpretation of unequivocal test results to support your pre-existing worldview! The fossil record clearly proves that amber jam jars are impossible'.

The shorter man produced a knuckleduster;

'The fossil record's full of holes! Where's the missing link? You're the one who's desperate to see your entrenched ideas affirmed by questionable evidence, ya bastard!'

The larger man head-butted his fun-sized opponent;

'And where are your amber milk bottles?! The evidence I've seen is the same as you have ya sonuvabitch! But only one of us continues to believe in a demonstrably false belief!'

The shorter man bit his adversary on the leg;

'It's narrow minded bigots like you who refuse to accept anything that doesn't fit some implausible series of coincidences that miraculously produced humans out of pandas and monkeys!'

'You're the ones who dragged pandas into this, not us!'

'We were merely extrapolating the theory of the intelligent design of the natural world proposed by Darwin! How else do you explain the fact that dolphins have nipples? As a fluke?! Or is it because they were intelligently designed that way?'

'Intelligently designed to do what?!'

There was quite a lot of blood by now; both men were beginning to tire.

'The mind of man is simply unable to fathom the intentions of the designer. Perhaps it was done to impress us?'

'So who designed the designer eh? Answer that ya cocksucka!'

The shorter man pulled a gun;

'That's completely outside the scope of this knife fight! If you won't play by the rules, neither will I'.

The taller man grabbed for the gun and the pair of them started rolling around in the style of a cliché.

'You make up the rules as you go along. And you only believe in things you wish were true!'

'And you're more interested in attacking the beliefs of others than defending your own inconsistencies!'

'You cannot reason with unreason!'

The gun went off. Both men laid still. People ran screaming from nearby cafés at the sound of the gunshot. So the tourist who'd been filming it all on his smartphone quickly seized his chance to go for a mochaccino.

16. Red Herring Performance Appraisal

*T*he fighting spread across borders. Adverts were plastered across London buses.

One side of the bus had a photo of a smiling Pope. The other had a smiling Blimey.

Smiling, reclining on a sun-lounger and dripping wet. Blimey that is, not the Pope.

The world's major cults had started haemorrhaging followers to Redstar's MIRAJJE. And more and more atheists had started believing what they were seeing.

The traditional two party system of science and religion was being prised open by an interloper with loads of popular support. Which is really the worst kind of interloper.

The battle against Redstar escalated every half hour; on soap operas, on chat shows, on chat operas. This was the survival of the fittest all over again. Every opinion for itself.

Each side rolled out their celebrities to fight it out for the public's allegiance. But MIRAJJE had by far the better performers. Organised religion had their uniformed imams and rabbis while the science club had a bunch of malformed muftis who'd never been on TV before. What chance did Professors Kronenbourg and Carling have against the American Tom Hanks and Mr T? Hanks had won two Oscars!

This was the survival of the fittest looking.

Maybe the cutest and the cuddliest creatures didn't survive in the wild. Maybe the cutest and the cuddliest were just vegetable lambs to the slaughter. But things were different on TV. On TV you had your bookworms in their brown suits and mustard stained shirts with their long fingernails and their haircut apathy. Their weird science.

And then there were the Blisciples; with their entertainingly supernatural causes for the amber jam jar and their short skirts and their attempts to free the blinkered minds of the scientists. To open up the doors of perception and increase consciousness.

Increased consciousness wasn't something that the Agency was particularly keen on. I knew this because I'd received a pictogram of a naked (but mercifully youthful) Mick Jagger, and Judge Judy. I had to spell it out for Smith and Rashid; someone from the Office of Reality Enforcement would be sent to judge my performance. I had no idea who. But I had a bad feeling about it. Rashid had a bad feeling about it too. Because of how the Agency had wanted to execute him. Because of how the Agency had only stopped wanting to execute him once I'd told them I'd already done it. We all agreed; we needed to finish Redstar before someone from the Agency arrived to finish us. There was only one option left to us now.

We were going to need a downpour of red-herrings.

'A downpour of red-herrings?'

This, of course, was Smith. I increased her consciousness;

'Redstar is winning the argument, because arguments aren't won by the truth, they're won by the most skilled bullshitter'.

'That's lucky for people in your line of work then'.

It *was* lucky for people in my line of work.

'So it's a battle between those who want to conceal the truth and those who want to invent it?'

'The truth isn't important right now. The more people Redstar signs up the more will want to come along for the ride. If lots of people believe what he's saying, then it must be true. Winning arguments is an art. And Redstar's surrounded himself with actors and popstars; he's surrounded himself with artists'.

'Bullshit artists' said Rashid.

'Exactly' said I.

'We need to surround Redstar with people who are terrible at winning arguments. We need to replace his bullshit artists with our batshit artists'.

After a quick call to the Office of Confessions I arrived at the CNN studios to meet Jacques and Igor who were going to run through a standard 'lunacy by association' play. I handed them their cash and my scapegoats went into hair and make-up before being called into the CNN Panic Room.

Portia Ferrari turned to camera three and introduced Jacques and Igor as 'Samuel Signwriter' and 'Lady Elizabeth Balls' from the International Flat Earth Research Society.

Portia flashed her glow in the dark smile and explained how;

'You were originally booked to appear via satellite link,

but you don't trust satellites, is that correct?'

'That's correct. They take a lot of misleading photographs. And that satellite delay; it's very fishy. We prefer to use a couple of tin cans and some string'.

'And what is it about satellite photography specifically that you find misleading? Or is it all photography?'

'Just satellite photography. And wedding photography. Some of these satellite images; they appear to suggest that the Earth *isn't* flat, to a layman at least'.

'And what is it that you do Samuel?'

'I'm a dental hygienist'.

Portia had a fifteen page pamphlet in her hand;

'But you wrote this right? 'Earth is flat and that is that'?'

'Yes. I'm expanding it into a screenplay'.

'And Chuck Redstar is affiliated with your organisation?'

'Of course. We're working with Chuck to tackle these so-called 'scientists' who are really just witchdoctors and magicians. All of this 'science', it's just a lot of weird ideas with no relevance to factual things like fried chicken and football and soap'.

'They claim to help the world but what have these scientists ever invented?'

Added Lady Elizabeth.

'...Didn't you guys fly here?'

'We flew here on a plane but it wasn't built by scientists, and it flew here in a straight line, because the world is flat'.

'And this is a view shared by Chuck Redstar?'

'Let me tell you what Chuck told me last night. Everything began with the creation of creation...'

Portia dimmed the CNN Panic Room lights as Lady Elizabeth hushed her voice;

'First there was the water, and then there was the land, floating on the water, and then the people who could stand up on the land because the water was flat. And then there was the amber jam jar. And there couldn't have been any jam jars if the world wasn't flat. They'd have just rolled away. So you see, this all proves that the amber jam jar is real'.

Everything Lady Elizabeth had said was complete balls, but it fitted together nicely, the flat Earth and the SOOPA. So now if you wanted to believe in the amber jam jar, you had to believe that the world was a flat disc and that Australia was not in fact, down under.

I'd hoped this would knock the wind out of MIRAJJE's sails. Unfortunately it only succeeded in garnering enough attention to turn the Flat Earth Society into the UK's fourth largest political party. People didn't just treat the truth as if it were an intruder, they treated the truth as if it were an intruder and they were a Norfolk farmer with a shotgun.

Most cable news viewers weren't sure what to believe.

Most cable news presenters weren't particularly clear either;

'Now Gabriel. Can you explain this to me again because I'm really not getting it? Am I just being stupid?'

This was MSG News. And this was Anne Punter.

'You're not stupid Anne. But it is very easily explained'.

This was Greg Upcharge, a leather-faced, rubber-necked news sub-contractor employed by various MSG shows as an expert. Think of Greg as like a PE Teacher. He didn't only teach PE, he taught Geography or Economics too; one of those subjects you read aloud from a text book. Greg was health expert to 'Sunday Brunch', food expert to 'Red Carpet Live!' and fashion commentator for 'Living Lifestyle'.

Greg was appearing on Public Opinions as an expert on philosophy. Or psychology. He couldn't remember which. But that didn't matter, because he had a teleprompter and an earpiece. The only bits of Greg that the station employed were the tan and the haircut.

'If you look at the stats then they really tell two stories.

Opinion is divided over whether having more or less people believe in your theories makes those theories more or less believable'.

'So the group with the least followers could be right?'

'Right. And the group with the most could be wrong. Like with the Nazis. Or astrology. A lot of people believe it, but it isn't true'.

There was a scream. The camera panned around and caught a blue-eyed blonde as she fainted in front of a weather map.

'So you could argue that these mass assumptions, these *massumptions,* are less likely to be accurate?'

'That's right Anne. Or you could argue the opposite'.

Anne tilted her head, like a confused Shih Tzu;

'So who is right and who is wrong?'

'I'm not sure Anne. I do know that smoking is bad for you, but I really only have a very superficial grasp of physics. I do know that Kimberley believes the stars control her destiny though. And she'll have the weather for us, right after this'.

The more liberal media faucets eventually found the confidence and the ratings to take on Redstar. Not because of my red herrings so much.

More because of all the orgies with Invisible Brian.

Redstar secured the services of the publicist Jordan Periscope (whom he'd met at an orgy) and Jordan explained how MIRAJJE had been unfairly criticised for its progressive attitude to women and girls with fake ids. These nineteen-year-olds were old enough to vote for political parties, so who was to say they weren't old enough for bunga bunga parties? Sure, sure, some Blisciples had gone a bit OTT, but to suggest they were formed entirely of sex workers was inflammatory and only partially accurate.

The Blisciples arranged a 'Tits Out!' parade along Sunset Boulevard protesting their First Amendment right to take their clothes off to have a good time. But when Pierce & Pierce, Pottery Barn and Pizza Hut all pulled their sponsorship deals Redstar was forced to publicly apologise and promise that the Blisciples would wear orange nipple tape in future.

Redstar had to appear on Face Talk and tearfully explain how Invisible Brian had been naïve, and unaccustomed to the parochial traditions of twenty-first century Earth.

Redstar announced that Brian had 'returned home'. But he'd left a gift.

Redstar's new and improved bandwagon was fifty feet long with polished wooden floors, a working fireplace and a fifteen-foot bar. The master bedroom had an en-suite rainfall shower and the pigskin trimmed driver's cab had been fitted with satellite TV. It had a custom glow-in-the-dark orange paint job (for health and safety reasons) and boasted 510bhp, a carbon-fibre spoiler and sport exhaust. It had an astroturfed roof terrace.

It had cost $1.9 million.

But it was worth it to Chuck Redstar. People looked at his bandwagon and thought; there's a guy who's going places.

The place he was going was the first annual Gladys Amber Jam Jar March.

Redstar had mobilised an orange army of Gladys loyalists to counter all of the bad press generated by those confusing test results. And those orgies.

Blimey Lowsey's amber uniform was on sale in every outlet store for five hundred miles. And everyone wanted one. Because everyone else was getting one. Sure it was a fad. But people liked fads. People wanted to buy an amber uniform and blend into the crowd. But in order to do so they needed an amber crowd to blend into. So they marched.

What started out as a FaceHerd page quickly exploded in the style of a teenager's house-party. As more people followed the page, more were obliged to like it.

You had to make a judgement call about your own judgement.

You had to ask yourself; what are the chances I'm right and everyone else is wrong?

You had to make a decision based on the evidence.

Maybe you'd recently lost your job at 'Bagel Shed'. Were you really in a position to contradict the choices that Angelina Jolie was making? Or maybe you had to work three jobs to feed your kids. Did you really have time to question Clint Eastwood's judgement? Wasn't it likely that Clint Eastwood had better judgement than you?

Were you the star of 'Pink Cadillac', 'City Heat' or 'The Rookie'?

No? Well then shut up and make a decision quickly. If you have to lie to yourself, lie to yourself. But pull on your amber pants.

And march with your mouth shut.

There was a war on. A war against the establishment. There were people in orange uniforms telling you this. You knew these people because they'd served you your mochaccinos. They'd measured your feet. They'd arranged your overdraft. Now they worked for MIRAJJE. They knew what was really going on.

Did you?

No. But you could see it. It was up there on the bandwagon rolling past you.

Quick. Don't waste any more time. Run. Catch up to that bandwagon and jump on it while you still have a chance. There's a guy up there with a megaphone.

Have you ever had a megaphone? Have you ever printed your own flyers?

These people knew what they were talking about. If you agreed with them, then you'd know what you were talking about too. You'd have all of the info because the people up there on the bandwagon were showering you with it.

'It won't last'.

I was explaining to Rashid why it wouldn't last as we argued over his disguise.

'Maybe Redstar's bandwagon looks pretty unstoppable when it rolls out of the showroom, but once it gets some dust and bird shit on it people will stop chasing after it'.

I needed to convince Rashid to wear a disguise.

Actually I needed to convince him to wear an anti-disguise.

I needed Rashid to wear something revealing. The reason I needed Rashid to reveal himself was because of the large crowd we'd be in the middle of. Rashid had a difficult face to make out in a crowd, because his face kept changing. I gave him a pair of dark glasses, a baseball cap and a false beard so I could recognise him even as his appearance kept changing beneath it all. I couldn't keep Rashid in our motel room on his own, and I couldn't stay there and keep an eye on him because of the mission. The mission came first.

The large crowd was waiting for the arrival of the bandwagon. I had to create a diversion. Fortunately for me between all of the rallies, the bogus test results, the Flat Earth Societies, invisible prophets, bandwagons, orgies and Elvis abductions I'd totally forgotten that I needed to return our fancy dress costumes. Which meant I could borrow Rashid's.

'You look good in that uniform...'

Smith said this and then turned red. And then turned white.

'...I mean, you finally look good in a disguise. ...You look convincing, is what I meant to say'.

Maybe the reason I looked convincing was that I'd impersonated a lot of police officers in my time. That and my rented Kawasaki. And my flat feet.

I repositioned some crowd control barriers in order to force the assembled news cameras and spectators to move to a vantage point where their line of sight was directly in line with where the sun would set. Then I got back on my Kawasaki, put on my mirrored sunglasses and rode down Sunset Boulevard, to where I could intercept the bandwagon before it rolled into town.

I flashed my lights and waved my arms and the bandwagon eventually came to a halt in front of me.

I boarded the bus and told everyone I was there to protect them from a nearby threat.

Redstar was singing in the rainfall shower.

Smith climbed on, posing as a journalist. I have to admit, she looked even more convincing than I did as a Highway Patrolman. Rashid posed as some looney waiting for a bandwagon. They put on their gas masks as I sealed the bandwagon's airlock and rolled a canister of sleeping gas into the bus.

Blimey Lowsey was already passed out but the other passengers soon joined her. I climbed into the driver's pigskin armchair and drove the bus down Sunset Boulevard. There was no way the news crews and spectators could distinguish the bandwagon's amber paint job from the setting sun. At the last possible moment I veered into an underground car park. To the watching spectators the bandwagon appeared to have disappeared into the sunset.

We offloaded our unconscious passengers onto an HGV LGBT parade float that my fellow officers had impounded that morning near Silver Lake. Then we left our passengers to awaken from their daydreams and drove the bandwagon down the Nixon Tunnel.

You didn't hear this from me, but the Nixon Tunnel is a gateway to another dimension. Stuff disappears down there all the time. If you believe the stories in The Sunday Spartan (and you should) a couple disappeared there in 1999 after pulling over to safely continue an argument over whether the man really knew where he was going or if he was just saying he did. It was also the scene of the vanishing of a bus load of Soviet marathon runners at the LA Olympics in 1984. None of them were ever heard from again. I know because my mentor covered it up. People were told that the Soviets had defected. They'd gone on the run.

The Nixon Tunnel had developed such a reputation that drivers routinely described periods of lost time, strange hallucinations and feelings of disorientation after spending extended periods of time in smog and traffic. Yep, the Nixon Tunnel was a real mystery.

I parked up and escorted Smith and Rashid to a safe distance. Then we watched the howling, swirling Nixon Tunnel Vortex descend and flush Redstar's bandwagon into an alternate reality. Smith seemed impressed with my disappearing of the bandwagon; Smith seemed to be giving me a lot of the credit. If you know what 'fawning' means, that's how she was behaving. I tried not to let my head swell and tried to explain what had just happened;

'...You know how a toilet works?'

Still, I felt a little anxious. We'd only recently come through a plot hole. These continuity errors were appearing far more frequently than usual. But I was hopeful that the disappearance of the bandwagon would at least disrupt the spread of Redstar's cult.

And buy me some more time with the Agency.

Time was not on my side. No it wasn't.

The bandwagon reappeared two hours later. Above the Hollywood sign. Which it promptly flattened. We stood there with everyone else, staring. People were on their knees praying to the bandwagon or the Hollywood sign or both. You could see people wailing and tearing at their ripped jeans. You could see Matt Damon in tears.

'It would appear that of the many things you know about the Nixon Tunnel Vortex, how it works isn't one of them'.

This was Smith teasing me in broken English.

'I said it works like a toilet. I just didn't expect Hollywood to be at the end of the sewer. If everything that disappears down the Nixon tunnel ends up here then Hollywood should be littered with damaged trash ...I just can't explain it'.

'Strange that you're not panicking more'.

I guessed this was more teasing.

I guessed this was Smith worrying that I was worrying about the bandwagon reappearing like this. Smith was just trying to make me feel better. But it wasn't working.

'Their magic trick, their bullshit, was better than mine'.

People were arriving by the bus load and everyone kept using the word miracle. But I wanted to get out of The Big Orange. I wanted to get into a dark room and have a lie down. Unfortunately I still had a job to do.

Maybe it was because Smith could tell what I was thinking.

Or maybe it was because I was telling her what I was thinking;

'This pretty much wins the game for Redstar'.

Or maybe Smith had learnt that I was a creature of habit.

Either way, it was Smith who put her arm around my shoulder, turned me away from Hollywood and suggested we go for a Happy Meal.

I sat in silence in the restaurant. Because my mouth was full. And because I was feeling utterly dejected. Smith kept trying to change the subject. But what was the point in being the only people *not* talking about the bandwagon? If it had stayed disappeared I'd have been happy not to talk about it; my job was to not talk about continuity errors. But there didn't seem much point any longer. Each time we saw a TV screen the bandwagon was on it.

The news cut to some Dickie surrogate who was frantically searching through the denialist's bag of dirty tricks he'd been handed;

'That wasn't a real bandwagon. It was a papier-mâché model! It was a hoax! I saw them building the papier-mâché bandwagon! It was James Cameron! And the Governator!'

New Dickie's number one problem was that the bandwagon's reappearance had validated what Redstar's Blisciples had been shouting at his predecessor all along.

If it was a magic trick then it had been a very convincing one.

And people tended to fall for very convincing magic tricks.

Redstar's bandwagon had crushed the Hollywood sign. And all of our hard work.

We'd gone to a lot of trouble injecting low fat jam into our fake SOOPA and fiddling the test results, but it was just like the Shroud; people only accepted your bogus results if they were in line with what they wanted to believe in. I feared that no matter what we did to debunk the SOOPA people would still believe Redstar. Because the thing people believed in now *was Redstar*. The SOOPA wasn't our target any longer. Our target had to be Chuck.

'We have to play the man, not the jam jar. If we can make people doubt Redstar, we can make them doubt the SOOPA'.

I told Smith. And Smith agreed. She told me;

'If we stop people believing in Redstar they'll stop believing in the jam jar'.

I told her I knew this because I'd just told her that.

If we could show everyone the real Norman Grinder then it wouldn't take much to put a halt to Chuck Redstar's bandwagon. If you got enough tears out of a clown their make-up started to run. Then people started to find the clown frightening.

And people didn't like frightening clowns.

We headed for Timberlake. As in; '⊗🎱💀! you Tim-ber-lake'.

As in; the town where Norman Grinder had spent his childhood.

We were in Timberlake trying to find something, or someone, to discredit Redstar.

We arrived at the old Grinder place. I rang the bell and the old Grinder wife came to the door in her dressing gown and her puffy jacket. I told Mrs Grinder that my name was Colin Jekyll and that Norman had been picked out of a hat of Playboy Magazine subscribers and won a celebrity G-string. I asked Mrs Grinder if her husband was in? If we could maybe take some photos of him accepting his prize? Mrs Grinder rolled her eyes;

'You can come in. But you must think I'm a damn fool if you reckon I believe your name is Colin Jekyll. I've seen you before. Your name is Madrid. Like in Europe'.

This caught me off guard. I wasn't even wearing my Dr Madrid disguise.

'I felt sorry for you, you being one of the few people Norman ever made to look more foolish than himself, but if you're looking for revenge then I ain't interested'.

The old Grinder place had worn carpet. A unique odour from the fridge that I couldn't identify. And posters of Belinda Carlisle and Debbie Gibson from c.1987.

Mrs Grinder made us some coffee that I couldn't drink and we chatted about things.

Mostly; Norman Grinder and what a disappointment he'd been as a husband.

Mrs Grinder explained how Norm had left her for Chuck Redstar in much the same way as Obi Wan Kenobi had explained to Luke Skywalker about his absentee father.

But Mrs Grinder couldn't tell us why Norm had turned to the dark side; she wouldn't tell us about the tragedy that had transformed Norm into a helmet named Chuck. She would only say that something had happened, something that had meant Chuck simply couldn't be Norman any longer. So he'd left.

Mrs Redstar was a forgiving woman. But she hadn't forgiven her husband;

'Being a fool ain't something you need to forgive. I'd never find the time to forgive every fool I ever met in this life. I just stopped caring about Norm the same time he stopped caring about me. We just weren't put on this Earth to care about each other'.

I wanted to tell her that I understood. And that it was a bit rude not to offer your guests a choice of beverage. But she cut me off;

'I'm sorry but I can't tell you anything more'.

'Because you still have a lot of affection for Norman?'

Asked Smith.

'Partly, yes. ...But mostly because he paid me not to talk'.

We left soon after that. We argued over the radio and whether Redstar was just a fool or a dangerous fool and whether one type of fool could be forgiven but not the other.

Then Smith and Rashid argued because Smith had told Rashid he was a dangerous fool and this was harsh on a seven-year-old and he threw a tantrum.

I said; 'There there'.

And; 'Why don't we put on that audiobook you like?'

And this calmed Rashid down sufficiently that he went all middle-aged and sombre.

We drove back to LA. And to Redstar.

But we were no better off than when we'd left.

17. Self adjustment

All of a sudden there was a shout and a crash.

Our motel room door flew off of its hinges and someone I vaguely recognised fell onto the floor with a large sheepskin-bound book in his hands. Maxwell Self stepped over his unwanted assistant, picked up the book and threw it at me.

It was a copy of The Principles of Reality Enforcement. The rulebook.

Self slapped me on the back;

'Remember this chap? You told me you always stuck to it you lying bugger. ...Pretty silly idea chap, flushing that bandwagon down a plot hole. Who knows where the crap we flush down those things comes out? Don't you know that's how a Norwegian yacht ended up in the middle of a desert? I wouldn't even expect such a poor effort from young Freddy here'.

He threw Ian a look that said; 'I loathe you'.

Then he looked Smith up and down as Ian set to work refitting our door to its hinges.

He needed to do that before he could close it again. Before Self could lock us all in.

'The bad news is the top brass have been sitting on their hands as usual, while all hell's been breaking loose, while you've been romping all over the shop with your lovely scratchie here. ...The good news is they've been persuaded to take a harder line with this Charlie and his cult. We're not going to be taking the diplomatic route any longer'.

I braced myself for some shitty news.

'I've come to take over from you chap'.

Self refused to stay in our motel room a moment longer than necessary and suggested I'd been bringing the Agency into disrepute by not availing myself of better quality accommodation. Even though I'd booked into the motel as Colin Jekyll.

An hour later we were sitting (uncomfortably) in the recently (and quite superfluously) refurbished Spielberg Suite at the Chateau Walmart in downtown LA.

Sure, sure, I was sitting uncomfortably, but I'd been relieved to get out of the motel. Because Rashid was on his way back from the hardware store. Rashid didn't like sharing motel rooms with his friends, let alone his enemies. I'd agreed that Rashid could get out of our motel room for a couple of hours on two conditions; i) he kept his anti-disguise on at all times and ii) he stopped at a hardware store and picked me up an electric McGuffin.

Self had no idea that my recent flouting of the rulebook had extended to sparing Rashid's life. I had no doubt he would combust Rashid without a second thought.

Yep, I'd *been* relieved. And then Smith had told me that she'd sent Rashid a text to let him know that we'd moved to the Chateau Walmart.

That revelation had made me want to check out. But the door to our suite was locked, so I just sat and listened to Self and tried to come up with a way out of this mess that I'd gotten us into;

'You could've told us what a mess you were getting into chap. This bloody jam jar's undermined everyone. People are fighting. And we don't want people fighting. Buying guns and ammo yes, but fighting, no'.

Self had taken his Mont Blanc ruler and crayon to a map of our troubles and traced a hard line from Redstar's embassy in LA all the way back to ⊗●☡!ling Timberlake. That was where Self and Ian had been before he'd thrown his scratchie through our motel room door. Self had been following us. And he'd brought back a souvenir to prove it.

Mrs Grinder was in the suite next to ours.

But I didn't think she was enjoying her stay.

Because she was handcuffed to the bathroom radiator.

The reason Mrs Grinder was handcuffed in the bathroom was; acoustics.

Also, it was small and damp and had no windows and was the closest Self could come to recreating the ambience of Guantanamo Bay in the Chateau Walmart.

Self was torturing Mrs Grinder with terrible cover versions. We listened to Celine Dion slaughtering 'You Shook Me All Night Long' and Take That's desecration of 'Smells Like Teen Spirit'. This is what's known in the business as 'butchering'.

Self sat on the toilet and looked me in the eye;

'Grinder was an academic, a sceptic. From what I could make out between her screams Mrs Grinder's husband spent his time trying to debunk the unexplained. Well you don't need me to tell you that he'd become rather irritable once he realised people would rather believe the lies in the yellow press than pay any attention to his research papers'.

Self didn't mention how we were responsible for the

lies in the yellow press.

I guess he didn't need to tell me.

'This Charlie Redstar realised people were too busy watching celebrities on ghost hunting shows to read his research papers. Well, if you can't beat them you join them chap. So our Charlie decided he'd create a miracle'.

You might have read about it in the Sunday Spartan.

The miracle Redstar created was called Phil's Hole.

It's what's known in hole circles as a 'bottomless pit'.

On November 7th 2000 a man named Phil Mein called into the Pedestrian FM 'Morning Shit-Shoot' and claimed that a hole of immeasurable depth had been discovered just outside of Timberlake. The reason Phil knew the hole was of immeasurable depth was because he'd tried to measure it with some string tied to an old Star Wars figure. But he'd run out of string after three thousand feet.

The other thing Phil claimed was that his hole was able to give life to inanimate animal icons. This was because when Phil reeled in his string his (mint condition) Chewbacca figurine had been replaced by a hot and bothered rat (v.poor condition).

People quickly concluded that the bottomless hole most likely led straight to hell.

And so for the second time in its history, the town of ⊛💣☠!ing Timberlake became synonymous with the name 'Hell Hole'.

Things had gotten a bit heated after that. There were allegations of negligent drilling against the local Kwik'n Save Mining Co. The Kwik'n Save Mining Co. (not to be confused with the marginally less negligent Kwik'n Safe Mining Co.) had drilled straight into hell.

The US military, NASA and the Mormons arrived to tackle the devil. They knew the devil was down there because Phil had lowered a microphone into the Hell Hole and recorded the tormented screams of the damned. But when it turned out to be just a Celine Dion cover version of The Damned people smelled a rat. And not one that had been miraculously transubstantiated from a plastic Chewbacca.

As the BSN started shipping replica holes a former colleague of Phil's phoned the Global Probe to expose the Hell Hole as a hoax.

And to expose Phil Mein as none other than Norman Grinder.

Phil's sceptical old colleague could prove all of this. Because Phil had given his agent and the Sales Pastor at BSN his phone number and address at the old Grinder place.

Phil had claimed his hole was proof of the existence of hell.

But it wasn't.

Phil had to get the hell out of Hell Hole quick. He had to change his name, twice. And move to Gladys. Where, in a plot twist Weird Norm could never have seen coming, he discovered a genuine 'miracle'...

Now that Self had evidence of Redstar's hoaxing chained to the bathroom radiator the Agency had everything it needed to debunk Redstar. All we needed to do was give people the facts about Redstar and they'd invent their own truth about the amber jam jar. They wouldn't be able to trust ~~Redstar's~~ Weird Norm's truth any longer.

Just between you and me, I was a bit surprised at myself for not having been more forceful with Mrs Grinder. For not having followed the rulebook.

I was a bit surprised at Smith too. Smith just sat there silently. Where were her fair and balanced arguments? Why wasn't she challenging Self's truth the way she had mine? It had to be for one of two reasons. Either I'd slowly persuaded her of the dangers of the truth over our past few weeks together. Or it was the gun Self was holding to her head.

He had the gun to my head too. Because this was Lee Harvey Oswald's magic bullet gun that Self had stolen from the Whitewash Museum. Reality enforcers had started raiding the Whitewash Museum when the armoury had run out of spontaneous human combustors.

There were a lot of enforcers out in the field, working to tackle their new arch-enemy; MIRAJJE. Having an arch-enemy was something that a lot of people were getting very excited about. Some chaps had been waiting a long time for an arch-enemy. The trouble was, the more the Agency turned its focus on the SOOPA the fewer enforcers were available to combat the day to day continuity errors and so more and more started coming to light.

There was the panic in Beijing when the Mars Rabbit touched down on the red planet and found a giant 'x' on the surface. And a chest full of Confederate gold buried beneath.

There was the panic in Mecca when the hidden tomb of a long lost imam was finally discovered. With an open case of beer, half a dozen packets of pork scratchings and a fruit machine inside it. The veil hadn't been lifted so much as ripped off. The mystery of the world was finally being revealed. All of the things that were hard to understand. That were beyond belief. All of the 'miracles' that were no longer being adjusted.

We'd always feared this moment. The panic on the streets. The total loss of composure. The loosening grip on reality. And that was just the news reporters.

These guys were more accustomed to standing across the road from some faceless building for hours on end. They simply couldn't cope with all of the weird shit that started happening. News anchors were torn between reporters competing for their attention by shouting or crying or wetting themselves. Who did you go to when

Warren Terror was broadcasting live from Sunderland where hundreds of people had vanished without warning but Warren Drugs was being chased by a poltergeist through Birmingham?

There were lions in Essex!

Reporters finished their reports or fainted and then it was back to the studio and an anchorman interviewing an empty seat where moments earlier an expert had been sitting before running from the studio. It wasn't fair on these experts. They shouldn't have had to explain things that couldn't be explained. That was our job.

But we were letting the side down.

Self saw all of this as justification for his hard-line.

Self saw his hard-line as justification for the gun he had on us. But this was no movie. He wasn't about to run through his plan so we could stop him. He'd given us his plan so we could carry it out for him while he held a gun to our heads. Self wasn't interested in living out the super-villain's fantasy. Self was an old school Reality Enforcer. He was all about the answers. No-one had any. But everyone needed some. So he was going to make some up.

Self was all about the common good. The big fat noble lie;

'We'll create a conspiracy and place Redstar at the centre of it. Then he'll be assassinated. The Office of Confessions are already casting for the role of 'cult member looking for revenge".

For some reason I was reminded of Tinkerbelle. I felt a bit sick, a bit jet-lagged;

'And the people in the MIRAJJE cult?'

Self seemed confused by my apparent confusion;

'Well, they'll be in the embassy. So, things should just work themselves out when it's pulled down shouldn't they?'

'You're not working in the Department of Health anymore. If you condemn dozens of people to death someone's going to start asking questions. ...And we're not hired assassins'.

'You assassinated that bally towelhead didn't you?'

Somewhere on TV a reporter vied for an anchorman's attention; standing outside the remains of the Screw-It hardware store as a green giant emerged from under the rubble of hanging baskets and scented candles and pre-packed sacks of rubble. The ogre was covered in green paint (Woodland Fern 3) but I could still recognise him. And so could Self.

It was that bally towelhead.

The report cut to some phoned footage of Rashid standing at a counter with an oil-fired McGuffin (and not the electric one I'd asked for). The shakycam shook nervously as a herd of Blisciples marched in and purchased cans of red, yellow and green paint. The ~~clerk~~ screenwriter serving Rashid asked the Blisciples what they needed all of the paint for.

'We're going to throw a rainbow all over the mosque on L. Ron Hubbard Way. Because they've been spraying black paint over Blimey's billboards for her new single 'Without my clothes".

I think I mentioned before, about Rashid's mood swings?

Well he looked like a very angry young man as he paid for the McGuffin and some heavy chains (an impulse purchase), then sprinted ahead of the Blisciples, pulled off his anti-disguise (in order to avoid being identified) and chained himself to the gates of the mosque.

'You should cover yourselves! You shame your parents!'

Rashid was all about the shame.

'You're vindicating centuries of repression!'

The Blisciples were all about the blame.

'If you want to get to this mosque you'll have to get past me! I am a human shield!'

A Blisciple threw her can of Woodland Fern 3 all over him.

The reason I'd asked for an electric McGuffin was because oil-fired McGuffins are notoriously unstable. Oil-fired McGuffins have been known to prematurely detonate if you accidentally drop the flux-capacitor on its widget. Rashid strained against his chains and hurled his McGuffin in the direction of the Blisciples. But this wasn't a murderous act. I don't think Rashid even knew what a McGuffin is used for. The McGuffin ricocheted off of a skip full of unsold soybean foam insulation and bounced into the hardware store car park.

And then the McGuffin exploded.

The force of the blast brought down an entire section of the hardware store roof. Fortunately it was the scaffolding section and so everyone escaped unharmed. The nearest Blisciples were thrown clear by the force of the blast and landed safely in the skip full of unwanted organic foam insulation. Only Rashid felt the full force of his miscalculated risk. The bits of mosque that fell on top of Rashid didn't leave a scratch on him of course. But once he'd managed to claw his way out from under the rubble he looked very angry. And fat. And green. And this was Hollywood. So everyone publicly applauded and secretly bemoaned the fact that a Puerto Rican had gotten the plum (and plump) role of the Incredible Hulk.

Of course Self was furious. Not because of the mosque so much. This was the guy who'd destroyed Mohammed's beard after all. No, Self was furious with *me*.

Because of the whole betrayal thing.

I'd never seen Self so angry.

Apart from that time when the Agency's stores had run out of yellow copy paper.

Oh and that time when there was a knock on our hotel suite door and there stood Rashid, covered in green paint and weighing twenty stone.

Self had Ian cover Rashid with one of the last few spontaneous human combustors that hadn't run dry already.

(In case you're wondering, Agency-issued spontaneous human combustors are battery powered. Although you can keep one running if you know how to hook it up to an electric McGuffin. You can hook it up to an oil-fired McGuffin of course, if you want to take your life into your own hands. But Self just wanted to take Rashid's life into his.)

Self took everyone out for a drive. It was all very De Niro; driving along with Rashid in the boot of Self's hired VW Vagrant begging for his life.

Maybe some people die harder than others, but everyone has their limits.

Everyone except Self. Self didn't have any limits. He had a spontaneous human combustor. And he was going to use it to adjust the Rashid problem.

I had to stop Self.

The problem was, I was handcuffed to the back door, and to Smith.

Smith was handcuffed to Ian. Ian wasn't handcuffed to anyone else though, Ian needed a free hand so he could keep his gun on both of us as I tried to convince Self not to take Rashid into the woods and set him on fire.

Just listen to my Self persuasion;

'This isn't what I was talked into when I joined up. You say you've people's best interests at heart. But this is all about self-interest. This isn't right'.

Maybe it came from the heart, but this speech was all about stalling the inevitable.

I'd raised my voice. Because I needed to get Self's attention. I had to take him on a diversion from the woods or waste-ground or harbour or wherever he was going to dump Rashid. I had to hit Self with my filibuster, to get into that of stream of consciousness politicians enter when they repeat your opinions back to you.

It's important to sound like you believe what you're saying.

But it's more important not to pause for breath and let someone else speak.

'This isn't a noble lie. Rashid isn't a threat to anyone anymore. He's been good as gold since he tried to blow up that plane. And it isn't our job to get him out of our world. It's our job to bring him back in. People can change, some more than others. Sure, sure; things were better in the good old days. But the past is the past. We need to think about the future!'

The point I was trying to make was; our job was to maintain the status quo, but you had to recognise that once the status quo had been made redundant, so had you.

I could see Self's knuckles whitening around the steering wheel.

He couldn't concentrate on the road with all of the shouting in the back.

'It distresses me chap, to hear you talk like this. I have been thinking about the future. And this panic just proves that we need stronger knowledge management. People don't know what's best chap, they don't know about the greater good and such'.

I wanted to accuse Self of totalitarianism.

But it's not easy accusing someone of totalitarianism when you're shouting.

Go on, try it. Try shouting 'totalitarianism'.

I lowered my voice and tried to reason with Self instead;

'Maybe people would be better off in a world where it's ok for things to be a bit confusing and unpredictable sometimes. And maybe to get there they'll have to panic a bit. But eventually they'll start asking themselves; 'what the hell was I panicking about?' By hiding the truth we just force people into the arms of chumps like Redstar'.

Maybe there's no way you could possibly know this,

but we'd pulled off of the main road while I'd been giving this speech.

Maybe you're just not seeing it, but Self was dragging Rashid into a clearing in the woods and aiming his spontaneous human combustor at him.

'If some of these miracles were allowed to slip through then maybe people could learn to live with the unfamiliar and the unexplained'.

I kept on moving my lips. But I dared not move anything else. Ian had his magic bullet gun pressed against Smith's temple. And mine.

Self cocked his combustor;

'Well... That's not really the direction the rest of us are headed in chap. It's down to us you know, to adjust other people's problems'.

I had my heart in my mouth.

Self had his finger on the trigger;

'Like your friend here. He just isn't normal'.

Maybe you're finding it hard to picture; the spontaneous combustion of a fellow human being. Maybe you'd rather not know the truth. Well don't worry.

I couldn't give you the whole truth even if I wanted to.

That's because when Self pulled the trigger and Rashid went up in flames he suddenly developed the physique of some stunt double or inadvertently steroid-enhanced Olympian, sprinted through a line of fruit and nut trees and disappeared from sight.

You couldn't tell what was beyond the fruit and nut trees, unless you ran through them. Then you could tell that there was a cliff beyond them.

By the time we'd discovered the cliff we could only just make out the fireball as it landed in the river below.

Unfortunately we were in California and the river had been dry for many years.

Smith and I surrendered our counterfeit passports and travel irons to Self and headed for the nearest Happy Meal.

Ian followed us, just in case we 'tried anything stupid'.

Although he didn't stop us from walking into McDonalds.

You don't need me to tell you that we'd lost our appetite. But the Happy Meal had never really been about nutrition for me; I paid no more attention to where it had come from than where it was headed. But standing in the queue and inhaling the charred fumes from the badly burnt burgers I found I couldn't shake the image of Rashid being combusted. Of being grilled. I reached for my loyalty card. It was hot in the restaurant. I was sweating almost as much as the lightly greased young girl serving me.

'I don't know how to say this... There was a complication...'

The sweat was pouring off of the young girl's face;

'We're only able to serve fillet-o-fish right now'.

People started wailing and moaning. People started reaching for the McSackcloths and Ashes. I explained that I'd lost my appetite and my server wiped a tear away and touched my hand softly. I took a complimentary thick-shake and joined Smith. I explained the situation but she already knew. Because of the truck driver next to her screaming;

'☺💣☠!fish?!☺💣☠! fish?!'

I tried to count backwards from ten as I walked down a staircase to my happy place but everything was flames and screams and for those reasons I couldn't calm down at all.

Because of Black Saturday.

'I was born in a fire in 1980. In the week they discovered the Rubik's Cube. On the day they invented the Kardashians. I was seven. An only child. And an orphan to boot. And my pants were on fire. In fact my pants never went out'.

'What are you talking about?'

Had I said all of that out loud? Judging by the constipated expression on Smith's face, I had. Judging by the expression on Smith's face, she'd either accidentally ingested some McNuggets, or she thought I was schizophrenic. Or nuts. Because of my multiple identities. My unreliable histories. You know, because of all the lying about my past.

Sorry about that. Sometimes the training just takes over. You end up ret-conning your own history. You adjust your memories. Repress your tragedies. Use a disguise.

But who had I been trying to kid?

Myself. I'd been trying to kid myself. I'd been doing it for years, but my fake past was of no use to me any longer, because the part of me that had been so comfortable with hiding the truth for so long, well, that part of me had changed its mind.

'Because of you'.

'Because of me?' asked Smith, a bit of colour returning to her face.

'The part of me that was so good at keeping the truth from others, it's the part you've been chipping away at. It's the part of me that was good at keeping the truth from myself'.

I went to live in the orphanage after Black Saturday. The orphanage was run by my aunt and uncle. I was their only orphan, but they did their best to recreate the ambience of an authentic Dickensian workhouse for me. Those stairs I leapt off didn't even have carpet.

I wasn't an orphan to start with. But I am one now. Because my dad was a dreamer. He needed a Reality Enforcer. Dad didn't agree with the consensus reality on house fires.

The problem with dad was that he believed in miracles. I can still hear him now, as he ran back into the house as it burned down, chasing after me, with mum chasing after him;

'⊗🎳☠!fish?!⊗🎳☠! fish?!'

It was nobody's fault, the fire. My electric blanket just spontaneously combusted. But I couldn't just leave my goldfish on the boil could I? I had an affinity with animals.

The headlines were wrong, as usual. The papers reckoned my parents had died because I'd tried to rescue my goldfish from the fire. But my parents had died because of Peter Principle. Some part-time pen pusher who worked for the council.

'It was a million to one chance'.

That's what the fireman had said. It was a freak accident. Because of the street signs.

The firemen had heard the alarm bells ringing. But they'd gone to the wrong address.

They'd arrived at 7 Principle Mews and dumped 300 gallons of water down the wrong chimney (much to the irritation of the family sitting in front of the telly eating dinner and watching The Towering Inferno).

'It's just, unbelievable'.

That's what the fireman had said.

But it wasn't. It was very easy to believe. Peter Principle was just lazy. And self-absorbed. That's why he'd named eleven new streets after himself. It was easier to copy Principle Road to create Principle Avenue, and Principle Close, and Principle Gardens. Principle Gardens. That's where we lived. 7 Principle Gardens.

Not 7 Principle Mews.

I guess it was around this time that my seven-year-old self decided the unbelievable truth was best kept hidden. It had taken thirty years, but it had all finally come to the surface because of the people being burned alive, and the fish. That and the epiphany I'd had as I tried to save Rashid's life. It turned out I believed what I was saying. Because of Smith. It seemed my days of burying other people's heads in the sand were over, and so were my own. My imagination had created a bunch of memories that I'd never shared with my parents.

I only wished that I had.

It was a real tragedy. My parents dying in that fire.

And my taping over my unhappy childhood with old episodes of Family Ties and Happy Days.

But I had to stop kidding myself that I was better off without the ugly truth.

I had to face up to the ugly truth and get over it. Also, I had to stop brainwashing others, kidding myself that I'd been doing other people a favour.

I had to face more hard truths than anyone should ever have to in a McDonalds.

I didn't want to follow orders anymore. I had to forgive myself for following orders.

The Agency was no good for me.

Also, the Agency wasn't especially good for other people.

Smith and I finished our drinks and stood up. Now that we were back on our feet we needed to finish this Redstar situation once and for all. But first we needed to stop Self. And at some point, probably after we'd had a short break, we'd need to stop the Agency.

Smith held the door open for me, and then she held out her hand;

'I tell you what, once we're done, you quit the Agency, and I'll get you a job at the Spartan. Then we can expose all sorts of miracles; I mean, you must know where the good ones are buried. ...And then we can still be partners'.

I picked the lock of a 5 door Honda Tranquillo that had been abandoned in the queue for the drive-thru, opened the passenger door for Smith and told her she had herself a deal.

Then I picked the lock of a taxi parked across the street and left the door open for Ian so he could follow us back to the hotel. At a discreet distance.

18. Rumour Grenades

Ring... Ring... No-one was answering the phones.

Ring... Ring... Ring... You get the picture.

There were two hundred worn out desks and two hundred worn out phones for two hundred worn out reality enforcers at the Agency. But everyone was out of the office.

Trying to tackle their new arch-enemy; MIRAJJE.

No-one was answering the phones because George and Stevens were on an encrypted conference call; telling us how they'd just finished redacting forty thousand copies of the Global Probe due to an outbreak of plagiarism. This was because the Global Probe had recently run a true story writing competition in an effort to recruit some cheap journalists.

Keith Ahoy had written in about the time he'd had to ditch his crimson hang-glider in the sea off of Grenada and how he'd spent the next five days clinging to a piece of old rubbish that had floated by.

Kevin Ahoy wrote in about the time he ditched his maroon hang-glider in the sea near Granada and then spent 127 hours clinging to a pallet of shipwrecked 'Roy Chancy, PCSO' DVDs. It was basically the same true story, with a different twist at the end.

Next up was a reboot of the winner of the 1993 Academy Award for Best Picture.

Hugo Posture (star of 'My Daughter's Dream' and 'South West Sincerity') had become the first A-list celebrity to be killed by a robot.

Posture had been campaigning against workers' jobs being lost at a Viagrador factory in Brazil when a crazed automaton on the assembly line had hit him on the head repeatedly and pushed him onto the rejects conveyor that led to the grinding pit.

To be fair to the robot, Posture had been asked not to touch anything, but he'd kept on pushing that robot's buttons.

George and Stevens had to reboot 'My Daughter's Dream' and 'South West Sincerity' so they could superimpose a multicultural Posture impersonator over the original.

Posture was a popular guy. He needed replacing.

You'd think people would notice, but they don't.

You didn't notice when the Agency replaced Paul McCartney did you?

Though Renee Zellweger, fair enough, you spotted that one.

The Agency didn't want people to start worrying about being killed by robots. People had enough to worry about. The thing that people were worrying about most was; what the hell was going on?

'The war has started'.

We were sitting in the Chateau Walmart with a gun to

our heads, trying to enjoy the soon to be deleted theatrical version of 'South West Sincerity'. Eventually there'd be nothing left on TV you could believe in. Eventually there'd be no way to suspend your disbelief.

Self was only half-right, about the war.

The war had started a long time ago.

It was more accurate to say that the ceasefire had ended.

And Self didn't want to take the diplomatic route any longer.

Redstar had rewritten the consensus reality. Now pastors and professors were fighting for Redstar's attention like a couple of peacocks wrestling over a female. They needed a theory to fit Redstar's new reality. They needed explanations for the amber jam jar and the bandwagon that wouldn't contradict their existing back stories. And they needed to make them sound convincing. The problem was, each time they invented an answer they found that their explanations were becoming more and more complex and less and less convincing.

Because people wanted simple answers.

Unfortunately the church had a script that was in need of an expensive reboot and the nit-pickers in the science mob had no imagination. They didn't know how to jump to a conclusion, they had to mess around with the hypothesis and the tests and the results first. But you couldn't test the hypothesis because there was nothing to test and that meant you couldn't get a result. And these guys were in the results business.

All these guys could do was argue over their explanations for the Martian gold and the bandwagon. Someone had to be right. And someone had to be wrong. The way you could tell who was right was; they agreed with more people than their opponent did. It wasn't important that people agreed with your results, only that your results agreed with people.

People like Chuck Redstar.

No-one was disputing that Redstar's bandwagon had materialised out of thin air and landed on the Hollywood sign. It had been there for all to see. But explaining *why* it had landed on the Hollywood sign, understanding why the bandwagon had travelled to Hollywood in the first place, that was different. The interpretation of the evidence, well it depended on who was doing the interpreting.

The thing about an amber bandwagon on the Hollywood sign was; it was quite an objective object. The thing about noted astral-biologist Christopher Caravan's assertion that this was the result of an inter-dimensional wormhole anomaly was; it was quite a subjective subject. One man's Caravan Theory was just another man's Fettuccini Paradox.

There were a lot of angry exchanges in the letters page of 'Good Scientist'. Nerdy bickering infected articles in Human Nature, Scientific Scientologist and MAD magazine. Traditionalists argued that 'Amber Jam Jars' and 'Damned Bandwagons' were not suitable topics for discussion. You didn't explain the irrational and the incredible; you swept them under the carpet where they belonged.

But once the publishers of Human Nature and Mad Scientist saw their circulation figures doubling they ignored tradition. It was easy; you just stopped printing the letters page.

You changed your typeface to 'Tabloid' and offered readers the chance to win a vintage replica 'Hell Hole'.

Meanwhile The Holy Times and Unscientific Scientologist saw their sales plummet. The church needed to offer you better explanations than the ones you were getting from your lab geeks. And they had to offer you better explanations than the ones in their script.

They needed to re-master the special effects. And then throw in some new ones.

The next month every religious periodical on the

newsstand had some spurious explanation for some new continuity error. And a coupon for a free Hot Wheels Bandwagon.

Nerd journals and holy newsletters outsold celebrity magazines for the first time since the nineteen twenties. People wanted to get their hands on the free bandwagon toys. People wanted to get their hands on the truth. The fact that the truth in one publication contradicted the truth in another didn't matter. People were just as confused about things as the journals and newsletters were, but they could still believe what they were reading because the journals and newsletters kept telling them that they agreed with Redstar.

Which meant that if you agreed with Redstar then they agreed with you.

And all of your friends who'd been telling you that they agreed with Redstar too.

Everyone agreed; they needed to figure out who agreed with Redstar the most.

And so, after a brief bidding war Anne Punter presided over the first televised 'Pseudo-Scientific Multi-Faith Smack-down!'

MSG News' largest audience in a generation kept half an eye on proceedings as one by one Jewish doctors, Atheist professors, Buddhist biochemists and celebrity lab assistants jumped into the ring at the Trump Taj Mahal and started flinging experiments at one another.

Maybe you caught Christopher Caravan's attempt to make the Hollywood sign disappear via a device that he referred to as an inter-dimensional wormhole facilitator and you and I would call 'a big curtain'. Or maybe you caught Dr Aldo Fettuccini's attempt to prove his paradox by spontaneously big-banging a bandwagon out of a herd of Aberdeen Angus, five hundred gallons of linseed oil and three-dozen large eggs.

Or maybe you didn't.

When Caravan claimed that a recent typhoon of four-eyed flying fish was linked to Global Warming he was immediately challenged by Fettuccini who claimed the four-eyed flying fish were in fact evidence of the exact opposite. The previous two months had seen the most severe flying fish storms since records began, but if you looked back further, before the records began, you'd see that the previous peak in four-eyed fish storms had been in 6000BC, and so in fact these four-eyed flying fish were evidence of an impending ice age.

The problem was, each fishy experiment conducted in the MSG news studios produced two totally different results; one to prove Caravan's theory and one to prove Fettuccini's. The problem was, you could pretty much draw any conclusion you wanted to from a cloud of four-eyed flying fish.

The only thing these experiments proved was that these experiments weren't proof of anything. Or that they were proof of everything. Like I said, it depended on whether you spoke to the guy who designed the experiment or the one trying to pull it to pieces.

The only people who didn't come out of all of this looking foolish were the physicists.

Physics stayed out of it.

They knew it wasn't worth the trouble; spending years coming up with a theory, then realising it couldn't explain gravity, the ending of 'Lost', or how gold is made.

Even Da Vinci had known how gold was made. He'd just been very badly decoded.

The bad news was that the situation was out of control. The good news was that 'out of control' was the best possible situation to chuck a rumour grenade into.

How to chuck a rumour grenade is part of every scratch-starter's basic training. Throw a rumour grenade into someone's past and it makes a real mess of their history. You get anecdotes and memories all twisted and mutilated and mixed up all over the place. You don't know what's true and what's not. Some people call it mudslinging. You just keep slinging mud until your target's past is completely muddied.

Take a moment if you want to write some notes in the margin about how I'd thrown a rumour grenade into my own past. But understand that I didn't have time for navel-gazing. I was busy inserting the fuse into the grenade we were going to chuck at Chuck.

This was one of those second generation rumour grenades you haven't heard of. It was full of AI and would have no trouble in dropping Redstar back into the Hell Hole. I just needed to feed my grenade some recently doctored photos of Phil Mein and it would throw up a whole mess of ret-conned proof that Redstar had been behind all manner of hoaxes.

Think of my rumour grenade as being like that bogus photo of the guy stood on the roof of the World Trade Centre as the first plane hit. You took an old holiday photo and cropped Mrs Grinder out and then you digitally framed Chuck within a bottomless pit.

This is what you call misinformation but people in the know call disinformation. They're synonyms. But they shouldn't be. The second volume of Redstar's diaries? The diaries you read where Chuck confessed to being Phil Mein? To creating the hoax? You know, those hoaxed diaries about the hoax? That's disinformation right there.

I sat down at the Spielberg Suite's writing bureau with a cold chisel, a pair of pliers, some black and blue wires and one red one to cut in case of emergency, and an old Commodore 64 with a modem. This was enough to make a rudimentary rumour IED.

Rumour grenades cost you next to nothing. You just needed a good throwing arm and access to the internet. Then you sent your rumour out into the virtual world and let it fend for itself. You didn't need to worry about whether your rumour would make it. There were your bloggers and your vloggers, your shock jocks and your Twitter players all queuing up to feed your rumour for you. Once you had a few people on board with your rumour it was just a matter of watching it snowball.

The more who have believed, the more who will believe.

People tend to assume that other people aren't as lazy as they are. That other people take the time to check their facts. Soon enough your rumour is part of the consensus reality. Whether it's true or not doesn't matter. For example:

'The US President has announced plans to convert more gas-guzzling Humvees into subsidised battery powered ambulances'.

Maybe this sounds innocent enough to begin with, but by the time the shock jock has relayed the blog post that relayed the tweet, the rumour has been simplified to:

'The US President is a French Muslim'.

The idea here is that people prefer brevity. And lies.

The Agency just had to make sure their lies were more convincing than Redstar's.

All the time I was busy cutting and pasting the rumour grenade together I could see the upholstered corner of our hotel suite out of the corner of my eye and Self taking Smith to one side and whispering a lot. This was exactly the kind of behaviour I'd expected from Self.

Which was why I'd hung Mr Freedom in that corner of the room.

During an incident which can only honestly be described as an outrageous coincidence I'd bumped into Mr Freedom's cage in the Chateau Walmart's Deus Ex Machina Italian restaurant. We'd had dinner together and then I'd invited him back to my room.

According to Mr Freedom, Self had been busy trying to

enforce his reality on Smith.

Also; Anne Punter had been right all along;

'He's a French Muslim! He's a French Muslim!'

I told Mr Freedom to focus. To tell me what Self had said.

'...Cheep ...Cheep'.

I figured out that Mr Freedom was trying to say 'chap'.

Mr Freedom was originally from New Zealand.

'...You've got to decide which side to play for cheep... Your friend is on the way out cheep... Canon and the Agency will be held responsible for the mamba jamba hoax'.

I needed Mr Freedom to paint me a picture. But I was out of paper.

And Mr Freedom was out of thumbs.

I could only guess that Self had ret-conned a yellow paper trail that would incriminate anyone more senior than himself in all manner of hoaxes and cover-ups that the Agency had been involved in over the years. I guessed there was some irony in the Agency's being incriminated in a deliberate conspiracy to keep the truth from the public.

It was either that or there was no irony at all. I sometimes get confused about irony.

Mr Freedom was confusing me too. Because of his Kiwi accent and his Pidgin-English. But I was pretty good with languages, and with animals, so I got the gist of it.

The gist of it was that I was in the frame for all of this.

'The old guard will take the blame for our hard work cheep... Then I'll be running things. I'm offering you a promotion cheep... And dinner at the Cock and Bull'.

This stank of reality enforcement. This was Self believing he could enforce his reality on Smith. This was Self offering Smith a step up the career ladder (and peeping up her skirt). And this was Smith looking down and agreeing. This was Smith telling Self he had a deal. Even though she already had a deal with me.

Basically the deal was; Smith would follow Self back to

the Agency and act like she belonged there. Smith was going to act like someone who wasn't an undercover investigative journalist. She was going to hang me out to dry in order to get behind the scenes at the Agency so that she could hang them all out to dry with me.

Any student of scapegoating will tell you the best situation to throw a scapegoat into is one that's already out of control. Your recessions, your depressions, your alien invasions. If the price of cotton falls? You go on a lynching. You find yourself a stereotype and turn them into a scapegoat. What you're looking to achieve here is basically some sort of unjustified and contrived and (if at all possible) prejudicial and violent relief from your troubles.

Being stereotyped was an occupational hazard of working for a clandestine cabal of intelligentsia striving to keep the truth from the man on the street.

But why settle for one scapegoat?

According to Mr Freedom, Maxwell Self had compiled a whole list of reality enforcers, civil servants and media magnates who'd been working with Redstar in order to hide the truth from the man on the street.

The plan was for popular children's TV personality and hand puppet Marvin Mole to hand the British PM a list of these bastards on top-rated children's TV show and surrogate parent 'Child Benefit!' The plan was for Marvin Mole to 'accidentally' flash Self's list to the cameras and then sell his database of names to local hearsay chasers and scandal bashers.

Raúl Greedo was on the list. And so was Elvis. I was on the list too.

I was also on Child Benefit! Behind some pixels. The pixels were the disguise that Self was wearing in order to impersonate me. I knew it was Self because I was watching Child Benefit! but I could hear him giving his interview from the bedroom next door. Self was blowing his own trumpet. And a whistle. Self was a bona fide one-man-band.

Self was admitting that I worked for the Agency and explaining how I'd been behind a whole host of hoaxes; the amber jam jar, the bandwagon, Milli Vanilli.

I felt exposed. The thin veneer of pixels that Self had on didn't even cover my arse. I wondered if anyone watching found it ironic that my face was pixelated but the photos of me shaking hands with Redstar and Saddam and Raúl were not. I wondered if *this* was irony.

We'd been in it together all along; Chuck and Frank and the Agency. Self really had it in for us. Fortunately Redstar and I had pseudonyms we could use. But the Agency wasn't so lucky. Self was going to bring the Agency down so he could rebuild it in his image.

The interview ended and the hand up Marvin Mole's backside slowly shook from side to side in despair and disgust. Self wiped the pixels from his face and nonchalantly walked out of the bedroom as we watched a commercial for the 'Post-Apocalyptic Dystopia Diet'.

It was all my fault. And Redstar's fault. And the Agency's. Our hoaxes had been designed to confuse society and create a state of perpetual panic. It was right there in the fake manifesto Marvin Mole had 'accidentally' tweeted to his followers.

I sat on the back seat of Self's VW Vagrant with the rumour grenade on my lap and a gun to my head as we drove from Miami airport to the Son of Deep Throat's house in Tampa.

Tommy was going to help fire off our rumour grenade. He just didn't know it yet.

Tommy was behind a locked door, playing along with an X-rated 'reimagining' of Spartacus on his Nintendo Wii. He let out a window cleaner's unconvincing denial and fell on his Wii sword as Self's scratchie kicked the door to his mum's basement in.

Self and Ian supervised Tommy as he sat at his tablet, removing conspiracy theories and whingeing. He was at gunpoint, so his whingeing was pointless. But he was the fifteen year-old co-founder of a conspiracy theory website and he really couldn't stop himself.

The computer program that Tommy was using was called GOD.

This was because, if you took the letters IBM, and you subtracted two letters from I you got G and if you added two to M you got O and if you added two to B you got D.

Tommy deleted the story exposing the fact that 'I can't believe it's not butter' is actually butter. He deleted the stories about the caffeine in decaffeinated coffee.

The Coke in Coke Zero.

Tommy was partly whingeing but also partly boasting about all of the hard work he'd invested over the years and the 'mad skills' which had meant that virtually all of his conspiracy theories had been circulated in the press verbatim.

Tommy's tale about how the Olympics were fixed was exactly the kind of story news agencies could've easily verified if they'd been so inclined. It was the fact that the Daily Mail had run a headline claiming that the discus had been fixed by a team from Reptilon that suggested they hadn't been too thorough in checking their facts.

Tommy put this down to his mad skills, but this was pretty typical of the Daily Mail. The Daily Mail had a bit of a 'no questions asked' policy when it came to scaremongering.

The news media loved a good conspiracy theory because in the age of social media these secret plots were one of the few things they could tell their audience that their audience hadn't already heard about the day before. Also, these plots were usually concerned with world domination by some super-villainous organisation who had members all over the place and probably living in that boarded up house in the next street along that always gives you the creeps, which meant that really, the audience was part of the story, and could text in (at £2 plus your standard rate) to play along.

Conspiracy theories tended to get lots of people following your newsfeed on social panic sites like MumsNet and SheepHerder.

I uploaded the rumour grenade onto the Sunday Spartan website that Tommy had hacked into. I could tell Self wasn't watching what I was doing. Self was agreeing which stories Tommy could keep and which he had to delete. The story about how the Olympics were fixed was ok with Self. Because Self detested physical exercise.

(Although he did renew his gym membership every year.)

Smith was watching though. So I started typing her an e-mail:

'Are you really going to throw your lot in with Self?'

I stopped typing, waiting for an answer. Maybe Self hadn't been watching what I was doing but he'd been cleaning out his ears. Smith leant forward and deleted my e-mail;

'Don't think I've forgotten what happened when you spat your chewing gum at me'.

Self looked over my shoulder. Smith looked over hers;

'I think my old partner's waiting for someone to help him out of a sticky situation'.

Smith leafed through a stack of Sunday Spartans as Tommy refused to delete a story alleging that Dick Cheney was just an actor who'd been paid to play an evil genius so people wouldn't panic that George W. Bush had just been making an awful lot of awful decisions.

People had needed to believe that someone was in charge.

People just hadn't been ready to believe that person was George Jr.

They couldn't suspend their disbelief.

It was far easier to believe that some smug git like Cheney was running things. It was far better to believe that some shady pack of utter bastards was running your life than to face the fact that you were living in a random, chaotic world and that your life had run hopelessly and totally out of your control. People who believed in conspiracy theories tended to be the ones whose lives were most out of their control. If there was a villain in charge there was always a chance you could overthrow him and start running things yourself.

The Bushes had paid the Agency to hire the actor who played Dick in the hope that the electorate wouldn't give junior too hard a time. Or impeach him. Like I said before, you don't want to be the person running things when things start running out of control.

Of course, the only reason the actor playing Dick had been cast as a villain was because Bush had only made bad decisions. If he'd stupidly made a lot of good calls Dick would've been a hero.

Sure, sure, Self was about to chuck a rumour bomb at his own shadowy organisation because he wanted all of those people whose lives had gotten out of their control to overthrow the cabal he'd framed as a scapegoat for all of the shit that had been going down recently. But Self had plenty of dirt on the Agency already.

He didn't need to upset the Bushes.

Or the US government.

If there's one thing you don't want to do if you're in power it's upset the US government. By convincing people without power that they were able to take it back from the Agency that had abused its own, Self was going to ascend to the golden perch of those he'd overthrown. But he still needed something for his golden perch to perch on top of.

Another thing Self needed were some anti-diarrhoea tablets. Or incontinence pants.

Or some sort of plug.

Because all of a sudden he started gushing over Tommy's stack of Sunday Spartans and then ran up the stairs to the bathroom in tears.

Self's scratch-starter looked down at the glass of ice tea Smith had prepared and started to turn a sort of green colour. Then he ran out of the basement too. Self had locked the bathroom door. But Ian had gotten into the habit of kicking doors down.

And it was a hard habit to quit.

Tommy put on some Rage Against The Machine. Partly to drown out the belching and farting from the bathroom, but also so that Smith could finally let me in on her plan;

'Did you get my hint? About the sticky situation? I was trying to tell you something'.

I'd figured it out straight away of course. Even if you hadn't.

But Smith seemed impressed with her subterfuge, so I feigned ignorance and pretended I'd thought she was betraying me all along and not just tricking Self into thinking that she was going along with him and I also pretended that the look of panic that had been on my face for the past hour was genuine and not a pretence because that's what it had been.

'It was all a ruse?'

Smith grinned as Tommy plugged his GOD tablet into the computer in front of me. Tommy had been lying too. Tommy hadn't been busy deleting his conspiracy theories. He'd been busy defusing my rumour bomb. And then GOD had taken my rumour bomb apart and put it back together again. With a couple of minor alterations.

Tommy had used his GOD programme to ret-con my rumour grenade. As well as a recent episode of Child

Benefit. He'd wiped those pixels right off of Self's face.

Tommy's artificial intelligence was smarter than mine. Smith was still grinning as she made the phone call.

Epiphany Smith picked up in the Spartan's offices;

'...Hello? Sunday Spartan, Sunday's boring without us. Mildred Smith speaking'.

'It's Agent X, Epiphany. ...From the Agency? ...Do you have the information we sent through? ...Well we need to make a couple of changes. ...The first change we need to make is the name Frank Canon. We need you to change it to Maxwell Self'.

19. Biased Lightning

*T*he headline on The Daily Express read: 'Bullshit!'

The face under the headline belonged to Maxwell Self.

Maxwell Self wasn't smiling in his photo in the paper. And he wasn't smiling in real life either. In real life Self was wearing a sort of tightly-clenched grimace.

Partly because he'd been implicated in a conspiracy to swindle the public out of the truth about jam jars and hell holes in conjunction with the fraudster Chuck Redstar.

Partly because he was suffering the effects of some bad tea Smith had served him.

And partly because he was desperately out of shape (his diet consisting only of cock and bull served for breakfast, lunch and dinner at the Cock and Bull Club) and struggling to outrun the posse of villagers who were chasing him down the Walk of Fame.

The rumour grenade had made a real mess of Self and Redstar.

And anyone associated with them.

The MIRAJJE spokesperson sat in her dressing room having her teeth painted and breasts inflated. She was up next on Face Talk, as soon as Andromeda Strain was finished with the sick and tired Agency spokesman who was trying to frame the revelation that they'd lied about Elvis as a simple case of terminological inexactitude. This didn't wash with Andromeda or her viewers tuning in from the world's airport lounges and motorway service stations.

The Agency's spokesman was one of the few people still sticking to the script.

But it was a lost cause.

Still, the Agency's spokesman continued to behave in that very ministerial way of refusing to admit defeat.

That very diplomatic way of refusing to admit there'd even been a fight.

George and Stevens knew they were in a fight though. Their opponent was an outbreak of laughing to death that had struck Rio de Janeiro. And Ipswich.

George and Stevens weren't trying to ret-con the fact that people had died laughing though, they were trying to ret-con the shows people had been watching when they died.

Dying of laughter wasn't impossible to believe.

But dying of laughter while watching Two and a Half Men?

George and Stevens barely had time to reply to my encrypted texts. They were hopelessly outnumbered. They were fighting a losing battle against a shit-storm of continuity errors. So instead of being kept in the dark, you probably heard about the nuclear submarine USS Unilateral accidentally torpedoing itself near Taiwan.

Where, in a neat twist, its 'no-frills' torpedoes had been assembled.

Trust me; you didn't get to hear about these things because of any lack of blood, sweat and tears on the part of the Department of Knowledge Management. Those brave boys over at the Office of Reality Enforcement had been working all hours trying to keep themselves (and their Self) out of the news. To distract you from the truth.

Reality enforcers were busy dispensing hallucinogens in the desperate hope that everyone would think what they'd been seeing were just the fragments of a bad dream.

The idea was to create a suspension of disbelief pandemic.

They dropped LSD25 into the mains water supply in cities across the globe to coincide with the theatrical releases of 'Zombie Gobblers' and 'Alien Settlers'. Once the hallucinogens got into people's bloodstreams they'd stop panicking about the rumour bomb implicating Self, Redstar and the Agency and start freaking out about gobbling zombies and illegal aliens instead. This is known in the business as 'covering all the bases'.

When everyone came down they'd ask;

'What was I panicking about? It was just a movie'. Or;

'I've realised that movies are a really bad influence on me'.

The rumour bomb would be swept up with the trash of communal consciousness and join yesterday's fears in the recycle bin.

And it would have worked. If it hadn't been for the French.

Yeah, the French. And their plastic bottles of mineral water. If only the Agency had taken into account the decline in the number of people using drinking fountains. They'd have realised the contamination of the water supply would only affect a minority of cinemagoers.

Disillusioned devotees of MIRAJJE watched the news. It was bad. So they laid siege to the embassy where Redstar had holed up with a few of his more loyal Gladys lieutenants.

'How does he know all of this?' I hear you ask.

Well there was no way I could have known at the time of course, I wasn't omniscient.

I already told you that.

It wasn't until later that I pieced together the sequence of events from witness statements, chat shows and FaceSpace posts.

And all of the phones in the embassy that Smith had hacked into.

Once the rumour bomb had gone off and those photos of Phil Mein creating hoaxes had gotten out (you know, the photos in that illustrated edition of Chuck's diaries) Redstar had been advised that he should either; i) defend himself by appearing on Face Talk and denying any of it had ever happened, or ii) defend himself with the embassy furniture by nailing it across the windows and doors in order to barricade them.

Only once Chuck and his followers were safely blockaded against the hordes outside did they decide to sit down and try to figure a way out of the mess they were in. And then they realised that actually, if you nailed your furniture across all of the exits, you couldn't sit down. And you tended to undermine your own escape plans.

But Chuck was desperate to get out.

His loyal followers had started sounding a little less loyal. The mood in the embassy had deteriorated to mutinous. And this wasn't going to be one of those good mutinies, where you were marooned on a tropical island full of single ladies; this would be more like one of those mutinies that involved walking along a plank.

Chuck didn't seem to be getting the respect he'd gotten in the past. Chuck was telling people that he wished he could be Weird Norm again. Even if he'd been the butt of their jokes he'd still been recognised when he walked down the street. Weird Norm had still been much better than being Norman Grinder, whom no-one had ever paid any attention to.

Chuck mightn't have been getting much respect from his inner circle. But on the flip side, they weren't trying to ram his front door with a Ferrari Segway. Chuck's lieutenants (like all residents of Gladys) knew that trying to ram someone's front door with an Italian Segway was un-American. It was rude. The correct way to behave was to squeeze all of your anger and your heartache into a tiny ball so tightly that eventually you transformed it into a shiny diamond that you kept in a pocket inside of you and never let out.

It was what was on the surface that mattered.

So really (even though Chuck was well versed in Gladys' social consensus for dealing with anger and frustration) he could pretend that the people trapped behind the sofas with him weren't anywhere near as furious as the people outside. Blimey Lowsey was outside with Kenny and Kevin Kardashian, flinging obscenities and what looked like half-digested falafels at the embassy's front door. But that was because Blimey wasn't from Gladys.

Christy was from Gladys. Christy just smiled and asked;

'Who'd like more English muffins? Maybe they can help us come up with an escape plan. The English are good at escaping'.

It wasn't as in your face as Blimey's lunch. But that was the difference between your rednecks and your white trash right there.

Another thing that people in Gladys frowned upon was holding onto bad feelings.

Christy felt sorry for Chuck. Christy felt sorry for Weird Norm.

Who was really to blame? Everyone had known Norm was weird, because of his name; they'd just gotten caught up in the moment.

A lot of people who were smarter than they were had trusted Weird Norm. George Clooney and Vladimir Putin had trusted Norm, so you couldn't exactly blame the residents of Gladys for getting swept along on the wave of euphoria.

And you couldn't blame Weird Norm either. Norm had been swept along on that same wave with them. He'd just been at the front of the wave all along, so now Norm was going to be the first to be sent crashing into the rocks.

No-one could stay mad at Norm.

Gladys folk just wanted to put an arm around his shoulder.

But Norm was starting to panic that one of these days they'd want to put their hands around his throat. They'd carry on feeling sorry for him, but eventually they'd start feeling sorry for themselves too. Eventually, everyone would start blaming Chuck for the mess he'd made of their lives.

Chuck had a wooden plaque on his desk that read; 'The buck stops here'.

But the Chuck couldn't stop here.

The good news for Norman Grinder was; he could leave Chuck. Norman could move on. He'd done it before. Why should Norm face the music? Norm had amassed quite a bit of money. Norm couldn't take all the credit for the hard work Chuck had put in, but he could take all of the money.

He just needed to get out of the embassy.

Maxwell Self needed to get into the embassy. Unfortunately all of the doors had been barricaded with sofas and beanbags. But fortunately for Self a barricaded door was like a red rag to a bull to Ian who couldn't stop himself from launching at it Jackie Chan style. At which point his boot broke clear through the embassy's front door and became wedged under the shoe-rack behind it. Self pulled his scratch-starter's leg as hard as possible but it wouldn't budge. Luckily for Self he'd been instructed by the same subterfuge instructor as I had.

As soon as he yelled; 'Fire!' Blimey Lowsey called her agent who quickly dialled 911 and within minutes fire-fighters were falling over themselves to prise Ian free and impress Blimey (whose Playboy centrefold had been pasted around their poles back at the station for weeks now). Self seized his opportunity and scuttled up a fire ladder towards an open window on the thirteenth floor of the embassy. He pulled it shut and locked it behind him before anyone could follow him through. Self knew it wouldn't hold though;

'Bring coffee tables! Bring Futons! We need to barricade this window chaps!'

Everyone from Gladys recognised Self straight away. He was the man who'd spread all of those lies about Norm. And about himself. No-one was quite sure why Self had spread all of those lies about himself too, but he had, so there you had it.

Redstar brandished a dado rail that he'd intended to nail across the window but which he was now planning to beat Self around the head with first. But Self had a plan;

'I've got some good news. I've a way for all of you to get out of this mess. Actually, it's a way for me to get myself out of this mess. Your getting out of this mess is really only a by-product of that, but there you go. In fact, forget I said that. I'm going to get you out of this mess because it's the right thing to do. I'm going to prove that Chuck is the real deal. I'm going to prove that the amber jam jar is genuine. Those test results were bogus!'

Self pulled a rolled up yellow report from his pants;

'I've got the real results! And the real amber jam jar!'

It was around this time that I received an encrypted pictogram from my employers.

The pictogram consisted of a photograph of someone's poo.

And one of a fan.

I found a secure ~~public convenience~~ payphone and called a stuttering George;

'Stevens is AWOL! It's the jam jar Frank, Stevens took it from the Whitewash Museum! He's working for Self now!'

I told George to stop panicking. It didn't matter if Self had the real test results. No-one cared. It was all too scientific. It was all just so unnecessarily confusing.

And the new season of American Idol was on. American Idol was simple.

'But that's just it. Self isn't just going to ret-con the test results so people can understand them! He's going to make everyone think that they care about them too!'

Self had reversed the polarity of the Department of Ignorance Management so they'd started ret-conning everyone's previous confusion about the SOOPA. The DIM had used a bootleg download of the GOD programme to create millions of astroturfed followers of Redstar on Ditto (a site where someone typed up to three words and then if you agreed with it you typed Ditto; you 'dittoed' them).

Millions of Ditto users suddenly appeared, and suddenly appeared to completely understand the newly released and absolutely genuine test results. And these weren't just any old users of Ditto. These users listed Shakespeare and Proust on the 'Books I'm Reading' tab. These computer generated intellectuals really cared about the test results that showed Redstar and Self had been right all along.

There hadn't been a hoax.

It had all just been another desperate attempt by the establishment (to which the whistleblowing Self no longer held any allegiance, but I apparently did) to discredit Redstar.

'We have to steal the amber jam jar'.

I winced and closed my eyes and counted to five.

But the plot hole I'd feared might open stayed shut.

I explained to Smith how this meant I wasn't contradicting my earlier statements that stealing the jam jar had been a bad idea. Things had been different back then. There hadn't been a set of genuine test results that proved the SOOPA was genuine. And there hadn't been a set of bogus results that proved the Agency had lied about it. If Redstar got hold of his truth and our lies he'd vindicate himself and leave the Agency holding the bullshit.

Sure, sure, all he owned was a very old jam jar. What that meant for the story of mankind? For the history of the world? Well it meant that Redstar would be the one who got to rewrite them, who got to replace the Agency's lies with his own.

He'd prove that the Agency had been lying to people all along.

I'd started to think this was probably fair enough.

Because the Agency had been lying to people all along. But there was a big difference between the Agency and MIRAJJE. MIRAJJE were the bad guys.

Smith reckoned this was a bit of a grey area. But I disagreed. I'd been telling her MIRAJJE were the bad guys for days. The number of civilian casualties caused by the Empire and the Rebellion was a bit of a grey area too, but you knew who to root for in Star Wars because you were told who by that crawl right at the start. You were told the Empire was evil in fewer words than you needed on Ditto.

We had to get the genuine amber jam jar and the genuine test results back from Redstar. We had to dash his hopes and shatter his dreams.

Please don't think I was being unreasonable though.

We were only going to steal the genuine jam jar.

We we're still going to leave him the fake.

The MSG News Omni-copter was broadcasting fuzzy

images of trapped MIRAJJE cult members rescuing their laundry from a line attached to the giant antenna that had been erected on the embassy roof to contact alien visitors and/or Heaven.

There were huge storm clouds overhead. There were goldfish falling from the sky, and clouds shaped like Viagradors. Typical drunken weather.

Half an hour later we watched the MSG Omni-copter land at the Four Seasons hotel. I already knew that Smith was better at disguises than I was (because of the impersonating an intern thing) and she had no trouble bluffing our way onto the helicopter by pulling on a blonde wig and swearing about liberals. I was Anne Punter's personal pilot apparently.

I had to convince the helicopter valet that I knew all about helicopters. The thing I knew about helicopters was that it was a good sign if your helicopter looked old and beat up. That was a good indication of reliability. If your helicopter looked brand new, how did you know if it worked or not? I didn't admit that I couldn't fly a helicopter to the valet though. I didn't even admit it to Smith until we were safely in the air;

'Can you try to find a YouTube video for flying a helicopter on your smartphone?'

Smith started screaming foreign vulgarities at me. I had to ask her to keep quiet so I could hear the guy on YouTube. It was easy to understand how planes flew because they had wings; like birds, and cane beetles, and other flying things. Planes were good at flying; they could even do it on autopilot. Ever made a paper plane? It just glided through the air right?

Bet you've never made a paper helicopter though have you?

Helicopters don't have wings. Like cane toads and bricks and pigs, and other things that can't fly. If you were flying a helicopter you were basically pulling strings and levers in a desperate attempt to keep something in the air that would much rather still be on the ground. Like me.

A gust of mice blew into the windshield as a bolt of lightning struck a tree in a nearby rooftop garden. The electrical storm was playing havoc with the helicopter's instruments. It was either that or Smith's smartphone. I felt something rise up from the pit of my stomach. Then I watched it hit the windshield. I was surprised at how similar a Happy Meal looked on the way out to how it did on the way in. But now I'd gotten that out of my system I felt better.

I had no idea where we were or what we were flying into, but through the fog of frogspawn I made out a neon sign on the embassy roof that read; 'Prophets: land here'.

We were greeted by a couple of dribbling cult members and introduced ourselves as the prophets Enoch and Elijah. Sadly neither of us were on the guest-list and so despite our clearly descending from the heavens they couldn't allow us in without checking first.

I needed to enforce their disbelief in the guest-list.

The facts were these: i) we were *surprise* prophets. If our names had been on the guest list it would've spoiled the surprise. ii) We were very late for the party. But how often did a prophet turn up at the time and place you'd been told they would? It never happened.

We abseiled down the elevator shaft and crept through the sleeping embassy. The elevator was working fine, but Smith had developed a bit of liftphobia since Dubai.

Smith walked into some wind chimes. I narrowly avoided a giant Jenga™ tower. I suggested we take off our shoes and socks so as to be as quiet as possible. I was pretty sure we'd find the genuine amber jam jar locked away in Christy's gun cabinet. But I was pretty surprised to discover that Christy had locked the fake away right next to it.

Actually, scratch that. I wasn't surprised.

The genuine SOOPA had a label that read; 'this is real'. The fake had a label that read; 'this isn't'. I could just make out a speck of diet blackcurrant jam inside.

Smith unlocked the cabinet and grabbed the SOOPA.

This is what's known in the business as 'a steal'.

Cast your mind back. Try to remember. Smith and I might have travelled through a plot hole into the past and prevented Rashid from stealing the amber jam jar. But that didn't mean we'd forgotten our returning it in the first place, or that Christy kept the key to her gun cabinet buried in an old croissant poked around the back. We hadn't forgotten about that at all. It was just the rat glue we'd forgotten about. Which was why I'd become glued to the spot. Fortunately Smith hadn't taken her socks off. Only her shoes. So I shooed her away;

'Take the SOOPA and get out of here'.

Smith looked terrified of leaving me. Probably because she couldn't abseil;

'Let me try to find some nail polish remover, or moonshine'.

'Leave me. I'll be fine'.

'Really?'

'Of course not. I'm just saying it so you won't feel guilty. But Self will combust you if he finds us. And I've had enough people I care about getting burnt coming back for me'.

Smith's face lit up, as a bolt of lightning struck the embassy roof;

'...You care about me?'

'...Enough not to want to see you set on fire. And I won't be able to put you out. I went to the toilet before we got in the helicopter. I always go before I travel'.

Smith smiled and started to undress. I thought that this really wasn't the time.

But she stopped undressing after taking her socks off.

'You've put me out more than enough. That's what

partners do'.

Smith stepped onto the rat glue. And then we heard a polite 'cough'.

We'd been caught amber-handed. And sticky-footed. Christy had a shotgun on us.

And a bit of pain-au-chocolat on her upper lip.

Seventy stories below us people in the street were staring up at the embassy roof and live tweeting what they could see. No-one was really sure what they were seeing; because they were all wearing sunglasses in the middle of the night. People were wearing sunglasses at night because of the lightning striking the embassy. Or because they were actors.

One by one everyone stopped looking up. They started looking at the superhero stood next to them instead. Then they started taking selfies with him. Much to his annoyance.

Some kid seventy stories below us was shouting; '...it's the Human Torch!' But he didn't look anything like the Human Torch. And his name was 'The Human Shield!'

'You burnt your costume' said the kid.

Self had tied Smith and I to the antenna on the embassy roof with some lingerie that had been hung out to dry. Like us. This was the same antenna that was about to conduct the lightning approaching us. I told Smith to shut her eyes. Because she didn't have her sunglasses. And because you didn't want to stare death in the face if you could avoid it.

I felt Smith's hand grip mine as she shouted something. But she was so nervous I couldn't understand a word of it. I let go of her hand and tried to loosen her lingerie.

I wondered if the person who'd designed the bra strap had heard about romance.

Smith was stuck fast. I tried to loosen my suspender belt instead.

Christy wanted to know why Self had to tie us to the antenna.

'I don't know... I'm the bad guy aren't I? And this just seems convenient. The helicopter is right there'.

Redstar was clutching the genuine amber jam jar. Christy clutched the fake. Self had told her she could keep it as a souvenir. Even though she really would have preferred the real one. But Redstar and Self had other plans. They were going to get on the MSG Omni-copter and get the real jam jar the hell out of there.

It hit Redstar like a bolt from the blue. The lightning.

Redstar hit the floor and started having a fit. Christy dropped her fake SOOPA which cracked up on the roof and rushed to his aid. But the lightning hadn't struck anywhere life-threatening. It had just struck Chuck's reason for living. It had struck the amber jam jar. And broken it into pieces. But not pieces of glass. The amber jam jar had shattered into pieces of plastic. And one of these pieces had the word 'Nestlé' moulded into it.

The genuine amber jam jar was a fake.

Prehistoric glass-blowing was one thing. But prehistoric plastic manufacturing?

That wasn't hard to believe. That was unbelievable.

Redstar was Weird Norm again. And worse than that; he was Norman Grinder. Redstar had truly believed the SOOPA was genuine. But it wasn't. It wasn't worthless. It was just worth about five cents. Chuck Redstar hadn't been struck anywhere life-threatening. But he was dead now. Chuck had gone and left Norman holding the plastic pieces of his shattered dreams.

This was completely unbelievable.

'What are you talking about?'

Smith didn't know what I was talking about. Smith hadn't been paying attention. Because I'd told her to keep her eyes closed.

I was easily the fourth most disappointed person on the roof. The first was Norman, who was shaking uncontrollably and threatening to jump off of it. The second was Christy, who was trying to shake some sense into Weird Norm and convince him not to;

'Maybe one day you'll dive into Shit Creek and save a deaf dumb and blind kid from drowning, and that kid will grow up to become the next Sarah Palin. You just don't know when your life gets to have its meaning. Sometimes you just have to bake cakes and wait'.

The third most disappointed person on the roof was Self.

But Self felt a lot less repentant than Weird Norm. Self was watching as the lightning struck closer and closer to the antenna. Not because he was waiting for us to die. Self was just worried about the MSG Omni-copter. The only people worried about Smith and I dying were Smith and I. Smith was nervous. And badly dubbed;

'Quel chemin à parcourir. Atado a un pararrayos debido a un atasco falso jar. ...Why didn't I just become an accountant like Sophia?'

'Sophia?'

'My older sister. ...She's about your age'.

Sophia Smith. My old sweetheart. And Mildred's older sister.

That was why Smith had reminded me of someone from my past.

It wasn't because Smith reminded me of my mother at all. ...Phew.

Sophia Smith; an accountant. I might have hooked up with a pen pusher. What a tragedy that would've been. Maybe I was tied to a lightning rod. But I'd started feeling lucky.

I yanked at Smith's pantyhose as hard as I could but they wouldn't come free. Smith shrugged her shoulders, as if to say; 'it's ok, shit happens'. Then she smiled;

'Ah what the hell. We had fun while it lasted right?

...You only live once'.

I had to agree, that was certainly true. Most of the time.

The lightning hit the roof. It missed the antenna. It missed the Omni-copter. It missed Self and Christy and Redstar. It just kept on striking the same spot. The same figure on the embassy roof. Once, twice, a third time. The lightning kept striking the Human Shield.

Rashid wasn't on fire any longer. Just smouldering. Because the river he'd landed in after he'd fallen off of the cliff had been dry. I already explained that.

There was nothing unbelievable about Rashid still being on fire, because of the dry river bed. Forget his spontaneous combustion and his surviving the fall from the cliff.

That's been explained already too. Just concentrate on the fact that the river bed was dry, and how that easily explains why Rashid was still smouldering.

That and his being continually stuck by lightning.

It wasn't widely known, but lightning could often be terribly biased. There were numerous well-documented cases of lightning striking the same person several times in one lifetime. You could try not to take biased lightning personally, but the truth was it really hurt.

And Rashid was being struck pretty much continuously.

On the plus side, he was getting closer to the antenna.

On the minus side, the closer he got to the antenna, the closer the lightning got.

Self made a dash for the Omni-copter. He pulled the cockpit door closed behind him. So he'd gotten out of the rain at least. But he immediately started grappling with the joystick in frustration. Self was going nowhere. The ignition key was safely in my pocket. And when I say safely I mean it was in the pocket of a man tied to an antenna in a lightning storm.

Suddenly there were flames all around us.

The lightning had spontaneously combusted the laundry basket next to us.

Rashid was struck by lightning and thrown against the antenna.

'Rashid! You have to untie us!'

Rashid was looking a bit stressed, a bit sunburnt, and quite a bit shorter.

He managed to loosen my bonds as he fell to the floor. That thirteenth lightning bolt had really gotten to him. I dragged him clear of the antenna fire and looked into Smith's glazed eyes through the wall of flames. I was going to have to do something about this.

I had to save Mildred Smith.

I had a moment of sudden realisation.

And abandoned her.

But I wasn't paralysed with fear like I had been when the Norwegian Queen went up in flames. Sure, sure, I was petrified. But I could still move. I ran to Self who was frantically trying to hotwire the helicopter. He looked up and saw me as I chucked the keys in his direction (having already made adjustments for the gale-force wind). Self caught the keys and started the Omni-copter just as the squall of rain and goldfish I'd been watching neared the roof. He cranked up the helicopter's rotor blades until they reached escape velocity.

The goldfish squall hit the roof. And the wash from the rotor blades directed it in Smith's direction, putting the fire out instantly.

Self spun out into the sunset with a fist-pump and a cackle. But I didn't care.

About Self getting away. Or that the sun had already set about an hour earlier.

I was done adjusting continuity errors.

I looked down at my feet. One of the goldfish had survived the fire. I quickly picked up my fake jam jar from among the fake amber that had cracked up when Christy dropped it. I let it fill up with rain and dropped the goldfish in. I couldn't stop smiling. And quite a lot of smoke had gotten in my eyes. I finally had a good memory of goldfish and fire.

I hoped the memories flashing before Rashid's eyes were good ones too. Because of how he'd saved Smith's life and mine. I leant towards him as he whispered something to me;

'I got my second chance. ...Do you think I redeemed myself?'

'Of course'.

Rashid stopped whispering and started shouting angrily;

'Then why the hell is Rashid being killed off? After everything we've been through, why in God's name am I being killed off now?'

Rashid suddenly appeared very old. In his mid-forties.

'Maybe he didn't recognise you. You'll have to ask him'.

'I think Rashid's going to see the other guy'.

I shook my head;

'I've seen a lot of crazy things in my life. But I haven't seen anything to make me believe in the other guy'.

'You don't think there's a subtle hint in Rashid's being struck down by lightning bolts? You don't think people will always remember the old Rashid?'

'Well you look twenty years older. And you act like it too. Everything before today, no-one will ever believe it was the same person'.

'But you will'.

'...I'm good at keeping secrets'.

Rashid went out as the hero.

Or, to put it more accurately, the Human Shield did. Rashid Rashid was the Human Shield's secret identity. It was an easy secret to keep. Not because he wore a mask or anything, but because Rashid had died looking about forty-five.

He'd changed a lot since the hijacking. Maybe he'd even been forgiven. Rashid was no longer a demon. The media needed a good guy to pit against the cartoon tyranny of Self in their docudramas and the CGI animations Chinese news networks used to dramatise events and which generated a Saturday morning spin-off; 'Human Shield Variety Hour'.

Maybe the complexities of Rashid's story couldn't be reduced to a traditional good guys vs. bad guys narrative. But you try telling that to a nine year-old who sleeps with his Rashid action figure each night.

Go on, just try it.

20. Seeing

*T*hings kind of went back to normal after that.

Continuity errors reached manageable levels again.

So you probably didn't hear about the Bolivian miners who dug up a series of metal discs. You didn't hear about how the mine caved in leaving the miners trapped underground for nine days with only a DVD player and those mysterious metal discs they'd dug out of the Precambrian rock. You didn't get to hear about how disappointed those Bolivian miners had been with the finale of The Sopranos.

You didn't believe it. But you didn't find it hard to believe either. Because you just hadn't been seeing things clearly. Yeah, things went back to normal. With one exception.

I wasn't adjusting continuity errors anymore. I had a new job.

Don't think I'd been fired. I hadn't. Sure, sure, I hadn't won any admirers by allowing my bogus intern to 'trick me' into exposing the Agency's secret history in the pages of the Sunday Spartan, but when I told the Agency that I couldn't adjust miracles any longer they just offered me a desk job at the Ministry of Culture. Selling the naming rights to historical monuments and world heritage sites. I turned them down. I took a holiday. But I wasn't planning a visit to Bridgestonehenge. The Hallmark de Triomphe. Or the Amazon Rainforest.

I went to visit some old friends...

I was reborn in the Outback in my forty second year. Picture me driving into the bush in a Toyota Magneto with Bishop Anger beside me arguing over what to listen to on the stereo. The Bishop wanted to listen to the local news. Apparently The Crooked Man was no longer a police station. It was an 'indigenous Koala art installation'.

I told the Bishop to put on one of his Cliff Richard CDs. I was done listening to the news. You couldn't believe a word of what you heard. It was always something unbelievable. But someone always had some bullshit theory to explain it. That hadn't changed, yet.

It hadn't changed yet because the Bishop and I hadn't made it to our destination. It was all about the destination for me (I was like the kind of person who found God on their deathbed). But it was all about the journey for the Bishop (the Bishop was more like the kind of person who went to church regularly).

People were still arguing over the bandwagon. And the Human Shield. People were still trying to explain the unexplainable to other people. No-one was on TV telling other people; 'You know, I really don't have any answers for you'.

People were terrified of those three terrible words.

I. Don't. Know.

Every day the questions became more and more complex and people became more and more ignorant. People couldn't explain what something was.

They couldn't see what something is.

They didn't know if something was really there.

For starters, no-one wanted to admit that they couldn't explain what the bandwagon actually was. Everyone could agree on what it appeared to be; it looked like a bandwagon. But people had called the manufacturers and asked them what they'd manufactured and they'd told them it was a tour bus. So how had it materialised above the Hollywood sign?

Lots of people had an opinion.

The only people who didn't were the physicists.

And anyone working for the church.

Those guys had been badly burnt.

After the events of the past few chapters most of the people who'd been telling you they had all of the answers had started shying away from trying to explain continuity errors. But they couldn't admit to not knowing. So they just issued a series of press releases stating that they were in the process of becoming certain about everything, but in the meantime the only thing they could confirm for sure was that they couldn't be certain of anything.

A lot of people were unhappy. They needed answers. They wanted to hear from people who were already certain. People who were sure of themselves.

But there were no easy explanations. Except for why people were unhappy. There was an easy explanation for that. It was Newton's Theory of Ignorance.

People were loath to accept the existence of anything they couldn't explain. People tended to deny the effect if they couldn't understand the cause (see: the bandwagon, see: global warming, see: the worldwide box office receipts for the GoBots movies). The only people who weren't unhappy were the ones who'd given up on anything ever being explained. What's that saying about bliss?

The reason Bishop Anger spent a lot of time on his Genesis step-master was; he ate a lot of pies. And so he insisted on directing me to a local diner that served his favourite.

We pulled up outside the Sunset Rock little roadside diner.

But I left the engine running just in case.

It turned out my first impressions of the Sunset Rock diner had been all wrong. It turned out women *were* allowed in all sections of the diner. As long as they were waitresses.

Ours asked if we'd booked. We hadn't but I could tell the Bishop was waiting for me to spin some yarn that would get us a table. Because he was staring at me and panting.

I opened my mouth but nothing came out. I was speechless.

Because our waitress was Mildred Smith. The original one.

'If you haven't booked I'll have to seat you in the toilets?'

This wasn't possible.

'Mildred?'

Smith looked at me like she looked at all strangers.

'It's Bronwyn actually? It says so on my name badge? It's why we have them? It's really the only reason we have them?'

Smith couldn't be in Australia because she was in England. And she couldn't be Australian because she was English. Maybe I'd been reborn, but Smith had been recast.

Smith obviously had no memory of her past life, before the plot hole. Smith didn't realise she was running up a huge bill at the Overlook Motel. Because she'd been given a new role. In a diner. By a plot hole. (Though on the plus side, her bill was peanuts compared to the one Mrs. Grinder was racking up at the Chateau Walmart.)

I was out there somewhere as well, probably. Not everyone got recast of course. Some people got typecast. I didn't want to think about what happened to them.

After lunch we arrived in West Wysolong.

Sharkbait and Nasty hadn't reached the rest of the world yet.

According to the barman they'd stuck around long enough to sell the locals several cases of Miracle Bitter (even though the label on the bottles said Bitter Miracle), but the locals in the Metropolitan were all behaving very soberly (though all still proudly insisted they were shitfaced). The Metropolitan was out of chocolate milk and I was feeling more relaxed since I'd quit my job. I was feeling more relaxed and I'd come to the end of my character arc. So I was basically a changed man. I tried a Miracle Bitter.

I enjoyed it more than I thought I would. It really got to my thirst fast.

Because it was water.

I thought about revealing this to my new drinking buddies. I thought about ordering another. To show them I could handle my drink. But everyone was hoping I'd just play along. Everyone was terrified of admitting they weren't enjoying their beer, because everyone in the pub assumed that everyone else *was* enjoying their beer. They were scared of being the first to admit they'd been duped by a couple of poms named Sharkbait and Nasty.

These were men! They didn't want to be duped.

Try it next time you're in a pub in the Outback if you don't believe me. Order a local beer and drink it and then loudly exclaim to the rest of the pub; 'this tastes like water!'

You won't will you? Well neither did I.

I'd never been good at challenging the status quo. But I was working on it. And I knew that as soon as I could speak out without fear of being punched in the face I'd do it.

Most people were terrified that they were wrong. But they were even more terrified of being the first to admit it. Human beings were the most intelligent, most attractive, most self-conscious species on the face of the Earth. They didn't like admitting when they were wrong.

Maybe Self had been right all along. Maybe there was a war on. But it wasn't between religion and science. It was between our vanity and our ignorance.

The Bishop was banging on about the rulebook;

'The one thing I've always said about the rulebook is it doesn't bear thinking about?'

You can listen if you want to. But I'd heard it all before.

My mind was drifting. I couldn't recall what the Bishop had just said. And I doubted our satnav could find a Casino in Las Vegas, let alone the Outback.

'How about a rulebook that only covers what we *don't* know? Is there one God? Are there three? Five? Is He smarter than MacGyver? As stupid as Wile E. Coyote? Is He a he, or a she? If He's a he, then is His name Jah? Or is it Geoff?'

The thing about God (or Geoff) was, He (or She) was unknowable. A bit of a recluse.

This is why no-one ever formed a religion based on having seen God. Religions are formed around your meeting someone else who tells you that *they've* seen God. The thing is; you have to give God a personality to make Him more believable. But you can't. So you give a personality some God instead. You can paint a picture for people of a personality. But you can't paint a picture of God. Because She (or He) is unknowable. I just said that.

Sure, sure, you'd like to get to know God better. But it's just never going to happen.

Maybe I'm tarring everyone with the same brush here, but chances are the only person you're ever going to get to know any better is yourself.

The satnav had directed us to a no-entry sign. Sure, sure, I'd stopped repressing my memories, but I still couldn't remember taking the exit for Wagga Wagga. One problem with the landscape in the Outback was; there wasn't any. It all looked the same to me. But there was a chance we were headed in the right direction. I figured it was a 50/50 chance. The Bishop was still talking;

'Want to hear a joke?'

'Sure, why not?'

'Three blind drunks stagger out of a bar and bump into a platypus? They're all like; 'what the hell is this thing?' So the first drunk leans forward and grabs the platypus' bill and he says; 'It's a duck!' and the second drunk grabs its tail and says; 'No! It's a beaver' and the third drunk grabs its belly and says; 'It's a weasel!' And they start arguing, until eventually the barmaid comes out and says; 'It's an animal stupid!'?'

'...What's the punchline?'

'That *was* the punchline? The joke is; they were all arguing about something they couldn't see, except the barmaid who could see it, but didn't know how to explain it? But she was still the only one out the four of them who was right?'

You didn't always need to know where you were going in order to get there. And you couldn't always trust your satnav. But I could see a Neapolitan salt lake that I recognised.

Heaven knows how I hadn't taken a wrong turn with the Bishop and the satnav constantly distracting me.

'Maybe she just *thought* it looked like an animal. I mean, this is a barmaid we're talking about, no offence, not a zoologist. How do we know she was seeing things straight? How do we know this barmaid's interpretation of events can be trusted?'

You know, in the same way the colour-blind couldn't be trusted not to panic during old horror movies.

Basically what we were discussing here was The Principle of Least Knowledge.

True knowledge wasn't impossible. But it was hard to come by. And you almost certainly didn't possess any. In fact, not only did you not know anything, you didn't even know that. You were best off just assuming that you didn't know shit, because the thing about knowledge was, what you didn't know couldn't hurt you, but what you thought you knew, probably would. That platypus might just come back to bite you on the arse.

We were on our way to see Titania. Bishop Anger had e-mailed me a photo he'd been sent of Titania. As soon as I'd seen her photo I knew I had to meet her.

Bishop Anger had heard about me quitting my job. He'd figured I was probably going through a rough time. And that meeting Titania might cheer me up. But the Bishop was still worried what I was going to do to her. Which was fair enough. I had a bit of a reputation.

I wasn't sure what I was going to do with Titania either. But I was pretty sure her owner wouldn't care as long as he got enough money out of her. Don't get me wrong, I wasn't going to hand over any money myself, but I was pretty sure Titania's owner would be able to sell his story. The Bishop bit into his Tim Tam and carried on talking;

'What do you think they'll make of her?'

It was impossible to say. The media were going to have a hard time framing Titania. They were going to struggle to explain why she behaved the way she did, why she looked the way she looked.

'Twenty bucks says there's an expert on MSG News convincing people he knows what he's talking about within a week?'

'Tell you what. I'll bet you forty that in a month's time

people will still be arguing'.

'You're on; there'll be a new story along well before then?'

'I'm not saying how long it'll stay in the news; I'm saying how long people will argue over it. Each bullshit argument will be countered with some other bullshit. The only thing that can threaten my forty bucks will be if the argument collapses under its own weight in bullshit'.

'Well it sounds like you're going to win forty bucks then? Unless you're not of course, and you just think you're going to?'

'Or unless I say the bet was for fifty'.

'No, you can't play like that? You're a reality enforcer?'

Not anymore I wasn't. What was the point of enforcing reality if you could never be sure that your reality was the most realistic?

There was a running joke at the Agency (back when I worked there) among people who were feeling stressed or generally having a terrible day. People who were having trouble sleeping at night used to say; 'Days like these make me wish I was in Area J'.

Area J was where we kept the frozen heads. There was John Wayne. And John Lennon. John Belushi. And JFK of course.

But not Walt Disney. That's just an urban legend.

'Maybe we're just a couple of old brains on ice?'

'So we're not lost? And you're not speeding?'

I was under the speed limit. Or at least I thought I was. It was either that or I was a brain in a jar in a laboratory somewhere, being convinced that I was under the speed limit.

'So if our brains are on ice what are our bodies doing?'

'They're probably in daytime television. Or politics'.

Seeing was no good without believing. If you didn't have a little belief in yourself there was no way you could ever really trust what you were seeing.

'...Before I was a Bishop I studied Buddhism? I experimented with a lot of other faiths while I was a student? I used to ask my Buddhist lecturer whether God existed or not? And he used to hit me with a stick? He would say; 'Maybe there is a God, and maybe he directed my stick against your arse'? Well it answered my question? I needed to worry a little less about what others believed and a little more about the stick that was hitting me?'

'Are you sure you should be saying this out loud?'

Bishop Anger turned the radio up. Just in case.

'Be careful not to ignore what's happening to you right now? Sometimes a little faith in yourself can be preferable to a blind acceptance of other's ideas?'

'I guess it's time to start hitting people with a stick then; just to keep them on their toes. When the occasional miracle slips through, some drunken weather or a cryptid, people will have to decide whether they believe what they're being told or not. They'll have to decide whether to follow the rulebook or not'.

'And what about you Frank? Do you still have your copy?'

'Of the rulebook? ...It spontaneously combusted'.

Sure, sure; I still told the occasional (white) lie.

We pulled up on the outskirts of the farm and stepped out under the warm Outback sun. The blue sky over the red earth and the resurrection bushes. We walked beside a rocky hill and through the fields towards the farmhouse, a beaten-up corrugated tin shack; like one of those new homes in Gladys. Except this was for real. There was no money left in the Bogan Station. All of the money was in the Casino bank.

I watched through binoculars as Cleaver wiped the sweat from his brow and accepted a bulging brown envelope from Anne Punter. Then I watched Anne interview him. I have to admit I still got a kick out of it, even though I was out of the picture. Out of the frame.

Titania was in the middle of the field.

Another solitary Vegetable Lamb.

I'd told Cleaver I needed to keep my distance from the media. Because of my reputation. My face wasn't likely to add much credibility to Cleaver's story following the fallout over the amber jam jar.

The Bishop and I watched the media circus interview Cleaver and his jackaroos and then I decided I'd seen enough. We turned to walk up the steep rocky slope behind us.

All around us was empty space. The empty red earth and the empty blue sky. It should've have been silent. But I could hear a strange noise as we reached the hill's summit.

Sometimes, just when you think you've seen it all...

You saw all of the empty space that was filled with lambs.

The first thing you heard was the lambs bleating. In fact this was all you could hear. The lambs bleating and gnashing their razor sharp teeth. And then, after that, came the only thing you could see. On the other side of the hill.

A vast cauliflower-coloured field stretching to the empty horizon.

Filled with hundreds of vegetable lambs.

21. Believing

Faith... Sure, sure, it's a good idea at the time.

But all good things have to come to an end.

Eating, drinking, breathing, faith; these things were almost certainly going to come to an end when you did. Maybe you'd finally start getting some answers instead. Maybe you'd find out you'd been right all along. Or maybe you wouldn't.

But I didn't want to rob the living of faith no more. If your faith was going to come to an end I didn't want to be the one to cause it.

Weird Norm didn't want anything to be his fault either.

If anyone was to blame it was Chuck Redstar.

But it turned out Chuck was totally blameless too. Redstar hadn't actually committed any crimes. Being gullible? That was people's own fault. The high court judge who presided over the 527 civil lawsuits against Chuck had said so. Redstar had sold people some replica jam jars in replica amber, so what the hell did they have to complain about?

Sure, sure, there was an investigation into the Agency too. Their alleged hoaxing of the SOOPA and all of the other bizarre continuity errors that had been reported. But all of these had been hoaxes perpetrated by Self. A rogue enforcer. A lone bullshitter.

Unfortunately Self couldn't be prosecuted either.

Mainly because he couldn't be found.

The Prime Minister set up a public inquiry into how Self could get away with something like this. It turned out you could get away with something like this if you ran away and hid. Or spent more time with your family.

It was one of those very short public inquiries.

Of course the suggestion that the Agency had been innocent of any wrongdoing was unbelievable. But that didn't mean people found it hard to believe. Because the investigation into the activities of the Information Reclamation Agency was conducted by the Information Reclamation Agency. No-one suggested the Agency didn't investigate itself robustly though. The Agency left no stone unturned. And then it cleared itself of any wrongdoing.

It was right there in the fourteen page document the Office of Confessions published via The Whitewash Museum Press.

If the Agency was guilty of anything it was only having been duped into thinking that Self was a trustworthy public servant. But it turned out he'd been a scapegoat all along. All of the time his managers had assumed he was fact-checking intelligence reports (for that was his job description) had been spent creating all of the elaborate hoaxes that people had witnessed (the amber jam jar, the submarine that torpedoed itself, Donald Trump).

Self had been on a one man mission to undermine the status quo. But he'd failed. Because all of these miracles had been hoaxed. None of them had been real, none of them.

The Agency really couldn't be clearer on that last point.

Like I said before; everything went back to normal. Everyone returned to their normal lives. Even Rashid returned home. Unfortunately he had to fly home in a coffin. With O'Brien Air (so he really was late for his own funeral). Maybe no-one knew Rashid's secret identity, but they knew he was British. Because of his dental records.

Normally it's difficult to identify someone's grave when their name isn't on it. But Smith and I found Rashid's ok. It was the only grave with lots of fresh flowers. The Human Shield had a lot of floral tributes surrounding his final resting place. Because he was a superhero. Rashid's grave had a lot of graffiti too. There was writing all over his headstone.

The only thing missing was his name.

'I was thinking about plot holes the other day...'

This was Smith reminiscing over Rashid's grave, under a bright grey British sky;

'If the Agency was convinced the SOOPA was genuine how did they miss that it was plastic? And the brand name? I was thinking; why hasn't a plot hole swallowed us up?'

'Why? Because the test results showed it was real?'

'Well, have you had a chance to look at them?'

'*I* don't have them'.

'Well *someone* must have them'.

Someone did.

But it wasn't the someone we were thinking of.

Christy looked up at the brand new sign over the café.

So many people were visiting Gladys now, she couldn't make do with that old sign she'd painted over. Christy needed a real sign.

Something that people who were looking for a sign

could find easily.

Everyone visiting Gladys wanted to have an Americano and a bagel at the red, white and blue 'All American Amber Jam Jar Museum'. Sure, sure, some people ordered stacks of chocolate chip freedom pancakes just so they could poke fun and tell Christy;

'You do realise there's no such thing as the amber jam jar? That it didn't exist? That it never existed?'

But Christy would just serve them a toothfull Gladys smile and explain;

'I still like to believe in the *possibility* of an amber jam jar. Maybe the one that was destroyed was a fake. But maybe there's still a genuine amber jam jar out there somewhere? I just have a feeling. And that feeling means a lot to me. I thought I might be happier if I gave up believing? But I just don't reckon I would be'.

It was difficult to know what to believe in. To know what was real and what wasn't. To know which feelings you had to trust. And which ones you had to ignore.

Christy knew she could trust herself in the kitchen.

She never put a foot wrong when she was baking.

And wasn't the brain she used for baking the same as the one she used for believing in amber jam jars? Christy tended to go with her gut when she was baking cakes. So why shouldn't she trust it when thinking about the meaning of life? If Christy's feelings about the amber jam jar and the meaning of life were just a bunch of random ideas then how come her baking never resulted in disaster? Christy had never baked a chicken-shit pie. She'd never served anyone a shaving-cream bun.

Christy couldn't be right about baking and wrong about everything else, could she?

A lot of people argued that the human gut was an unreliable narrator at best. A lot of people argued that the only narrator worth listening to was logic. Logic was like Morgan Freeman. It had a voice you could trust. But sometimes even Morgan Freeman could do something stupid. Sometimes logic could get it all horribly wrong.

What you saw. It wasn't always what you got.

A lot of scientists had faith too. In science.

But sometimes that faith could get misplaced for a bit. Like with Thalidomide and Windows Vista. But you had to find your faith again. You had to keep your faith in science, because science could sometimes come across a touch ~~theatrical~~ theoretical.

The story of science is one of those stories where it's best not to start at the beginning. No-one was around at the beginning, so no-one was really sure how all of this got started.

Our universal ancestor was a bit difficult to understand.

Which is why the lab geeks made her a woman.

There was a time when logic dictated there was no Eve. There was a time when Eve was the kind of woman you were just never going to meet. But then a lab geek found her!

Except her name wasn't Eve. It was LUA. And she wasn't much to look at.

She was a bit shapeless. A bit rough around the edges.

Maybe you've been taking the Bible a bit literally. But LUA didn't wear a fig leaf.

Because LUA was a single-celled bacteria.

Don't get the wrong idea. Lab geeks had come up with pretty much all of our good ideas. Lab geeks had found sugar in space. Space jam!

But they'd come up with the Millennium Bug too.

Don't get the wrong end of the stick though. Everyone else was coming up with stupid ideas as well. The church didn't always get it exactly right either.

There was that whole Inquisition thing. Executing astronomers. For saying that the Earth *wasn't* flat! But come on, the church admitted it was a mistake.

Four hundred years later.

It was 'their bad'.

Sometimes the people with all of the answers got things wrong. They just didn't like you knowing it. These guys were happy to keep feeding you a story they knew was wrong, because they knew they'd get away with it, as long as they made the truth sound harder to believe than their lies.

But just because something was hard to believe, that didn't make it unbelievable.

The fact was; you could keep your faith in the irrational. At least until it was proven impossible. That was kinda the whole point of having faith. If you couldn't always believe what you were seeing then sometimes you had to keep faith in what you couldn't.

Don't believe me? Then just ask any atheist.

Atheism was founded on a faith in something that couldn't be seen. Atheists referred to this intangible individual that they didn't believe in as 'God'. But there was currently no hard evidence for the nonexistence of God. Atheism was like one of those irrational beliefs that atheists are always up in arms about. Sure, sure it was wishful thinking.

But you had to keep the faith if you were an atheist.

Sometimes what you thought you were seeing, it wasn't really what you were seeing.

Don't believe me? Then just ask Christy. You could see something irrational or hard to swallow, but you could still put your faith in it, as long as you had some faith in your own judgement. You know; as long as you weren't the kind of person who was usually wrong about things. But Christy didn't need to worry about being wrong about things. Christy had test results that proved she was right. That proved Christy's amber jam jar was genuine.

You know; the amber jam jar that Christy had swapped with the fake she'd baked.

After that dream she'd had.

That dream Christy had woken from around the same time that Smith and I'd been tumbling through a plot hole. You know; that premonition of someone stealing the amber jam jar. The dream that had given her a nagging feeling the amber jam jar wasn't safe.

Christy had to swap the real jam jar for a fake'n'bake. You know; for safekeeping.

Christy was a good baker. And like all good bakers she had a copy of Da Vinci's 'Gioia Di Cucinare Codex'. Da Vinci's book was full of good recipes. It was basically the good baker's rulebook. Of course she'd wanted to make her fake look convincing. But there was one ingredient Christy hadn't had. A jam jar.

It was all the fault of the Swiss.

Yeah, the Swiss. And their European chocolate spread.

You couldn't do without it if you wanted to bake a genuine European pain-au-chocolat. But Nestlé insisted on using plastic jars for their chocolate spread. And so Christy had been forced to make do with a plastic jar instead of a glass one. That's why her fakery had been so obvious when her replica jam jar had been struck by lightning. But that was ok. Things had worked out. What you thought you saw, it wasn't always what you got.

Christy had the genuine amber jam jar locked safely away in a concealed pantry along with the test results. This is what's known in the trade as 'provenance'.

Christy couldn't tell anyone she had the genuine amber jam jar. Because it had never existed. But Christy could still see the genuine amber jam jar any time she wanted.

And she could believe what she liked.

We heard thunder in the distance. Smith ran to the Tranquillo to get her umbrella. And her cardigan. But I wasn't worried. I already had my cardigan on. And I'd stopped worrying so much in general. The hypnotherapy really seemed to be working for me.

It was either that or it was my recently acquired taste for watered down lager.

I was feeling pretty relaxed, about the thunder, and about the test results not picking up on the fact that the jam jar had been plastic. There was a perfectly rational explanation for why the Agency hadn't realised that the jam jar was plastic. And the amber immature.

The Agency was an agency. And government agencies didn't exactly have the greatest track record when it came to the stringent examination and assessment of evidence. Or fact-checking.

Of course the other reason I wasn't worried was because I had no idea (at the time anyway) that Christy had baked a fake amber jam jar. How could I have?

Maybe I'm repeating myself here, but I wasn't omniscient.

Just psychic.

Just kidding. I'd figured it out eventually.

There had to be another explanation. And wouldn't you know it, there was.

The fact was; Christy was a lot like me. She liked to collect souvenirs. Like the amber jam jar. And her backstage pass to Blimey Lowsey's Knoxville concert. Christy wore that backstage camera pass all the time. Even in her concealed pantry. Maybe The Real World had lost most of its audience a long time ago. But I'd renewed my interest in it.

To be honest (something I never used to be) I'd considered our road trip through the States to have been a bit of a nightmare. But Smith was all for tracking down the test results and leaking them to the Sunday Spartan. Smith wanted to re-live her glory days.

'You really want to go through all that again?'

'We had a little fun didn't we?'

Maybe a little. But there was no reliving the past (unless we could create another plot hole). I thought about telling

Smith how I'd figured out what had happened to our original selves when we fell through the plot hole. But she was working as a waitress at the Sunset Rock Diner and I was pretty sure this was the kind of thing that might upset her.

I wasn't a loner anymore. I'd figured out that sometimes you were better off just keeping the truth to yourself. But you didn't want to make a career out of it.

And I wasn't sure I could explain it to her anyway. Of the many things I knew about plot holes, how they worked wasn't one of them. There was a lot of confusion surrounding plot holes. There was a lot of confusion around the unexplained in general. People had been through a lot, what with the amber jam jar and those terrifying prehistoric rock records. People had started to doubt the debunking of one seriously out of place artefact would ever be enough to prove or disprove the existence of the phenomenal. People just had to decide whether they wanted to believe or not. And then they had to choose something to believe in.

'It's a difficult choice. Between a Ford Fallus and a Toyota Magneto. They both have their die-hard supporters. And the aftersales service packages are about the same'.

Smith was reminiscing again. About an earlier metaphor.

Smith believed in God (because she'd seen a lot of miracles). She just didn't believe in religion (because the church had been trying to cover them up).

I could hear Rashid's rebuttal. Not from beyond the grave, but from the other direction; Rashid had decided what to believe in a long time ago. I wondered how he'd have reacted to how things had panned out for religion in the past few weeks.

Religion was another thing that hadn't gone back to normal. Adam and Eve might've been the status quo three hundred years earlier, but they weren't any longer. And if there's one thing you couldn't accuse the church of; it was not moving with the times.

The world's religions had started rewriting their rulebooks.

The thing about most rulebooks now was; you had to stop taking things so literally.

You weren't supposed to worship the rules. You were just supposed to read them.

It turned out these weren't rulebooks at all. They were guidebooks. You were meant to take them out into the real world, not treat them as a world you disappeared into. The thing about guidebooks was; they started to become out of date fast. Guidebooks weren't great at providing up to date answers. But the places you had to go looking for them? They were usually the same. You just needed a bit of free time. And a bit of faith in yourself.

Of course that wasn't to say you could just ignore logic.

You didn't want to start being unreasonable.

Faith without reason was no use to anyone. Faith without reason was pornography. But reason without faith was masturbation. Sure, sure you could try to enjoy one without the other, but you might not end up feeling completely satisfied.

The Agency had been suffocating faith by trying to force a rulebook down people's throats. We'd been telling people we had all of the answers. But we didn't. Smith and I could give everyone some more questions though. The kind of questions other people couldn't answer for you. The kind of questions for which the only honest answer was; 'I don't know'.

People were going to have to learn to live with a more unpredictable world, and a more unpredictable God (or Geoff). The kind of God who was full of love.

But who sometimes held the most persistent grudges.

We said our goodbyes and left Rashid's grave.

We heard the thunder.

But we didn't see the bolt of lightning strike his headstone.

My alien neighbours were selling up and shipping out. I could see them outside, in the middle of the night; painting their kitchen extension the colour of Mars. I was back home. Some things had stayed the same. But some other things had changed. For instance; someone or something had been siphoning water from my pond. Or drinking it. I was concerned about my fish. But the black water had gone. What was left was very shallow. But very clear.

I looked at the goldfish I'd been trying to keep alive. Then I looked at the goldfish next to it. There'd been two goldfish all along! I just hadn't been seeing things clearly.

It had been me and the one fish for so long. But now the house was getting crowded.

'How does it feel having a lodger who can speak English?'

This was Smith. With the teasing, and the perfect dubbing.

It was 3am. It was pretty late for Smith to be turning up at the house. But she had her own key (and her own bathroom). I grabbed Smith a Marvel Burger from the freezer, threw it under the grill (from a record distance) and asked her how work was.

'I got stuck in a revolving door. Almost blew my cover'.

Smith had a bit of a commute. From the Negli-Gen Research facility near Loch Ness where she was currently undercover. Smith was investigating Negli-Gen experiments testing the interaction of human consciousness with various household appliances (toaster ovens, vacuum cleaners etc.). Smith had received a tip off from the Son of Deep Throat who had licensed the facility his GOD.v2 operating system. Negli-Gen engineers and cleaning ladies were reporting a 'conscious bond' with DVD players and digital radios. It only occurred once or twice in every ten thousand experiments, but it was pretty significant by most statistical standards. Stereos became louder if you'd been drinking. Kettles and toasters became lethargic when people were in a hurry. In other words, these appliances were responding to human emotions. Or not. It was a pretty controversial study. And science was complicated.

And what was I doing while all of this was going on? I was booking a flight to Simpson Airport, Alaska. I had to stop Maxwell Self from combusting body errors. I knew Self was back at work because thirty-nine left feet had washed up on the shores of Homer. The feet belonged to twenty-two men, thirteen women and four 'TBCs'.

Most of the feet were wearing Nikes, although two were wearing Hi-Tecs.

Some of the Nikes were probably fakes. All of the owners were probably dead.

There'd been a hoax involving some Pumas stuffed with raw chicken (or raw pigeon), but two local Bigfoot hunters had already confessed to that.

But I knew it was Maxwell Self. And I knew that I had to stop him.

Of course, nobody else knew what the hell was going on. But everyone had a theory.

A couple of severed left feet wash up, the media frames it as a boating accident. You get a dozen, and they start talking about a plane crash. But when you get thirty-nine severed feet all bets are off. It could be sea trolls. Or crutch manufacturers.

But no-one was talking about spontaneous human combustion.

You could flick between the channels or surf between Face Talk and Public Opinions. They both had reporters on the scene, holding trainers. Neither had a damned clue what had happened, but they had to speculate. They had to give you a convincing explanation.

The truth wasn't important. But then it never was. The media could speculate until the pigs started to fly. They'd spend hours speculating about other people's feet. Maybe some of us had stopped trying to wing it, but the news media hadn't learnt a thing.

The headline on The Express read; 'Hotter than Madrid!'

The Daily Mail claimed it was; 'Colder than Moscow!'

The Sun told you it was; 'Just right!'

We no longer lived in an age of darkness or enlightenment. We didn't live in a world with one right answer to the question anymore. We lived in a world where there were two right answers for every question. This was what people expected to see, other people arguing over their hypotheses, their feelings, their beliefs. That was your status quo right there.

The war was just beginning. Not between religion and science. This was a war between your truth and theirs. It was time to live without other people's bullshit.

It was time to try to live with the truth.

And maybe the occasional miracle.

www.ingramcontent.com/pod-product-compliance
Lightning Source LLC
Chambersburg PA
CBHW022206030726
47494CB00021B/1715